ANTEBELLUM AWAKENING

THE NETWORK SERIES
by Katie Cross

Mildred's Resistance

Miss Mabel's School for Girls

The Isadora Interviews

Antebellum Awakening

The High Priest's Daughter

War of the Networks

ANTEBELLUM AWAKENING

Katie Cross

KW

Antebellum Awakening

Young Adult Fantasy

Text copyright ©2014 by Katie Cross

Cover designed by Seedlings Online at www.seedlingsonline.com
Typesetting by Chris Bell, Atthis Arts at www.atthisarts.com

Published by KCWriting.
Visit www.kcrosswriting.com for more information.

ISBN (paperback) 978-0-9915319-3-6
(ebook) 978-0-9915319-4-3
(hardcover) 978-0-9915319-5-0

Visit the author at www.kcrosswriting.com

For my second grade teacher Terry Felts

Who loved an awkward, frizzy-haired little girl.

Acknowledgments

Sitting down to write the acknowledgements is quite honestly the most difficult part of writing a book. I'm a little more than terrified that I'm going to forget someone pivotal.

Let's be honest here. The biggest thanks of all certainly goes first to the Miss Mabel's School for Girls fans that kept the book going. Without your excitement and enthusiasm, this would be a much lonelier process. I've said it once, and I'll certainly say it a hundred thousand times more: Bianca has the coolest fans.

No author is an island. I have the most magnificent team of designers, editors, proofreaders, typesetters, bloggers, and beta readers that a girl could ask for. Jenny, Robin, Catherine, Bailey, Kella, Atthis Arts, and all the others that helped, thank you for bringing your honesty and talents to my door. Your awesomeness helped make Antebellum Awakening as perfect and beautiful as it is today. To all the many beta readers that contributed, thank you for your selfless time donation and honest opinions.

To the artists of Read Write Muse, and now my new family of Blue Monkeys. Thank you for all your unfaltering love, support, beta reading comments, and giggles when we're all staying up far too late to chat on Facebook. I love each and every one of you. There's no one else I'd rather go into business with than you.

To the followers at KCrossWriting that keep me endlessly entertained with your witty comments about my frizzy, out-of-control hair that closely resembles Camille's: thanks for the love and support! A special thanks to Sam-Bam for her young prowess with words and helping me refine and hone the blurb on the back. She deserves the credit for the chills and glitter the last line gives.

Then there are the people who not only put up with me in a professional regard, but in every other facet of life. I can't name everyone in my family that has supported me, or else I'd have to write another novel, but know that I love you and think of you always.

Husband, love yer face.

Prologue

The carriage rolled away from the graveyard with a *clack clack* of wheels on the rocky dirt road. I stared out the window, watching the trees of Letum Wood fade by in spears of gray and black, like the shadows in my heart. Low clouds blew over from the south in a blanket of gray foam.

Mama's gone now. The dark gloom I felt stirred the magic near my heart. *It's time to move on. Don't think about her death anymore. Keep the past in the past.*

Sometimes I wished I wasn't so honest with myself. Perhaps I could pretend that Mama would come back from death, that I could delay going on with my new life without her. But no, I couldn't. The pain would never let me forget her entirely, though I knew I'd try.

"Does your father know that Miss Mabel did not remove your Inheritance Curse?" the High Priestess asked, breaking our stony silence with her gravelly voice. She sat across from me, her beady eyes black in the fading daylight, her short gray and white hair swept back from her face in little wisps. The mention of Miss Mabel tightened my stomach.

"I don't know," I said. Wrapping up my old life, closing the cottage I'd grown up in, and reeling from the shock of Mama's death had sapped all of Papa and my strength. I hadn't even thought about the curse that would kill me on my seventeenth birthday just six months away. What did it matter? Mama was dead, and so was my heart. My own death would certainly hurt less than the moment she died in my arms. "I don't think we've talked about it."

"Yes or no?"

"No."

The High Priestess fell quiet for so long I thought she'd forgotten the subject. She could have easily used magic to transport back to Chatham Castle and resume her duties as leader of the Central Network, but she stayed with me. I wondered why. I'd chosen the lengthy carriage ride simply because I didn't want to go back to the castle. Without Mama there, it wasn't home.

Close the door, Bianca. Stop thinking about her.

"Would you lie to your father and tell him that Miss Mabel removed the curse if I asked you to?" the High Priestess asked.

My eyes lifted to hers in surprise.

"Lie to him?"

She nodded, as if she asked this kind of thing every day. I couldn't believe it. Tell my father a lie? I'd never lied to him before, and couldn't even fathom how to successfully go about it. He was a master of disguise, a man who lived in the shadows to protect those living in the light. I'd have to live with my falsehood every day, remember my guilt every time I saw his face.

"Why would you want that of me?" I asked in a hoarse voice.

"The Central Network is walking into a war," she said in her crisp, punctuated inflections. For a woman as powerful as the High Priestess, nothing got in the way of business, not even mourning. "Your father is one of our greatest hopes for getting out of it intact. If he knows that Mabel still has power over you, he'll throw all his attention into stopping the curse, even at the cost of the Network. I can't let that happen."

"What about me?" I asked. The High Priestess locked her sharp eyes with mine. "I'm just supposed to let the curse kill me?"

"Of course not. If you lie to your father, I will promise to personally find a resolution to your Inheritance Curse. You will not die at seventeen."

"You can't promise anything when it comes to Miss Mabel," I said in a bitter whisper. Just saying that name sent a tremor through my heart, like a lion waking with an indignant bellow.

"There are ways around your curse, I think. In fact, I'm confident enough that I'll take a vow," she said, her eyes as serious as they'd ever been. Surely she wasn't considering such a thing! Could anyone stop a witch as cunning and powerful as Miss Mabel? The longer I studied the High Priestess, the more convinced I became. If anyone could defeat my old teacher, it was the High Priestess. I may not have understood her, but I respected and trusted her.

"A vow?"

"Yes. I'll take a vow—this moment—to resolve your Inheritance Curse before you turn seventeen."

The vow would seal her to the promise. Not with her life, like a binding, but with a part of her magic. If she didn't complete the vow, a portion of her power would wither away inside her. For a witch with responsibilities like the High Priestess, an unfulfilled vow could be devastating.

But lie to Papa? Just thinking about it made my heart ache, even if I couldn't deny the truth of her words. He'd throw his life into saving me, perhaps try to find a way to offer himself up as an exchange. Miss Mabel would grasp at such an opportunity.

I sucked in a sharp breath at the thought.

Offer himself as an exchange for my life. That's exactly what he'd do. He'd hunt down Miss Mabel and give himself for my freedom. I'd lose the last of my family. My own resolve hardened in a flash, thick as a stone. I wouldn't fail another parent.

"Yes," I said, resolute. "I'll lie to Papa."

She nodded once, and I saw a flicker of relief pass through her eyes.

"Do not speak of this without my express permission. There are ears at Chatham Castle that are not friendly to us. Of the ten Council Members, I only trust a few."

"Yes, Your Highness."

She leaned forward and extended her right arm. I lifted my hand and gripped her forearm; she held onto mine.

"I vow to resolve your Inheritance Curse by your seventeenth birthday," she said. Magic, flowing from the place her skin touched my fingertips, zipped through my fingers and arm, into my shoulder. It settled in my heart and my head. Both of our arms glowed with a warm, yellow light.

"I accept."

The magic swirled and then settled in my heart with a calm little sigh. Satisfied, the High Priestess released me and leaned back against her seat. The carriage rolled on, carrying us through foggy Letum Wood, and onto my new life.

I swallowed back the tears.

Time to start over and forget the past.

Forest Dragons

Two months later.

I didn't know grief lingered in the sunlight.

It would sweep all the caverns of my heart with the power of heat and fire, reminding me of Mama and all I'd lost. Her face lingered in the back of my mind even though I tried not to acknowledge her. When the worst of the melancholy moments took over me, not even the blue spring sky or the fluffy clouds piled high like wisps of cotton could remove the darkness inside. Grief was my new companion, the wraith that haunted my heart. I hated it, and clung to it at the same time.

"Why aren't there Guardians patrolling the gardens?" my best friend Camille asked with an annoyed sigh. "Aren't they supposed to be protecting the castle grounds?"

A light, cool spring breeze accompanied us around the gardens of Chatham Castle, which loomed high in the distance behind us, soaring with turrets and stone. A crimson and gold flag flapped from the second highest tower in the same wind that brushed my hair off my shoulders. Gardens lay in lazy grandeur around the fortress like a long skirt of pastel flowers. Behind the flower beds and lawns was Letum Wood, the great forest of imposing trees and rolling hills, puffed out in new buds of green. We passed a small mound of pink spring flowers, and I trailed the tip of my finger along a teardrop petal. It felt soft and silky.

I cast Camille a questioning glance.

"Is that why you wanted to go on a walk? To talk to Guardians?"

The quick rise of color to her apple cheeks gave her away. She looked straight ahead and tried to force a nonchalant voice.

"N-no! I just wanted to enjoy the lovely spring air. It is a bit chilly though." She pulled her light blue cape farther over her shoulders when another soft gust of wind brushed against us. A moment later she pointed to a small queue of maids and butlers a few paces away. "Oh, look! They're setting up for the spring luncheon with the High Priestess. I'd love to eat with her. I have loads of questions I want to ask. Who d'you think does her hair? Does she pick out her own dresses? They're horrid sometimes, aren't they?"

I followed her gaze. The High Priestess was meeting with the southern Coven Leaders at noon. If the gossip I listened to in the castle meant anything, she wanted to address the rumors that the Southern Network had called their army to assemble near the sprawling stone wall that separated us, which meant that our lower covens could be in danger from an attack. I had little hope that good news would come from the meeting.

Servants bustled around in black uniforms with gold and red embroidering, carrying platters of food and pitchers of apple cider. They put together several long wooden tables adorned with vases of spring flowers and the finest bone china. Silver spoons and forks glittered in the sunlight. A white canopy hung overhead, suspended by no ropes or twine, but the magic of the butlers held them up. The canopies protected the tables from the warm sunshine, which seemed such a waste to me. Why eat outside if they wouldn't enjoy the gentle heat?

"The luncheon should be starting soon," I said, eager to get away from what would be a collecting crowd. Although informative, most of the talk would be political arguments, and as riveting as watching grass grow. It was something my friend Leda would swoon over. "Let's go this way."

Camille followed as we turned and headed across the spongy grass, toward Letum Wood's shadows. Sprawling gardens, gazebos, and flower-laden trellises still separated us from Letum's dark trees and tall awning, but even so, I felt a small tug of comfort just knowing I was going to be near the wild forest. I'd grown up under the murky trees and my heart longed for it with a homesick little pang.

No, I firmly reminded myself. *That's part of your old life, not your new life. Stay away from Letum Wood.*

The trapped magic in my heart swirled restlessly at the thought of never going back to the gloomy canopy. The closer we meandered to the thick foliage, the more the back of my throat ached.

"Let's talk about the Anniversary Ball!" Camille said with a spring in her step that made her dishwater blonde curls bounce. "Henrietta and I picked out the perfect material for my dress! I know the ball is still four months away, but that will give her plenty of time to work on it. The design is exquisite, Bianca!"

"Oh?" I feigned interest, my eyes trained on the forest. A rustle of leaves in the upper canopy caught my attention in a windless moment. What could be moving that high? "What color?"

Happy to find someone who showed the slightest regard, Camille prattled on about lace and ribbons and the perfect material. My eyes remained locked on Letum Wood. The movement of leaves rippled through the foliage, moving across the forest. A bird, perhaps? No, it would have to be quite large. I steered us slightly to the left, toward the break in the hedge that would let me see what animal lurked so close to the castle.

"Then I told Luther that I wouldn't go with him," Camille said with a little sigh, speaking of one of the many Guardians enamored with her. "There are too many Guardians I'd want to say yes to, and not enough time. I'll have to dance with all of them, I guess. Oh! We better turn back. We're at the back hedge now."

Indeed, we stood at a hedge several feet taller than us and as wide as I was tall, the last protection between the dangers of Letum Wood and the castle grounds. Occasional breaks in the hedge allowed movement to the forest. We lingered at one such spot, peering down the rolling, grassy knoll that led right into Letum Wood.

"Can we stay just a second?" I asked, meeting her eyes. I'd hate myself later for letting myself remember all the old times, but being this close weakened my resolve. *I won't go in. I'll just try to see the animal that's scurrying around.* "I want to look at it, that's all."

She hesitated, then nodded once. Camille seemed to understand my random needs and tumultuous bouts of emotions since Mama died better than anyone. She lost her parents at a much younger age. Knowing she'd made it through gave me hope on some of the darkest days.

"Just for a minute," I promised, scanning the green depths. For a moment I could smell the fresh pine, hear the chitter of a squirrel, and feel the rush of blood moving past my ears as I ran down a cool dirt trail. How I missed it!

The movement in the leaves had ceased and didn't seem to come again. Just when the longing to return to the cool, misty forest nearly overwhelmed me, when I was ready to turn away and put it behind me for good this time, the deep foliage of the forest stirred and shifted. I grabbed Camille's arm.

"Did you see that?" I asked, breathless. To see a creature in Letum Wood in the light of day was a rare occurrence. It could be nothing more than a game of chase among a few large rodents, but Letum often hid far greater things. "Something is moving in the trees. Something big."

"Don't say that," she muttered, shifting her shoulders as if something cold hung there. "You have the worst kind of luck lately. What if it's a lion? They sense beauty—I'm sure of it—which means I'll be the first to be eaten."

I rolled my eyes. "Lions don't come out during the day. Look! It can't be the wind. It's moving again."

The leaves shifted anew, accompanied by a low snort that sent clouds of steam billowing into the clearing. The hair on the back of my neck stood up. Perhaps lingering hadn't been such a good idea.

"Uh, Bianca?" Camille whispered, "W-what is that growling sound?"

A massive shape with a long, supple neck and shiny scales that gleamed a blue-black in the sunlight slipped into sight. The graceful creature hung back, barely discernible, until a long tail with two sharp spikes flickered out of the trees like a whip. When a pair of yellow eyes peered out from the darkness, I sucked in a deep breath and shoved Camille behind me.

"A forest dragon," I whispered.

"Then look away!" she screeched, whirling around and pressing her hands to her eyes. "If it looks you in the eyes it will paralyze you and eat you for lunch!"

The eyes blinked once, then retreated into the forest, while the ebony tail, flecked with sapphire, twitched but remained visible. He was shifting positions.

"His eyes are gone," I said.

"Did he leave?"

"No." Forest dragons were surly and prone to anger, usually catching their prey in the dead of night by sneaking up with panther-like precision, or so the legends said. I felt less than comfortable finding one in full daylight. They hadn't even been seen in centuries, at least not by anyone who lived to tell the tale. Some witches questioned whether the legends surrounding them had ever been real. So why would a forest dragon come out in the daylight now?

"Okay," Camille whispered, panic edging into her voice. "Okay, okay, okay. We just need to get out of here, that's all. Will it come after us if I start running? What if I scream?"

The lemon-colored eyes reappeared from the dark depths, staring right at me. A little shiver skimmed my spine, but I didn't look away. I felt no spell, no desire to move toward it, as the stories claimed. Instead, I felt unusually calm.

"Don't scream," I whispered, listening to the little instinct inside. "I don't think it wants to hurt us, and I'm not sure it's seen you. Back up to the other side of the hedge."

The dragon stepped forward, moving out of the tree line and into the sun with lazy grandeur. His chest alone was three times taller than my height, with a willowy tail and long wings that folded onto his expansive back like sheets of leather. I squinted against the bright reflection off his glittery scales. I needed a plan.

As soon as Camille is safe, I thought, *distract the dragon so he doesn't fly after her, then transport to Chatham.*

"Go find a Guardian and tell him what's going on, Camille," I said, keeping my gaze locked on the dragon's queer eyes. Now that he stood in the sunlight, they had faded to a shade of burnt orange. "Can you do that?"

"Y-yes," Camille whispered. "Right. Calm. Calm. Calm. I'm calm. I'm calm. Can't you just transport us out of here?"

Camille hadn't learned transportation yet, so she didn't know I couldn't take another witch with me. "Transportation doesn't work when two witches are touching. Just run back to Chatham. As soon as you're safe, I'll transport over and meet you near the back door."

She swallowed and nodded.

"O-okay."

The sound of her retreating footsteps on the grass reassured me. As long as I kept the dragon's attention, he wouldn't follow her.

"It's you and me, dragon," I said, a bold tone creeping into my voice. His head lowered closer to the ground. The gaping nostrils at the end of his angular face constricted and widened as he sniffed the air, his eyes still trained on me. The magic inside me had swollen since he stepped out, expanding until it filled my chest. I'd have to keep the powers under close reign or risk losing control, with consequences no one wanted. "Are you going to hurt me?"

The dragon's eyes narrowed at the sound of my voice. I fell under no spell meant to lure me within range of his massive claws; the dragon and I simply stared at each other. It was as if we were old competitors returning again, sizing each other up, uncertain what the years had changed. Despite the obvious danger, I couldn't deny that he was a magnificent creature.

"Beautiful," I whispered under my breath. The dragon growled suddenly and snapped his head to the right. His pupils constricted into thin slits. I followed his gaze to a glint of light on metal that hadn't been there before.

Two male witches crouched near the hedge at the top of the grassy hill. One had a special bow and arrow pointed right at the dragon. His arrows, nearly four times the normal size for hunting, were tipped with silver. I straightened with a gasp.

Poachers.

The poachers seemed to have a great deal of trust in the legends surrounding the use of a silver arrow when hunting forest dragons. When shot right into the heart of the beast, the silver would paralyze the dragon in mere moments. If the myths weren't true, these poachers would have one angry dragon on their hands.

If they were true, they were going to kill an innocent forest dragon, a creature that hadn't been seen in hundreds of years.

My magic brightened in fury, feeling hot and cold at the same time. I had to stop them. But how? It was two against one, and I was only a sixteen-year-old girl. My anxiety thickened the magic in my chest. If I didn't do something, the powers would take over and I'd lose control.

The crouched witch notched his arrow, forcing my final decision. Acting without thinking, a particular specialty of mine under pressure, I shot past the hedge and sprinted onto the grass. The second witch, nearly buried in the bush in a poor attempt to hide from the dragon, had his back to me and didn't see my approach.

"Stop!" I yelled. "Stop!"

Startled by my sudden cry, the first witch jerked up, releasing the arrow. It went wild, landing with a dull thud in a sapling near the edge of the forest and splitting it in two. I plowed into him, knocking him onto his side. The collision made me lose my balance, and I rolled a few paces down the hill.

"What are ya thinking!" the witch bellowed, his face turning red. He pushed off from the grass and barreled toward me. "I had a perfect shot! Mangy girl—"

"Alvyn," the second witch yelled, trying to extricate himself from the hedge. "Don't do anything stupid! If we're caught—"

"Don't say my name, ya fool," Alvyn yelled over his shoulder, nearly apoplectic. "We've got to get rid of her now. She's a witness!"

"You can't kill a forest dragon!" I retorted, leaping clear when he reached for me. The dragon let out a bellow behind me, sending a plume of fire into the air. A wave of heat rolled past my shoulders and stirred my hair.

"Really?" Alvyn sneered. The putrid smell of fermented ipsum rolled off his breath. "Who do you think you are?"

"I'm Derek's daughter," I hissed. Perhaps all this building power gave me a reckless confidence, or maybe I was terrified, but admitting who my father was wasn't going to help. "If you lay one finger on me, he'll kill you with his bare hands."

"Derek's daughter? Good!" Alvyn sneered, an odd light in his eyes. "I hate Derek as much as I hate dragons. The rest of the Central Network will thank me for getting rid of ya."

For such a burly man, he charged toward me with surprising speed. But even he couldn't match the force of the power boiling in my angry heart. I stopped fighting the magic and let it slip away from me in a current.

Time slowed. Every breath I took echoed in my ears. Alvyn's thick face closed in, an arm's length away, when Camille's distant shriek echoed behind me. The world dimmed into darkness.

Everything happened in one long blink after another. Alvyn reached for my neck. *Darkness.* A glowing white ball of heat formed in the air, forcing him a step backward. His eyes widened; his face turned away. He stumbled back a step, and then the light burst. *Darkness.* The world spun by in shades of green and sky blue. *Darkness.*

"Bianca!" Camille's shrill, panicked voice came from far away, as if traveling through water to reach me. "Wake up!"

Sharp pain burst into my head. My stomach roiled. I felt a pair of hands tug on my arm.

"We're both going to die if you don't wake up!" Camille screeched right next to my ear. "Wake up! I can't drag you up this hill! I'm not strong enough!"

The fear in her voice roused me. Disoriented and dizzy, I pushed up into a sitting position to find the forest dragon standing ten paces away. Hot breath swelled from his chest and puffed out of his wide nostrils, caressing us both in a ripple of heat. His thick tail swung out like a rope loose in the wind. The narrow, sharp angles of his face moved closer, peering at me. When a low growl rumbled from some-where inside his deep chest, I scrambled backwards, putting myself between the dragon and Camille again.

"No harm here," I said to him in a low, soothing voice. He grunt-ed, glancing between Camille and me. I couldn't have been uncon-scious for very long. "What happened, Camille?"

"I ran back to make sure you were okay," she said in a tremulous voice. "I screamed for the butlers, then when I turned around you were gone and I was scared that something happened to you. I-I didn't know what to do so I ran back!"

"It's all right," I said in a calm voice, my eyes still locked on the dragon. "Where are the poachers?"

"Those two witches? They're lying on the grass. I think they're knocked out. They might be dead!"

"I'm going to stand up, and I want you to follow but stay behind me. Understand?" I asked.

"Yes."

"Here we go."

We stood together. The dragon's nostrils widened when he sniffed the air, but he didn't move toward us.

Great job saving his life and nearly losing your own in the process, Bianca, I thought. *Wonderful idea. Dragons really don't care about morals, do they?*

You saved at least one innocent creature, my heart replied. *Even though you didn't save—* I cut the thought off and turned my whole attention back to our sticky situation.

The dragon's ears quivered. His great head swung to gaze back over his shoulder. I took advantage of the break from his stare to check on the poachers. They lay prostrate on the ground, their arms thrown wide and eyes closed. A few streaks of black smudged their faces.

Blessed be, I thought with a flutter of fear. *I really might have killed them.*

"Bianca?" Camille asked again, her face averted to the ground to avoid the large eyes peering down at us again. "What about the dragon?"

"He won't hurt us," I said, my eyes flicking up to meet his intense gaze. "He won't. I can feel it."

"Are you mad?" she breathed. "It's a dragon!"

"Maybe," I whispered, and thought that maybe the grief had finally taken my last ounce of sanity.

Guttural shouts broke the tense silence. Five Guardians appeared in the air surrounding Camille and me, pressing their backs to us. Two witches in plain clothes appeared near the edge of Letum

Wood carrying the corpses of forest creatures. The dragon, smelling the decaying bodies, instantly ducked his head and swiveled toward the offering.

"That's it," one of the witches taunted, shaking the dead animals and side stepping into the woods. Zane. A Protector that often worked with my father. "Come get this nasty little skunk. Whatta treat, huh, dragon? Just for you!"

The forest dragon slipped into the trees after the carcasses, disappearing with nothing more than a rustle of leaves.

"Are you all right, Miss Bianca?"

Brecken, a Captain of the Guardians, called to me from near the poachers. His curly dark brown hair bounced as he stepped toward us with a determined stride, his bright blue eyes looking us over in concern. His wide set of shoulders stood out from beneath the half-armor of leather and metal that Guardians wore on patrol. The Guardians were a massive, all-male force that protected the castle and the Network, a veritable army of witches trained to fight and defend.

"Yes. I'm not hurt."

"Ya don't belong here!" a weak voice cried. "Coven Leader Clive is right! They should exile ya and yer father and send ya to the Northern Network where liars belong."

I looked up to find Alvyn shaking a fist at me from where he lay in the grass, his face pressed into the ground by the heel of a Guardian. Another stood over him, a drawn bow and arrow pointed at his head.

"Silence!" the Guardian barked, then kicked Alvyn in the ribs. "Traitors don't get to speak to anyone but Derek."

I turned to Brecken.

"Traitors?" I asked, grateful to turn the conversation away from Papa and I. Ever since the Central Network found out Papa's secret—that he'd flouted the unbroken tradition that the Head of Protectors give up family life—hatred for us had run deep in some regions. Witches could be unusually attached to the traditions of old. Some believed that upholding the rules laid down by our forefathers established safety in our land. I agreed with them to some extent, but not on every account.

Despite Papa's unpopularity, the Guardians remained steadfast in their loyalty to him. "I thought they were just poachers?"

Brecken's lips formed a grim line.

"Trying to kill a forest dragon when we teeter on the brink of war?" he asked. "The act of a traitor. They probably work for the Western Network."

And Miss Mabel.

The thought tightened my fists so hard my nails bit into the skin.

"Let's get you back," Brecken said, with a glance at both of us. He held out an arm to motion us to the castle, and I saw the tattoo of a shield on his inner wrist. Instead of a circlus like mine, Brecken bore the Mark of the Captain. "Your father will be hearing of this by now, no doubt, and will want to see you himself. I'll walk you back."

He motioned for us to follow with a jerk of his head. Camille, who had remained mostly silent, bounded forward to walk at his side, her eyes bright.

"I'm Camille," she said, eyeing him with an appreciative little grin. "I don't believe we've met before."

Her rambling voice died into the background as I trailed behind the two of them. Thanks to Brecken's grim reminder of Miss Mabel's presence, my mind fixated on the one place I didn't want it to go.

It was a place far from the spiral staircases and wide stone halls of Chatham Castle. The little old manor in the shadows of Letum Wood, Miss Mabel's School for Girls. The whole drama of my last day at the school unfolded in the space of two breaths. Me in the attic with my evil teacher Miss Mabel, using defensive magic against her in a battle for my life. Then Mama stepping in to protect me, and Miss Mabel killing her in one decisive move.

No. I stopped the flashback before it re-ignited the restless powers within me. The magic had had enough exercise for one day.

An Internal Weapon

I passed through the opulence of the Royal Hall later that evening with a feeling of trepidation. The impending meeting with the High Priestess had loomed in my mind for hours. Would she be angry with me for defending the forest dragon? Had I done something wrong? Papa would be waiting as well, and it would be a relief to have him at my side. He was the only thing left that made me feel safe.

Two Guardians lingered near the staircase, protecting the deserted hallway I started down. I didn't mind the solitude because it gave me an opportunity to think.

Paintings of past High Priests and Priestesses covered the wall in gilded frames. All wore the same shade of crimson in the portraits, the Central Network's color. Their faces held similar echoes of the stoic determination that I saw in our current High Priestess. Perhaps they all knew something that the rest of us, who didn't lead, never would. Something besides the strange desire to tie themselves to a desk and sit through meetings for their whole lives. I shuddered at the thought.

I checked to make sure the nearby Guardians couldn't see me, then crept up to the High Priestess's door and pressed my ear to it. It was the perfect eavesdropping opportunity, and since I was the topic of conversation, I suppressed the pang of guilt rather quickly. I whispered a spell under my breath to magnify the sound and used my exceptional hearing to tune into the room.

If an important, secretive meeting had been going on, or if the castle had been unusually full of witches and visitors, the High Priestess would have cast a protective incantation to block nosy witches like me. Since I had little to do with Network security or the fear of upcoming war, I hoped she wouldn't have taken such precautions.

The gravelly voice of the High Priestess worked through the elaborate door first.

"—the natural result of Marie's death."

I jerked away. The sound of Mama's name shocked me, as if they'd touched a poker to my heart. It had been several weeks since I'd heard it spoken out loud. My heart thudded in my chest as I attempted to recover my calm. I let out a long, slow breath and tried again, placing the shell of my ear back on the cool wood.

That's what you get when you listen to conversations you aren't invited to, I thought in a moment of self-chiding.

"She misses Marie . . . how do I help when she won't even speak of her? I'm not sure . . ."

Papa's muffled voice moved in and out. His back must have been to the door. I could picture him pacing in front of the desk, trying to figure out why his daughter wanted to save a dangerous dragon. I didn't blame him. Even I wondered.

"I'm most concerned about her safety," the High Priestess said in a grim tone. "Things are getting ugly here."

"We could leave . . . Go north—"

"Absolutely not. What would leaving do?"

Her words trailed off and I clenched my fist in frustration, only able to make out a low murmur with a few words in between. The High Priestess would never let Papa leave. Her vow to save me from the curse was proof she'd do just about anything to keep him here.

"Yes," Papa said, pulling me back into their conversation. "Some outlet . . . I haven't pressed her into getting a job because I wanted her to have space. . . Doesn't run anymore."

My heart twisted again. So Papa had noticed.

Just two months ago on the day Mama died, Miss Mabel blackmailed me into signing a magical binding, a contract in which I agreed to complete one unknown task. After I signed the binding, she killed my mother. She hadn't assigned me a task yet; I'd been waiting for two months without word. I figured she would assign me to kill the High Priestess. What other reason could she have had? But because the binding's protective magic prevented me from speaking about it to anyone, no one knew of my tie to Miss Mabel. At one point, the High Priestess had had her suspicions that Miss Mabel was going to put me under a binding, but I didn't know if she still suspected it was done. If she did, she didn't let on. Unfortunately, if I didn't complete the task, I'd die.

In the meantime, my birthday approached fast. It stood just four months away, and brought with it the culmination of my old family curse. If the High Priestess didn't fulfill her vow, the curse would kill me when I turned seventeen. I had four months left to live and two ways to die.

To top it off, Papa had no idea.

"—help control the power," the High Priestess's voice jarred me back into the present. "We need to help her protect herself. I can't trust every Coven Leader or Council Member anymore. I'd feel a lot better if Bianca could do more than throw around a couple of blighters to defend herself. Mabel isn't dead yet and I don't think we should act like she is."

The stark reality of the High Priestess's words struck a chord of fear deep inside me. I lived in a castle filled with Guardians and Protectors, not to mention with Papa, one of the most talented witches in all of Antebellum. Yet, the High Priestess still feared for my life. Safety was an illusion, something cursory that one thought of but never found. After watching Mama die before my eyes, I figured I knew that better than anyone.

"Merry meet, Bianca."

A quiet, amused voice came up from behind me with all the presence of a ghost. I jumped and whirled around to find Merrick, my father's apprentice, standing there. His freshly washed hair rested against the base of his neck in a ponytail. The blonde strands nestled amidst the light brown looked bright in the light of the nearby torch. A shadow of brown stubble covered his tanned, handsome face and made his eyes look as green as the spring leaves outside. He wasn't much older than me, something close to twenty-two or three. As a fledgling, almost-accepted Protector, Merrick spent a lot of time with Papa but rarely interacted with me. He was always focused on whatever task Papa had given him.

"Oh," I said, pressing a hand to my galloping heart. "You startled me. What are you doing here, Merrick?"

His face twisted into an expression of wry irony.

"The High Priestess summoned me."

A little envelope with the High Priestess's writing flashed between his fingers.

"What are you doing here?" he asked, glancing between me and the door. I opened my mouth to defend myself, but realized I had no good explanation. He'd caught me.

"Ensuring the success of my future," I said. To my surprise, a little grin filtered across his features.

"You may want to step back then," he said. "Or else your future is going to involve a black eye."

Better safe than sorry. I obeyed. The doors cracked open as I stepped away, spilling a sliver of light into the hall. I shot him a silent, grateful look. The thick wood would have smacked me in the face, revealing my eavesdropping in the worst way.

"Both of you may enter," the High Priestess called. Merrick stepped back to allow me in first, and I ducked inside.

The dying light of day ringed the edges of Letum Wood just outside. Four open windows allowed the cooling spring air to spill in. Scrolls and pieces of parchment sat on the High Priestess's massive desk, limp from the humidity of the day, as if they were melting. There were no books in her office. She kept them all in a side closet, with the simple explanation that offices weren't libraries. Pictures lined the walls instead, covering the dull gray stone and leaving the impression of a quiet room of art. The High Priestess waited until I stood just across from her desk to address me.

"The grief over losing your mother has made your magic stronger," she said with a direct stare. The door to her office closed behind Merrick. "I'm not sure how I feel about you being so bold while your powers are out of control."

That's a surprise, I thought of saying. *I'd assume that everyone likes a girl who will step in front of dragon and throw herself onto a dangerous poacher.*

"My apologies, Your Highness," I said, ignoring her reference to Mama. She rolled her small, dark eyes. Small talk did not exist in the High Priestess's world, and this habit of getting right to the point was one of my favorite things about her. I was grateful to get this over with. Papa moved to stand near the window. He cast me a quick wink, allowing me to release some of the anxiety in my chest.

"Don't get ahead of yourself just yet," she muttered. "You may not have reason to apologize. I spoke with everyone involved with the incident."

"What did they say?" I asked.

"All the witnesses had the same story. You stopped Alvyn from shooting the forest dragon. When he tried to attack you, you used magic to cause an explosion. It sent you rolling down the hill while Alvyn and his accomplice were knocked out."

A poor choice of weapon on my part, I thought with a frown. Now that time had passed, my back and shoulders felt sore and tight from the tumble. I'd have a bruise or two to deal with later.

"Well?" the High Priestess demanded, pulling me from my thoughts again. "Is that what happened?"

"I believe so, Your Highness. I don't remember much."

Her eyes narrowed.

"Why did you want to save that dragon?"

My jaw tightened. "He hadn't done anything wrong. Killing him for being alive seemed a bit . . ." I trailed off, meeting her eyes. "Ruthless."

"It's a dragon, not your mother."

"It's a life," I snapped. "And I saved it according to my conscience."

The magic, now itself resembling a roaring dragon, calmed enough that I could think. Ever since Mama died the magic made me restless and fidgety, keeping me up into the late hours of the night while I stared at the ceiling, missing Mama with an ache so terrible I thought I'd break. There were days I couldn't control the powers, and those were usually the days when my grief felt the strongest.

Papa shot me a sharp look of reprimand.

"I'm sorry, Your Highness," I said with a true pang of guilt. "I didn't mean any disrespect."

The High Priestess released a long breath and let the error slide.

"Your conscience led you right and I thank you for it."

My eyes snapped back onto hers. "What?"

"You did nothing wrong in defending yourself, and you managed to save a dragon in the meantime."

"But I lost control of the magic."

"Yes, but you saved your own life, and possibly Camille's. Alvyn admitted to your father that he planned to kill you."

A little shiver of fear skimmed my spine when I met Papa's suddenly turbulent eyes. So Alvyn had faced Papa. For a moment I felt a flash of pity for the poacher.

"He actually confessed to wanting to kill me?"

The High Priestess gifted me with her piercing stare. "He had to. Veritas is a very powerful potion, as I know you are very aware."

No arguments here, I wanted to say, recalling the terrible memories of the Veritas potion I carried with me from my time at Miss Mabel's. Veritas caused a crippling vertigo and nearly unstoppable desire to speak your deepest wishes. No one could withstand the Veritas without years of calculated exposure.

"What will happen to him?" I asked.

"He dies tomorrow."

Her simple response startled me, and I could only stare at her for several moments, blinking.

"Dies?"

"Yes. Both of them earned it. I will not allow traitors to live. Enough of the poachers, let's talk about our plan for you. Until Miss Mabel is dead I will fear for your safety, Bianca. Chatham Castle is not the safe place it used to be, unfortunately."

The rush of panic took me by surprise.

"You aren't going to send me away, are you?"

"Of course not," she said with a frown. "You'd be less safe anywhere else. Besides, your father has a plan of his own."

She looked over to Papa, silently giving him the conversation. His forehead had puckered into deep grooves that smoothed out as he spoke. The fast, clipped inflections of his tone comforted me.

"She's right. Ever since your mother died your powers have grown, B," he said in a quiet voice. Worry flickered through his gaze for just a moment, then disappeared. He straightened up, standing to his full height. "Mabel isn't under our control yet, which means you need to learn how to fight in order to defend yourself should the occasion arise. You have to learn something more than how to use blighters in a Mactos."

Blighters, Mactos, defend yourself. All these words took me back to my time with Miss Mabel. I'd stood alone against her in a Mactos, a magical fight where blighters, little balls of energy, were used as the main weapons. Just remembering that day flamed my already agitated powers. I swallowed. "Papa, I haven't done anything to make the magic so strong."

"It's not your fault," he said, sharing a glance with the High Priestess. "It's to be expected with grieving. I thought the magic would work itself out if I gave you time to process losing your mother, but that's obviously not the case yet. Perhaps you just need more time."

I flinched at the reference to Mama and remained silent. I didn't know what to say. Papa dealt with everything through logic. Forward movement. Never looking back. Emotions placed on the back burner to deal with the current situation. When he grieved, he did it in private, away from the light and other people. I didn't doubt he mourned as deeply as me, but he did it in such a different way that I sometimes felt as if I were drowning in a sea of despair while he stood on the shore.

Papa continued, pulling me from my thoughts, "You need to be able to defend yourself from witches like Alvyn or, heaven forbid, Mabel when she shows up."

His use of *when* and not *if* sent a violent shudder down my spine.

"That's why we asked Merrick here," the High Priestess said, turning her eyes onto him. He stood several paces behind me with his hands folded behind his back, so silent I'd forgotten he was there.

"You have served as an apprentice to Derek for nearly two years, is that right?"

"Yes, Your Highness," Merrick responded.

"You have three months before the Protectors can vote on whether or not they will accept you. Is that also correct?"

Merrick nodded once. Every male witch that hoped to serve as a Protector had to survive an initial training period that lasted an entire winter. If the witch passed and still wanted to be a Protector—and most did not—they spent two years as an apprentice. At the end of the two years, the Protectors voted on whether they would keep the candidate or not. Few enough made it past the initial training period and even fewer were initiated after the vote. With only thirteen people allowed at one time, the Protectors were one of the most exclusive groups in all of Antebellum.

"I'm assigning Merrick to teach you sword fighting," Papa said. "He'll continue with his regular duties, of course, but will also instruct you every day. Our hope is that through learning how to fight physically, you will not only learn how to protect yourself, but also give your emotions an outlet."

Merrick's shoulders tightened, but like most Protectors, his expression never changed. I suspected he may resent it; he probably saw it as a babysitting duty rather than an educational experience.

"The magic took over you today, and you nearly exploded." Papa's chocolate eyes latched onto mine. "Since you refuse to talk about your mother, we'll try giving you a physical way to express your emotions."

I turned away from his intense gaze. He was right: I wouldn't talk about Mama. The ability to control the madness in my heart? I would work for that, especially if I could avoid speaking about her. Having a solid distraction from the grief and madness in my mind would be even better. I'd start immediately, if they wanted.

"Yes, Papa," I said. "I'll try."

"Do you have any questions?" the High Priestess asked.

I had so many I couldn't narrow them down. Should I be worried about my safety all the time? Did Alvyn work for Miss Mabel? Could my powers even be controlled?

"Why did those witches want to kill the forest dragon?" I asked, voicing the first that came to my tongue. "Forest dragons haven't been seen in centuries."

The High Priestess's lips pressed into a thin, pale line.

"Hunting them for Mabel," she said, and left it at that. The confirmation of my fear stirred the magic inside. It felt like a dragon just starting to wake up. Perhaps dragons weren't just the threatening creatures in Letum Wood. Perhaps the magic made me part dragon now, roaring and raging on the whim of my internal fury.

"Your first lesson begins in two days. That will give Merrick time to rearrange his schedule and prepare the lessons. Go away, all of you," the High Priestess said with a flick of her wrist. "I have work to see to."

Papa walked up to my side and hooked an arm around my shoulders while Merrick led the way to the door.

"Come on, B," Papa said. "Let's go get dinner."

We shuffled into the hallway without a word, leaving the quiet office behind. I cast one last glance over my shoulder to see the High Priestess already buried in a new correspondence that had just flown in the window.

The Witchery

The Witchery was an abandoned turret that my three friends—Leda, Michelle, and Camille—and I had claimed the week they'd arrived. No one challenged us for it. No one really seemed to want it.

Leda and Camille came to live at Chatham Castle a month after Mama's death. Although I didn't remember much of the first few weeks without her, I knew that I'd slept through most of it. One day I woke up to Leda glaring down at me, fists on her hips, and Camille hopping for joy. The High Priestess had arranged for them to be with me, doing their classes at the castle with Miss Scarlett occasionally checking in. Their presence had been a definite balm for my aching heart.

Our explorations of the castle during the long winter days led us to an old wooden door, behind which a set of winding stairs led to an abandoned room. The turret rose so far above the ground that we could see all of Chatham City and the blurred edge of the rolling horizon from the arched windows. I couldn't imagine how no one seemed to notice it had been empty for years. Of Chatham's ten turrets that speared the sky, it was the tallest and widest.

Leda and I came to the conclusion that a vengeful witch had cursed it so no one would go in. Chatham Castle, and all her inhabitants, tended to be a superstitious lot. Perhaps my spreading of the rumor that the ghost of Esmelda—the first High Priestess of the Central Network—had been seen there helped maintain our privacy.

The next morning after breakfast Papa informed me my lessons with Merrick were to start the next day, then ruffled my hair and headed for his office in the Gatehouse. I cleaned up, changed into a fresh cotton dress, and headed for the many steps of the spiraling turret staircase. The tips of my fingers skimmed the walls on either side. Every few steps an arched window about knee high spilled light on the stairs, allowing the fresh air to sing through.

I released a content little sigh. Though the world might crumble around us, the Witchery was always a safe place.

"Merry meet!" I called to my friends when I gained the upper stair.

Leda sat curled on a window seat, her white-blonde hair reflecting the sun like strands of snowflakes. She had a pert little nose that turned up just slightly at the tip, giving her a girlish mien. An ancient book with frayed edges held her attention, as usual. She didn't bother to look up when I entered, so I ignored her. Leda was a friend better tolerated if she chose when to speak. Asking her a question she didn't want to answer only led to a reply I didn't want.

"Merry meet, Bianca," Camille replied. "What did the High Priestess say last night? Are you in trouble? I hope not! Even if I do think you're crazy for saving that dragon."

She stood at the window opposite Leda, where she always watched the Guardians when they trained below. The clash and clang of sword fighting drifted up from the lower bailey, which took up half of the front of Chatham Castle's walled interior and swept over to the left side.

"Who were you looking at?" I asked instead of answering.

Tiberius, the Head of the Guardians and Papa's best friend, stood on the Wall, looking down on his charges in the lower bailey like a great bird assessing his prey. Swords and shields glinted in the sunlight as the Guardians sparred. I wondered if Merrick would have me doing the same kinds of routines. Would I learn how to use a sword as well as the Guardians did? I was already skilled with my shield. Perhaps that would give me a small advantage.

"No one in particular," Camille said with a wave of her wrist, but her eyes narrowed. "Tell me, Bianca, what do you know about Brecken?"

"Brecken?"

"Yes. The Guardian that walked us back yesterday? I tried to get him to talk but he barely said a word." Her lips pulled down in an un-characteristic frown. "I can't figure him out. I've never had a problem getting a Guardian to talk to me before. They're all so excited for the attention of a lady they practically beg me to speak."

I laughed and stepped away from the window. She had all their affection-starved hearts in her sweet little hands. All except one, it sounded like.

"And who can fathom a Guardian that doesn't swoon over your every word?" I asked with a dramatic flair. Camille didn't notice my sarcasm.

"That's what I was wondering!" she cried, throwing her hands in the air. Then she sat down with a happy sigh, her trouble expression disappearing. "Oh, Bianca! Living at Chatham Castle is so much better than school! I'm going to die of jealousy when I have to go back to that wretched old manor in the fall and you get to stay here."

"I agree," Leda said, piping up. "Bianca, it's a waste that you should be here with a library so extensive when you don't even like studying."

"Maybe I'll pick up reading just to spite you," I said in a light-hearted tone. "Then I'll write out book reports and send them to you so you're maniacally jealous of me."

Leda shot me a playful glare from her two differently colored eyes; one was an olive green, the other a light straw. Behind her lay a rigged-up bookshelf, nothing more than an old rotting board held up by two cracked pots. Most of the books she'd smuggled out of the library lay stacked in perfect piles along the shelf and wall. A skinny little bed with tucked covers and a white pillow hid behind the tattered sheet she kept pulled to separate her area. Leda took her own space very seriously.

Camille's side of the turret looked like it had just weathered a windstorm. Dresses and ribbon clotted the floor and rained from the divan. The doors to an abandoned armoire she'd brought up with the help of a few Guardians were thrown open and belched even more clothes onto the ground. A bouquet of pale pink spring flowers, a gift from one of her many Guardian admirers, wilted in a small vase nearby. She'd forgotten to water them again.

"Merry meet," another voice said, huffing from climbing the stairs.

Michelle's burly frame appeared in the doorway, accompanied by the shuffle of her heavy feet. She was tall and hefty for a girl, raised in southern Letum Wood with a family of five brothers that worked as foresters and ran a farm to sustain themselves. Her broad shoulders, disappearing eyes, and thick facial features made her look awkward and boyish. She had been a third-year at Miss Mabel's School for Girls when the rest of us were first-years.

Fina, the main cook for Chatham Castle, hired Michelle once Miss Mabel's School for Girls closed down. After Mama's death, most of the students had been pulled from the school by their parents. With rumors of war threatening from the West, Miss Scarlett finally cancelled the school year until the fall. Because Michelle was so talented in culinary means and wanted to pursue a career with food, Miss Scarlett allowed her to take the final tests.

As a result of her early graduation, Michelle was hired on at Chatham Castle after earning her marks and spent most of her free time with us. Though she had quarters of her own, she often slept on oversized pillows piled into a kind of lumpy mattress on the Witchery floor. Because the school was closed, Leda and Camille continued their lessons with private instruction from Miss Scarlett once a week.

"Why didn't you levitate the platter up, Michelle?" Leda asked, flummoxed that anyone would do physical labor if magic could do the work for them. Her puny muscles testified to her bookish ways.

"Oh, I don't mind." Michelle shrugged. "Papa had us do almost everything without magic growing up. He thinks that witches are too lazy now."

"I'm starving!" Camille declared, pouncing on the platter. "This smells so good! I want to eat it all. Did you already eat with your father, Bianca?"

"Yes," I said. "But go ahead."

The four of us sat down in the middle of the turret at the old table we'd dragged up from an abandoned meeting room a couple of floors below. Camille had filched a red and gold Central Network banner with a dragon roaring out of it for the wall. She hung it right next to a white flag she'd started to embroider with the goal of saying *The*

Witchery, but she'd gotten bored halfway through, been distracted and messed up on the C, and now all it said was *The Wits*.

"Have you heard anymore from the High Priestess about your vow?" Leda asked. They were the only ones that knew about the secret vow between me and the High Priestess, and Leda checked in often.

"No," I said in a clipped tone. It was the last thing I wanted to talk about. "I haven't."

"Are you getting worried?" Camille asked, her concern evident between mouthfuls. "I am. It's been two months already."

"Not yet. We still have loads of time."

"Right, loads." Camille rolled her eyes and reached for the loaf of brown bread. Leda snatched the crock of butter before Camille could take it and Michelle grabbed a chunk of ham. "Just a few months, really."

"We might have found a way to control my powers," I said, hoping to break apart the current discussion. Talking about my almost-certain demise rarely brought me joy.

"Really?" Michelle asked, her small eyes lighting up. "How?"

I filled them in on the conversation with Papa, Merrick, and the High Priestess, including Alvyn's interrogation and murderous intent. "Papa thinks physical work will help me release my emotions and the powers. I start tomorrow," I finished, leaning back.

"Oh, goodness. That's frightening about Alvyn." Camille blinked, pausing with a slice of bread halfway to her mouth. "But training with Merrick? He's very handsome. I'd never be able to concentrate on the lesson. I'd just want to stare into those green eyes."

Her gaze went distant for a second, then she shook her head and bit into her bread with renewed vigor.

"Do you want to do it?" Leda asked, carefully cutting her bread into small, bite-sized pieces. I could see the cogs in her mind spinning. Of the four of us, Leda was the logical planner. A vengeful witch set the Foresight Curse on Leda when she was a baby, which meant that she could see possibilities for the future. They pressed themselves upon her—she certainly didn't want them—quite often. On rare occasions she would share the future chances with us, but most of the time she wisely kept them to herself. Her gaze went distant and I knew she was looking ahead, into the future, but wouldn't tell me what she figured out.

"Yes, I do. It will be nice to have something else to think about."

My sentence hung in the air like a bird stilled in flight. They knew what I didn't say. *Besides my mother's death.*

"I also want to know why Miss Mabel has witches hunting the forest dragons," I said, clearing my throat.

"I'll ask Nicolas," Michelle said, then instantly blushed. "H-he's a friend of my mine in the kitchen. He's obsessed with dragons and has worked at Chatham since he was young, so he'll know all about them. He talks about them all day."

"Nicolas, was it?" Camille asked with a sly smile. "You should go with him to the Anniversary ball!"

"No!" Michelle said, averting her eyes. "I-I would never . . . I can't dance o-or talk to him for very long."

"Well I can't wait to go!" Camille leaned back, her eyes glowing. "I've always dreamed of wearing a beautiful gown and dancing all night. And the food!"

She draped a lazy arm over her stomach and gave a satisfied sigh.

The High Priestess had deemed it mandatory that I attend the ball, or I would have found a reason not to go. I wondered if that would change now that safety was of greater concern. Leda would have outright refused if Miss Scarlett hadn't told her she had to attend as part of the curriculum for her second year.

It'll be a perfect chance to execute the manners I've taught you, she'd said a few days before, setting her sharp eyes mostly on me. *You'll not get another chance like this for months, even years.*

"I certainly won't be dancing for very long," Leda said. Crowds of witches activated her curse, overwhelming her with a headache and making it almost impossible to function. "I'll stay just long enough for Miss Scarlett to see me, and then I'll leave."

"Will you be able to go, Bianca?" Michelle asked.

"Yes, of course," I said with a wicked smile. "I'll go dressed as a Guardian and show off my newfound talent—sword fighting."

They stared at me, aghast for a moment, then we all dissolved into

a fit of girlish giggles that faded into the sweet perfume of the beautiful spring day.

Running Pains

A message fluttered into my bedroom the next morning, bringing the early tendrils of sunrise with it. The night-stained sky, with all her fading stars, winked at me from the skinny window on the opposite wall. I closed my eyes and groped blindly for the folded messenger paper hovering over my face until I caught it in my palm. With a groan, I forced myself to sit up. It took several moments to wake up enough to comprehend the message.

Meet me on the Wall in twenty minutes.
—Merrick

Yawning and half-blind from sleep, I stumbled into an old dress with long sleeves, left my feet bare as usual, and crept through the silent halls of Chatham Castle, braiding my hair as I went. A few maids, as weary as I, stumbled through their morning routines, ignoring me.

The air felt chilly when I stepped out into it, prickling the edges of my skin. The Wall, a protective structure several stories high, ringed the front and sides of Chatham Castle proper. Its top had a walkway wide enough to permit three or four carriages abreast. Most Guardians assigned to duty at Chatham Castle lived within the Wall. They called it the Ranks. The Gatehouse, where Papa and Tiberius worked, sat in the middle of the Wall, above the entrance from the road.

Merrick straightened as I neared. The early morning light made his eyes look bright and alert. Despite the early hour, he looked refreshed, as if he'd been awake for hours. I stifled another yawn at the thought. It was my first lesson. Surely he'd go easy on me.

"Ready to begin?" he asked. His deep voice rolled with a long rumble. His hair was pulled back in a ponytail as usual.

"I don't know," I said, my voice betraying my suspicion. "What are we doing?"

He grinned. Perhaps he liked it when people didn't know what to expect from him. He certainly had enough of that mysterious, vague air.

"We're going to run," he said.

"No!" I cried with a sharp intake of breath. Even the thought of running seemed unbearable. "I mean . . . I don't run anymore."

His eyes narrowed. "You can't run?"

"I-I mean to say that I haven't run since—"

The words stalled in my throat. *I haven't run since Mama died.* But even that was a lie. I had run. The day after burying Mama I headed into Letum Wood out of desperation, hoping to get away from my overwhelming new life. It had been a mistake. A terrible, terrible mistake.

"Since Marie died?" Merrick finished for me. My heart reacted with a painful ache. I folded my arms across my chest.

"I won't run."

"Yes, you will," he said without an ounce of sympathy. "It's our first lesson and I need to figure out what you're capable of before I plan the rest out. I know you used to run all the time. Derek told me."

Like Papa, Merrick spoke with even, calm logic. No emotion, no judgment. Just fact. It was infuriating. How could anyone live in a world of black and white, especially now?

"I already told you," I said, folding my arms across my chest. "I won't run in Letum Wood."

He paused, narrowed his eyes, and studied me. I wasn't sure which was worse, not knowing what he was thinking or getting the sense that no matter how hard I protested, I still had to run. Merrick didn't seem like the type to back down.

"Look, I can't run," I said, pleading. "You don't understand."

33

"You're right," he retorted. "I don't understand. Why can't you run? You look capable."

My mouth opened but the words faltered.

I see Mama when I run and I can't bear it.

No, it sounded insane, even in my head, though it was the truth.

A rousing start to our first lesson, Bianca, I told myself. *Two minutes in and he thinks you're a coward. If you tell him the truth, he'll think you're mad. Why don't you just start screaming like a shrew and really impress him?*

"Yes, I used to run all the time, but I stopped. I-I don't want to run."

"So you're afraid to run?"

The insinuation prodded my powers, raising them from their slumber with liquid fire.

"No!" I yelled. Forcing myself to calm by inhaling a long breath through my nose, I leveled my voice. "I'm not afraid of anything."

"Really?" he asked in a dry tone that told me I'd just revealed too much about myself. This was rapidly slipping out of my control. "Is that why you're reacting like a two-year-old?"

"I am not!" I stomped my foot. Merrick raised a single eyebrow. I wanted to call it all back, to rewind the morning and start over. I was acting like a small child. But I was desperate that he understand. I would not run.

"I'm not afraid of running," I said in a too-calm voice, dropping my arms to my sides. "I just don't like it."

The lie almost didn't come out. It felt as thick as sap on my tongue. In truth, I needed to run. I could feel it in my bones, in the ache of my muscles. My body longed for the freedom of movement, for release and euphoria. But I couldn't risk seeing Mama's ghost on the trail again, calling to me. Running through Letum Wood would revive all the memories I'd been trying so hard to keep buried. I'd never endure that kind of pain. My heart was just too frail.

He thought about what I said for so long that the silence became cumbersome. I opened my mouth to speak and closed it again. A few Guardians stumbled into the high bailey below us, laughing raucously over a joke about a gypsy.

"I'm sorry," he said. I drew in a breath of hope. Mercy! He was going to show mercy and think of something else for me to do. My body nearly collapsed with relief. Perhaps Merrick wasn't as ruthless and intense as I had thought. He continued, "But it's time to face your fears and start running again. Let's go."

All my hope disappeared. He took off at an easy lope down the stairs on the outside of the Wall that led down to the gardens. I didn't even have a chance to protest. His pace didn't slow to a walk; he sped up. He couldn't so much as put a friendly arm around my shoulder and say, "Let's go easy on you this time." No, none of that. He simply started running.

"Merrick, wait!" I called, starting after him. "Please?"

My cries went unheeded. Dread filled my stomach. I had to follow him or he'd tell Papa and the High Priestess. They'd demand an explanation. I'd have to talk about Mama again, and explain how frazzled the grief had made me.

I see Mama's ghost in the woods now, Papa. I refuse to think or talk about it, so this is your only shot to learn how crazy I am now.

Forced to move forward, I let out a heavy sigh, following behind at a jog more worthy of a walk. My sluggish muscles moved with all the grace of wooden sticks at first. I felt like a toddler learning how to walk for the first time. Each step thudded heavy and leaden. I marveled that I ever used to run at all. Had it only been two months? It felt like so much longer.

Without saying another word, Merrick led us right to Letum Wood, canceling any hope I'd harbored that we'd run around the gardens.

"Keep up," he said, ducking a low branch with a lithe side step. His body moved graceful and fast like a cat. "I don't want to get separated while we're in the forest."

The rocks in the trail cut into the soft bottoms of my feet, and I mourned the hardened, calloused skin that once protected them. My heart beat uncomfortably hard and fast. When I didn't adequately dodge a root, the hem of my dress snagged, and I spilled onto the trail, scraping my foot on an exposed stone and rolling onto my back.

"Wretched dress," I muttered, shoving the skirt away from my face. Dirt coated my sweaty arms. My skin already felt sticky and flushed with heat. A scrape on the front of my leg dribbled blood onto my ankle. I ignored it and climbed back to my feet, purposefully keeping my eyes on the trail. Maybe I wouldn't feel as homesick if I didn't look at the trees, or study their brilliant green color. I'd just act like I wasn't in Letum Wood at all.

Focus solely on the trail, I told myself. *Nothing to see but dirt and rocks.*

Merrick paused ahead and waited while I pulled myself back together. Seeing that he was watching, I pushed up and started to run again.

Prove you aren't weak, Bianca. I chanted to myself in a loop, using it as a mantra. *Prove you're not afraid.*

Merrick and I fell back into jogging without a word. I kept an eye on the trail snaking ahead of me, waiting to see patches of white in my peripheral vision. Despite my determination to only focus on the trail, every now and then my gaze flickered to my surroundings; I couldn't help it. Letum's call was far too strong.

Drapes of moss coated the thick tree trunks and crawled with blooming vines, leaves, and flowers. Branches clogged the air, soaring so far over my head I couldn't make out the sky. It was dense, tall, and thick, but still beautiful in the way that only Letum Wood could be.

The earthy scent of pine provoked the memories first. They flittered through my mind like the birds chasing each other through the canopy, stretching their wings after a long winter slumber. In between the flashing tree branches I thought I heard Mama's voice on the wind, calling to me. I pushed the thought away, forcing it back.

Don't think about her. If you think about her, you'll miss her. Allowing the memories only allows the pain. Protect your heart. Live without pain.

Before long I was gasping for breath, shuffling over the larger roots while Merrick hopped them. My tight muscles had loosened after the first few minutes but clamped back up when we hit the rolling hills. It took most of my concentration just to breathe, winding through the trails taking us away from the castle. Before long the path shifted, looping back. Merrick said little, but I could sense him change his pace when I really struggled, allowing me a short reprieve to catch a few extra gulps of air. But even with this extra time, he didn't go easy on me.

Just when I thought I had control, when the memories had retreated so far in my mind I couldn't feel their power, a flash of white stole my attention on the trail ahead. I looked up, and the magic flared in my chest with a burst of renewed strength.

A woman stood on the trail in front of me. Her loose linen dress shifted in the breeze, trailing down her slender, lithe figure. Gentle strands of the blackest hair rested on her shoulders, fluttering with the wind. She held a hand over her eyes, as if to shield them from the sun. My heart skipped a beat. I skidded to a dead stop, breathless. Merrick ran past Mama as if she didn't exist, disappearing around a tight corner in the foliage.

"No," I whispered, numb. "Not again."

The woman smiled and called my name.

Bianca! Come home now. It's time for dinner.

My heart knotted into a painful hole in my chest and I looked away. *No!* I wanted to scream. *Leave me alone! Let me move on!* But the words stuck in my throat, dammed with unshed tears.

I heard the sweet giggle of a little girl and spun around to see a small child with matching black hair and bare feet run up to Mama's side. Mama picked her up and spun her around. Me. The little girl was me. Their gauzy, ethereal figures danced and twisted together.

"No!" I pressed my palms to my eyes. Every beat of my heart caused me physical pain. Playing on the trails of Letum Wood with Mama were my earliest memories. They haunted me now, reminding me of all I'd lost. "Go away!"

When I dropped my hands, the memory had faded, leaving nothing but a gentle giggle rolling through the air. I stood in the middle of the trail, panting. The power ballooned inside me, threatening to break free. I pushed it aside, forcing my mind to other things. Anything but Mama.

"Think of something else," I whispered to myself, shoving the hair out of my face. "Say something in the Declan language. Curro. Tine Curro—"

"Bianca?"

Merrick crested the hill in search of me, the corners of his mouth pulled down in concern.

"Are you all right?"

"F-fine!" I said, stumbling forward, trying to shake it off. "I'm fine. I—"

The words stopped. How could I explain what happened without sounding like a lunatic? *I saw a ghost of my mother on the trail. Oh, I was there too, but I was only five.*

"Why did you stop?" he asked.

His green eyes narrowed, looking more curious than annoyed. Perhaps he saw the way my hands trembled, or heard how my voice jumped around, unsteady and fearful.

"I-I don't know. It was nothing."

His forehead furrowed into deeper lines, but he didn't say anything. Before my thoughts took a drastic twist into an overwhelming, paralyzing depression, I caught his gaze and said firmly, "I'm done."

I whispered the incantation to transport and a comforting darkness embraced me. Pressure bore down on my eyes and face until my legs struck ground and I fell onto my side near the hedge boundary back at Chatham Castle. I exhaled in relief and climbed back to my feet.

Merrick transported next to me without a word, his jaw tight. I scrubbed all thoughts of Mama and Letum Wood away, thinking instead of soaking in a tub of ice water until my lips turned blue. Blue, yes. Cold. Frigid. Numb to pain.

"Tomorrow," Merrick said, his green eyes distant. I wondered what he was thinking about my odd, frantic behavior. Would he tell Papa? "Same time. Meet me in the Forgotten Gardens."

"Tomorrow," I repeated, and walked away as fast as I could.

"Ready for breakfast, B?" Papa called.

I came out of my bedroom and entered the main room of the apartment, shaking out my wet hair. A cold bath had shrunk the jittery feelings from the run to a manageable size, and my powers had retreated. I'd all but forgotten the brief encounter in that vague place we'd gone.

Papa's apartment was sparse, but it felt like him, so I loved it. A brick fireplace filled the wall on the right, swathed with decorative bundles of willow boughs tied with twine. Two mustard-colored divans clustered around the fireplace on a woven black and tan rug. A few matching pillows plumped up the window seat overlooking Letum Wood, where I often curled up for naps in the sunshine. Swords and gleaming knives filled the rest of the walls. A pair of crossed spears hung above the door leading to the balcony.

Guardians bustled in the lower bailey below, preparing for their first training lesson of the day. Despite the early hour, the clang of swords kissing drifted up to the apartment. I glanced down with a grim face. The Guardians trained around the clock now, preparing for war with the West.

"Thanks for waiting, Papa," I said, settling into a wooden chair. A tray of food sat on the small table we'd used since I'd arrived. Before I lived with Papa he'd always eaten in the Gatehouse with Tiberius. Now we ate breakfast together every morning that he wasn't on a mission. A loaf of fresh bread, four eggs sunny side up, a crock of strawberry preserves and another jar filled with butter awaited. My stomach growled in anticipation. It had been awhile since I felt hungry. Perhaps the running inspired my lacking appetite.

"Here's your fork," Papa said, and we dove in. Fina had stopped sending up plates with our food because we never used them. It had always been like that, even when Mama was alive.

Plates, Papa always said with his roguish smile, *are for formal occasions, not family.*

"How'd the lesson go?" he asked, squinting at me through the bright sunshine that rose above Letum Wood.

"Great," I said, slathering a thick piece of warm bread with butter that instantly melted. "We went for a run."

"Was it hard?"

My annoyance wasn't contrived. "Yes. I've lost a lot of my endurance."

Papa stared into the lower bailey with a tight jaw. I wondered what he'd think if I told him the truth. Part of me wanted to talk to him about everything that had happened. About my hatred of living in Chatham Castle, missing the forest, wanting to see Grandmother's little shop, the Tea and Herb Pantry, again. But I wouldn't, even though I knew he wanted me to. He'd tried hard enough to get me to open up about how I felt. Talking about it only brought pain, so I avoided it, even though I saw the same agony in his eyes every time I refused.

It's for the best, Papa. You'll see.

At least, that's what I always told myself. Thankfully, Papa didn't question me further about the run. His thoughts had moved on already.

"And what do you think of Merrick?"

"He's heartless," I quipped. Papa tilted his head back and laughed. It was a deep belly laugh that rolled out in long waves. I smiled, unable to stop myself. Papa's mirth relaxed some of the tension in my shoulders, and for just a moment, the strained magic eased off inside me.

"He's focused," Papa corrected with a wink. "Not heartless. I chose him for the job because I know he'll get results. He must. His career as a Protector depends on his success with your training and he knows it."

I thought that over and chewed a bite of Fina's pillowy bread.

"Where does Merrick come from?"

"You'll have to ask him," he said vaguely. "He doesn't talk much about himself."

Papa piled two of the eggs between slices of bread and bit into it. I pushed my questions about Merrick aside and turned to more worrisome thoughts.

"Has the Council said more about removing you as Head of Protectors now that the secret is out?" I asked.

When the High Priestess asked Papa to become Head of Protectors, he was unmarried but deeply in love with Mama. Unfortunately, tradition as set forth by the first High Priestess stated that the Head of Protectors, the Head of Guardians, the High Priest, and High Priestess, were not allowed to be married or have a family. Their jobs demanded total focus. Guardians and Protectors could marry and have children, but they would lose their chance for leadership.

Papa could have taken the job and left Mama behind without a word of explanation. No one knew about her. But he refused to leave her. He divulged the truth to the High Priestess. He would take the job, but he wouldn't leave Marie. If she'd allow it, he'd shoulder the position of Head of Protectors and keep Mama a secret, only visiting when his responsibilities as Head of Protectors allowed.

To his surprise, the High Priestess eventually agreed. It was a terrible breach of tradition, one they both knew would incur severe consequences if discovered, but the High Priestess was willing to risk it. I came along less than a year later.

Papa had lived a double life, sneaking away to be with us whenever he could while leading the most talented band of brothers, or spies, that Antebellum had ever known. Mama and I were his best-kept secret until she died, and then the world and the Council found out the truth.

"No. They won't remove me from the Protectors right now," he said, swallowing a bite and forcing an easy tone. "Not with the Western Network tripling the number of West Guards at the Borderlands between our Networks. Don't worry about it, B. You focus on learning how to defend yourself."

"Yes, Papa."

A knock on the apartment door echoed through the room. Before I could stand up to answer, Tiberius welcomed himself inside. His curly blonde beard hung down his chest in a long plume and wagged whenever he spoke. He resembled a brick wall with his beefy shoulders, paunchy belly, and ham-like arms. A pile of envelopes tied by string preceded him, falling onto the table with a thud.

"More reports from the Borderlands," he said, striding over. "Our man is reporting increased activity from the West Guards."

Tiberius grabbed three pieces of bread and the last egg and threw himself into a chair. Papa shifted back into Protector mode, his eyes sharpening as he grabbed the envelopes.

"Please come into our apartment and eat our breakfast," I said to Tiberius with a wave of my hand over the food. "Don't mind us."

"I will," he said, helping himself to a spoonful of preserves, which he spread on his egg before jamming the bread back together and biting into his sandwich. I laughed in spite of his horrid manners. His suspicious, bulbous eyes regarded me.

"I hear you're learning from Merrick now," he said through a mouthful of food. A few flecks of bread came out with his words.

"Yes."

"What, you want to become the only female Protector?"

"Maybe," I shot back. He snorted.

"You and your father have broken enough traditions," he said. "I don't think you should try to shatter that one. Although you, of all witches, probably could do it."

Amongst the many traditions of the Central Network was another unbroken law: No female could serve as a Guardian or Protector. There were legends of women who had tried to convince the leaders to make an exception, but the tradition remained solid.

"Sounds like a good challenge to me."

Tiberius gave a *humph* and dove back into his sandwich. Papa sorted through the envelopes and broke the wax seal on the thickest. The more he read, the deeper the stress lines around his eyes became. I watched the transformation with great sadness. Papa's eyes flew up to Tiberius from one letter he'd just opened.

"They are certain the West Guards are unloading big wooden crates full of shovels at the border?" he asked in concern.

Tiberius nodded. "Zane just got back from one of your little spy circuits. He's waiting for you in the Gatehouse to brief. Sed sum fin ith happneeng."

I dodged a bit of egg yolk flying from Tiberius's mouth and looked to Papa for clarification. The number of West Guards congregating at the Borderlands had been increasing for some time, but nothing definitive had taken place yet. At news of this development, my stomach churned with fear.

"What could they be using shovels for?" I asked. Papa hesitated.

"Tiberius and I think the Western Network is going to try to divert the Borderlands River to their Network. It will cut off the water supply to our crops and possibly throw us into a famine."

My eyes widened.

"Can't you stop them?"

"It's speculation at this point," Papa said wearily, running a hand through his dark brown hair. A few strands in front stood up on end. "At least it was until Zane observed the shovels. If they are planning on digging, it'll take them awhile, so we may have some time to figure out a plan." He shot me a look. "Please don't speak of this to anyone, B."

"Of course, Papa," I murmured.

The two of them stood.

"Love you, girl," Papa said, a hint of longing in his voice. "You look like your Mama today."

He placed a kiss on the top of my head, squeezing my shoulder with a firm hand.

"I don't love you, rotten female child," Tiberius said, lowering his massive hand onto my face and pushing me away. But his touch was gentle and he shot me a wink. "I don't even *like* you, but I'll tolerate you."

The two of them trooped out the door, leaving a still apartment in their wake. My powers welled back into a tense knot in my chest, and I leaned into my palm with a sigh.

Have You Missed Me?

The halls of Chatham Castle were equal parts elegant and simple, cluttered with the occasional sofa, stuffed chair, or small table. Paintings lined the wall, and elegant drapes and greenery covered the space near the floor-length windows. Camille and I had become experts at picking the locks on closed doors to find forgotten rooms in the long halls. It gave me a little thrill that I missed but rarely sought out anymore. Despite my less-than-busy lifestyle, I often felt exhausted with the littlest task.

After breakfast I made my way to the Witchery through a back hall I rarely used, and paused to inspect an elaborate wall sconce with twisting golden leaves like the ivy in Letum Wood. Next to it, a detailed painting of winged creatures painted directly onto the wall caught my attention.

"What are these?" I whispered to myself, running the tips of my fingers over the distorted faces that were half-bat, half-human. Their fangs dripped with red blood and their beady eyes looked dull and lifeless. I stared at them in both revulsion and fascination.

"What are you doing up here?" A shrill, annoyed voice caught up with me from behind. "You don't normally walk down this hall."

Oh, Mrs. L, I thought as soon as I heard the nasally hum behind the tone. *You grace me with your pinching presence yet again.*

Mrs. L had been the housekeeper at Chatham Castle for so long no one remembered when she started. She had piles of grayish blonde hair on top of her head that towered like a pillar of clouds. Her thin lips, bony hands, and slender frame were as tight and anxious as her personality. Not only was she the best housekeeper in the Central Network, but she also kept abreast of every scrap of gossip. Nothing passed her notice.

Not even my walking habits, apparently.

Her particular vendetta against me started when I met her in the winter while trying to earn my first mark by attending the Esbat, a monthly meeting for Network leaders. In order to get into the meeting I had to insult her. Unfortunately, Mrs. L did not forget anything.

I kept my eyes on the hideous bat-like creatures while she came up behind me. I tried to figure out an escape plan. Would running away be too obvious of an escape? Yes. She'd holler at me, lest I fall and bleed on something. Transporting? I could just disappear in the middle of the conversation. No, she'd track me down. Enduring the crotchety old housekeeper was my only option.

"Mrs. L, do you know what these are?" I asked, pointing to the painting and feigning a deep interest in the work. Mrs. L came up to my side and studied it with her head tilted back.

"Clavas," she said with a sniff. "They transform into humans from their bat-like form. Very powerful fighters. It's Almorran magic and hasn't been used since the Networks were formed. This painting has been here since the castle was built, actually, and depicts the Almorran witches using Clavas in the Mortal wars. The Clavas almost killed Esmelda, you know."

"Jikes," I muttered and she shot me a sharp look.

"Watch your language, young lady. It's not attractive to use profanity like that."

I turned back to the painting.

"Almorran?" I clarified. "Are you sure?"

The Almorran witches had been our ancient enemies. They lived back in the time when witches co-existed with mortals before the five Networks formed. The Almorran Priests exiled the mortals, sending them across the ocean to their death or salvation, no one knew. Brutal curses and dark magic were the Almorran legacy.

"Of course I'm sure!" she said.

"Yes, however did I doubt you? Thank you for that explanation, Mrs. L, but I really must be going now! Merry part."

"Wait, where are you going?" she demanded. "I don't trust teenagers. They have no control over their impulses, especially teenagers without parents around."

No wonder we don't get along, you old bat, I thought. *I have no control, and you need too much.*

I ground my teeth together and forced a warm smile.

"I'm just going to see my friends, Mrs. L. I'll save the subterfuge for another day."

"Where are your friends?" she asked, her eyes darting around. "They aren't up at that turret, are they? I watch you girls. I know you're conspiring up there."

"Conspiring?"

"Yes, conspiring! That pale girl takes books up there all the time. What is she trying to learn? It's odd that she studies so much. I don't like it."

"I agree, Mrs. L," I said in a droll tone. "Leda is odd. Perhaps she's trying to figure out the composition of your cleaning potion. You should talk to her about it. One can't be too careful."

Before she could respond, everything went black.

The floor fell out from underneath me and I plunged into darkness with a gasp. The usual pressure of transporting bore down on my closed eyes and chest, as if something heavy sat there. I felt the weight, and then it disappeared. I fell onto a rock floor with a heavy thud and curled onto my side with a cough. I'd just transported somewhere, that much I knew for sure. But where? And how? Transporting another witch was a power reserved just for High Priests and High Priestesses, and I hadn't . . .

"Merry meet, Bianca darling. I've been waiting for you."

I froze. The low drawl, the smug tone, the chills it brought to my spine, could only mean one witch.

I pushed off the floor and leapt to my feet, coming face-to-face with the witch I'd kill if I had the power. Miss Mabel stood before me in all her alluring, evil glory. Her crimson lips twitched into a full, teasing smile. Wisps of blonde hair stuck out in organized disarray from a loose bun behind her right ear. The luminous blue eyes that haunted my dreams now blasted me with the power of an arctic wind.

The moment we made eye contact, magic came to life in my chest with a dangerous scream.

"Welcome to my new home," she said, spreading her arms out. "I've missed you very much."

"Miss Mabel," I said with a tight voice.

An expansive room with jagged red rock walls opened up behind her. There was no wall to my right, just a room leading to a balcony that made the area bright. Beyond it lay an endless expanse of yellow and red sand. The hot sun spilled in beams on the floor, sucking the moisture from every breath of air. Instead of walls, fluttering gossamer drapes edged with yellow lace separated the room into sections. Bookshelves on the left, warbled with carved designs in the dark mahogany. Decorative pots embedded with sparkling pieces of glass on the right. An elaborate painting of fire on the far wall straight ahead. Miss Mabel had transported me to her new lair in the Western Network.

"Have you missed me, Bianca darling?"

"Not particularly. How did you transport me here? It cannot be done with our magic."

The words *our magic* lingered in my mind. She must be using a dark magic that I didn't know how to block. There was no other explanation.

"Lovely outfit," she said with a chuckle, purposefully ignoring my question. "I'm a little surprised you aren't wearing pants and leather slippers. They are still your favorite, aren't they?"

I'm surprised you're not wearing horns.

"They're being cleaned," I said casually, clenching my hands into fists. The power hummed in my chest, dangerously alive in her presence. I didn't know how long I could control it. Once it took over, I wouldn't be able to stop it from acting.

She smiled in her demure way.

"I'm glad to see you still have something of a wit. And your courage, too. I hear you had a little encounter with a dragon the other day. How very sweet of you to rush in and try to save it. You're always trying to control the things you have no control over, aren't you, foolish girl?"

My nails bit into my palm.

"I didn't try to save it. I did save it."

"For now."

A long silence stretched between us. We stared at each other, sizing up, assessing. Could she feel my hatred, my power? Of course she could. Only a fool wouldn't sense the crackling tension.

"It's difficult keeping the power under control, isn't it?" she asked. "I can feel your struggle."

"I don't know what you're talking about."

She laughed again, a trilling sound that grated on my nerves. What I wouldn't give to be rid of her! But even I wasn't foolish enough to try to fight her. I wasn't ready, not yet. Last time I tried to fight her—

No, just focus on making it out alive, Bianca. Just focus on surviving right now.

"I used my exceptional magical power and transported you here for something simple, really," Miss Mabel said, interrupting my internal dialogue. "No doubt you thought I'd forget about our little agreement, though I never forget anything."

She snapped her fingers in a lazy motion and a familiar book appeared. The *Book of Contracts*. It held our binding, complete with my signature. I struggled to keep my face impassive the way Papa always could.

"You're going to set the task," I said.

"Yes."

"Fine. What is it?"

She made a tsking sound through her teeth.

"Are you in a hurry?"

"Yes," I shot back. "I have a life to live."

"Not unless you listen to me." Her eyes flared in a sudden rush of passion. "You seem to have forgotten that I am my grandmother's magical heir and the only witch alive that controls your curse."

A hot pain clamped around my throat, paralyzing my voice like the grip of a pair of searing tongs. I gasped. My hands wrapped around my neck, but nothing was there. She smiled.

"Now pay attention, will you?" The burning spasms that choked me subsided, and I wondered if the heat of the West compromised her usually suave control. She resumed with her usual tone of indifference. "It would be very wise of you to do what I tell you. Matters such as this cannot be rushed."

The nearly silent sound of someone padding into the room stole my attention. I tuned into the sound and sensed movement behind me. Gentle, even breaths. An adult, based on the low shuffle of the footfalls. Most likely a female. Twenty paces away. Miss Mabel's head instantly jerked up and she focused on the witch over my shoulder. The smooth lines of her perfect neck twitched. Whoever stood out of sight had not been invited. I almost spun around to see who was there, but didn't want to take my eyes off Miss Mabel for even a second. The fiery discomfort still clinging to my throat reminded me of how unpredictable she'd become.

Miss Mabel glowered at the shadows with glittering eyes.

"Let's talk out here, shall we, Bianca?" she asked.

Miss Mabel sauntered away, barefoot. A white cotton dress, so thin it was almost scandalous, drifted in the hot air around her legs as she walked. Lace spread across her neck and upper arms, revealing snippets of her tan skin. Finally gathering my courage, I looked over my shoulder and saw only gauzy drapes and rock walls. The whisper of someone transporting away hovered in the air, then faded.

She strolled to the balcony outside and stopped just within the shade. A sprawling city bustled below, filled with early-morning vendors, the fair-haired and blue-eyed witches of the West, and horses. There were no trees here, just a dense green scrub brush on the red cliffs and white stalls that the witches used to hide from the blistering sun. Buckets of dates, coconuts, and long white robes were scattered through most of the market. This had to be Custos, the largest city in the Western Network.

Above us soared more red rock, honed and refined into the smooth, waving walls of a castle. Skinny threads of red, yellow, and orange color ran through the layers of rock. Pictures of dragons and desert serpents were carved around the windows and painted black. The castle walls extended up several stories more and then blended into the mountain.

The Arck, I thought. *The legendary castle of the Western Network.* It was the only castle in all the Networks built into a mountainside like this. Legend stated that a waterfall fell five stories through the middle of the High Priest's chambers and supplied the witches with their only constant water source. Judging by her sprawling chambers here, Miss Mabel was no servant. I wondered how much power she held. Almack, the Western High Priest, had been deathly sick for months now. Was Miss Mabel trying to take over upon his death?

"Do you see what I command now?" she asked when I came up next to her, staying out of arms reach. "It's beautiful, isn't it?"

Whether she spoke of her rule over the city, or the city itself, I couldn't decide.

"You command?" I asked instead, trying to play it cool. "I don't remember Almack empowering you as High Priestess."

"Trivialities," she said, brushing me off. "I was destined for it, Bianca."

"What about Dane? He comes to power when Almack dies."

Her eyes glittered with a smile, making her look nearly mad.

"Perhaps."

The magic had grown so frantic that my usual analytical abilities failed. When the lightest of tingles started in my fingertips, and the pressure of keeping the power contained began to cause me pain, I knew I had to get out.

"Let's get this over with," I said. "What's the task?"

"You're much braver than you used to be. You certainly never demanded anything of me at school."

If bravery meant uncontrollable power, a churning gut, and a skittish heart, then yes. I had a bit more of that.

"Living through your worst nightmare tends to make etiquette less important," I muttered.

"Very well," she said, opening the *Book of Contracts.* "I will set your task."

"How do I know that the task you assign me is the one that will fulfill the contract?"

"The binding responds, you see?"

The *Book of Contracts* had flipped through its pages and now lay open to mine. The ink of her smeared thumbprint gleamed a blood-red color on the bottom of the parchment, seeming fresh.

What if I ripped the contract out? I thought. *Could I destroy it?*

"Your task," she began, interrupting my thoughts, "is to kill the next High Priest of the Central Network before you turn seventeen. Should you fail to accomplish this assignment, you will die. Should you succeed, your Inheritance Curse will be removed, and you shall live."

The words appeared on the contract as she spoke them.

Your task is to kill the High Priest.

This unexpected turn was more confusing than shocking. I blinked several times, staring at the page. We didn't even have a High Priest. What advantage would she gain?

"The High Priest?" I repeated. "We don't have one right now."

"Not yet, but Mildred is searching. The Central Network has never gone into a war without full leadership. Not even Mildred would break that tradition." She looked at me from the corner of her eye with a sly grin. "Although she has broken another rather important tradition, hasn't she?"

My heart pounded, filling my ears with the sound of rushing blood. I wouldn't do it.

"I'll never kill anyone for you," I said in a hiss, loathing her more and more with every word. The magic was breaking through the already weak guards in my heart. Any minute now and I'd lose control.

She shrugged.

"Fine. Then you'll die. It's up to you."

"Why not the High Priestess?" I asked, desperate. "Why the High Priest?"

Miss Mabel chuckled.

"Oh, Bianca, I wouldn't pass on the pleasure of killing Mildred for the world."

I really studied her for the first time. Despite her languid expression and unreadable eyes, a few stress lines marred her face. She could do all the transformative magic she wanted to make herself appear young and beautiful, but she couldn't hide the anxiety.

Did you ever feel fear? I thought of asking, but wasn't certain I wanted the answer. *Or do you run on anger? Is that your source of power? Who could you hate so much that you'd be this terrible?*

I'd spent my life questioning Miss Mabel's actions but never her motives. Now, for the first time, I realized that her evil must have a purpose beyond ambition to rule the Central Network. An overwhelming wave of power made me lose visual clarity, forcing me back to the terrible reality of my situation. With magic this strong, I'd black out entirely. The magic would work through me with no way to stop it. I steeled myself to battle the power, but my energy waned.

"Then why are you doing this?" I asked.

There was too much vulnerability in the question, too much raw emotion I couldn't control, and I hated myself for it. The magic seeped out of my heart, spreading through my chest and arms. If I let it go, would it destroy her? Or would it just destroy me?

"The same reason I do everything," she said. "Leverage."

"You lie," I whispered. Her face blurred. I gripped the wall to keep from falling. "You want power."

"Don't we all want power? Are you and I so different, Bianca? Both of us have someone we hate, someone we'd be willing to do anything to get rid of. The real question is: which of us wants it more?" she asked, turning away. "I'll see you soon, I'm sure."

The world went black when she sent me into the darkness again. The pressure of transporting pressed on my face and eyes. I recognized the velvet underbelly of the canopy of Letum Wood over my head just before the magic overcame me.

Darkness.

A Jagged Weakness

"See that Guardian there?" Merrick asked, pointing. "His body is low and his legs are far apart. Now look over here. That Guardian crossed his legs and now . . . he just fell on his arse and everyone is laughing at him. Never cross your legs. It's asking to be embarrassed."

Merrick and I stood on top of the Wall the next morning, hidden back in the shadow that Chatham Castle sent over the lower bailey. Masses of Guardian hopefuls teemed in the deep stone pit, fighting each other with the wooden swords that meant they were new recruits. Furious cries rang through the air now and then, a sure indication that some inattentive trainee would later be nursing a bruise or a splinter.

Good thing they don't have real swords yet.

The spring air sat heavy on my shoulders, thick with fog and threatening a chilly rain. It felt good to have a cool day. Even though I'd faced Miss Mabel two days before, the desert heat still felt real on my face. After my unexpected visit, I'd awoken in Letum Wood with scratches on my hands and feet, and no idea where I was. I had to transport back to Chatham Castle. Sleep had been elusive for the past couple days, adding to my weariness. To my relief, I didn't see Mrs. L again.

Seeking a bit of security, I pulled my deep blue cloak closer around my shoulders but left the hood down. Camille had woken up early to tuck my hair into two braids against my head, ensuring it would be out of my way for either a fight or a run. But it had been in vain.

Merrick and I had been hidden for an hour, studying proper fighting technique. Or, more realistically, how not to fight.

"Watch that one," he said, pointing to a different fellow on the other side. "He seems to know what he's doing. We'll start working on new footwork patterns tomorrow. Learning a sword is pointless without them."

"Are you going to make me practice with the Guardians?" I asked, a disturbing image of fighting with the burly boys flickering through my mind. One gangly Guardian stumbled over his own feet, fell to his knees, curled into a ball, and pled for mercy. *Then again,* I thought with a wry look, *perhaps it wouldn't be too bad.*

"No. I'm teaching you a different sword fighting style, but the basics are the same."

"Why?"

He thought it over for a second. "If you are truly training to fight Miss Mabel, then she'll expect you to be trained to fight like the Guardians. Teaching you a different style may give you an advantage."

"Oh," I said. "I hadn't thought of that."

"Tradition isn't always a good thing," he said with a grim tone. "Keep that in mind."

"What do you mean?"

He shook his head with stoic disregard. "It's not important now. Our current task is just to get you ready for it. Focus on that."

I was grateful when he finally released me for the day, hoping the Witchery was empty so I could have a chance to iron out my thoughts. I trudged up several winding staircases and down the lonely castle halls. An abandoned Witchery waited for me and I let out a sigh of relief.

Several notes cluttered our rickety table. Michelle was working on an order of orange rolls in the kitchen. Leda was in the library writing an essay for her political history class, and I'd heard Camille laughing with a couple of Guardians as I walked through a back hall. Despite the pervasive silence, the solitude was welcome.

I dragged a thick wooden box filled with blankets and herbs to the window and sat on top, my knees pulled into my chest, protecting my heart. The wind blew the scent of Letum Wood into the turret. I closed my eyes and savored the sweet smell. Calm moments like these made me remember Mama in a way that didn't hurt quite so much. It was one of the rare days when the grief took second place to better memories, and didn't sit on my chest quite so much.

I felt so calm that I gave into the rare weakness of thinking about Mama, recalling the smell of lavender on her linen dresses. She had liked the light touch of the material, the way it never felt heavy or restrictive. Although she had stayed home to raise me and run the Tea and Herb Pantry with Grandmother, Mama had been a free spirit.

Just when the daydreams about home started to feel real, when I began to convince myself that I still lived in the cottage deep in Letum Wood, I jerked out of it to the sound of Miss Mabel's voice.

Your task is to kill the High Priest.

My eyes darted around the room, and then I realized I'd started to fall asleep in the mild spring air. I straightened and pushed the hair out of my face. Try as I might, Miss Mabel's voice wouldn't leave. Her task echoed through my mind over and over and over.

Your task is to kill the High Priest.

Though today's memories of Mama were gentle, I was grateful for something else to focus on. I started to formulate a plan. There were only two ways out of the binding: figure out a way to destroy it or die. No matter what happened, Miss Mabel wouldn't get me without a fight. I ran the pad of my thumb along my bottom lip as I pondered over our meeting. Miss Mabel had said she hated someone as much as I hated her. It had to be the High Priestess, the only witch with more power than her.

The flash of inspiration I had when I'd seen the contract again for the first time ran back through my mind. Would a binding have any power if there was no evidence of it? Could I steal the binding and destroy it?

My heart hammered at the thought. If it were possible, I'd have to go to the Western Network under my own power, find the *Book of Contracts*, search for mine, destroy it, and get back before someone noticed. If the West Guards caught me, they'd kill me on the spot. If Miss Mabel caught me?

I shuddered at the thought.

The tattoos staining the skin of my right wrist called my attention. I gazed down on the circlus, a ring containing the three marks that I'd earned at Miss Mabel's School for Girls. It represented three areas of magical expertise: the Esbat —an advanced course in leadership and ancient languages—Advanced Curses and Hexes, and Advanced Defensive Magic.

Staring at the circlus reminded me of the night I earned the last two marks, when Miss Mabel killed Mama. A rush of fury stirred my heart to even greater passion. What did it matter if Miss Mabel caught me? I was going to get that binding. What did I have to lose?

I only had a few months left to live anyway.

"Merry meet, Bianca. What did Merrick make you do for today's lesson?" Michelle asked me when I walked up to her table the next morning. She sat in front of a plate of biscuits, gravy, sausage, and toast. The servants' dining room moved around us, the one area of Chatham Castle that never seemed to sleep. It bustled with harried servants and dissonant Guardians, and was the main battleground for the eternal war between Mrs. L and Fina, the head cook.

Tables of varying size had been scrunched into every available spot in the broad dining room, which was almost as big as the ballroom, and made movement chaotic and difficult. There was no intimate space here, and it never emptied. Different shifts of workers kept it in constant flow. A table half the width of the room stood near the eight foot tall fireplace. Four kitchen workers kept the massive table constantly full of fare. The dining room made it easy to disappear into the melee but still keep track of everything going on. This morning I'd wandered there in search of Leda.

"Push-ups," I said, sitting across from Michelle and recalling that morning's training with a grimace. A careful attempt to shift my already sore shoulders only resulted in greater pain, so I stopped moving. "Lots of them. And footwork. I had to repeat the same movements at least five hundred times."

Michelle's nose scrunched. "Sounds miserable."

"Thanks," I said, buoyed by her empathy. "Where's Camille?"

Michelle motioned behind her with a jerk of her head. In a moment I spotted Camille's bushy blonde hair, pulled away from her face with a glittering headband. The broad shoulders of the Guardians clustered around her dwarfed her short, but increasingly slender frame. Her chubby teenage cheeks had begun to lose some of their girlish roundness since she'd moved to the castle. All the attention from the Guardians left her in a happy glow most days. When she tilted her head back and laughed at something one of her admirers said, I smiled to myself.

"They are all so in love with her," Michelle said, following my gaze. "Except for Brecken, I think. She mentioned something about him ignoring her yesterday when she tried to get him to take her on a walk in the gardens."

Sure enough, Brecken sat at the far end of the table, oblivious to Camille's presence. He wasn't lost on her, however. I noticed her eyes dart his direction every now and then, especially after she let out a witty comment that earned guffaws from the rest of the Guardians.

"It's good to see that someone is immune to her girlish charms," I said. My mind turned back to my original purpose. "Have you seen Leda?"

"No," Michelle said, her forehead scrunching together. "She was gone by the time I came down here this morning."

My mind churned. Where would Leda have gone so early? Michelle woke up before the sunrise to get working on the fresh loaves of bread, a time of day when no one stirred. The librarians would have opened the library just fifteen minutes before I came to the dining room. What was Leda up to?

"Oh," I murmured. "Interesting."

Michelle lapsed into her familiar silence and I was glad. She only spoke when she had something pertinent to say and I loved that she held little expectation for conversing. Sitting with Michelle was easy.

"Okay, well, I'm going to the library," I said after a few more minutes when our intermittent chatting died down and Michelle finished up her meal. "Are you still on duty?"

She nodded and said, "I'll see you after work."

After waving to Camille and winding my way through the maze of tables and bodies, I headed toward the library to begin the first phase of my big plan to free myself from Miss Mabel. First, I had to find out if bindings could be destroyed before they were fulfilled. After that, I would figure out a way to infiltrate the Western Network. If I were caught, they would kill me.

When I walked through the stained glass double doors that led to the three-story book sanctuary, I found Leda and Miss Scarlett sitting together at a table near the outer fringe of the room, their heads bent in deep discussion. I made a mental note to ask Leda about her early morning activities later.

"I want to try," Leda said in a low tone. "But I'm afraid that my curse will become a problem if Council Member Jansson finds out that—"

She stopped, her spine stiffening, and gazed right up to me.

"Merry meet," I said in a jovial tone, wondering why Leda had any business with Council Member Jansson. He was a middle aged, black haired witch with a constantly bland facial expression who oversaw both Chatham City and Chatham Castle. Most of the affairs of the castle went through him.

"Merry meet, Bianca," Miss Scarlett returned, tugging on the edge of her jacket, as if it could have the nerve to wrinkle. "I heard about your experience with the dragon. I'm glad you and Camille came out of it unscathed."

"Thank you, Miss Scarlett. So am I."

Miss Scarlett looked no different today than any other day. She wore a blue dress with her hair swept into a bun at the back of her neck and a crisp white jacket with long sleeves over it. The red bracelets she never took off sang each time they clanged together on her wrist. I'd never seen a piece of fuzz on Miss Scarlett's clothes or a hair out of place. If I had, surely it would have been a sign of the end of the world. Miss Scarlett was as steady and timeless as the wind.

"Why are you talking about Jan—"

"We're learning about the political history of the Southern Network as well as current events," Leda blurted out, her nostrils flaring. "Would you care to join us and write an essay on why the Southern Network army needs metals found in the caves of the Western Network?"

"Lots to do today!" I said, taking a step back. "Hope you have some fun."

"I'll see you later," Leda said dismissively and turned back to her paperwork, but not before a look of relief crossed her face.

Well played, Leda, I thought. She wanted to get rid of me, and she had. But why? She was definitely up to something.

"Now, the Southern Network has always been known for their talent in crafting weaponry," Miss Scarlett began, and her voice soon droned into the background.

I ventured further into the library, past the circular, elevated desk that sat in the very middle of the room. Several librarians bustled inside of it, sorting cards, books, and slips of paper. The walls filled with dusty tomes gave off the scent of aged paper and ink. I perused the stacks with a disinterested eye. *Treating Fungus, How to Properly Age and Preserve Mushrooms*, and *All About the Mansfeld Pact* ran past my eyes. It wasn't until I found a book entitled *Bindings and Such* that I felt a glimmer of hope.

A librarian passed by, ignoring me. I settled on the floor and cracked the book open, flipping through the table of contents. Old, nearly illegible handwriting covered the fading pages. I had to squint, working to read every line.

"The many types of bindings," I read under my breath. "Eternal bindings. Inherited bindings. Bindings for children."

Nothing on the list appealed to me. After combing through the book without success, I shoved it back onto the shelf and grabbed another from nearby. *How to Fight in a Mactos.* But that dealt primarily with magical fighting and blighters. I pushed it back.

An hour later I had a walloping headache, a suspicious librarian tailing me at every turn, and no progress on my goal. Could a binding be destroyed? I began to have my doubts. If it could, I found no evidence of it, which disheartened me. A male voice the next row of books over stopped my perturbed thoughts in their tracks.

"Derek deserves to be exiled," it said.

My powers woke with a sudden start, surly and ready to fight. I paused, waiting, trying to identify the witch on the other side. There were no slats in the shelves in this section of the library, so I couldn't peer through the tops of the books to see who stated those traitorous words with such ease.

"You're taking on a big cause," said a different voice with little inflection. Another male witch. Older, if the drawling tone meant anything.

"Yes, perhaps. But it's a worthy cause, no doubt," the first voice replied in a rush. "Derek lied to the entire Network! Our first leaders set up the rules against leadership having family for a reason. He willingly defied that tradition. Willingly! It's insulting, that's what it is, to all that went before him and made the sacrifice."

"Some will argue that he still did his job well."

"He fulfilled his duties, yes. So what? He lied the entire time. The real question is this: In a time of war, how are we to trust Derek to make the right decisions?"

A long paused stretched between them.

"The question is one you may choose to act on however you feel is best, Clive. I cannot stop you, but I would advise you to have a plan. The Council will not accept a petition that is poorly executed or presented."

Clive.

The very name sent a cool chill through my blood. Clive had been the Coven Leader over Chatham City for the past five years. Because Chatham City was the biggest city in the Network, its Coven Leader had a lot of power. Usually, the Coven Leader eventually became a Council Member. No doubt Clive wanted to pad his career by getting rid of Papa, hoping to advance into the Council upon the next vacancy.

"I have a plan," Clive said with a self-assurance that made me want to punch him. I balled my hand into a fist instead. The magic burned behind my ribs like a pile of coals. "Starting tomorrow, with your approval of course, I'll begin holding rallies all across Chatham City. Once I gain the requisite 50,000 signatures from the occupants of the city, I'll bring the petition to the Council."

"You're talking about Derek Black," the deeper voice said. "Not an initiative to change taxes. You may meet some resistance."

"I respectfully disagree. Derek is no favorite anymore, Council Member Jansson."

Since Jansson oversaw Chatham City, it made sense that Clive was speaking to him about this. I hadn't spoken with Jansson directly, but saw him working often with the High Priestess and Papa.

"You know of Derek's waning popularity better than anyone," Clive continued. "I wouldn't be able to get five hundred people to sign something in support of him. But to remove him? I'll get plenty of signatures. Chatham is foaming over it."

And so are you, I thought, wanting to rake my nails across his face. *You dirty snake.*

"I came here today to ask for your support," Clive said when Jansson didn't reply. I whispered a cloaking incantation and stole to the edge of the bookshelves as the icy spell ran down my body, concealing me from sight. When I peered around the corner to see the two of them standing together, conspiring, my anger ignited again.

Jansson drew in a deep breath.

"As your leader, I urge you to be cautious. Everything you do reflects on your career in some way. But as you are petitioning the people for their opinion, and are free to have your own, I cannot withhold my support to continue."

"Thank you, Council Member," Clive said with audible relief. "It's greatly appreciated."

The building power slipped out of my control for only one second, but it was enough. Books exploded from the shelves near Clive and Jansson, raining on top of them in a fall of paper and ink.

"Jikes!" Clive shouted, leaping out of the way. Jansson deflected a few volumes that almost tumbled onto his head with a quick spell. A final tome several inches thick caught Clive on the shoulder. Two librarians rushed to the scene, clucking and pecking after the torn pages like a bunch of hens.

Take that, Clive.

With the librarians cleaning up the mess, Clive and Jansson started walking toward me. Clive's rat-like face, wide ears, and sharp nose contrasted with the droopy skin and mild, rounded features of Jansson's face.

"Haunted, I tell you. Just like the southern turret," Clive muttered, brushing his fingers through his hair to straighten it. "Or that batty old librarian did it."

I retreated as they neared and pressed my back to the bookshelf. Clive, already jabbering about his plans for the first rally, soared past. Jansson, however, glanced over his shoulder.

If I hadn't had so much faith in the integrity of my magic, I'd have said he looked right into my eyes.

My breath came fast, hot, and with great pain the next morning.

I jogged along a well-worn trail in Letum Wood that the Guardians used for training runs. Merrick remained just behind me, trailing at my heels like an overeager puppy. The last tendrils of night still clung to the heavy canopy of Letum Wood, reluctantly giving sway to the rising sun's greater power. The air was cool and crisp.

The steep hills with jagged spines made of boulders and roots challenged my weakened leg muscles. Despite my two-month break from running, I found my body eagerly gobbling up the familiar motions of pounding down the trail. I was used to pushing past physical fatigue. Although it would take time to gain my speed back, in essence the running rhythm was already returning in full force. My mental capacity to face Letum Wood, however, was as feeble as ever. I felt like my body was a traitor to my mind. I didn't want to enjoy running again, but I couldn't help the small sense of elation it brought me. Papa spoke of running as an outlet for my emotions, but he was wrong. It only made them stronger.

"Faster," Merrick said, barely winded. "Push yourself."

Irritated, I picked up speed, but the burst cost me. I'd never be able to maintain this pace and fight back the memories, so I slowed down again. Avoiding the recollections was my first priority.

Flashes of white ghosted by me in Letum Wood every now and

then, sometimes followed by a stray giggle. I held them off by translating words into the language of the Ancients, forcing my mind to conjugate verbs over and over. But I wasn't stronger than whatever power I fought. Any moment now and Mama's memory would plague me again.

The sway of the canopy high above mocked me as I scampered past, tripping over roots and nearly breaking my toe. A few birds hopped from branch to branch, staring at me with their heads cocked to one side. I allowed myself an occasional glimpse into the darkness now and then, wondering if my dragon friend was near.

All the forced thoughts that ran through my mind came to a sudden halt when a familiar little girl with gray eyes ran onto the trail in front of me, her ghostly hair waving behind her.

I skidded to a stop with a gasp. Even though I expected the memories, the shock was still brutal. The child hopped up and down, trying to catch a butterfly with gauzy green and blue wings. Mama stepped out of the forest.

No, Bianca, she said, rushing over to the little girl. She grabbed her hands and pulled them down. *Don't hurt the butterfly. If you hold still, it'll come to you.*

My heart raced, my blood pumped, and the magic stirred with painful stabs, threatening to slip away. I turned, unable to bear it.

"What?" Merrick asked, gazing around. "What's wrong?"

"Stitch," I lied through a gasp, doubling over and grabbing my side. "I just need to gain my breath."

"Breathe through it, then. You need to keep running."

I hesitated. The memories would continue to come. I could feel it in the violent surges of power.

"No," I said in a panic, my eyes squeezed shut. "I'm done."

"No, you're not. Let's go," he said in a firm tone.

Explaining my real reason would be far more painful than dealing with Merrick's disapproval, however it stung.

"I can't, Merrick," I whispered. Tears choked my throat, but I forced them back. *No weakness. No tears.* "I'm done."

See? Mama's voice asked, resurrected from the deepest, most vulnerable parts of my mind. *If you're patient, the butterfly comes to you. It's beautiful, isn't it?*

I wanted to scream just to hide the sound of her voice. The tears building up in my throat threatened to explode in a violent sob.

It was real once, my heart whispered. *You can't deny that.*

But it's not now, I thought. *She's gone. Mama's in the past.*

"You can't keep giving up."

I opened my eyes and looked at the trail through sweaty tendrils of hair. A memory of Mama and Papa together in Letum Wood stood a few paces away, their gossamer existence as fragile as my own control. They murmured quietly together, their hands clasped. The unsettled power stirred like a mighty storm, robbing my ability to temper it.

"I told you I can't do this," I said. "I'm done. This was far enough."

"Bianca—"

"No! I'm done. I'm not ready for this. I told you I wasn't."

Merrick opened his mouth to say something, but I didn't wait around to hear it. I transported back to Chatham Castle, landing in the middle of my bedroom. Once I recognized my arched window and the plumes of deep blue satin draped around the four-poster bed, I pressed my back to the wall and sank down with an unsteady breath. The tears surfaced, stinging the insides of my eyes. I pressed the heels of my hands to my eyelids, refusing to let them out.

I will not be weak.

I. Will. Not.

Isadora

"Bianca, I already went over the rules with you," Leda said with a long-suffering sigh the next afternoon. "When you're playing *Networks*, a Guardian can't take out a West Guard on their own. They only move forward across the Network Line, remember?"

I glared at the pieces of the well-loved board game. My half-slain row of Guardians and dying handful of Protectors stood facing Leda's double row of West Guards. She hadn't lost a single one yet. Her eyebrow lifted in a gentle smirk. No matter what move I made, she'd be able to kill my High Priestess. Since she'd killed my High Priest at the beginning, I'd have no one left to ascend the throne. She'd won this game and she knew it. I just had to find a graceful way to admit it.

"Oh, fine," I growled, pushing the last of my Protectors into a new position. "Take over."

With a little shout of glee, Leda waved her hand. "West Guard to High Priestess," she declared. A West Guard pawn slid forward and knocked my High Priestess over. The rest of my pieces wilted on the spot, as if someone had taken a flame to them. I let out a long, bitter sigh.

"You win again, Leda."

"Yes. I always do," she said.

"Well at least you're humble about it."

"I think you're mad for playing against Leda at all," Camille said, pulling a lollipop from her mouth with a *pop*. "She's been playing *Networks* since she was a little girl."

Leda grinned and swept the pieces, now restored to their previous form, into the velvet bag.

"I'm particularly fierce when I play as the West Guards," she said. "But I use more strategy with the Eastern Guards. The Eastern Network has excellent political strategy."

I straightened my back, working out the kinked muscles as I stood up. Rain drizzled from the sky, settling on the cobblestone outside with a gentle patter. Fog crept toward the castle from the depths of Letum Wood with a slow, easy crawl. The sweet scent, cool air, and low murmur of the rain made me sleepy. But there was little time for sleep. I had a plan for today.

"I love rainy days," Leda said as she pushed the checkered marble board onto a shelf near her own window and looked outside with a sigh. "I think I'll go into the library and curl up with a good book. *Advanced Algebra* should hold my attention. Don't bother me."

Camille, who lounged on a set of massive pillows on the floor in her knickers and binder, acted as if she were gagging and rolled her eyes. Leda didn't notice and trounced down the stairs, humming under her breath.

"I hate it when it rains," Camille lamented. "There's nothing to do. I'd much rather walk through all the pretty gardens."

"I like the rain," Michelle said quietly. She sat in front of a large scroll, transcribing recipes from a book she'd borrowed from Fina. "We were always glad when it rained at home because it was good for the crops, and that meant we'd have food."

Camille sucked loudly on the sweet candy and moved farther down a fashion scroll she'd bought in Chatham City on her last weekly visit. The discarded wrappers of several caramels littered the floor around her.

"Aunt Bettina used to make me do extra homework on days it rained. She said that rain meant I had to be quiet since I couldn't go outside and give her a break."

Once I saw that the two of them were occupied, I grabbed my cape from a rack near the door, slipped into the turret staircase, and padded barefoot down the stone steps without them any wiser. Camille's voice continued to drone on behind me. Out of sight, I closed my eyes, whispered the transportation spell, and fell into the waiting darkness. It whisked me away, bearing down on my chest and face, and dropped me in the middle of the forest.

The fading aftermath of rain choked the air when I struggled to my feet in a copse of trees far from Chatham Castle.

"Jikes," I muttered, batting several tenacious branches away from my arms and making a mental note to talk with Papa about learning a more precise way to transport. Once I caught a glimpse of the trail off to the side, I battled my way through the thick, wet brush. Tendrils of hair flew around my head in a wild halo from the humidity, but I didn't care. Bigger monsters than a poor hairstyle awaited me. I moved onto the nearby trail, hopping over mud puddles and moving from stone to stone.

Isadora's little cottage soon appeared in the foliage, although nothing moved inside. Surely the old Watcher was home. Except to sort out the next first-years for Miss Mabel's School for Girls, Isadora never left her cottage in the trees.

At least I didn't think she did.

I didn't know much about Isadora, not really. Not the way my friends did. Their interviews with Isadora were far different than mine. Every student that wanted to go to Miss Mabel's School for Girls had to meet with her. She had the ability to see and understand a witch's motivations and personality in ways that others could not. With such power and talent, she kept the school and the part of Letum Wood that surrounded it safe from the dangers of the forest.

Shaking off a little raindrop that dripped down my neck, I walked down the verdant path that led to her quaint residence. The wood groaned beneath my feet when I stepped onto the porch, surprised to find the door open.

"Come in, Bianca," Isadora called with her creaky voice. "I've been expecting you."

Of course you have, I thought, stepping inside to find Isadora's foggy, unsmiling eyes staring at me.

"Open the door," she said. "Let the sweet smell of rain come in."

I followed her directions, casting my eyes around the empty walls of her small home. A little bed was tucked into the corner, a table with two chairs stood in the middle of the floor, and potted plants filled three open windowsills.

"Where's your china?" I asked, seeking the piles of plates and cups she used to display. They'd decorated every wall only a year ago, when I first came to her cottage. The house seemed barren without them.

"Put away," she said and motioned me to the table. The bony ridges of her knuckles stuck out in sharp angles when she folded her hands on her lap. The skin looked soft and translucent, freckled with age spots. I wondered how long Isadora had been alive. "Sit down. We'll have some tea."

A plain set of white cups with steam rolling off the top waited. I glanced at them with an inward grimace. Hot tea sounded as welcoming as a boiling bath on this already humid spring day.

"Don't get ahead of yourself," she said with a sidelong glance at the cup. "It's not what you think."

To be polite, I lowered myself into the chair and raised the cup to my lips, pulling on a quick sip. It tasted ice cold and minty, and sent a cool shiver down my body.

"You're here because you have questions about your binding with Miss Mabel," she said before I could get a word out. The chilly swallow of tea nearly drowned me.

"W-what?" I asked, coughing. "You know about—"

The protective magic of the binding cut me off. I couldn't even make reference to it or Miss Mabel in any way that may lead to the binding. While I had expected Isadora to know what was on my mind, I didn't think she'd jump right into it. I fidgeted at the thought, wondering what else Isadora saw in my messy, bruised heart. Did she know what I saw when I ran, or how out of control my powers were now?

"Yes," she said, lifting her eyebrows and taking a draw from her cup. "I do know about the binding."

My friends told me Isadora had been kind to them during their interviews before she accepted them into Miss Mabel's School for Girls. But she'd been nervous around me, maybe even frightened. Now she regarded me the way I'd look at a dangerous animal: with a healthy amount of uncertainty. Did she sense my simmering powers the same way Papa did? Being this close to the school again agitated the magic, like the turmoil of emotions in my chest had again become a dragon, only this time it paced back and forth.

"How do you know?"

"I know many things," she said.

"Will you answer my questions?" I asked tentatively. Suddenly every word I spoke seemed to matter more than it did before. Although I couldn't make reference to the binding out loud, Isadora would know what I wanted to ask.

"You can't overpower the magic of a binding when it's been sealed in blood," she said, anticipating my first question. "Nor should you try. It would be foolish, don't you think?"

It took me several moments to soak that in. "Yes," I finally murmured. "It would be foolish."

Overpowering magic was one way to take control, but I already knew I didn't have enough strength to overcome Miss Mabel's advanced skill. I ran my fingers along the saucer, enjoying the cool, polished sensation of the porcelain while I tried to figure out what question to ask next. I hadn't expected this conversation to go so fast.

"Do I have options?" I asked, barely able to squeeze out the words before the cold magic crept up my throat.

"Perhaps."

"I'm desperate, Isadora," I whispered, thinking of the next High Priest. If the magic overpowered me then I could commit the heinous act of murder without knowing. My resolve to conquer the binding doubled. "I'll do whatever I can."

"I know," she said.

"What if I—"

The magic stopped my question. *What if I could destroy the contract?*

She stared at me again, but this time her eyes looked distant. She was rustling through my brain and heart, fleshing out all my insecurities and fears, finding the decisions I would make that could lead to bad ends. I wondered how close to the darkness in my heart she would go. She blinked twice, then shook her head.

"In answer to your question, yes. If the contract is destroyed, the binding will no longer exist."

Hope, sweet and pure, surged through my soul.

"Yes?" I asked, breathless, needing verbal confirmation. It couldn't be that easy.

Isadora paused.

"Remember that she's quite cunning, Bianca," she said quietly. "You've underestimated her before."

What little confidence I still had in myself shattered. "Yes," I heard myself whisper over the bellow of my powers. The reminder of my responsibility in Mama's death struck a crippling blow, resurrecting my anger and despair all over again. "I know."

You were weak.

"Miss Mabel knows the limitations and weaknesses of the magic. She knows that she must keep all her bindings near or risk losing them. Getting to your binding would be very difficult."

The word *bindings* echoed in my head and I shuddered to think of all the other witches Miss Mabel held in her control. Was that how she had become so powerful? I recalled the protective way she held the book in the attic four months before, and again in the Western Network.

"It seems quite hopeless," I said in a strangled voice. My life, and the future High Priest's, hung in the balance. Even if the High Priestess found a way around my Inheritance Curse, what would it matter? I wouldn't kill another witch for Miss Mabel, so the binding would claim my life.

The wrinkles around Isadora's eyes softened for the first time. Her voice reminded me of my grandmother.

"You'll never beat her with sheer power," she said softly, "but there are strengths you possess that she does not. Every witch has a weakness. Those who seem to have none are often the most flawed of all of us."

"What strengths?" I scoffed as the magic expanded in my chest with a painful lurch. Pretending that I wasn't mourning Mama had leeched my strength. "Sarcasm? Running? I can't even do that anymore."

I leaned forward and put my head in my hands. Why wouldn't this all just go away? The silence continued for several moments until I looked up.

"How is Miss Mabel doing all this evil?" I asked. "How is she so powerful? She—"

She transported me.

Isadora shifted in her chair. "She's using Almorran magic," she said with a troubled frown, and I knew she understood my thought.

"Almorran?" I murmured, recalling the Clavas in the painting.

"Yes. Dark Almorran magic like your binding is something Mabel has always been interested in. It would also allow her to transport you against your will because you aren't powerful enough to block her, like the High Priestess or your father could."

The idea of Miss Mabel resurrecting an ancient dark magic in order to gain control shook me. She would stop at nothing. But for what? What was her end goal? There had to be a reason.

So my only hope is to destroy the binding, I concluded to myself in a grim thought, unable to speak it aloud. "There's no way for me to combat Almorran magic right now," I said instead. "I don't know enough."

Isadora's expression didn't change.

"The possibilities are always shifting, Bianca. One never knows what could happen when you least expect it."

"Should that comfort me?" I asked, puzzled by her cryptic words.

"That should comfort all of us," she said with a final sip of her tea. "No future is set in stone. Now, I have a few things to do this afternoon. Thank you for your visit."

"Yes. Thank you for having me, Isadora," I said, pushing away from the table.

She didn't stop me. I wanted her to call after me, to tell me the secret behind saving myself. To say I was clever enough to steal a binding set by one of the most powerful witches in the world using a magic so old that some believed it had never really existed. I stopped at the doorway but didn't turn around. Behind her cottage lay the beginning of the land owned by Miss Mabel's School for Girls. I shivered, thinking of the painful memories. Letum Wood cast a long shadow on days like this.

"Are you going to tell the High Priestess what you know about me?" I asked, peering out the door to the dripping forest. It would be so much easier that way. Then I wouldn't have to bear yet another secret, another burden on my strained heart. But would she? Isadora didn't have to act on what she saw.

"Who said she doesn't already know?" she asked.

I whirled around.

"Does she?"

Isadora peered into my eyes. "That's not for me to say. Mildred knows many things that I do not."

"She suspected that Miss Mabel would—"

The words stopped again, just short of hope. *She suspected that Miss Mabel would bind me into an agreement.* Maybe the High Priestess was already anticipating a traitorous action. If she knew, she certainly gave no sign of it.

"Regardless of whether Mildred knows or not," Isadora said, "I will not be the one to tell her. Sometimes the most obvious courses are not always the safest."

Disappointed but not surprised, I closed my eyes, took several breaths, and pressed forward into the gray fog that had settled in behind the rain. Isadora had her own reasons for her silence and I had to trust that it was for the best.

I ducked away from the little cottage and into the wispy fog, grateful to return to Letum's expansive ceiling. The dragon inside cooled as I walked further away, my cape billowing out behind me.

Sanna

"We're going far into Letum Wood for your lesson today," Merrick said the next morning.

We stood in the middle of the Forgotten Gardens on the edge of the castle grounds. They surrounded a dilapidated stone building with no roof that had been crumbling into ruins for years. Ivy and vines from Letum Wood had slowly been pulling it into the forest. New leaves sprang from the dead, dried vines of last year, coating the decaying walls in a layer of fluttering green. Every now and then bluebirds peeked their heads out and chirped, dancing along the wall with the promise of spring.

"Far into Letum Wood?" I asked. "How is that any different from the other runs?"

"It will be much farther than we've gone before."

The hope for an adventure ran through me like a little thrill. But then a nagging reminder of Mama's ghost tugged on the moment, reminding me that running was no adventure anymore.

"You look quite refreshed today," I said in a dry tone, elevating one eyebrow. "Sleep well?"

A light dusting of stubble touched his cheeks with a golden shimmer, highlighting his bloodshot eyes. He rubbed a hand over his face to push aside his hair. He wore it down today, and it hovered above his shoulders like strands of sand.

"You're brave to taunt the witch who controls how hard you have to run," he said, mimicking my dry tone. I snorted with false bravado.

"I'm not afraid of you."

But a little flicker in Merrick's eyes told me that perhaps I should be.

"Let's go," he said, nodding toward the creeping fog of Letum Wood. "We've got a jaunt to get there."

"Do we have to run?"

"What else do you recommend?"

I hesitated. "Not going?"

His tolerance for my attitude took a considerable dive.

"We're going."

I grabbed his arm when he turned to leave.

"But I can't run!"

"Why?" he demanded, staring at me. I hadn't expected such a vehement response. I could sense something behind his question.

"Because."

He lifted an eyebrow. "Because what?"

Because it hurts too much.

"Are we really having this conversation again? I just can't."

"Yes, we are having this conversation again because I want you to tell me why you refuse to run."

My heart hammered in my chest. For a second, the words hovered on the top of my tongue, but I dismissed them.

"There's no reason. I just can't."

The muscles in his face relaxed into a disappointed frown. "Well, you're going to have to figure it out on your own then, since you won't let anyone else help you."

He pulled away and continued on to Letum Wood. I scrambled after him, feeling a little like a failure. "What are we going to do?"

"Test a few things," he said, starting to run.

The early morning mist had just started to rise from the gardens, leaving a coating of dew on the hedge and grass. At first Merrick kept us at an easy lope, skirting along the edges of Letum Wood, for which I was grateful. Once we turned and plunged into the forest, Letum Wood's trees loomed high and shady. I watched for a pair of bright yellow eyes in the murky trees and thought I heard a snort in the distance. Trying to find the dragon gave me something to think about besides the memories lurking in the back of my mind.

By the time we wound through several back trails, crossed forgotten roads, and waded a low creek, we were in a different part of Letum Wood, one that didn't incite such strong emotions in me. The trees were spread out here less densely, making it feel open compared to the confinement of the forest near Chatham. It felt like a vise releasing from my chest, allowing me to breathe freely.

"This is where Sanna lives," he said, motioning with his head to a small cottage. A chimney on the south end piped out a lazy stream of gray smoke, and two open windows faced us, their white drapes fluttering out into the fresh spring air. "Sanna is a friend of mine that lives out here all by herself."

"You have friends?" I asked, feigning surprise.

"Only a few," he said with a very brief grin. "Come on. You'll like Sanna. She's special."

I wasn't sure what surprised me more: the thought of Merrick having something to do outside the Protectors or seeing the old woman hobble onto the porch with a cane as knobby as Grandmother's hands used to be. She wore a simple brown dress with a necklace that glittered ebony and orange. It only took me a few seconds to realize that she wore a string of dragon scales.

"Special, you say?" I eyed her necklace again. Either it was an old family heirloom, passed through many generations, or Sanna was the only living Dragonmaster in Antebellum. I dismissed the idea. Dragons hadn't really been around in centuries: the Dragonmasters were long gone.

Then again, I reasoned with myself, *I didn't exactly imagine that forest dragon.* A shudder climbed my spine. What was happening? Almorran magic, dragons in Letum Wood, West Guards in the Borderlands. What more?

Merrick smiled. "She's special for her own reasons. Anyway, we're going to help her split wood."

"Wood?"

"Yes. It burns better than stones."

I followed behind him with a growl, annoyed that he'd bested me in the silent game of wits. If Leda found out how quickly Merrick could silence my own personal brand of sarcasm, I'd never live it down.

"Merry meet, Sanna!" he called with a blithe smile. "Staying out of trouble?"

"Merry meet yourself. I'm probably having more fun than you!" Sanna bellowed back. I'd expected her speech to betray her age like Isadora's did, but she sounded young and spry. Merrick laughed and turned off to the back of her cabin. I ignored him and followed the footpath leading to her front porch, crossing over a small wooden bridge above a tinkling brook. I was curious about this woman in the woods.

"You must be Bianca," Sanna said as I approached. "Merrick told me that he's your teacher now."

Unlike most female witches, she didn't curtsy. Instead she held out her steady arm and waited for me to grip her forearm in my hand, like a Council Member might do. Her eyes, cloudy and dim, gazed past my shoulder without seeing. I realized with surprise that Sanna was blind. How could she live alone? Especially here?

"Merry meet, Sanna," I said, taking the offered arm. Her soft skin and braided white hair reminded me of my grandmother. She wore an old shawl across her thin arms. A peek over her shoulder and into the open door of her house revealed an old wooden table, a braided rug on the wooden floor, and a large claw on the wall that looked like an ivory scythe. My throat went dry.

This little old lady in the woods owned a dragon talon. *Special indeed,* I thought, grateful she couldn't see my shocked expression.

"What'd you come here for?" Sanna asked.

"I'm not entirely sure," I said, distracted by her necklace now that I stood close to it. Small beads of bright orange gleamed from the black scales. I wondered how long it had been in her possession. "Merrick said something about chopping wood?"

"They're heart scales," Sanna said, and I glimpsed a knowing grin on her face. For a woman who had no sight, she certainly knew what was going on. "I got them from a very special dragon when I was a little girl. They shed these scales from near their heart when they are young, you know. For the rest of its life, a dragon will loyally serve whoever gets its heart scales."

"Oh," I whispered, glancing from her necklace and back to her eyes. "It's beautiful. You are a Dragonmaster then?"

"No, I'm a fairy," she snapped, and I stared at her in open-mouthed surprise. Then she burst out laughing, a belly-deep cackle that made me smile, albeit hesitantly. "Of course I'm a Dragonmaster! You're not very sharp, are you?"

"But you live out here alone," I said, running my eyes over the forest. I'd grown up in a safer part of Letum Wood, but even there the dangers had been very real. "How are you a Dragonmaster by yourself?"

She snorted.

"What you're really asking is how am I the Dragonmaster when I'm so old and blind?"

"Yes," I admitted, feeling sheepish. "I guess that's what I'm asking."

She tapped the side of her head.

"It's all in their heads."

"Whose heads?"

A heavy line furrowed her forehead. "The dragons, stupid girl. The dragons! You don't get out much, do you? Didn't you just graduate from Miss Mabel's School for Girls? I'm surprised my sister let you in."

"Isadora?" I asked, my mouth dropping. "You know her?"

Sanna rolled her eyes. "Know her? The woman is my twin. She's the hardest sister to grow up with you'd ever meet. She anticipates the punch line of every joke."

"I didn't know she had a twin."

Sanna snorted. "Figures. She never talks about personal things. She's much too high and mighty that way. I broke a china teacup once and she took years to get over it."

"We'll be done in no time, Sanna," Merrick interrupted, striding around the corner with two axes resting on his shoulders. "I'm glad we came today. You're almost out of wood."

I was grateful he showed up at that moment. I needed a chance to recover. Sanna and Isadora were twins? Two more different witches never existed. Isadora, who was always proper and calm, the sister of this loud, obnoxious witch before me? Impossible. I shook my head to clear the collecting thoughts. An aged, blind Dragonmaster? None of this made sense.

Merrick shoved an axe into my arms as he walked past.

"Let's go," he said briskly, swinging the other ax off his shoulder with smooth, practiced grace. "You'll want to get started soon. A girl like you will need as much of an advantage as you can get."

"A girl like me?"

Sanna gave a low whistle. "Sounds like a challenge!" she called out with another bawdy laugh.

"We are each going to make a pile of wood and see who wins," Merrick said when I stepped off the porch and joined him. He'd already grabbed a rotten log from nearby and pulled it near a stump. I tested the weight of the ax in my hand. It didn't feel too heavy.

"What's the prize?" I asked.

"If you win, I'll let you transport back. If I win, we run without complaint."

One less chance to run into Mama's memory and flounder in a magic I couldn't control?

"Deal," I said.

"I'll show you how to do it," he said. "Watch."

He grabbed a log, lifted the ax above his head, and brought it down with a mighty swing of his arm. The wood broke into equal parts and fell to different sides of the stump. I laughed under my breath.

"Easy," I said. Merrick's eyebrows lifted innocently as he bent over to gather the pieces. He took a few skinny shards that had split off to keep for kindling.

"You think so?" he asked.

"Indeed. You better get to work," I said, spinning on my heel toward another splitting stump. "You wouldn't want a girl to beat you."

Sanna chuckled and moved into her house with all the confidence of someone with perfect sight. Papa used to split firewood for us all the time. When he wasn't around Mama used an incantation her father had found in a family grimoire, and the logs simply fell apart into perfect pieces. How difficult could it be?

Extremely, it turned out.

Aiming the ax correctly was the first hurdle. Most of the time I missed the wood completely and shaved the side or hit the stump, or even the dirt. One poor attempt embedded the first inch of my axe into the wood. No matter how many times I pounded the log onto the stump, it wouldn't budge.

"Jikes," I muttered, wiping a bead of sweat from my forehead. I had nothing to show for my sweat. Merrick had stopped chopping to watch my struggle, his modest, neat pile mocking me.

"Need help?" he asked.

I wasn't sure if it was the magic that felt hot inside or the sting of my pride. The heat crept into my cheeks.

"No! Well . . . not help, exactly," I corrected. "I can do it! The ax just won't work right."

"So you can't do it?"

The heat from my chest turned into an ugly glare his direction. He abandoned his ax with an effortless grin and grabbed mine. "You want to use momentum to break the log," he said. "Not just your arms."

He adjusted my grip on the ax handle, taught me how to keep my dominant hand fluid, and walked me through my first attempts at swinging it above my head and down.

"Use your back," he said, observing my first pathetic attempts. "Good."

The first three strokes missed the wood. I reset my grip, and the fourth hit true.

"Ha!" I cried, abandoning the ax and stacking the three pieces into a little pile with no small amount of pride. "Take that."

My victory, however strong, was short lived.

Within twenty minutes my arms trembled violently. I could lift the ax, but each swing grew weaker. Merrick's rapidly-growing pile dwarfed mine. I envied his fluid, synchronized movements. Set the log, step back, swing the ax, pick up the wood.

"I'm losing my grip on the ax," I said, looking over my shoulder at him. "My hands aren't strong enough to hold it."

"You can quit if you want," he said unsympathetically.

I eyed the depressing difference between our piles. Running home had already been decided. I'd never win. Why waste the energy chopping wood if I'd just have to run anyway? Merrick wiped the sweat from his eyes and looked right at me.

"Since you're too weak to keep going, of course. In that case, you should probably take a break. Maybe go check on Sanna. Drink some tea. Or you can just do it with magic since you're not strong enough physically."

He was baiting me; I knew it. I recognized the sarcasm in his voice, and I couldn't help but feel rankled. The idea of not following through on the task made the magic come alive inside me with a little jolt of anger. I wasn't so weak that I had to use magic. I straightened so tall I thought my spine would snap. I didn't want to face ghosts while I ran, but that didn't mean I wasn't capable.

"I can do it!" I growled, and set back to work. Twenty minutes later the blisters on my palms burst. Merrick, still hard at work, didn't see me stop to tear off the bottom of my shirt. I wrapped the scrap of fabric around my hand and used my teeth to pull the knot tight. I started again, I hoping he hadn't noticed.

I'm not weak.

Amidst the grueling, repetitive motions, my mind wandered. The swirling magic in my chest pulled me back to Miss Mabel, the High Priest, and my Inheritance Curse. Too tired to push the thoughts away, to focus on *not* focusing on Miss Mabel, I let the thoughts flutter through my mind in random bursts.

Your task is to kill the High Priest.

The thought brought my defenses down for half a second, letting the magic slip from my heart in a quick pulse. A familiar tingling sensation shot through my arms when I brought the ax down on the log. The wood flew apart with a violent crack, shooting four separate pieces into the yard. I jumped with a yelp, narrowly avoiding the thickest piece. One hit the side of the cabin and clattered to the dirt, while another broke a branch off a tree several paces away. I looked down to find that the ax had bitten into the stump all the way to its top.

"Blessed be," I muttered, tugging on the handle. The stump had swallowed the ax head whole. My head swirled as I tried to understand it, and I finally used an incantation to work the ax head free. Merrick, realizing I'd stopped, threw an armful of logs onto his pile and wiped his palms off.

"What happened?"

I thought about telling him that I'd accidentally used magic to chop the log and didn't know how, but decided that I might sound even more out of control.

"Nothing," I called over my shoulder, setting the ax on the ground and heading for the well before he could ask for details, unable to get away fast enough. "Just need some water."

The cool water parched my throat. I sat down on a nearby boulder and took long draws until my stomach started to hurt. How had I buried the ax in the stump?

I finished with my drink, and unnerved by my own inability to figure out how the moment of strength came about, I dumped the rest of the water bucket over my head and returned to the porch.

"We're all done," he said. "Stack your logs with mine. I'll let Sanna know."

I suppressed my sigh of relief and did as he said without word, water dripping down my back and ears. Sanna had walked onto the porch by the time he returned and pressed a small parcel into my trembling hands.

"For the trip home," she said. "You're bound to be hungry. It's good. Isadora sent it over."

"Thank you, Sanna."

Despite my sweaty skin, she reached up and patted my face with a bit more slap than I expected.

"You're a good girl. You'll get him one day. Thanks for the free labor, Merrick!" she called as he returned from the shed. The warm hues of her rare necklace caught my eye again.

"Yes," I said, smiling at her even though she couldn't see my face. "I'll come again. Thank you, Sanna."

Merrick and I started off at a walk down the winding trail through the trees, crossing over the little brook that trickled past her house. I opened the parcel to find a large slice of pound cake. I broke it in half and offered Merrick the bigger slice. He waved it away.

"Don't you feel hunger?" I asked, irritated that he came away so unfazed. My ravenous stomach threatened to eat itself, and the broken blisters on my hands pulsed. This run would be miserable. He ignored me, so I devoured the whole piece. Once the pound cake disappeared,

I peeled the fabric off my hand to tighten the makeshift bandage. Blood had soaked through the fabric.

"When did that happen?" Merrick asked in surprise, his eyes narrowing on my injuries. Embarrassed, I just shrugged.

"Awhile ago."

"You should have said something."

I kept walking, not knowing how to respond. *I don't want people to know I'm weak because I can't afford to fail again. If I fail this time, the High Priest will die.*

A long silence fell between us as we walked, heading into the great maw of Letum Wood. Thinking of the run ahead, and the living memories that possibly awaited me in the forest, made my stomach hurt. Perhaps I shouldn't have sucked down that pound cake so fast.

"It helps your hand-eye coordination," Merrick said, breaking the silence. I turned to him in surprise.

"What does?"

"Chopping wood. It also strengthens your back, stomach, and arm muscles so that when you learn how to use a sword you're strong enough."

"Oh," I said, chagrined that there had been a purpose behind the exercise after all. "How did you meet Sanna?"

"During my training as a Guardian," he said. "I was lost in Letum Wood and fell into a creek in the middle of winter. I stumbled into her house, nearly frozen to death, and she took me in. I've been coming back to help her ever since."

"You were a Guardian?"

He nodded. "I rose quickly through the ranks from Guardian, to Captain of the Guards, and then I tried out for the Protectors. Now, here I am, waiting to see if it happens."

I could tell there was more to the story by the way he set his jaw. Before I could inquire, he motioned to the trail with a nod. He'd tied his hair back again with a leather strip, but several tendrils had worked loose while he chopped wood. He peered into the forest.

"You ready?" he asked. I shook my head. The very idea of having to fight the memories again while feeling so tired drained my already depleted energy reserves.

"No," I admitted.

He hesitated, staring at me with those cool green eyes.

"You worked hard today, so I won't force you to run back," he said. "You can transport."

Relief rushed through me like a cool breeze.

"Thank you."

He nodded once, but even as I dropped into blackness, I couldn't miss the concerned look that crossed his face.

A Broken Mirror

"I'll do the algebra homework, Leda. I will. I promise," Camille said three days later. "I'll work on all the algebra rubbish that Miss Scarlett is forcing me to do over the summer, but you have to tell me how I'm going to use it in real life!"

Leda started to answer Camille's challenge but stopped, her face crinkling into thought.

"Yes, Leda," I said, from where I lay on the Witchery floor, lounging on the large, overstuffed pillows. "How will Camille use algebra in everyday life?"

"Very well," Leda said, taking up the challenge by clearing her throat. "I'll tell you how you'll use algebra in real life."

"Wonderful," Camille said, setting down her pencil. "I'm waiting."

Leda cleared her throat again. "First of all, there's a lot of practical application," she said, pausing to chew on her bottom lip.

"She's stalling," I sang under my breath. Leda silenced my surfacing laugh with a sharp glare.

"Well?" Camille asked with a bit more backbone than usual. Her confidence had certainly grown the past few months. "What's the answer?"

"Oh, you'll use it!" Leda said in a quick rush. "You'll use algebra all the time."

"Yes, so you say. But how?"

"Take sewing, for example," Leda said, her self-assuredness growing. "Yes, think of sewing. You have to know lengths for sewing, right? And angles for . . . for dresses."

Camille's eyes narrowed. "Angles for dresses," she repeated blandly. "I don't know about that."

"Oh hang it, Camille," Leda burst out. "You don't have a choice. It's required curriculum. Whether or not you'll use it doesn't matter. You still need to learn it to pass your first year. Now get to work."

Camille let out a dramatic sigh and stared at the parchment with loathing. She muttered something under her breath that sounded like, "Won't need algebra to marry a handsome Guardian," and turned back to her studies.

Eyes closed, I enjoyed the sensation of not moving after a grueling morning lesson with Merrick. Though it had been several days ago, the experience at Sanna's ran through my mind, and I replayed the way the magic moved through my arms and gave me a burst of strength. Every day I awoke, planning to tell my friends about what happened, but could never bring myself to do it. If even I didn't understand it yet, how could I expect them to?

A steady flapping sound came from the turret stairs. All of us gazed at each other in question.

"What's that?" Camille asked.

"If it's a witch," Leda said in a threatening tone, "they better leave now. I don't want anyone else coming into the Witchery but us."

The sound grew louder and was joined by two more pairs of shoes.

"Hello?" I called, climbing to my feet with a grimace. My swollen, aching leg muscles protested. Running the stairs in the lower bailey had taken its toll. I peered into the dark stairway to see only faint movement.

"Yes, move aside. Yes, yes. Move aside, please!"

A short, buxom woman bustled in wearing a light blue dress and a kerchief to match. She had cheeks so red they reminded me of cherries, and made her plump face fringed with strands of yellow hair look very merry. Her bright eyes matched her dress. Altogether, she looked entirely like a dinner roll. Round, soft, and squishy.

Camille leapt up from her chair, sending her scroll of homework flying. "Miss Henrietta!" she cried. "What are you doing here?"

"You'll look lovely in this deep blue, won't you? Eyes like a thunderstorm," Miss Henrietta said to me, inviting herself in. She gazed around, her eyes nearly disappearing into her face when she squinted.

"Goodness, so bright. So, so bright. All right then, come along, Bianca. I need to see you. Yes, yes. Come."

Her assessing gaze roved over my body and she started to tut under her breath. Two girls wearing matching black dresses with golden lace trim streamed into the room, their eyes trained on the floor. They stood next to each other against the wall and waited without making a peep.

"A little more work than I thought. Move aside. Yes. Yes, yes. Oh, that horrid fabric won't do!" she muttered, touching my dress with the tip of her finger.

"Are you here to sew a dress for Bianca?" Camille asked, stepping forward. "See? She certainly needs the help, just like I told you."

I shot Camille a perturbed look but she smiled innocently. Henrietta looked up, then returned to her offended perusal of my dress.

"Merry meet again, Camille," she said. "It's always nice to see you. Go over there, Bianca. Stand up. Up, up!"

Henrietta scooted me toward the table. A chair slid out and moved into the middle of the room.

"To the chair!" she commanded. "Yes, yes, good."

Bewildered, I shot Leda a desperate glance, a plea for help. She smirked, tucked her legs underneath her, and disappeared into the book, *Easing Into the Political Realm*.

"Take that horrid thing off her," Henrietta commanded the maids. I realized with a start that she meant my dress. The two girls stepped forward and peeled the dress off, leaving me in my knickers and binder.

"Wait!" I cried. "What are you doing?"

They attacked me with a mass of material, slipping it down my body in soft folds of fabric, silencing my squawks of protest. It turned out to be mostly the shell of a dress. The sleeves were too long, the waist too wide, the neckline jagged, and the bottom frayed at the hem. Even incomplete, it took my breath away.

"The High Priestess sent us," Henrietta said, circling me, an army of needles following in the air behind her that Camille had to dodge.

The two witches with her began to poke, fold, and prod, occasionally snatching a needle from the air to slide into the dress. "This is what you are to wear for the Network Ball. I've been able to do most the basic work on it, but needed to check my measurements."

"Ouch!" I muttered when one of the girls pricked my hip with a pin. She averted her eyes to avoid my glower.

"It's a special material," Henrietta said, her lips pursed. "Quite rare, and imbued with a special magic that keeps you cool and prevents sweat stains in the heat of the summer. It's all the High Priestess wears."

"What is it?" I asked, running my fingertips along the seams. It felt much softer than silk to touch, but light like linen. I never wanted to take it off.

"It's called linea. It originally came from the Eastern Network."

Linea. I'd heard of it before. It was the strongest of fabrics and exquisitely expensive. I pulled my fingers away, frightened even to touch it. If it came from the East, it meant this material must have been over a century old. There hadn't been any trade amongst the Networks since the Mansfeld Pact, a treaty that banned trade, interference, or the conducting of business across Network borders. We remained self-sufficient instead. Although there was an underground market for this sort of thing, the High Priestess would never wear material that had been obtained illegally.

"I can't wear this," I said, meeting Henrietta's eyes in a panic. "I'll destroy it. It must be over a hundred years old. I can't even pour tea without spilling."

"Or worse," Leda called.

Camille stood on tiptoe and pulled a leaf fragment out of my hair. "She's right, Henrietta," Camille said. "Bianca's a mess."

Henrietta acted as if she hadn't heard and pointed to my leather shoes, shooting a glance at the red-haired maid. The girl seized my ankle and removed the shoes immediately.

"Hey!" I clambered after her, nearly falling off the chair, but Henrietta pushed me back into place. "Those are mine! Papa made them for me."

Henrietta cast a revolted look at the slippers. "Although I think they should be destroyed, I won't throw them away. We're just taking them off for the fitting so we can get a proper hem. The High Priestess chose this particular fabric from her stores just for you. You'll wear it, and you'll like it."

"I'll destroy it."

"It's a hardy material. Don't worry. You'll not get it so dirty that I can't clean it up."

Just you wait.

The maids continued to pin and re-pin the hem, tailed by the cloud of needles. When they poked me again near the ankle I let out a yelp, then growled at them.

"Abbee, the mirror, please," Henrietta said.

One of the seamstresses left and reappeared with a long mirror drifting in behind her. Henrietta turned me toward it with a self-satisfied smirk.

"See?"

When I looked into the mirror to see the dress, the girl in the reflection startled me. The dress's elegant sapphire color blended magnificently with my dark hair and gray eyes. Though unfinished, the curves of the unfinished material set off my girlish figure to give me an older, matured bearing.

Camille beamed.

"It's not even done yet and you look beautiful, Bianca!" she cried, grabbing my hair and twisting it onto my head in various positions. "We could curl your hair and put it here, like this. Ooh, or this! It would be so pretty."

"With a little work on that wild mane you should clean up well enough for the ball," Henrietta murmured.

Their words slipped through my mind with all the permanence of a gust of wind. Whatever they said, I didn't care. All I could see was my reflection, and what I saw made my heart's dragon stir with a little cry of pain. I didn't know why the powers started building when I ran my hand along the high waistline, enjoying the fabric's silky touch. Not even I, the girl with blisters on her hands who loved to run in pants, could dispute the grace that a dress of this caliber lent to a forest-child like me.

Mama's gray eyes whirred through my mind, seizing my chest in a sudden rush of angst. I gazed at myself in the mirror again, staring hard.

Just like Mama. I look just like Mama.

In a breath, the magic slipped away from my heart for just a second, leaving with a faint tingle before I reined it back in a moment later. The mirror split with a loud *crack*, creating an intricate web of edges from top to bottom. Only pieces of my hair and dress remained visible, showing in glimpses of blue and black.

"Oh dear!" Henrietta cried, startled. "Oh dear, dear, dear. What happened? I don't know what happened. My lovely mirror! Abbee, this is your fault!"

"No!" the small redhead cried. "I wasn't even touching it."

Both Camille and Leda shot me sharp looks.

"Quite strange," I said quickly. "I'm sure we can find you another one, Miss Henrietta. The gown is gorgeous. Thank you for working on it. Would you like me to take it off now?"

"Yes, I suppose," she said, shooting Abbee a dark look. "Let's be on our way now, girls. We have a mirror to fix and a few more dresses to finish. I think I know an incantation to reverse this. Camille, we'll have your ivory gown finished in just a week or two."

The garment flew over my head in a violent flap, almost knocking me off the chair and leaving me standing in my undergarments. It gathered itself together and fell in a drape across Henrietta's shoulder.

"Well, merry part," Henrietta said, her troubled gaze lingering on the mirror as it floated out of the room ahead of them.

"Thank you, Miss Henrietta," I called, feeling a twinge of guilt over her mirror. The three women disappeared down the stairs.

"Oh, Bianca," Camille cried, collapsing onto the couch behind her. "That dress was beautiful! You looked lovely. But why would you break that mirror?"

"Can you toss me my clothes? I didn't mean to. It just . . . it just happened. I don't want to talk about it."

Camille pitched the gray dress back to me, a dreamy gaze in her eyes. The comfortable smell of lavender washed over me when I put my own bland dress back on, but I couldn't deny missing the soft, flowing feeling of linea on my skin.

Despite the heaviness in my heart, and the agitation left over from my burst of power, I felt the tension dissipate once Henrietta left with the broken mirror. There were no mirrors in the Witchery to remind me of whom I looked like.

Leda turned a page in her book.

"I think next time we should have a magnet ready," she said without looking up. "Then we can suck all the pins away before they poke you to death with them. That's probably why you broke the mirror."

Camille and I looked at each other, then all of us burst into laughter, making me forget Mama's quiet gray eyes.

Mildred's Resistance

"Do me a favor?" Papa asked the next afternoon as I walked out of my bedroom, still bleary-eyed from a nap. He gathered a couple scrolls from the table near the bay window. I shrugged, then grimaced. My neck and back muscles were sore from an intense hour of climbing up and down trees. Merrick had remained ahead of me, as usual, and dropped pinecones on my head. For every pinecone I didn't catch, I had to do ten push-ups. He claimed it helped with my hand-eye reaction time and strength, but I suspected he just liked torture. Sap still clung to the bottom of my feet and my palms with sticky persistence.

"Sure," I said, yawning.

"Will you take this to Council Member Stella?" he asked, waving a scroll at me from the other side of the table. "I want to make sure no one else reads it."

I grabbed it from the air. "Yes, Papa."

"Thanks," he called over his shoulder, rushing off to a meeting with the Protectors. "Love you, girl."

I rubbed my face, pulled my hair from its ponytail, and headed out of the apartment.

It took a brave soul to lead the southern covens that flirted with the border of the Southern Network. Winter brushed that part of the world for much of the year, leaving them with a short growing season in the summer and fall. Ice, wind, and frost were the way of life down there, from what Michelle described.

Fortunately, Stella was just such a brave and bold soul, ready to lead and eager to work.

Her close friendship with the High Priestess and love of outlandish scarves set her apart from the other Council Members. Her warm personality always drew people to her; it was rare to see Stella alone or unhappy, despite those around her. I envied her ability to do and feel whatever she wanted without restraint. Sometimes when I watched her I felt like a caged bird.

A dark purple door came into sight halfway down Council Hall. Sparkling jewels dotted the front of the door, accompanied by a golden pattern of swirls and whirls across the edges to give the impression of a snow shower of diamonds. Singular, just like Stella. The handle shimmered with purple gems and swung to admit me before I could knock.

"Come in, Bianca," she called in a friendly voice. "I'll be with you in just a second."

Stella stood at her desk, while an assistant with limp blonde hair and red-rimmed eyes hovered nearby. I stepped just inside the door, running my eyes over the comfortable room. The cherry wood desk and bookshelves gave a warmth to the stone, even though snowy paintings of the south decorated the walls. Blue-green plants crawled along the windows in little fountains of color, and an expansive purple rug lined with white and blue thread covered most of the floor.

"Send a message to the villages on the Southern Network border," Stella instructed her faded, hunched assistant. "They must wear those bracelet charms I sent. The Southern Network has assembled their army and those charms will help protect our witches if there are skirmishes"

Stella's graying auburn hair tapered back in an elegant, coiffed bun at her neck. An outlandish pink and yellow scarf draped her shoulders and chest in plumes of gauzy chiffon.

"Come in, Bianca," she said again, looking over the top of her glasses with a warm smile. "Dyana and I just finished."

Her assistant slinked by me without making eye contact. If she could get a job as an assistant, surely Leda could find some kind of place in the political realm.

"What can I help you with today?" Stella asked.

"I came with a scroll from my father," I said, extending it to her. "He asked me to bring it over."

Stella smiled and took the scroll.

"That's very kind. Thank you."

I smiled, curtsied, and turned to leave.

"You look like your mother in that gray dress," she added. "It matches your eyes."

I stopped. I wanted to walk away, to pretend like I hadn't heard, but my heart wouldn't let me. Against my better judgment, I circled back around.

"You knew her?" I asked. She smiled, the wrinkles around her eyes creasing.

"Yes. I knew Marie and your grandmother Hazel. Hazel was quite young when I first met her in one of the Resistance meetings. Her father, William, was the local leader and a very good man. You're a lot like him, but you look like Lily, his wife. She had rich, beautiful hair just like yours."

"Really?"

"Indeed. Both you and your grandfather have shown great amounts of courage in frightening situations."

"I didn't know you were part of the Resistance," I said, eager to bleed information from her. Perhaps she knew something about Miss Mabel.

"Indeed," Stella said. "Mildred and I were best friends before she overthrew Evelyn. We started working together in our early twenties, a couple of years after I graduated from Miss Mabel's."

My jaw dropped. "You went to Miss Mabel's?"

"Yes, but that was when the elder Mabel ran it, not the Miss Mabel you've been unfortunate to know."

All my terrible memories of Miss Mabel ran through my mind in a blur. I suspected that her grandmother Mabel, the woman who started the school, couldn't have been much less frightening.

"What was Mabel like?" I asked.

"She was very proper and put together," Stella said in a distant tone. "Her dresses were always new, and her hair perfect. Pleasing her was a futile task. She expected perfection from all her students and was a surly old girl, really." Stella laughed quietly to herself. "It was a difficult three years to say the least. Mabel made extraordinary demands of her pupils, but she got the best of us."

"Sounds familiar."

"Yes," she agreed, matching my wry tone with another little laugh. "Very familiar. Miss Mabel is a lot like Mabel in more ways than one." She tapped her chin in thought. "In fact, I think I have something that you may be interested in. It's not a book I've ever lent out. You may be one of the only witches I trust to read and keep the secrets therein safe. Follow me."

She led me to a bookshelf on the other side of the room, ran her fingers along the edge and finally pulled a book away.

"Here it is!" she cried, brushing the dust from it. "Goodness. All this dust. The maids aren't very thorough, are they?"

I accepted it from her. It was heavy and broad, with thick pages and a neat, slanted writing inside.

Mildred's Resistance.

"It's written by an anonymous historian and accurately details most of what went on between Mildred and Evelyn. They were, at one point, friends. All three of us were."

"Friends? With Evelyn?"

I couldn't picture a woman like Stella, so friendly and good, close with Evelyn, the tyrant who would have destroyed the Central Network if Mildred hadn't taken over.

"A tremendously arrogant lot we were," Stella said, laughing. "We worked together as assistants here at Chatham. A little like you, Camille, and Leda, only we were older. All of us set out to change the world."

"And the world did change."

"Mildred succeeded in changing it," Stella said in a sad tone. "I guess you could say that Evelyn did as well, except not for the better. She didn't start out as a monster, you know. She chose her path through a complicated twist of bad decisions. Despite what she became, I don't think anyone really sets out to betray her friends or her Network. Mildred thinks differently, of course. I tend to believe better of people than she does."

"Did Evelyn try to get you on her side?" I asked.

"Oh, yes," she said, her expression souring. "Very much so. But in the end I stayed with Mildred because I knew she had chosen the better path. Losing Evelyn was a terrible loss."

"I'm sorry that happened to you," I said, unsure of how to continue. She squeezed my arm with the sweet, gentle touch of a friend. A little wave of peace ran through me like a sigh of wind. I craved more of the kind touch, which made me realize how much I missed Mama's frequent hugs. It amazed me how easily disoriented I got without Mama's stability to cling to. Little moments, like a sympathetic gesture, suddenly meant so much more.

"You may be surprised what you find in that book," Stella said, pulling me back out of my thoughts. "I believe your family is mentioned in there."

My eyes widened. "Really?"

"Yes!" she declared with a warm smile. "It wouldn't be complete without mentioning them. They helped Mildred a great deal during the Resistance, and were loyal from the beginning. I know she still appreciates all they did to help her. I'd be pleased to hear your thoughts on the book when you finish."

"Of course," I replied. "I'll bring it back when I'm done. And thank you for telling me about my family."

Stella put her hand around my shoulder as we strolled to the door.

"I had a son once, you know," she said, her voice laced with a deep sadness. "Your fortitude and determination remind me of him a little."

"Where is he now?"

"Gone," she said with a melancholy tinge. "He died when he was very young, but I'd never seen such a stubborn child."

I looked away, suddenly unable to meet her eyes. Any wind of grief triggered something dark and frightening inside of me.

"Oh, dear," she said, pressing a hand to her heart and searching my face. "I've made you sad. I'm so sorry."

"No!" I said, meeting her eyes with a sheepish smile. I didn't want her to feel bad. "You didn't."

"Well, I'd never want to," Stella said with a bolstering smile. "We are all mourning something, Bianca. All of us. Keep that in mind, for you are never alone in your grief. Anyway, thank you for your assistance. I hope the rest of your day fares well. I'm sure we'll see each other around Chatham. At least, I certainly hope we will."

"What are you reading?" Papa asked at breakfast the next morning, setting a loaf of bread and a block of cheese out on the table. My stomach growled.

"I haven't started yet," I said, setting aside *Mildred's Resistance* and straightening my stiff back muscles with a grimace. My body was already starting to tighten up after an early lesson with Merrick. We'd spent the time practicing footwork, lifting heavy logs, and working me into a frenetic appetite for food. "Stella loaned it to me yesterday."

"*Mildred's Resistance?* I've heard of it but never seen a copy. I think that may be the only one." His eyebrows lifted halfway to his hairline with a pointed glance that clearly said *control your usual luck so you don't destroy this book.*

"So using it to start a fire later tonight is out?"

He smirked and threw a piece of cheese at me. It hit my cheek with a slap. A morning breeze made the herb pots hanging from the balcony ledge bob up and down. Basil, and a hint of rosemary, drifted on the wind. Papa sawed away at the bread with a long knife, handing me the first warm slice. I tore off a corner and took a bite. It tasted slightly sweet and soft, like chewing on a cloud. I sighed in contentment and sank farther into the chair.

"Everything going okay in the Borderlands?" I asked, studying his face. Tiberius had come for Papa in the middle of the night. Papa had returned to the castle with a fat lip, a cut on his jaw, a purpling bruise, and no explanation. His eyes flicked to mine.

"Do you really want to know?" he asked. The deep, rolling timbre of his voice made me shudder.

"Yes," I said, although I wasn't sure.

"No, it's not going well at all. They started digging an exceedingly large trench last night."

"Trench?" I questioned, and he nodded. "So your suspicions were right. They are going to divert the river."

"Yes. What I can't figure out is their magic. They've found a spell that can control hundreds of thousands of shovels. They have Guardians supervising, but for the most part the West Guards aren't doing anything. Because they have so many shovels at work, and because the work is so well synchronized, the trench is growing fast." He dragged a hand through his hair, his eyes focused on something in the distance as he worked through the problem. "They must be using an older magic."

My mind sped back to my encounter with Miss Mabel and Isadora's words rang in my head. *She's using Almorran magic.*

"What is your plan?" I asked, wishing I could tell him what I knew. If I mentioned Miss Mabel at all he'd grow suspicious, and that was the last thing he needed right then. He rubbed his face, infused with a sudden weariness.

"We're going to siphon off as much water as we can," he said. "Probably start creating a river of our own further above them."

"Near the Northern Network?" I asked in surprise. The small tract of land we called the Borderlands lay wedged between us and the Western Network, but it also reached our border with the Northern Network.

"Yes," he said, and left it at that.

"It's a good plan," I said. "At least you're doing something."

"It was Zane's idea. He has a tactical mind. Anyway, if it doesn't work we have a few other things in mind."

His tone sounded dark, and a grim feeling creep over me.

"Is there any active fighting yet?"

"Not yet. I think Dane wants to weaken us first. He knows we can stand against them from a military perspective, but not if our witches are starving and in a panic. It's smart. I'd do the same thing if I were in his position."

His casual mention of Dane, the acting High Priest for the Western Network, made me shudder. Almack, the actual Western High Priest, was still deathly sick. The war would truly begin once he died. Unlike in our Network, the Western Network only allowed one governing witch at a time, and the ruler was always a male. No woman had ever taken power in the West. Would Miss Mabel be the first High Priestess? It seemed likely, if Dane could be manipulated. She seemed to think he could; perhaps she held a binding over him as well.

We ate the rest of our meal in the quiet, content to just be with one another.

"See you later, girl," he said, planting a kiss on top of my head once he finished. "Love you."

"Love you, Papa."

Once the apartment door closed, I grabbed *Mildred's Resistance* and hauled it onto my lap, eager to get the grim thoughts about the war with the West out of my head. *Mildred's Resistance* was like new. The edges of the heavy cover had frayed a little, but the pages looked undisturbed, as if someone had carried it around often but never read it. I turned to the first page.

Dear Reader,

This book is written by an unknown author. That's the name I've chosen and it's the only name you'll ever know. My identity is not nearly as important as yours.

Suffice it to say that you may trust me; everything in this book is true. I tell the story of the people of the Resistance and all that it meant at the time. Perhaps it means something to you now, but it will never mean anything to you like it did to us.

The Resistance wasn't an explosion. Rather, it was a slow burn that turned to flame and then to fire. As to blame, I ask you to draw your own conclusions, for you now hold the truth in your hands.

Sincerely Yours,
*   The Unknown Author*

The next page began:

Mildred was a young girl, only she didn't know it.

I read a few paragraphs, skimming through the beginning of the

High Priestess's life. Unable to focus on the story, I skipped ahead, searching through the words. I would read about the High Priestess later. For now, I was on the hunt for something, although I didn't know what.

Several minutes of perusal later, my eyes snagged a word.

Mabel.

Startled, I straightened, my interest rekindled. The original Mabel started popping up quite often. When Evelyn became High Priestess, Mabel gave the school to her granddaughter Miss Mabel and took a job as Evelyn's personal assistant.

"Mabel, you old devil," I whispered. I dog-eared the pages she appeared in as I continued to read. The more often Mabel's name appeared, the darker the picture seemed to grow. She must have had an awful personality.

Her countenance hides the ice beneath.
Sharp eyes in a pretty face.
Selfish soul beneath all that beauty.

Miss Mabel's blonde hair and ruby lips flashed through my mind. *Selfish soul, indeed.* The dreaded grandmother had rubbed off on her protégé. I shook away the terrible feeling, hoping to keep the dragon in my chest at bay.

The sun crept higher in the sky, forcing me indoors. I sprawled out on a comfortable divan, hidden by shadows. If Leda could see me so enthralled by a book, she'd die with happiness. I slipped through the pages, uncovering scattered snippets of information as I went.

As time went on it became clear to all that there was more to Mabel than a smooth voice, but whether Evelyn realized it or not was another matter entirely.

Rumors swirled that Mabel had kicked her daughter, Angelina, out of her house when she came home pregnant. No one could confirm it, and Mabel never spoke of it. When anyone tried to ask, she placed a hex on the witch who broached the subject. It rarely came up twice.

99

Mabel fled the final fight, leaving Evelyn to battle Mildred alone.

The execution of Mabel was particularly sad, as there was no one there to attend her or keep her company in her final hours. No one showed remorse at her passing. Any attempt to contact her daughter or granddaughter was futile. They both rejected the messages.

By the end of the book, I had little doubt that Mabel had been a horrid, evil, conniving woman: characteristics she shared with her granddaughter. Perhaps a potent evil ran through Miss Mabel's blood. But what of Miss Mabel's mother, Angelina?

Even a book this detailed couldn't give me all the information I wanted, and I couldn't ask the High Priestess without inciting suspicion. I drew in a deep breath and slammed the book shut. Before I moved forward with my plan to destroy the binding in the West, I needed to visit someone. Someone who knew Miss Mabel better than anyone else.

Miss Celia.

Miss Celia

Merrick called to me from across the Forgotten Gardens the next day.

"This is going to be your new best friend," he said. "Bring it with you every day."

I lifted my gaze just in time to see a long piece of wood hurtling toward me through the air, and caught it just before it kissed my face. The smooth wood snagged one of the healing blisters on my palm, causing a smarting pain. I bit back a grimace and glared at him instead.

"Good catch," he said with a surprised smile that almost offended me.

"A wooden sword?" I asked, studying it. It was thick and heavy, whittled from a light yellow wood. Its shape resembled a sword, but it was too thick to be real. The sword with which Papa had taught me a few things with as a young girl was nowhere near as hefty.

"We'll use it to practice. You have to earn a real sword. This one is weighted and heavy. Learning it heavy makes it easier to use the actual sword."

Earn a real sword? I wanted to ask. *With what, bruises?*

Merrick held his own wooden sword in his right fist. His white shirt stretched tight over his broad shoulders, and he had pulled sandy hair away from his tan face. I hadn't really paid attention to it before, but Camille was right. Merrick was handsome in a rugged, intense kind of way.

"Why do I have to earn a real sword?"

"So I know you won't cut your own leg off," he said in his usual dry tone. "Let's review the footwork we've been going over the past week. Show me a forward attack, and then a lunge."

The sun shone around us in the early morning light, echoing off the ivy screens of the walled garden. We had almost total privacy out here on the edge of the gardens, close to Letum Wood. Only the birds fluttered around, keeping us company. The sweet hold of spring had slowly started to fade into the hot days of summer. Although the mornings and evenings still smelled like honeysuckle and carried a cool breeze, the days were getting warmer, and this morning was no exception.

We reviewed the footwork, although the heavy weight in my hand often distracted me. Merrick introduced a new footwork pattern for me to practice the rest of the day, and then we started into swordplay.

"You're going to need to be fast," he said, grabbing a stick from the ground, "and accurate. Having a sword to defend yourself won't mean anything if you can't hit your target."

He tossed the stick straight up, swung his own wooden sword, and cut the stick into two equal parts with very little effort. After the experience chopping wood at Sanna's, I knew this would not be easy.

"The wooden swords aren't sharp," I pointed out.

"No, but if you're fast you can break it. I'll give you a few swings to start practice. A block, a lunge, and swing, for example. You'll practice on this dummy."

Off to my right stood a figure cloaked in a white sheet. The fabric fell away, revealing a four-limbed wooden figure with a grotesquely painted face and a distorted frame. Many swords had bitten into its wood.

"What is that?" I asked.

"This is Mikhail, or so the Guardians dubbed him. He's the practice dummy for sword work."

"Mikhail? Named after the Southern Network High Priest, Mikhail?"

"The very one," Merrick said, walking toward it. I followed just behind. "He just stands there and doesn't do anything while all the Guardians work around him, a shocking resemblance to the South's High Priest."

I would have laughed if Merrick hadn't looked so serious. Focused on the objective as usual, he immediately began to demonstrate several new sword movements while I mimicked him.

"Practice again tonight," he said, casting his eyes over the dummy. "We should be able to use Mikhail for a couple of days. Oh, and carry those back with you."

He pointed to two buckets filled with rocks.

"Why?" I asked, already dreading it.

"Because I said so."

I glared at him. No doubt he enjoyed having someone to boss around. As an apprentice, he probably had very little power of his own. I couldn't begrudge him a little flexing of his control. I'd probably do the same thing, but I didn't have to like it.

"Can I ask you a question?"

He looked back at me, his green eyes bright, almost dazzling, in the full sunshine.

"Yes."

I hesitated. Ever since my visit with Isadora I'd been contemplating what she said. *There are strengths you possess that she does not. Every witch has a weakness.* I hoped that putting the question to Merrick wouldn't bring me, or my intentions, too much attention.

"Do you think physical strength could match magical strength in a fight?"

His brow wrinkled.

"In what regard?"

I wanted to ask him outright: *I cannot beat Miss Mabel with magic; she is too powerful. Could I kill her with physical force before she kills me with magic?* But I couldn't for so many reasons. How I loathed the dark secrets of my heart.

"Oh, just an idle question." I kicked at a clump of grass nearby, certain that my lackadaisical response made him more suspicious than ever. "So many witches rely on magic that I wondered if, or when, we fight the war, we could triumph through non-magical means."

Merrick thought about the question, and I was glad to have a moment to recover my wits. *Oh, just an idle question?* That must have been the single most suspicious thing I could have said. I would have smacked my forehead if my arms weren't so tired.

"Yes, I think it can," he said. "The Eastern Network has fought battles entirely without magic in the past, and triumphed. While I think it presents its own challenges when the opponent does use magic, it's by no means a death wish."

"I agree," I said, hoping to close the conversation. But my heart sped up just a little. Is that what Isadora had meant when she told me I had strengths that Miss Mabel didn't? Perhaps I really could destroy the contract and win my life back. Maybe by learning sword work with Merrick, I could physically fight Miss Mabel for my life.

Could I meld the two? Magic and sword work? There must be a way. I thought back to the day at Sanna's, when the magic slipped and buried the ax in the stump.

"Can magic and sword work be used together?"

"Together?"

"Yes," I said. "I mean, could a witch use magic to make her sword work better?"

He pressed the tip of his wooden sword in the ground and leaned on it, looking me directly in the eye.

"What you're really asking is if Miss Mabel came after you again, would you be able to win if you were using a sword and she was using magic?"

At first his straightforward response scared me, but having it out in the open felt better.

"Yes," I said, averting my eyes. "That's what I meant."

"It depends on if she knows how to fight with a sword."

I looked up at him again, an unnatural desperation in my voice that I couldn't control. "But could I use the magic to make my sword fighting better? She's too powerful for me to defeat any other way. A physical fight would be my only chance."

I'd said far too much, with too much emotion. I could see the surprise in the way his face wrinkled and his eyes focused on me. But I couldn't take the words back so I waited, holding my breath.

"Magic can give strength and power to skills that you learn if you can figure out how."

"How do I do it?" I asked, breathless.

He shook his head. "I don't think you can."

"What? Why not?"

"Because there's more to sword fighting than swinging your arm and having good footwork." He tapped his head. "Sword fighting is all about what's up here. Until you're ready to let go of whatever is holding you back, you won't be able to really learn."

His words set fire to my rage, making the hair on the back of my neck stand up. What did he know anyway?

"You think you know me so well?" I hissed. "Nothing is holding me back! I'm learning just fine. I executed each task today just as you ordered me."

"I didn't say your footwork was a problem," he said in a calm, unapologetic tone. "Your footwork is fine."

"Then what is my problem?"

"I can't tell you that. Only you can."

I growled, grabbed the two buckets, and left without another word.

With Leda and Camille occupied by their studies, I took the opportunity to visit Miss Celia—one of the teachers at Miss Mabel's School for Girls and Master of the kitchen—later that day.

Without girls to fill the school, the usual bustle and hum of life had drained away. No stray giggles. No candles in the windows. It made me feel decidedly lonely as I approached the old manor. Even with the bright sun illuminating the green strands of ivy, it looked bleak and forgotten.

I pushed the creaky iron gate open with trepidation. My eyes flickered to the attic and then away again. Magic stirred within, annoyed by the sudden flood of memories. I turned the power away and opened the heavy front door.

A tall, expansive foyer with a silver chandelier greeted me. I ran my eyes over the twirling stairs, the ivy carved into the railing, and the crimson rug that ran along each step. The comforting sound of

Miss Celia humming drifted through the empty corridor, pulling me from the dark reveries the magic threatened to pull me into. Smiling, I closed the door behind me and called out. If I startled Miss Celia she'd clobber me with a rolling pin.

"Miss Celia?"

The humming ceased.

"Who's there?" she called back. I followed her voice down the hall and turned into the kitchen on the left.

"Oh, blessed be!" she cried, her rosy cheeks lighting up. "Bianca, what are you doing here?"

Miss Celia looked the way she always did, with a little pouf of gray and white hair on top of her head and her favorite old apron with flour splotches, covering her torso. Her wrinkled, kind face lit up in a smile. I recognized a familiar rectangle of dough on the counter in front of her. She must be making a batch of her famous cinnamon buns! Good timing indeed.

"Merry meet, Miss Celia," I said, laughing. "Are you busy?"

"Not too busy to talk! Come in, come in and have a seat! I'd love a little chat. Heaven knows it's too quiet here with only me and Scarlett around. How are you?"

I obeyed, taking a seat on a stool near the cupboard where she worked the dough, not realizing how much I had missed her. When she didn't have forty hungry girls to cook for and a gaggle of students coming in and out of the kitchen all the time, she seemed more like a friend than a teacher. We dispatched with the trivialities about my time at Chatham Castle quickly.

"And Camille?" she asked. "How is she enjoying the castle?"

"She's the center of attention with the Guardians," I said. Miss Celia's eyes sparkled.

"Yes, yes I can see that. Sounds like a lovely time. And Leda is holed up in the library doing classes, I hear."

"Yes, and Michelle is the pride of the kitchens."

Miss Celia waved a hand through the air, spreading a slight puff of flour as she went. "Of course," she cried. "Michelle is one of the brightest girls I'd ever met, that's why I recommended her so highly to Fina."

"Miss Celia," I asked, making sure to keep my tone light and sweet. "I came for a specific reason. May I ask you a few questions?"

"Of course! Ask me anything."

Ha! We'll see about that.

"It's in regards to Mabel."

Her countenance dropped a little, suddenly not as bright as it had been.

"Miss Mabel?" she repeated, forcing nonchalance. "She's been quite busy these past few months and I haven't—"

"No," I said, pulling *Mildred's Resistance* from my bag and setting it in front of me with a loud thud. It sounded like the final gong before a death blow. "Her grandmother."

Miss Celia paled beneath her flushed cheeks, her rolling pin poised just above the dough. She stared at the book for a second, and her eyes darted back to mine.

"Why?" she asked in a faint voice.

"I need information."

Miss Celia dropped the rolling pin and turned away, dodging some of the cast iron frying pans and copper pots suspended from the ceiling. She opened a long cupboard and fumbled through several glass jars of spices with a trembling hand.

"I'd prefer not to talk about her, if you don't mind," she said in a clipped tone, dissolving her previous joviality.

"But I do mind," I said, sliding off the stool. "I need to know about her, and you worked with her all the time. You are probably the one person alive that knows her best, except Miss Mabel. Please, Miss Celia?"

She cast me a suspicious look from the corner of her eyes.

"I can't imagine why anyone needs to know about her. She was not a nice witch."

"Because I need to find out more about Miss Mabel," I said. "Learning about the original Mabel may give me some more clues."

"Why do you need to know more about Miss Mabel?"

"I-I just do, Miss Celia. Please help me?"

"I don't know," she said, fidgeting with a small bag labeled *basil leaves*. Her eyes flitted around, avoiding me. She stuffed the bag back inside and shut the cupboard. "I just don't know."

"We both know what Mabel really was," I said in a low tone, although no one could overhear us. "I need your help if we are ever going to make right what she's done."

Miss Celia looked at me. I let her search through my eyes, silently pleading. She finally capitulated.

"Oh, fine!" she muttered with a familiar snap in her voice. "But only for a few minutes while I finish my rolls. Then I have things to do. Heaven knows I hate talking about her. What do you want to know?"

Relieved, my shoulders dropped back.

"Thank you," I said. "Tell me what she was like. Anything you can remember."

Miss Celia let out a huff, making it clear once again that she wasn't happy about it, grabbed a can labeled *cinnamon* and pattered back to her pastry dough. I walked back around the oak table to face her and leaned against the smooth wood, giving her my full attention.

"She went by May. She had hair like a raven, black and shiny, just like yours. Her eyes were sharp." Miss Celia gave a little shudder. "I remember her wearing a lot of black, though she was as vain as a peacock."

Miss Mabel's sultry beauty drifted through my mind. Miss Celia, sprinkling a generous helping of cinnamon and sugar on the dough, continued on.

"She wasn't a warm witch. She was very business-like and demanding. Luckily she didn't care much for simple matters like groceries and kitchen work, so she let me manage it and left me alone to handle the meals. I didn't have to interact with her much, really."

"How did she treat Miss Mabel?"

"The same way she treated everyone else," Miss Celia said, shrugging. "She had high expectations and little compassion. Miss Mabel and May were far too much alike. By the time Miss Mabel could talk, the two of them were in a continual power struggle. Miss Mabel didn't want to listen, and May wouldn't tolerate anything but total obedience."

"That explains a lot," I muttered.

"They constantly fought. Miss Mabel grew to be a very bitter young woman because of how difficult May was to live with. May was always spouting off big ideas and plans, but she rarely followed through with them. I could never decide which of the two of them had more vanity, and which one wanted power more. "

I perked up. Vanity was a given. But their mutual desire for power had me intrigued.

"What do you mean by *power*?" I asked.

"May loved controlling things, and people. Unfortunately, so did Miss Mabel. The two of them were constantly trying to control the other one. Even as a young child, Miss Mabel could be extraordinarily manipulative to get what she wanted. The good gods know I tried teaching that child the right way, but she just didn't care. Once Evelyn appointed May as her personal assistant it was a welcome relief. Miss Mabel took over the school and May left to live at Chatham Castle."

I thought that over while Miss Celia cut the large rectangle into smaller sections. A little residual flour and cinnamon dusted her hands and apron. My gaze drifted over the warm brick walls of the kitchen, past the large hearth and fireplace, to the windows edged in black and the sky beyond.

"Did you ever meet Miss Mabel's mother?" I asked, knowing it would be tenuous ground. Angelina seemed to be an apparition, a ghost. The lack of information about her made me curious.

"Angelina?"

"Yes."

"No. I was here the night Angelina left Miss Mabel on the doorstep. I was the one that heard her crying first. May had already kicked Angelina out by the time I arrived. She was a wild child."

"What do you mean?"

"May had a hard time controlling her. Angelina was quite talented with magic, according to some of the teachers that knew her. Far more powerful than her mother, and May didn't like it."

"Sounds like May didn't like anything," I muttered. Miss Celia agreed with a little hum. Her fingers flew over the dough, deftly accomplishing their goal.

"Miss Mabel told me that her mother looks just like May," she said in a musing tone. "Black hair, a curvy figure, and eyes that could cut right through a witch."

An unusual jolt hit me in the gut, leaving me breathless.

"Miss Mabel knows her mother?"

"She must." Miss Celia shrugged. "Although she never really talks about Angelina. Maybe she saw a painting of her?"

"Is there a painting of Angelina?" I asked, leaning forward. Although I couldn't explain why, something told me that Angelina had something to do with this.

"No. May wouldn't allow it."

"And you never met Angelina?" I confirmed and she nodded. "Do you know who Miss Mabel's father is?"

Miss Celia shook her head. "No, and I doubt she knows either. If she does, she's never mentioned him."

My thoughts churned like the foam of a wild river as I watched Miss Celia roll the pastries into small buns and set them in perfect rows. The buttery little blobs would soon swell, a little like how my brain felt with all this new information.

"Were you surprised when Mildred executed May?"

"No," Miss Celia said with a guilty little sigh. "A bit relieved, perhaps. Like I said, May was not a good witch. Miss Mabel was downright giddy the day May died. She twirled around the school singing for the whole day."

"Have you been happy working with Miss Mabel?"

"Yes," she said with a sad little smile. "I couldn't have children of my own, so it was like I got a chance to be something of a mother. I raised that girl since she was a wee baby and I'll love her till I die. Anyway, she's good to me. The wages she gives me for working here are enough to meet my needs. She trusts me more than May ever did, anyway, and lets me do my work."

I had my doubts that Miss Mabel could trust anyone, but didn't say it to Miss Celia. A maternal warmth had crept into Miss Celia's tone, despite the apparent fear, as well as love, that she felt for Miss Mabel. I wondered how it must feel, to have both terror and compassion in your heart for the same person, knowing you raised her to be something that she never would be. Whether or not Miss Celia saw

Miss Mabel for who she really was, I couldn't decide. Perhaps she didn't want to see.

My headache began to throb. All this thinking of Miss Mabel made the magic burn in my chest. The sound of footsteps came down the hallway, accompanied by the familiar chime of Miss Scarlett's bracelets.

"Well," Miss Celia said with a sudden, forced brightness in her tone that told me she'd say no more, "I've got some cinnamon buns just about ready to take from the oven. Why don't you take one back with you?"

"Yes," I said, grateful to be done with the conversation. "I'd love that."

Miss Scarlett entered the kitchen with all the warmth of a grizzly bear.

"I thought I recognized your voice," she said, straight-backed and rigid as usual. Her hair lay in a braid today instead of its usual bun, which made me wonder if even Miss Scarlett let loose just a little when the students were gone.

"I had a pining for a cinnamon bun, Miss Scarlett," I said with a smile. "I dropped in on the hopes that she'd have some."

Miss Celia beamed, all vestiges of darkness from our conversation erased.

Farther Than Yesterday

I found Michelle at the Witchery table by herself, writing a letter to her family, when I returned from visiting Miss Mabel's. She smiled in greeting.

"Merry meet, Bianca."

"Where is everyone?" I asked.

"Camille is eating lunch with the Guardians in the dining room. I saw her when my shift ended. She had a bunch of books around her, but I don't think she was getting much studying done."

The cinnamon roll sat heavy in my stomach. I pressed a hand to it with a happy sigh. The sweetness of the thick layer of frosting Miss Celia had smeared on top lingered in my mouth with the warm flavor of fresh vanilla bean and sugar.

"Leda's probably in the library," I said. The information Miss Celia had given me on May and Miss Mabel wouldn't help me destroy the binding, which meant I still had one more thing to research. "I need to run to there myself. Would you like to come?"

"Sure," Michelle said, quickly folding the messenger paper. When she finished it popped up off the table and zipped out the open window, headed off to her family in the southern covens.

Michelle spoke quietly about her day as we went down, providing a low chatter to my whirling thoughts. She mentioned Nicolas telling her about recent dragon conspiracies while helping her with a heavy bag of flour, and then talked about a new apricot turnover recipe Fina wanted her to try when the apricots were ready. I nodded every now and then, only distantly aware of what she said. My mind spun back to my conversation with Miss Celia and then to the West. Was Miss Mabel's mother Angelina still alive? Should I go to the West and destroy the binding tomorrow?

"Are you sure Leda will be in the library?" Michelle asked.

"No," I admitted as we stepped through the stained glass doors and into the expansive library foyer. "Leda's an enigma most days."

"She's been gone a lot lately," Michelle said, her thick forehead furrowed into lines. "I can never find her, especially in the afternoons. It's odd."

"Yes," I said with a little sigh, having noticed her absences myself. "But everything about Leda is odd, isn't it?"

Michelle agreed with a shy smile.

We walked through the foyer and into the main library. Books lined the three-story walls at every crack and seam, crawling to a stop at the ceiling, which formed a dome painted with murals of Letum Wood. Even in Chatham Castle I couldn't escape the vines and leaves of the forest. The quiet hush of the librarians and the bustle of witches walking by filled my ears. Ladders moved along rolling tracks by the bookshelves, following the librarians as they walked from spot to spot.

I spotted Leda the moment I walked in. Books, scrolls, jars of ink, and molted feather pens filled a table built for ten in the middle of the library. Leda sat in the middle of the organized array, her lips moving wordlessly as she read from one book in her lap, then turned to look at another sitting on the table next to her.

"Can you see her in between all the books over there?" I asked Michelle, pointing her direction. A daunting tower of books blocked Leda's head the closer we walked.

"It's hard to tell."

"Look for hair," I said. "You can't miss anything so white."

Leda's head popped up, armed with her usual thin glare.

"I heard that."

"Oh good," I said. "You're alive. I thought the scrolls drowned you."

"Are you here to study with me?" she asked with an arch look. "If not, leave. I have no time for you."

"Right," I scoffed, running my eyes over the towers of books and scrolls. "I came to study because I just love it. What are you working on today?" My eyes caught on the gold lettering of a tome nearby. *The Political History of Antebellum Before the Reformation.*

"I'm finishing up my political history class. Miss Scarlett is going to test me tomorrow. She had to go back to the school to get a copy of the exam."

I know. I just saw her, I almost said, but stopped just in time and reached for the book instead.

"Stop touching things, Bianca."

Despite her protests, I pulled *Policies and Procedures of the Central Network* from the top of a pile. It landed on the table with a heavy thud.

"Be careful!" she muttered, shooting me another glare. "That's borrowed."

"Grief, Leda. You're only seventeen. Did anyone tell you that? We're supposed to be off getting in trouble, not reading about policies and procedures."

She sniffed with an air of haughty importance.

"You do that enough for all of us."

Ignoring her jab, I ran my fingers over the old cover and peeked inside. Several styles of handwriting filled the pages, testament to the many years, and many Councils, the book had been through.

"Where did you get this?"

"That doesn't matter," she snapped, trying to snatch it back. I turned and blocked her with my shoulder, perusing the writing. "Just give it back! You can't ruin anything or I'll be in trouble!"

You could use a little trouble, I thought.

A movement in the corner of my eye caught my attention, and I looked up to see Camille walking next to Brecken. Without his Guardian armor on, he was hardly recognizable, but his dark curls were unmistakable. Something he said made Camille smile with a warm flush and jabber in excitement.

"What's this?" I asked quietly, setting the book aside. Leda snatched it, then followed my gaze, the color returning to her face.

"Camille is in the library?" she gasped, her mouth going slack.

"She's in the library with Brecken," Michelle corrected quietly, as if we were observing a deer. "Doesn't she hate him?"

"She adores him, but I thought he didn't like her."

"Doesn't look like it," Michelle said. "Not with that smile on his face."

"Let's find out. Merry meet, Camille!" I called, waving to her. A nearby librarian hushed me with a quiet hiss. Camille jerked to attention and froze mid-step in the library walkway.

"Oh, merry meet," Camille stammered, her cheeks and ears blooming a bright red. "W-what are you doing here?"

I cast an eye at the algebra book tucked under one arm and then up to Brecken, who smiled and nodded, as if strolling around the library was a common thing for him.

"You didn't show up for your algebra class with Miss Scarlett today," Leda said with impressive haughtiness, as if Camille's slack approach to education offended her on a personal level.

"I-I was busy," Camille said, tugging on her skirt.

"The date for the test hasn't changed. You'll still have to pass even if you don't show up for classes."

"I know," she said simply, readjusting the scrolls in her arm to hide the book beneath them. "I-I'll be ready."

Brecken took a step back with an awkward wave.

"Well, I'd better be going. Merry part, ladies. Camille, I'll see you later."

She stared after him in surprise, managing a weak "Merry part" to his back. She remained that way until he disappeared from the library. When she looked back at us she struggled to put an innocent smile on her face.

"Want to go see if Fina will let us have some of her fizzy water?" she asked with a hopeful tilt of her voice.

"All right, what's going on?" Michelle asked, looking to where Brecken had gone and back at Camille. Camille opened her mouth and hesitated. Her shoulders slumped.

"Oh, fine," she sighed. "I can't keep it from you any longer. Brecken is tutoring me in algebra."

Leda's eyes widened. "Really?" she asked.

Camille nodded. "Yes. He stumbled on me during a . . . well, let's just say I was having a bad day and couldn't figure out an equation. He prevented me from throwing the book against the wall and taught me how to do the problem. Then I asked him to tutor me."

Her cheeks bloomed bright pink yet again. I grinned.

"It's all part of your plan to win his heart, isn't it, Camille?" I asked in a droll tone. She ran a hand over her curls and straightened her dress.

"I'm sure I don't know what you're talking about," she said with a purse of her lips. "Anyway, all this studying has me parched. Fizzy water or no?"

"Sure," Michelle said. "I'll go."

"I need to work on my homework, and write a paper," Leda said, giving Camille a perplexed look, as if she still couldn't figure this situation out, and motioning to the five open books and three scrolls on the table around her. "It's due tomorrow. I'll be working on it all night." Leda turned her back on us as if we didn't exist anymore.

"Can I meet you there?" I asked, remembering the purpose behind my visit to the library. "I need to look something up."

"Sure." Camille shrugged. "We'll see you there, Bianca,"

I started for the back corner, motivated by the promise of the sweet drink. A collection of maps covering the walls of a quiet little nook soon caught my eye. Most of them had decayed, written with ink on old pieces of leather, showing the boundaries of Antebellum before the Networks formed. I reached out to run my finger along the side of one particular map and heard a deliberate *harrumph*. One of the pesky librarians stood behind me, her arms folded across her chest.

"Sorry," I whispered, eyeing the *Absolutely No Touching* sign above the map and smiling sheepishly.

Several long skinny drawers lay below the wall maps. I grabbed the tarnished brass knob on the one marked *Western Network* and tugged on it. The librarian, seeing that I gave no further signs of subterfuge or destruction, moved on.

Alone now, I pulled all the maps from the drawer and spread them on the only table in this lonely part of the library. Their burned edges left a smudge of black on my hands, and the rest had aged into a golden yellow. They all showed the vast desert sands of the West. Only four cities really thrived there, aside from the capital Custos. It sat in the middle, a heart for the emptiest Network in Antebellum. There was no map of Custos as a city. Due to the violent changes in weather, Custos evolved constantly, making it almost impossible to peg down. The only stable thing there was the Arck, and even it was built into the red rock mountain.

"There you are," I whispered as I came across an old, hastily drawn map of the Arck. The lines of the map were so faint I could barely make them out, but I saw what I thought would be Miss Mabel's chambers. I shuffled to the next scroll and found a few rooms on the floor above Miss Mabel's. There was no label indicating what they were, but their small size made me think they were the maids' quarters.

Whenever I decided to go, I would try to transport somewhere near Miss Mabel's room, but not in it. That much precision would be tricky, as I'd never been to any other part of the Arck before, not to mention the question of my unrefined transportation skills. The risk that I could land at any random point in the Arck and be discovered by a West Guard made me shudder.

Don't even think about failing, I told myself with a bolstering exhale. *Just do what you have to do.*

I pushed the drawer closed, wincing when it shut with a loud *crack*. Leaving before the librarian could scold me, I walked out into the main aisle and passed Leda's table. An empty chair remained, her scrolls neatly stacked and her books organized into several clean, even piles the same height. I stared at the vacant seat, puzzled. Didn't she have a paper to write?

With a shake of my head, I brushed it off. I'd have a private chat with her later. I left the library with the slow simmer of my powers burning inside, always ready, always waiting.

"Come on!" Merrick called over the sound of my gasping breath. "You're faster than this!"

My legs flew down the dark trail, whizzing past gargantuan tree trunks and blankets of lush moss, but it still wasn't fast enough.

Merrick stayed close on my heels, barely out of breath. He knew he was already pushing me beyond my physical limits. What he didn't know about was the bubbling volcano of magic raging in my chest, threatening to explode.

Don't think about Mama. Don't think about Mama, I chanted in my head. The memories pressed on me as they always did, but I wouldn't give them the space they desired.

"Keep it up," he called. "We're going farther than yesterday. We have to hit the hill and make it to the top."

Farther than yesterday, I thought, switching mantras. *Farther than yesterday.* Yesterday we ran this same route, but a vision of Mama twirling me in the air on my fifth birthday stopped me at the bottom of a hill. No matter how hard I had tried, I couldn't get past her. She stayed in the air ahead of me, giggling with an apparition of me as a young child. So I'd given up again. I'd turned around and left without an explanation, frustrated, out of breath, and lightheaded. Merrick said nothing about it or my fit from several days before. I sensed he was trying to give me space to work it out, but I wasn't sure I was even trying.

Farther than yesterday.

Yes. I can do it. I can be stronger than the magic. If I ignore the pain long enough, it'll go away.

The hill Merrick spoke of appeared in a break of the trees, looming like an ugly monster. I expected to see the glimpses of white, to hear the giggle on the breeze, but nothing met me but silent, quiet air. It was as if the trees themselves waited. High above, in the top of the canopy, a few black streaks painted the tree trunks in thick stripes. The leaves had withered, leaving broken bald spots.

Dragons, I thought, then leapt a large boulder, tucking my feet beneath me. The nimble movements had become second nature again, although they brought me little joy. I spent too much time fighting the memories to appreciate the inertia of moving across the ground.

The tug on my muscles told me that we'd started up the hill, and I put all my concentration into moving higher. I thought of the ax, how I'd used the magic to give me strength. I tried to turn the powers into my legs, channeling it to make me run faster. Instead of obeying my command, the magic flared, sending a barrage of memories through my mind. *Dancing in the kitchen. A flour fight. Mama humming in the rocking chair.*

"No!" I yelled, startled by the intensity of the pain that ripped through me. I grabbed my head, hoping to erase the image of Mama in my mind. "No!"

The magic grew so hot, so fast that I lost almost all control. The edges of my vision went blurry. My heart drummed on the back of my ribs.

"Bianca!" Merrick yelled. "Stop!"

Startled, I skidded across the ground to find a massive claw blocking the trail ahead. The movement of a heavy tail swept my legs from underneath me. I fell to my backside and scrambled back.

"Whoa!"

A forest dragon stared at me with a lowered head and narrowed, darting eyes. Hot, steamy breaths blasted through the already sultry air. I barely registered Merrick stepping in front of me, his eyes averted to the trail.

"Don't look at it!" he commanded. "Transport back to Chatham Castle right now."

But I was looking at the dragon, and it worked no spell over me. The creature shook his black, angular head, the wide chasms of his nostrils widening and closing. He had a familiar tint of blue running through his body.

"Merrick, this is the same one from before," I murmured.

The dragon looked from Merrick to me, the heat emanating off his body in long waves. His eyes had constricted, making his long face look suspicious and uneasy. He shifted, stamping his feet.

"Just go. You can't know that," Merrick said, his eyes flickering up toward the dragon and then away again. He was right. I couldn't know that.

"Are they all violent?" I asked. "Because, if it is the same dragon, he hasn't hurt me yet."

Despite the danger I was flirting with by looking a forest dragon in the eye, I still admired the sleek, beautiful creature that lived in the deep shadows. As if he understood what I said, the dragon snarled and snapped his jaw, glaring at me in undisguised malice.

"Guess they are," I whispered, pushing back a little farther.

The dragon tramped about the brush, his footfalls shaking the ground. Merrick fell to his knees; I had to grab onto a tree branch to stay upright. The forest dragon tilted his long head back and shot a blast of fire into the air, setting flame to the verdant canopy above.

"Go!" Merrick yelled. "Transport back to the Forgotten Gardens."

Frightened into action, I obeyed, landing flat on my back with a heavy thud. Merrick appeared a few seconds after me, landing in an easy crouch. My hands trembled at my sides and my stomach felt queasy. I sat on the crumbling edge of the fountain wall and drew in a deep breath. This encounter with the forest dragon hadn't been as sedate as the first. Perhaps they were creatures I should invest a healthy amount of fear toward.

Merrick pushed his sandy blonde hair out of his troubled eyes. He stared at the ground, setting his hands on his thighs. His jaw was tight again, angled with tension and worry.

"What is it?" I asked, wiping off the moisture on my forehead with the back of my hand. Merrick looked back to the forest, then to me. He shook his head.

"It doesn't make sense," he said. "Why are they here? They must be coming out for a reason. Forest dragons don't just start interacting with witches, especially after centuries. They hate witches."

The edge in his tone sent a little shiver down my spine.

"I didn't even know they were real until a few weeks ago," I said quietly.

His face dropped into a frown.

"I'll talk to Sanna about it out later," he said, returning to his usual intense focus. "Come on, let's pair some footwork drills combined with attacks and blocks. Grab the two rock buckets and follow me."

The Monster

The next day came and went without incident. Merrick and I didn't speak about the dragon, and I was glad. Too much lay heavy on my mind already.

After a grueling morning workout carrying heavy stones to the top of the second-tallest turret, reviewing the same footwork a mind-numbing number of times, and using my wooden sword to spar with Merrick, I joined Camille and Michelle on their weekly trip into Chatham City.

Camille had dressed up in a pale pink dress with ivory lace and a small string of fake pearls, her hair pulled into a sweet, fluffy ponytail that rested on her left shoulder in long ringlets. I probably looked bland in my long-sleeved green dress. I'd been hoping to hide the ugly bruises from my lack of sword skills. My hair fluttered around my shoulders as usual.

"I just love going shopping in Chatham City," Camille said with a happy smile as we walked along the straight-as-an-arrow road that led from the castle to the gates of the town. "I'm almost out of caramels, so we'll stop at Miss Holly's Candy Shop first. Then we'll go get a few ribbons for my ball gown at the dressmakers."

Camille's prattle faded away and I let it, peering into the darkness of Letum Wood on either side of us. Was the dragon watching from deep within the forest? A few witches on horseback passed us with a nod. Two young boys, obviously Guardian hopefuls by the way they loitered around the gate, stared with open mouths as Camille sashayed by with near-poetic grace. If she noticed them, she gave no sign.

Chatham City was an old, soot-stained world with steep gables and cobblestone streets. Torches stood at intervals along the roads, which teemed with people and stray dogs. Despite the questionable puddles, stench of burned coffee, and occasional piles of refuse, Chatham City had an endearing personality. Whether it was the constant hum of life, the tall brick houses with flower pots and white shutters, or the scrollboys on every corner trying to sell the latest *Chatham Chatterer*, I couldn't tell.

"Did Leda pass her Political History test?" Michelle asked as we passed under the soaring arch and into Chatham City. A few Guardians waved to us. When one winked at Camille, she shot him a haughty look, but a pleased little smile danced on her lips once he was far behind us.

"I think so," I said. "She started her next class already."

Leda had politely informed me that morning that she'd prefer putting a fork in her eye to visiting Chatham City, so we left her behind, dutifully working away in the library.

We picked our way carefully through the streets, avoiding the horses that clopped by within inches of us. The air smelled of pastries and burning wood. A walking merchant tried to shove a pile of scarves into my face, pleading with me to buy, but I ducked away. Camille ignored the low whistle of a few homeless grubs.

"Oh," she said, coming to a stop near a blacksmith shop. "What's going on here?"

A sea of people loomed in front of us, crowding around one man standing on a platform at the street corner. The queue took up the entire road, blocking the horses and carriages that wanted by. A couple of frustrated drivers hollered, but no one paid them any heed.

"Our Protectors will soon be dying under his command if we don't do something about it!" shouted the man on the platform, his face reddening from the effort. I recognized him in an instant.

"Clive," I muttered with a grim purse of my lips. The angry little dragon in my heart roared to life, instantly on guard. A thick Chatham City accent started to burn through Clive's words, although I didn't recall hearing it when he spoke to Jansson in the library. "It's one of his rallies to get signatures against Papa."

"The High Priestess doesn't want us ta know, but the fighting has already begun! The Guardians are in the Borderlands as I stand in front of ya, facing the West Guards."

A low murmur of disbelief rippled through the crowd. My stomach churned.

"He's lying," I whispered to Camille. "The fighting hasn't begun yet."

Camille looked at me with a worried expression. "Are the West Guards in the Borderlands?"

"No . . . and yes," I said, thinking back to my conversation with Papa. For good measure, I tacked on, "They aren't in the Borderlands, they're just along it on the other side of the border."

"No one's going to care whether they are fighting or not," Michelle said, glancing around. "The fact that they are so close is bad enough. Let's get out of here. I have a bad feeling."

"Wait," I said, pulling away from Camille. The restless crowd surged around us, nearly knocking me down. "I want to hear what he says."

"Tiberius!" A voice shouted from the crowd. "Tiberius leads the Guardians! He's never lied ta us!"

A chorus of applause and cheers followed the response.

"Yes," Clive agreed with a charming smile. "Tiberius has been good ta us. Is it too much ta ask that we trust our Head of Protectors just as much as we trust the Head of Guardians?"

"No!" the crowd roared.

"Bianca," Camille said more firmly, grabbing my arm. "Let's leave. I don't think we should stay. What if someone recognizes you?"

"What about Derek?" Clive demanded when the shouts died. A chorus of hissing sounds filled the air. Their collective menacing took on a new personality, filling the air with something vile and horrible. Two men near me snarled.

"Liar!" they shouted. "He lied ta us! He broke our tradition!"

"We can never get that back can we?" Clive bellowed, whirling around to face all sides of the audience. "He broke the tradition set by Esmelda. He's not to be trusted!"

"Wait," I said, breathless, knowing I should listen to Camille but unable to leave. "They're talking about my father."

"I know," Camille said, distressed. "That's why we need to go."

Michelle locked eyes with me.

"She's right, Bianca. It's not safe."

"The West is coming!" Clive yelled. "They are almost here, knocking on our borders. We need protection! We need a Head of Protectors that will take his job seriously. I'm just like the rest of ya! I've got a family ta take care of."

Another round of furious grunts echoed through the crowd. Every shout and mistruth they called out expanded the roiling anger inside me. The magic grew more and more unstable. Above the crowd bobbed a thick scroll and quill, moving from hand to hand to gather signatures.

"And now he's keeping his daughter at the castle!" Clive cried from the box. "He's insulting us as a people! He breaks the rules, and then shoves it down our throats!"

"The High Priestess is letting him!" someone shouted.

"Exile them!" a woman only a few paces away called. "Send Derek and his daughter ta the North."

Cackling pockets of hostility erupted behind me.

"Bianca, come on," Camille insisted, true fear in her eyes now. "Come on!"

"Yes," I said, swallowing. "Let's go."

Relieved, Camille and Michelle turned to go. Someone stumbled into me from behind, drunk with brewed ipsum, and sent me flying into the crowd. My friends faded into the teeming mass of brown and black cloaks. Witches shoved me back and forth, yelling and laughing at the sport, until someone had pity and set me on my feet.

"There ya go," he said, the smell of ipsum rolling off him. "What's a pretty young witch like you doin—"

He stopped when I looked up at him, blinking in surprise. His eyes narrowed, then grew wide.

"The good gods," he muttered under his breath and tightened his grip on my arm. "You're Derek's daughter."

"Let me go," I said, frantic. "Let me go!"

"Well," he breathed with a lurid grin, his bloodshot eyes looking me over. "Let's have a bit of fun. Look who I have here!" he cried, waving his arm. "Look what good ol' Joe has found!"

"Let me go!"

"No, I don't think I will," he said. "She's here! Coven Leader Clive!"

Desperate, I slapped him across the face with a crack that echoed through the air. He stood there for a second, stunned, while I jerked my arm from his grasp. His bloodshot eyes bulged.

"Cheeky little girl," he muttered, grabbing the back of my neck so tight it hurt.

"Let me go!"

"I'm not overly fond of bratty vixens like ya. Makes ol' Joe kinda angry."

Angry? I thought. *You'll never be as angry as me.*

"Leave me alone!" I gasped again, the force of my powers overwhelming me. My fingertips tingled. "You'll regret it if you don't."

"What, is your Papa going ta hurt me? She's here!" he yelled, hollering like a pig. "Bianca Monroe!"

The witches nearest us whirled around, at first annoyed at the commotion. But as soon as they saw me their eyes popped open and they joined the battle cry. Another pair of arms grabbed me. I stomped my heel into the toes of my new assailant. He yelped, but didn't let go.

"Bianca is here!"

"Derek's daughter!"

Clive stopped speaking and gazed toward us, seeking out the source of the unrest. The drunk man grabbed my arm and shoved me into the crowd. Someone else grabbed my arm. They pushed me deeper into the queue, toward Clive, who sneered from high on his perch. The crowd began a low chant as the warm slime of someone's spit slid down my right cheek. I wouldn't be able to fight the magic much longer. It would take over, creating something dangerous, perhaps harming everyone around me. Maybe even myself.

"Get the girl! Get the girl!"

"Take her over there!"

"Let's hear from her, eh?" a witch reeking of ipsum shouted, stumbling over his own feet. "Maybe she can tell us secrets about her scoundrel father. She looks like a real tart, doesn't she? Just like her pretty mama must have been!"

His words echoed in the red, bitter chambers of my heart. Time slowed. I calmed. The dragon in my chest bellowed with heat and fire and pain.

Just like her pretty mama must have been.

I lost the battle and the magic ran free.

In that moment everything went oddly quiet. The screams of the apoplectic crowd became a dull roar in my ears. In between all the capes, waving arms, and jeering faces I made out a snippet of bright blue sky. *This is it. The magic won.*

I processed what happened next in snatches of time, completely unable to control the outcome.

A stranger reached for my neck. I threw out with a hand to stop him and something flashed. *Darkness.* His body lay on the ground. *Darkness.* A sea of astonished faces stared at me, gaping and terrified. *Darkness.* Several pairs of hands trying to pull me to the ground. My legs kicked. *Darkness.* A white explosion. *Darkness.* Witches on the ground around me. Pulsing pain in my head. Blood on my hands. *Darkness.*

Then Merrick's calm, steady face appeared. He grabbed my arm and pulled me from the ground. A shock ran through my body, breaking the trance.

"Come on," he said in a low voice. "I'm here to take you back."

He helped me stand up, untangling me from the ten or more witches lying on the ground around me. Screams filled the streets. Eyes, hundreds of eyes, looked at me.

"Follow me," Merrick said, grabbing my arm. He kept his intense green eyes on the crowd. I could feel how tense his muscles had become, waiting for someone to spring out at us. Several witches stepped out of his way. No one tried to stop us as we wound through back alleys, headed for Letum Wood.

The next thing I registered was trees. A green canopy. Moss. We ran through Letum Wood, the trees flashing by us, chests heaving. My legs moved so fast my heart couldn't keep up as we darted through the forest, outrunning a monster.

Faster. Faster.
I stumbled, already knowing the monster was me.
Darkness.

Silence

"**S**he's waking up, Mildred."

The voice swam through my head. It took me two tries to grasp what it meant. Mildred? Once I started slowly surfacing, like coming up from deep water, the words started to make sense.

"She better do it soon!" the High Priestess snapped. "Or I'll give her a reason to wake up. Foolish girl."

My eyes fluttered open. I lay on an uncomfortable divan in a room I didn't recognize. The white walls were trimmed at the top with golden leaves. Papa's silhouette stood near a floor-length window, his hands folded behind his back.

"Bianca?"

The High Priestess's sharp voice hit me like a slap. A mighty headache split my brain, walloping the sides of my head like a giant with a club. I groaned.

"Derek, I think she's waking up," Stella's quiet voice said from right next to me.

"Are you ready to grace us with your presence yet?" the High Priestess asked in a haughty tone. "I'm done waiting. We have a mess to clean up. I don't have time for this."

I closed my eyes against the daylight and shrunk into the divan, wanting to disappear. My memory returned in an instant. *Crowd. Merrick. Darkness. Bad.*

"No," I said.

"Too bad," she snapped. "Get up."

"I have something here for you, Bianca," Stella murmured. She rubbed it on my temples, filling my nose with the cool smell of peppermint. "Sit up slowly," she instructed.

The High Priestess paced back and forth, her maroon dress rustling as she prowled like a caged animal. Stella put a hand on my shoulder and helped me sit up. The world swam. I closed my eyes and leaned into my hands.

"Are you okay, Bianca?" Papa asked. He crouched in front of me now, a mixture of concern and hesitation on his face.

"Yes, Papa."

"Nice little display," the High Priestess said. "Whether or not you realize the scope of the campaign Clive has been launching against your father, I'm here to tell you that you've just made it much, much worse. Your show in Chatham City today earned Clive all the signatures he needs to bring it before the Council. 10,000 in one day! It's absolutely unheard of."

"What did I do?" I asked, a knot forming in my throat.

"You defended yourself as you should have," Papa said, casting a warning glance at the High Priestess. "But in doing so you injured ten witches. No one died, but they won't recover quickly. It's what they deserve for dragging you into the crowd that way."

His voice was hard, without remorse or compassion. Perhaps I had done what I should have to protect myself, but the number of injured witches seemed enormous. Had my powers grown so much? I forced the thoughts to slow.

"Besides," Papa said, putting a heavy hand on my shoulder and straightening. "Most of them were drunk, and over half that crowd was part of the Factios."

"Factios?" I asked with a grimace. He squeezed my shoulder.

"I'll explain later."

"Mildred," Stella said in a low tone. "Take a deep breath. I'm sure Bianca has an explanation."

The High Priestess shot her an acid glare but did as she asked. When she spoke again her voice had calmed.

"Merrick, Brecken, Camille, and Michelle have already told me what they saw and heard. I want to hear your version of it before we go down to my office. Begin."

With a stiff voice I recounted the events, starting from the moment we heard the rally, including everything that was said, and how the power had taken over. I ended with the last few snatches that I remembered, including running through Letum Wood with Merrick. Stella rubbed a hand over my back, whispering a blessing under her breath. The headache began to retreat, eventually fading into a nag that disappeared completely.

"Thank you," I whispered, sending my gaze her way for just a second. She squeezed my shoulder with a warm smile.

"Is that all?" the High Priestess asked.

"Yes, Your Highness."

"Clive is waiting for us in my office to discuss the matter." She set her hawk-like eyes on me. "You will not say a single word. Not. One. Word. Do you understand? It's going to take some careful negotiations on my part to get you out of this with all your limbs. Chatham City is foaming at the mouth."

"Yes, Your Highness," I whispered again.

"Follow me."

I stood up, Stella and Papa next to me. He hugged me to his side, and I leaned into him. The High Priestess turned around and held her finger to my face.

"I don't trust your powers or your mouth, Bianca. For obvious reasons. I'm putting you under a silencing incantation."

A fading tingle wrapped around my throat. When I tried to speak, nothing came out. I nodded, mute. Satisfied, she circled back around and started to walk, muttering under her breath.

Clive, that disgusting pile of a witch, waited inside the High Priestess's office with a thoughtful look on his face. The High Priestess came to an abrupt halt a few steps in.

"What are you doing in my office?" she demanded.

"Waiting, Your Highness," he said with a dip of his head.

"I did not invite you in. Get out."

Stunned, he hesitated, looking at Stella, who had the same annoyed expression on her face, then slowly walked past us into the hall. Once there, he turned around, hovered for a second, and tapped on the open wooden door.

"Um, may I . . . may I come in?"

"When I'm ready," the High Priestess replied.

Stella, a hint of a smile on her face, nudged me to stand with her behind the High Priestess's desk. I didn't fail to notice the strategy. In reasserting her authority by ordering Clive out, the High Priestess had shifted the power balance in the room back in her favor.

My stomach gave an uneasy lurch. My life would almost certainly end in a few months. Clive couldn't do much to hurt me. But I feared what this meant for Papa. My heart lodged in my throat and stayed there.

The High Priestess pushed around a pile of scrolls, divided a mess of letters into two piles, and murmured under her breath. In short, she didn't really do anything. When Clive edged toward the doorway the High Priestess shot him a sharp look. He moved back, lingering in the shadows again. Marten moved into the room without invitation and walked up to her desk.

"Your Highness," he said. "Forgive my intrusion but I have some paperwork for you that cannot wait. Here are the letters and . . . a few other items of interest."

Marten set the papers on the desk in front of her. The High Priestess glanced at them, then jerked her eyes up to his in surprise. Her eyebrows lowered into a question and he nodded once, grim.

"Yes," she said, taking the top paper into her hand, her expression troubled. The paper disappeared. "Thank you, Marten."

He left the room without another word or backward glance. I wondered where he went. Marten seemed to slip in and out of life here without making a single ripple. It seemed awfully covert for an Ambassador, and I wondered what he really did.

"Move it," a deep voice commanded Clive, and before he could obey, Tiberius lifted him out of the way. He strode over, stood on my left side, crossed his arms over his chest, and glowered at the office door. Papa stood a few paces away, near the window, deep in thought. Clive, looking a little paler than before, swallowed but stood his ground.

"We are waiting for Jansson," the High Priestess announced, looking at everyone but Clive and myself. "Then we may begin."

Jansson stepped up to the doorway only a few moments later. He stood there, awaiting permission to enter.

"Yes, please come in, Jansson, Clive."

The two of them moved into the room and stood across her desk from us. I met Clive's gaze and kept it, striving to keep my face as eerie and impassioned as Papa's. He looked away first.

"Well?" the High Priestess demanded, lifting her thin gray eyebrows and glaring at Clive. "We're here at your insistence."

Clive stepped forward.

"I have respectfully submitted the signatures needed to go before the Council in an appeal regarding the matter of removing our current Head of Protectors."

"That has nothing to do with you being here," the High Priestess snapped. "You're here for Bianca, not Der—"

"I beg to differ," he interrupted. "I believe the two problems are linked."

Stella gasped. My stomach turned to jelly. Had he just interrupted the High Priestess?

Jansson shot Clive a look of warning. Tension tripled in the room as Clive, realizing his mistake, stopped talking and deferred his gaze to the floor.

"I suggest you get to the point," the High Priestess said in a cold tone. "Before I kick you out of my office."

"Indeed, yes. Thank you. Your patience is exemplary. I'd like to address the grievance against Miss Monroe regarding the violence in downtown Chatham City just a few hours ago. I apologize for the delay. I would have liked to address it immediately, but—"

"List your grievances," the High Priestess said.

Pompous donkey, I thought, noticing Clive's Chatham accent was all but gone now. I looked at the clock, confirming the time. It was well into the evening, which meant I must have blacked out for several hours. I wondered if Merrick had to carry me back all that way.

"The first grievance," Clive began, happy to oblige, "is inciting violence in a public place. Two, responding violently without sufficient cause, and three, denying the citizens the right to express their opinion."

I pressed my lips together in livid disbelief. *Without sufficient cause? Inciting violence?*

"Denying the right of expression?" the High Priestess questioned. "Please, do explain how Bianca's self-defense in an openly violent crowd suppressed anyone else?"

Clive's eyebrows lifted halfway up his forehead.

"Yes, Your Highness," he said in a low voice. "The witches at the rally felt that they couldn't be honest about their opinions of Derek with her in attendance. Obviously they were right, as we see from the many injuries inflicted."

"Yes, yes," she muttered impatiently. "What eyewitnesses do you have to support your claim?"

"I have twenty, Your Highness."

He stepped forward with a small scroll. She pulled it open to skim it, rolled her eyes, and set it down. I wondered how many of those witnesses had been under the influence of ipsum. All of them, perhaps? Papa's mouth twitched and he shifted his weight. I could tell he wanted to say something, but held back.

"What is your desired outcome for the grievance?"

"Ultimately, Your Highness, all I ever want is the safety of my people in Chatham City."

"Don't try to impress me."

"Send her away," Clive said, his voice sharpening, now both demanding and tight. "At least until such time as she can prove herself in control of her emotions."

Clive met my eyes again, and this time, he did not cower. My fists tightened. *So that's your game,* I thought. He hoped that by sending me away Papa would go with me; that he'd break under the pressure and give up his job.

Sneaky, underhanded snake.

The High Priestess turned to Jansson without a ruffle in her composure. "As Clive's supervisor, do you agree with his grievance and expectations?"

My heart stalled in my chest while Jansson thought over his reply.

"Clive is free to make any grievance he wishes," he said slowly, "but I feel that there is enough evidence that she acted in self-defense to say the punishment may be too steep. I recommend that Bianca be restricted to the castle grounds and asked to do work hours with Mrs. L."

My heart both lifted and fell at the same time. Work hours with Mrs. L? I'd prefer exile.

"Your Highness, the real question here is whether Bianca is receiving the attention she needs in order to deal with her grief," Clive interjected. "With her mother gone, it's only natural that her father should step up and fill the empty spot in her young life. Quite frankly, I doubt that's happening and this uncontrolled temper is the result. Perhaps we should look at giving Derek more of an opportunity to take care of his daughter."

Both Tiberius and I started forward, but Stella yanked me back before my foot touched the floor. Tiberius snarled low in his throat. Clive didn't move, but looked for all the world like a small animal trapped in a cave of lions.

"Your opinion was unsolicited and therefore not received," the High Priestess said with a withering gaze.

"Does that have anything to do with the fact that Bianca is a favorite of yours and has received your official pardon before?" Clive asked.

"Silence, you fool!" Jansson hissed under his breath.

Papa stepped forward, his face hardening into furious lines. My powers surged, gaining more strength than should have been possible. Stella reached over and put a hand on my arm. A cool feeling flooded my body, settling me.

"Be still," she whispered and the magic obeyed.

"This is the third time you've spoken out of turn during one meeting, Clive. Should you feel the need to speak one more time in my presence without invitation, you will be placed under impudence and banned from your position as Coven Leader for the rest of your life," the High Priestess said in a calm, dangerous tone. "I am, quite frankly, insulted at your insinuation."

"I didn't mean it in that way, Your Highness," Clive stammered, shuffling back a step under the terrible power of her beady eyes. "I would never wish to insult you."

"I'm not convinced. You are banned from Chatham Castle for one month and will not be allowed to attend meetings or events. Should we have this problem again, I will exile you without hesitation. We'll see what you think of your own opinions then."

Clive's face fell. He opened his mouth to respond, but Jansson put a hand on his shoulder.

"In addition," the High Priestess continued in a cold tone, "I recognize four names from this petition as wanted witches from the Factios. I expect your full cooperation in finding these criminals. Bianca is hereby restricted to the grounds at Chatham Castle. Leave my office this instant." She turned to Jansson. "If I have any further problems from him, the responsibility for it rests on your shoulders. I suggest you control him if you want to keep your job."

Jansson nodded once and steered Clive from the office with a bit more force than necessary. Tiberius flexed his hands and wrists, trouble brewing on his face.

"Spineless coward," he muttered, ensuring it was still loud enough for Clive to hear. Papa drew in a deep breath, and the tense muscles in his shoulders relaxed. The High Priestess removed the incantation that held my throat hostage.

"I'd like those names, High Priestess," Tiberius said. "I've got a hankering for a Factios bust, if you don't mind."

"What's a Factios?" I asked.

"They are a recent problem from within the last year or two, possibly connected to Mabel," the High Priestess said in a weary tone. "Factios is just a name. They are a group of organized criminals living in Chatham City stirring up trouble. They're also a bunch of sodden idiots, although they must have some kind of intelligent leadership amongst them."

She waved a hand at the scroll with a disgusted look and sent it flying to Tiberius, who tucked it into his pocket with a happy little pat.

"Always glad to plan a raid, Your Highness," he said in a jovial tone. "It keeps the captains and me happy. There's nothing more fun than busting the ugly mug of these Factios members." Tiberius shot me a wink as he gave me a light slug on the shoulder that knocked me into Stella.

"Maybe I'll have you teach the Guardians how to fight since you fended off an entire crowd."

I couldn't even smile, but Tiberius didn't notice. He nodded once to Papa before swaggering out of the room and shutting the door behind him with a violent slam that rattled the paintings on the walls.

"I'm sorry this happened, Bianca," the High Priestess said in a voice that was—to my surprise—calm. "I was not angry at you, you must understand. It's not safe for you outside the castle anymore. Your restriction is a safety measure, not a punishment."

"Yes, Your Highness."

She studied me for several long moments, then let out a quiet sigh and turned to Papa.

"Derek, please send for Merrick. I would like to talk to him in private. Stella, please remain behind. I have something to speak to you about. The rest of you may go."

The paper that had disappeared earlier reappeared in the High Priestess's hand. Papa put a hand on my back and escorted me away as the High Priestess handed the paper to Stella, a frown on her face.

All my friends waited for me in the Witchery.

Camille paced back and forth across the width of the turret, tugging on the ends of her hair in agitation. "You're okay!" she cried as soon as I walked inside, throwing her arms around me.

"Relatively."

She pulled away with tears in her pretty hazel eyes. "We've been worried sick! We searched the crowd forever trying to find you before they did something terrible. They were chanting and screaming. I was so scared."

"We were really frightened," Michelle said with a little shiver. "I caught a glimpse of you just as they started dragging you toward

Clive. If Leda hadn't told Merrick, I don't know how we would have gotten you home."

"Leda?" I asked, whirling around. She sat on the edge of the divan, her pale hands folded in her lap.

"I saw glimpses of it," she said. "I was in the middle of talking to Janss—in a meeting, and I just up and left without a word of explanation. Luckily Merrick and Brecken were on the Wall, talking. As soon as I told them what I thought might happen, they transported."

I collapsed onto one of the large piles of pillows, surprised to find my knees so weak. The images of the rabid crowd and being thrown around flapped through my mind, wanting to be processed, but I wasn't ready and pushed them away.

"Thank you," I said, meeting her gaze. "I don't really know what happened, but I don't think I would have gotten out of there alive without Merrick."

She moved over and sat next to me on the pillows, a sure sign that she had been worried.

"All I saw was a bright white light," Camille said, joining us. Michelle came next. The three of them surrounded me. The Witchery walls closing in around us settled the rankled fear in my heart. *Safe.* My muscles began to relax, and I felt exhausted. "A lot of people started screaming, some started to run. Then Brecken showed up. He pulled Michelle and I away. Merrick slipped past him into the crowd to find you."

"The last thing we saw was Merrick pulling you from the ground and the two of you running away. Brecken walked us back to the castle," Michelle said.

"I don't remember half of it," I said, shaking my head. "But I'm glad that the two of you made it out okay."

"What did the High Priestess say?" Leda asked.

I recounted everything. When I finished, Camille's look of disgust reflected my feelings.

"Clive is a horrid man!" she cried.

Michelle's upper lip curled a little. "At least you didn't get work hours with Mrs. L," she said in a quiet voice. "At that point I think you'd want to renegotiate for exile."

The four of us looked at each other, then broke into smiles. The knot in my chest released just enough that I could breathe freely for the first time that day. When Camille and Leda's conversation dwindled into algebra lessons and simple potion making, I closed my eyes, leaned back against the pillows, and let their words and voices lull me into a safe place again.

Not Entirely Mad

"Papa, where's Merrick?"

I stood outside Papa's office in the quiet Gatehouse that night. He looked up from his scattered, messy desk. Candles bobbed in the air around him, shedding light on books and paperwork. Outside the sun sank into the horizon, fading behind the shadows of Letum Wood.

"I haven't seen him," he said, his eyes looking bloodshot and fatigued. "Not since he spoke with the High Priestess a few hours ago."

My teeth bit into my bottom lip. That conversation was the reason I wanted to find him. "Did he get in trouble because my powers aren't under control yet?" I asked, fearing the worst.

Papa hesitated and slowly shook his head.

"No."

The reserved tone in his voice told me all I needed to know. Merrick's fate was as tied up in whether I regained control as mine was. It was a terrible burden.

"Any news from the Borderlands?"

The drawn, tired lines returned to his face.

"Yes. The West has successfully started to draw water from the river. The High Priestess is following the directions in the Mansfeld Pact and sending a formal message to them tonight."

"Is this the first she's sent?"

He shook his head again.

"No. They've ignored all the others."

"If they ignore this one?"

"Then we defend ourselves by whatever means necessary."

I had so many more questions but kept them to myself. I'd caused him enough stress already.

"Thanks, Papa," I said and pushed away from the door. Tiberius grunted at me when I passed his sparse office, which was filled by a table large enough to seat all of his Captains of the Guard. He sat in a large seat in the middle, paperwork belched out around him. I wanted to ask him if he knew where Merrick was, but he waved me away.

I returned to the apartment and curled up on top of my silky bed-spread, the darkness and still air sending me to sleep.

Merrick was leaning against a broken fountain near the Forgotten Gardens when I found him the next morning, hauling the two buckets of rocks that he still made me carry every time. It never got easier—he kept adding heavier rocks—but my grip strength had increased dramatically. The predictability of a familiar routine comforted my anxious heart.

"Merry meet," I said quietly, setting down the buckets. His eyes looked nearly blue in the morning light. His jaw was tight and tense.

He straightened. "Ready to train?"

Panic jolted through my heart. "Did the High Priestess get angry with you? Did she blame you for my loss of control? Because it's not your fault!"

"What she said or didn't say isn't important. This isn't about me. This is about you dealing with your grief."

I stared at him in disbelief, unsure of what to say.

"You aren't angry?"

"Why would I be angry?" he asked. Despite the even tone, he was unable to hide the tension in his white knuckles and tight shoulders. The High Priestess had put pressure on him, I was certain of it. "You defended yourself against a dangerous mob."

"But I lost control. I haven't . . . I haven't figured out how to control the power."

For the first time since he started teaching me, an exasperated tone crept into his voice.

"You don't figure grief out, Bianca. You go through it. Grief is a mess that you can't clean up all at once. It takes time and patience, not logic and fact."

"But my grief is dangerous," I said, struggling to keep the tears from filling my eyes. Where had this sudden onslaught of emotion come from? Unable to bear his intense gaze, I looked away. Eye contact was little more than a willing vulnerability. "I'm going to hurt someone if I can't control it."

"Then stop trying to control it."

I paused. "What do you mean?"

He let out a long breath.

"My father died when I was twelve," he finally said, the muscles of his jaw flexing as he looked out across the Forgotten Gardens to the dark heights of Letum Wood. A few lazy flower petals drifted from the wall behind him, landing on his shoulder.

"Twelve?"

"On my birthday, no less. We were hiking a mountain and a storm came in. I didn't know how to transport yet so we had to hike back down. The rain moved in so fast we could barely see. When you're up that high, the hair on your arms stand up before the lightning strikes and the thunder is so loud you can't even hear yourself think. We started back for home right away, but a flash flood swept through the mountain when we were halfway down. I woke up the next morning, lying on a rock. I couldn't find my father anywhere. My leg was broken, so I couldn't move. I sat there on the rock, waiting to be found."

"How long did you wait?"

He shrugged, the distant quality of his voice receding a little.

"It's hard to tell. I was in and out of consciousness. I kept waking up to call for my father, trying to let him know where I was. Eventually one of the witches from my village found me. I woke up at home, my leg healing, and my father dead."

I thought about what he said for several moments, unsure of what to say. It felt best not to say anything.

"I blamed myself," he said with a shake of his head. "It tore me apart for years. I replayed that day over and over again in my head, wondering what we could have done differently. I thought it was my fault because I didn't know how to transport. I refused to feel the grief. I worked until I was so tired that my body had no choice but collapse into an exhausted sleep. By the time I turned fifteen, my powers were nearly out of control."

"What did you finally do?" I asked.

"I got tired of fighting it. I just let it happen."

"Let what happen? I don't understand."

"Eventually you will," he said. "Until then we'll continue to focus on our goal of learning swordsmanship."

"And the goal of controlling the magic?"

He shrugged. "Just let it happen."

I held my breath. Could it really be that simple?

"Are you sure?"

"Emotions are power," he said. "The more you fight them, the more they fight back. Take a break today. Think it over. Put the High Priestess and any expectations out of your mind. We'll start up with training again tomorrow."

The Gatehouse lights burned bright that evening.

I stared out at their long flames from the darkness of the empty apartment high above. The candles waited to be lit, an untouched dinner sat on the table, notes from my friends remained unopened. No doubt they wondered where I'd been all day. I ignored all of it, wanting to be alone. I couldn't get Merrick or Miss Mabel out of my head.

Emotions are power.

It's difficult keeping the power under control, isn't it?

Just let it happen.

No matter how I tried, I couldn't imagine what Merrick meant when he said *let it happen,* so I stopped thinking about it. My mind slid to Miss Mabel instead, to the binding, to my seventeenth birthday. The thoughts suffocated me. I had to get out of the room. I needed to do something. I drew in a bolstering breath, struck with sudden inspiration.

Tonight.

I knew it was crazy. I knew it was a spontaneous, poorly thought out idea. But I didn't care anymore. I had no control over any other part of my life, but at least I could take care of this one thing. Before common sense caught up and told me I wasn't ready to face Miss Mabel or destroy the binding, I quickly prepared.

The thought that perhaps I shouldn't have isolated myself for so long today snuck into my mind. I felt like I was going mad. Then again, maybe I was. Maybe insanity was just a slow creep away from reality, so subtle the nightmare wasn't recognizable until the monsters were too strong. I tied back my hair. What did monsters matter when I only had a few months left to live? The High Priestess would come through on her part and end the Inheritance Curse. But I wouldn't kill the High Priest for Miss Mabel, so I'd die anyway.

I slipped into a pair of breeches I'd filched from the laundry and bound my hair into a braid that fell between my shoulder blades. My powers bubbled under the surface with such violence that I almost stopped myself from going. Then I caught sight of myself in a stray mirror. The flash of my gray eyes reminded me of Mama. I had to go.

For added protection, I strapped a sheath to my forearm and slipped a small dagger into it, hoping I wouldn't have to use it. The silent halls of Chatham Castle seemed to echo when I walked the long corridors on bare feet. The quiet shadows snuck up the walls like hands trying to grab me, to keep me in the castle. *Reckless fool,* they seemed to whisper.

No going back, I thought. *Time to free myself.*

The shadows shifted. I heard the scuffle of a foot and Leda appeared out of the darkness. She grabbed my arm and shoved me against the wall, the strength of her skinny frame surprising me. The shock of my head slamming into the stone reverberated through my skull.

"Don't!" she hissed. "Don't do it."

"Don't what?" I muttered, rubbing the offended spot and glaring at her. "Jikes, Leda. Did you have to slam me into the wall?"

"Don't do it."

"Do what?"

"Whatever you're doing."

"Why? What have you seen?"

"Nothing," she said. "Nothing except that whatever you've decided to do involves Miss Mabel."

My eyes widened. "You can see her?"

"No. Not really, anyway," she said taking a step away, as if standing too close caused her pain. "That's just it. I can't see anything. Nothing but gray and black, just like last year at school. Just like . . . just like the afternoon your mother died."

"I can't explain it," I said. "I have to go."

"Please, Bianca!"

"No!" I cried and the torches near us popped into bright flame. Her queer eyes stared at me through the flickering shadows, narrowing in question. We watched each other until she took another step back. I wasn't sure what emotion hid behind her annoyance, but it looked an awful lot like fear.

"I have a bad feeling about tonight," she said in a tremulous voice. "It's bothered me all day."

"I have to do this, Leda. I don't expect you to understand."

Unable to bear it, I turned and left her in the hallway behind me, headed for the cover of darkness in the Forgotten Gardens.

A chorus of long, soulful wails welcomed me into the Western Network.

They sent my heart into a wild spin, matching the drums that pounded in the background. Why such loud mourning? Chills skirted my skin.

I've had a bad feeling about tonight all day, Leda's voice rang out in my head.

Life is full of bad feelings, I reassured myself. *Let's just get this over with.*

The transportation spell had left me crouched in a long hallway somewhere in the belly of the Arck, folded in red rock and shadows. The floor under my bare feet felt cold and dry. I whispered an invisibility incantation and stepped to the wall to gain my bearings. The hall stretched to my right and left, disappearing in dark twists and turns. A few torches illuminated the area with yellow light. It smelled like cloves and spice.

Right or left?

I didn't let myself debate long. It would be better to keep moving until I could figure out where the spell put me. I headed to the right, hoping it led outside. My bare feet didn't make a sound as I padded down the halls at a wary jog. My powers were on alert, but still, my ears picked up nothing except the exaggerated screaming from outside.

The wall eventually gave way to a dead end, with a square window that reached my waist. I ran to it to find a familiar sight: the market I'd seen above Miss Mabel's chambers. My eyes locked in on her balcony. I was a floor above and just to the right of her personal quarters. But the balcony was too small for me to transport to with my imprecise skill.

This is going to hurt, I thought, surveying my option. There was a subtle slope to the wall, and I thought I could climb down; the side was uneven, with rocks sticking out and divots pressing in. My eyes flittered over the ground six stories away. I'd have to be very careful.

Don't think. Just do it.

The scuffling of two witches walking in unison helped me find the motivation to climb over the window. *West Guards.* On patrol, no doubt. I did one more quick assessment of where I would put my feet, lifted my legs over the window, and slowly lowered myself onto the first bump.

The red rock was firm to stand on, but loose dirt shuffled beneath my feet as I moved to a divot in the wall. I moved as far to the left as I could go before encountering a wall that jutted out. From here, Miss Mabel's balcony was a straight shot down. The two approaching

West Guards stopped at the window and peered out. I pressed myself against the gritty wall and willed my heart to quiet. If I didn't move, they wouldn't be able to see me.

"Pity," one of them said, drawing out the *i* so it sounded like *peety*. Their accent was strangely soft and lilting compared to the hoarse, rough dialect of Chatham City. "Almack was a good leader."

"He was sick for so long. It's good to die when you're not strong anymore," the other said.

My eyes widened. No wonder the Western Network was mourning. The whole world would soon join their wail, I imagined, when we all went to war.

The divot my right foot stood in started to lose integrity, and my body slid down the rock. I held my breath and tightened my grip on the two pieces of jutting rock my hands clung to. A little stream of dust dribbled down the wall, and a West Guard looked my direction with a sharp glance. I held my breath, thankful I'd had the wits to make myself invisible. All the work with Merrick had strengthened me, but I wouldn't last forever.

"Let's go," the other said, softening the *t* so it sounded more like a breath. "We have work to do."

The first Guard narrowed his eyes, still scrutinizing the spot where I grasped the wall

"Yes," he whispered. "Much work."

They disappeared and I let out a breath of relief just as the rock supporting my right foot and almost all my body weight gave way. I stifled a scream as I started sliding down the rock face, grappling for a new hold with my fingertips.

I skidded along the wall so fast it was little more than a blur. One second I was falling along the wall, plummeting toward the balcony floor, and then a flash of darkness, a moment of pressure, and I stood in the middle of Miss Mabel's quarters.

I gasped. I'd transported right into her lair without knowing if she was here or not.

I froze, waiting for her condemning voice or for a maid to scream, but nothing happened. Feeling almost sick, I darted to the nook of bookshelves on the left and slipped behind the last shelf, tucking myself into a little corner. My gaze swept the room as I waited, but I saw and heard no one. My wild heart eventually began to slow. That brush with death had been a little too close. I whispered the invisibility incantation again; it hadn't carried through the transportation.

Focus. Don't lose your concentration now.

I reviewed my plan, listening for any suspicious noises.

Listen in. Find the book. Tear out the binding. Immediately transport back to Letum Wood.

A sultry breeze flapped Miss Mabel's sheer curtains into the room. The sun was sinking low in the western sky, lighting the sand on fire. I drew in a deep breath. *Sandalwood. Cumin.* The smells reminded me of Miss Scarlett's classroom. I turned my focus to listening to the sands around me. Nothing to hear but the mournful singing and pulsing drums.

A set of bookshelves stood across from me. I took a deep breath and padded closer, skimming all the titles. *Almorran Traditions. Dark Magic from the Depths. Monsters of Antebellum.*

The *Book of Contracts* was not with the rest of her gruesome library. *Of course,* I thought, canvassing the room again. *She probably sleeps with it.*

My eyes fell on a small alcove off the main room where a massive bed stood in between the fluttering curtains.

There, I thought. *She'll keep her Book of Contracts there.*

A low murmur of voices came from somewhere near the hall. I froze, but they were still too far off to make out the words, which meant I still had a few moments of stolen time before I'd have to leave for good.

Once I made it into the bedroom, I paused in the doorway, taking it in. Rolled black pillows littered the sprawling bed. Tawny drapes that contrasted with the red rock walls danced in the air. A gilded mirror with elaborate carvings flared out like arms of the sun. The elegant simplicity was so Miss Mabel that it unnerved me. Her personal chambers felt oppressive and made me nervous, like crouching in a cave I couldn't stand up in. I shifted my shoulders, as if that would shake it off, but it remained.

The voices in the hall were closing in. My eyes fell on another bookshelf, filled with scrolls of various sizes, a jar of white ink, a vial of veritas, and three extravagant peacock quills. No *Book of Contracts*.

I paused to listen again. The low drone of voices that had been far away sounded suspiciously close. Two females. I could barely make out their words now.

"A simple task . . . Many places to search . . . Can't you handle it, Mabel?"

My heart fluttered. Miss Mabel was on her way back. They were still a few moments away if my guess was correct, so I threw myself into searching every nook and cranny of the room. I'd transport at the last possible second. The spell was ready on my tongue. The *Book of Contracts* wasn't under her bed, or in the far cupboards. It didn't hide behind the other books.

No! I thought desperately, shoving aside a few dresses. *It has to be here!*

The two voices turned into Miss Mabel's main room. My heart pounded. Wasted! All of this would be wasted if I didn't find it.

"I know I'm right, Mabel darling," said an unknown voice with the light accent of a woman. Slightly condescending in tone, and punctuated with a crisp dialect I didn't recognize. "I'm always right. Surely after all these years you've learned that."

"I'm looking for it," Miss Mabel hissed. "Why don't you try for awhile?"

"I shouldn't have to do it if you were competent. Honestly, how difficult can it be to find a book? We can't afford a longer delay, not with the Central Network fighting back and Derek still in as Head of Protectors. Two simple tasks, Mabel. Find the book and get rid of Derek. That's all I asked of you. Looks like I'll have to do it myself."

Now, I thought. *I should transport now.*

But I didn't, because they were talking about my father, my Network, my world.

"I have it under control."

"Is that why you have a little stranger rifling through your bedroom?" the new voice asked in a little purr, setting my powers on fire. A feeling of fear pinched my heart, like someone had pulled a string through it.

"She's nothing I haven't handled in the past," Miss Mabel said tersely. "I'll take care of things here. Leave, and don't rush back."

"I'll leave you to it, darling," the voice said. "She's obviously quite brave for someone so young. Perhaps we should try to recruit her. She might do a better job than you have."

"I told you to leave."

The whisper of someone transporting away was the only reply.

A surge of fear welled up within me as I whispered the transportation spell. But the welcoming blackness didn't come. Panicked, I tried again and again, but it felt like my magic was hitting a wall. Nothing happened. Miss Mabel must have a protective shield on her room that allowed witches to transport in, but not back out. A veritable trap that explained the oppressive feeling I'd had.

"Come out, come out, Bianca darling," Miss Mabel called, her voice closing in. "Or I can come find you."

This was it. I wasn't getting out. I tightened my jaw, drew in a deep breath, and yanked an unlit torch from the wall. If I couldn't get away, I certainly wouldn't cower. The sound of Miss Mabel's hem sliding over the floor rustled into the room. I released the invisibility incantation and gripped the torch in my hands, holding it like a club.

"Miss Mabel," I said, dipping my head in greeting.

She stopped at the foot of her bed, her eyes narrowed. Her blonde hair swung loose on her shoulders, skimming a scandalous dress of sapphire silk that brightened her eyes, making them shine. A slip of black lace peeked out from underneath the top layer. Held fast in her left arm was the *Book of Contracts*. I swallowed back the dry taste of humiliation and fear.

"Merry meet. Why don't you stay right there for a little while?" she asked.

An invisible force pushed me into the wall and tightened around my neck, cutting off my airway. The torch fell from my arms with a loud crack and rolled across the floor.

"Nasty little trespassers deserve to be punished for their stupid ideas, don't you think?" Miss Mabel spat. "Especially a witch with such poor execution. You thought I wouldn't notice you here? Fool!"

The invisible band around my neck constricted. My arms flailed for purchase, my toes stung from the weight. No matter what I did, I couldn't breathe. All my weight sat on my throat.

"So," she drawled, setting the *Book of Contracts* on her bed and moving toward me with her usual slow saunter. "You thought you could come steal my book and destroy your binding, did you?"

The *Book of Contracts* flapped open with a burst of hot wind. My hair whipped across my face, partially obscuring her wild, bright eyes. I'd seen Miss Mabel in many forms, but never had she appeared this dangerous, this . . . furious.

"I'm going to assume that you are still determined to not kill the next High Priest?" she said.

The pressure around my throat loosened just enough to allow me breath. I coughed, pulling in large gulps of air. "Never," I finally muttered.

"You don't want to live?"

"Not at that cost."

Standing so close to her, knowing that my life was in her hands again, was almost too much to bear. I didn't know I could hate someone so much. The magic in my chest pressed against me. What would happen if I let the power go?

The band around my throat disappeared. I pitched forward, landing on my hands and knees in front of her.

"That looks better," she quipped, taking a step back. I coughed so hard I nearly vomited. Catching my breath, I glanced up. The *Book of Contracts* lay just out of reach on top of the bed, still rustling in the wind. When the pages finally settled I saw my name.

I, Bianca Monroe, swear to complete an unknown task . . .

With a flick of my wrist, I pulled the hidden blade from my sleeve, jumped to my feet, and drove the tip of the dagger into the *Book of Contracts*, stabbing right into her bloody thumbprint. Pain burst through my hand, shooting up into my shoulder and down my body. I let go with a cry. An explosion threw me back, tossing me as if I were a rag doll. I slammed into the wall and bounced to the floor, smacking the rock with the side of my head. Her laughter was earsplitting to my hazy mind.

"You are a bit reckless lately, aren't you?"

When my vision cleared, I saw my blade resting next to the *Book of Contracts*, melted all the way to the hilt.

"A courageous try," Miss Mabel said, chuckling in a way that frightened me. "But never good enough."

"I'm not afraid of you."

"You should be afraid," she said, regarding me with her lazy gaze. "As I'm sure you overheard, I'm not the only witch out there who wants the Central Network, so I'm not the only one you have to fear. Don't be so stupid next time, silly fool. You'll die when the binding's time runs out, or you'll prove yourself useful. Merry part, Bianca. I do look forward to our next visit."

I fell down into the blackness that transportation brings, where the pressure made me feel alive and the rush of air was so painful I screamed. The darkness won, claiming me as her own.

Color of Goodbye

Miss Mabel sent me to Letum Wood.

After disentangling myself and clumps of my hair from a pile of brambles, I stumbled through the trees to find the lights of Chatham Castle glowing in the distance.

"Just get inside," I whispered to myself. "I'll think about it all later."

I had to focus. I needed to get inside without a Guardian detecting me. I skirted the back hedge and dodged a pair of Guardians walking their rounds by ducking behind a sculpture of some forgotten High Priest. They had passed by me, unaware of my presence, when a low bugle broke the quiet night. My eyes jerked up to the castle, suddenly aware of how many Guardians stood at the top of the Wall.

The bugle was an ancient calling system used in times of war or distress. It could be heard across the entire Network, calling every Coven Leader to Chatham Castle. I headed for the Wall at a jog. A familiar head of curly blonde hair waited at the top.

"Camille!" I called, running up the stairs. "What's going on?"

Camille threw herself into my arms with a cry.

"Are you okay?" she asked, pulling away to study me. "You look so pale. Is that blood in your hair?"

"No, I'm fine," I said, gesturing to the lower bailey below. "What's going on?"

Brecken stood behind her in his half-armor, holding onto the hilt of his sword with a white-knuckle grip. His eyes darted around the Wall and the high bailey, barking orders to the occasional Guardian.

"They just sounded the bugle," Camille said. "We're waiting for the High Priestess to come out now."

"Leda?" I asked. "Where is she?"

"I don't know!" Camille wailed, wringing her hands. "I was out here and—"

"Camille! Bianca!" Leda called from halfway up the stairs with Michelle at her heels. "Did we miss anything?"

"Not yet," I said.

Leda gave me a dark look, but I saw the relief behind it.

"All right?" she asked quietly, glancing at my head. I touched it with my left hand and a few spots of blood came away on my fingertips. I nodded once.

"Bad feeling?" I asked.

"I guess we can see why."

A small group of witches gathered in the bailey below us. Their voices echoed off the Wall, making the crowd seem twice as big. Every now and then a new witch would transport in with mussed hair, wearing a robe and a sleepy expression.

Tiberius walked amongst the Guardians at the front gate, eyeing every witch that entered. Protectors were probably hiding in plain sight, wearing casual clothes and having transformed small details of their face. A bulbous nose, thick eyebrows, and a new hair color made them a totally different witch. As masters of disguise, they blended in flawlessly. I wondered if Merrick was with them when the second bugle sounded. It came from the second-tallest turret, where the scarlet and gold Central Network flag flapped in the wind.

"One more," Leda said. "One more call and the High Priestess will come out."

All of us remained silent, absorbing the currents of tension running through the walls. Even Camille didn't speak as she grabbed my hand and waited with wide eyes. Snippets of conversation below filtered up to us.

"Must be bad news."

"Think the High Priestess is okay?"

"I'll bet something happened in the Borderlands."

"Perhaps the war has finally begun."

The ringing tones of the third bugle seemed to take forever to come, and when they did, even longer to finish. The High Priestess stepped out the main doors and stood at the edge of the first floor. Most leaders spoke from the balcony three stories higher, but Mildred insisted on standing amongst the witches, elevating herself only enough to be seen.

From this distance, the High Priestess looked every inch a leader and a witch without fear. She held her head high, her shoulders squared. I wondered if her knees ever trembled, or if she too feared the things she couldn't control. Miss Mabel's words came back to me.

I wouldn't pass on the pleasure of killing her for the world.

"Witches of the Central Network," the High Priestess called. Her voice projected over the bailey and the crowd of Coven Leaders, carried by a special incantation. "I have ill tidings to bring you tonight. We have just received word that Almack, the High Priest of the Western Network, has passed from this life."

Camille clenched my hand. I returned the gesture, recalling again the long, mournful wails in the Western Network. I didn't have to force a concerned look.

"Almack's life was one of leadership and service. He brought peace and prosperity to a constantly restless Network. The West shall mourn the loss of his company."

So will all of Antebellum when we go to war.

"In order to commemorate his life, we pay tribute tonight."

Four archers stepped forward, Merrick amongst them, reminding me that for all the time we spent together, I knew very little about him. Flaming arrows blazed to life from their bows, burning with a bright white center. White, the color of mourning, of passing. The color of goodbye. A lump rose in my throat, remembering Mama's funeral and the crowd of white gathered around her grave. As one, the archers leaned back and tilted their arrows at the ready.

I leaned in toward Leda.

"Why would the High Priestess order the bugle to announce Almack's death tonight?" I asked in a whisper so quiet only she would hear. "It will only alarm the Network."

"If the West is smart they'll attack immediately," she whispered.

"Use the element of surprise. The High Priestess will meet with the Coven Leaders once this is complete to prepare."

"Then why would she honor a witch she doesn't know?" I asked. The Mansfeld Pact bound us to never deal with another Network's business. Most leaders had met each other but that was all. Only Ambassadors were allowed to cross borders, and even then only on invitation in case of a diplomatic need or question.

"It's a sign of respect," Leda said. "Maybe even a defiant stance, really. Mildred may be trying to send a message to Dane."

Tiberius called out a command in the Guardians language, drawing my attention back to the bailey. He stood just behind the High Priestess now, his burly body dwarfing her. The shadows behind him shifted just a little, and I saw Papa. Despite the distance, his eyes connected with mine. Knowing he was close gave me courage.

Four women surrounded the archers, wearing white robes and holding burning candles. A mournful chant came from their lips, belted out in tones of reckless grief, consuming the crowd, the bailey, the Network. The arrows continued to burn. The arms of the archers were slick with sweat, their muscles trembling.

Then the singing stopped and the arrows flew, one at a time in each direction, soaring into the black night. The faces of the Guardians on the Wall flashed in the passing lights of the arrows.

The terrible silence of the bailey seemed to roll.

"What now?" Camille asked, her voice faint. "What happens now?"

No one answered.

By mutual, silent understanding, all four of us silently piled the pillows onto the floor and lay near each other in the Witchery that night. I was grateful to be close to them instead of in the apartment, alone. Papa was already gone, shuffled into meetings in the Royal Hall that would last through the night. Camille held my hand as we stared at the ceiling. Michelle curled up on her other side on the edge of the nest we'd made. Leda lay to my right, silent, her eyes staring at one fixed spot on the ceiling.

"I guess we'll go to war now," Leda said, breaking the silence. Camille sucked in a sharp breath. My own thoughts strayed to Papa and Tiberius and Merrick. What would it mean for them?

"Everything will be okay," I said, but my voice sounded wooden.

"I have five brothers," Michelle whispered. "I hope they won't have to fight."

My heart twisted for her. Camille reached over and took Michelle's hand. We continued to stare at the ceiling as if the answers were written there. Camille dropped into sleep first. Michelle followed with her husky, quiet snores, leaving just Leda and I behind.

"Your feet are cut up," she whispered, curled up on her side and facing the window, her back to me. "You hurt yourself wherever you went."

"Yes."

She fell silent, and I offered nothing more. Several angry scratches crossed my feet and toes. A scrape decorated the side of my shin from the fall down the Arck and a cut from hitting my head against Miss Mabel's wall bled a little above my ear, but overall I was unscathed.

"What is going to happen now, Bianca?" Leda asked, and I thought I heard a note of fear in her voice.

"Can't you see that far?" I asked, turning to look at her back. The old seams in her nightdress from home had started to fray, barely holding together. I wondered if coming from a family that could barely afford clothes made her feel small in the judgmental world of politics.

"I won't let myself," she said.

The moonlight spilled across Leda's figure. I studied her white-blonde hair, then turned to look at the ceiling again.

"Do you have that much control over the curse now?" I asked in surprise. "To prevent yourself from seeing certain outcomes?"

Her shoulders tightened. "Maybe . . . I don't know. I'm tired. Leave me alone."

Her hasty retreat from the conversation startled me. Leda pulled the light blanket from her waist to cover her head and tucked into a little ball. Minutes later her breathing evened out.

I turned back to stare at the ceiling. My thoughts lingered on the echo of the bugle and the chilling words that struck my heart.

We'll go to war.

They haunted me into my dreams.

The Dragons Are Out

Chatham Castle held her collective breath the next morning, waiting to see what news would come from the West. The *Chatham Chatterer* updated every fifteen minutes with a new article. *Guardians on Guard in the Borderlands! Almack's Dead, Thousands Mourn. Will the High Priestess Announce Our New High Priest?*

The obnoxious headlines never stopped, so I shoved the scroll out of sight. Merrick sent me a message canceling our lesson just as the sun crested the forest, and I was glad. I wouldn't have been able to focus.

I pulled on a light blue dress and headed out of the turret toward the Royal Hall with my hair in a braid, hoping to catch some gossip on my way to talk to the High Priestess. I didn't know if she'd hear me, but I had to try. Now that an ominous threat of war hung over the Network, my fear for Papa tripled. Would they try to get rid of him as soon as possible? Could the High Priestess stop them?

The Guardians at the grand stairs cast me a suspicious glance when I walked into the Royal Hall, but they let me pass when they recognized me. Chatham Castle teemed with nervous bodies.

That was too easy, I thought.

"You may not go in!" Donald chirped as I neared the High Priestess's office. The door closed with a quiet click. "She's meeting with Council Member Jansson right now. What are you doing here anyway? No one is supposed to be in the Royal Hall."

"Council Member Jansson, you say?"

"Yes." Donald's desk sat outside the office today, practically in front of the double doors. He kept adjusting his legs in little squirms, looking as if he were ready to get comfortable there. I'd have to play this very carefully.

"Oh, that's all right," I said in a breathless tone. "I'm just so glad I found you. Fina is having a problem in the kitchen. She's concerned about . . . er . . . a few letters she's received since last night."

"Fina is a capable woman. She's never needed my help before."

"The letters are from the local farmers that are distressed about the war. She's so busy coordinating food for all the unexpected guests that she just can't deal with it on her own."

He didn't even look up.

"She'll work it out. I'm not to leave."

I glared at him and bit my bottom lip.

"B-but she sent me for you, specifically," I said, trying to infuse panic in my voice. "She must respond immediately, or . . . or—"

He looked up, his long face expectant, like a horse waiting for his oats.

"Or what?"

"They won't send food any longer."

His eyes tapered in a suspicious glare. "They must send food. They are under contract."

I shrugged. "I agree. But they are refusing. They want to keep the food for their villages and families if there's going to be a war. Not to mention the water shortage that's already hitting the fields." I let out a dramatic sigh. "A food crisis on top of all that's already happening! What a shame."

He simmered on it for a second, his face pinching together. I cast a nervous glance at the door. This had to hurry or I'd miss the whole meeting!

"No, they're bluffing. Fina won't let them do it." He waved the matter off. "Now leave me alone. I have work to do."

"Very well. I'll go tell Fina you said that it wasn't important enough to address," I said in an even tone. "Thank you for your time, Donald."

He looked up as I started walking away with a mild expression of panic.

"I didn't say that. Don't tell Fina I said that!"

"What can I do, Donald? She wanted me to bring you to help her sort the issue out. Clearly, you are too busy."

He chewed on his bottom lip. "You said she sent for me specifically?" he checked again.

"She said you were the only one maintaining an even head today, and that your decision would be the most trustworthy with the High Priestess tied up."

The flattery worked. He cleared his throat and straightened the collar of his shirt with his spindly fingers.

"Well, I have been pretty calm, if I do say so myself."

I nodded in willing agreement. He cast an uneasy look at the door.

"But I can't leave while the High Priestess meets with Jansson. I'm supposed to keep other witches from disturbing them."

"I could sit here while you go," I said, as if the thought had just come to me. "I have a few minutes to spare."

He studied me in wary indecision before finally giving in.

"Very well. I shall be quick."

His long body took awhile to unfold and start walking toward the stairs, stretching my patience. I sat down after he vacated the desk and stared innocently at the wall-sized painting across from the office. He cast one look over his shoulder, remained satisfied I hadn't moved, and disappeared.

The moment his steps faded away I jumped to my feet and ran to the door. If I stood almost pressed against it, I could pick up every word. Just in case, I muttered an incantation under my breath, one that made sounds expand, and kept my eye on the hallway.

"Yes, I'm aware that the Western Network has successfully diverted most of the river. Derek said they were able to save a small amount, but it will only help the northern farmers. I plan to bring the matter before the Council for discussion later tonight."

Jansson's even tone followed. "Very well. Two more items of business. I wanted to speak with you personally in regards to the Derek issue before the Council meets on it. I come at no one's behest but my own."

The Derek issue?

"Proceed," she said.

"With war nearly inevitable now that Almack is gone, the Council Members are planning on reviewing Clive's petition tomorrow. Their first priority now that Almack has died is to have you put a new Head of Protectors in place. It doesn't look good for Derek, Your Highness."

"No, it doesn't."

"I've spoken to all of the Council Members. I know of at least six guaranteed votes to exile Derek. The rest are undecided but one. Stella votes to keep him in office."

His words made my heart turn cold in a way I never could have imagined. Six out of ten already? The odds were against him.

"It's exile they want?" the High Priestess asked. "Not just removal?"

"Exile," he confirmed.

A silence stretched through the room, filling me with dread. "I can't say I'm that surprised," the High Priestess said with a low breath.

"Forgive me if I sound impudent or am speaking out of place," he said. "But I would strongly advise you to not divide yourself from the Council over the issue of the Head of Protectors. There are some witches on the Council that would not hesitate to invoke the old rules and pull you out of office alongside Derek."

"The old rules?" she repeated. "Those have never been used. Not since the Networks were formed. They feel so strongly about it?"

"Some of them do, Your Highness. Though I'm not sure that their motivations are entirely pure."

His cryptic response gave me chills. Miss Mabel must have Council Members on her side. Miss Mabel, or the woman she was working with.

"Thank you for your help, Jansson."

"Your Highness, I have one other item to bring to your attention. This I do on behalf of the Council and not myself."

"Go ahead."

"If a High Priest is not chosen in three days, along with a new Head of Protectors," he continued, "the Council has requested that I inform you of their plans to invoke the ancient Rule of Settlement."

My gasp came out before I could stifle it, and I slapped both hands over my mouth. The Rule of Settlement declared that the ten Council Members could vote, on an eight out of ten majority, to put a High Priest or Priestess in office if the current leader had not done so already. At its best, it was a protective mechanism to ensure we always had a leader. At its worst it was a political slap in the face, an insinuation that the current leader didn't know well enough to choose the right counterpart. The High Priestess's unchanged tone rang out as clear as a bell.

"Three days, you say?"

"Yes, Your Highness."

"Thank you for delivering that message, Jansson. You are dismissed."

Before I had a chance to resume my innocent position on Donald's chair, the door popped open and hit me in the face. I fell back onto my bottom. Rupert, Jansson's assistant, peered out around the door. He had an orange mustache that came to a point on either cheek and wore his red hair slicked away from his face.

"Sorry, miss," Rupert muttered, casting me a suspicious eye. "What were ya doing right there?"

To my shock, Leda came out next. Her mouth dropped when she saw me on the floor, then she quickly clamped it shut and moved out of the way. Jansson followed behind her.

"I'm sitting here while Donald takes care of an issue downstairs," I said, probing the stinging flesh of my nose. "I stood to stretch my legs and the door flew open at me."

Rupert offered his hand, but I ignored it and climbed to my feet myself.

"Council Member," I said, bobbing out a curtsy. Jansson gave me a startled glance, nodded, and turned to walk away. Rupert cast me a once-over as well, rolled his eyes, and departed at Jansson's side.

"What are you doing?" Leda hissed, taking a step toward me.

"Me?" I cried in a low voice. "What are you doing with Jansson?"

She looked over her shoulder at Jansson's and Rupert's retreating forms and bit her bottom lip.

"I work for Rupert now," she said.

"What? Why?"

"I'm trying to get my foot in the door for a job once I finish my marks," she said, as if it should have been obvious. "Jansson is the busiest Council Member of all, and the one with the most influence, so Miss Scarlett helped me get a job as the assistant to his Assistant. If I do a good enough job, Rupert will help me try to get a better job next year once I have a completed circlus."

"Is that where you've been disappearing?"

"Yes, of course," she said quickly, glancing around again.

"Oh," I said, breaking into a smile. "That's wonderful!"

"Yes, but don't tell anyone yet! I'm in a trial period to see if they really need me or not. Please?" Her gaze turned pleading. "I'd just die of embarrassment if it didn't work out."

"Of course not," I said. "Good work, Leda. I'm proud of you."

She edged a few steps backward.

"I-I have to go. Don't tell anyone!"

She quickly whirled around and dashed off after them. Her bag bulged with scrolls, quills, and the lumpy edges of ink bottles. I stared after her in disbelief until the slap of Donald's large feet started up the stairs. Startled back to action, I dashed into his seat and lounged back, pretending to be bored.

"There you are!" I cried the moment his perplexed face came into view. He opened his mouth to speak, but I brushed past. "Sorry, don't have time. Merry part, Donald!"

He called after me, but I quickly slipped away.

I wandered down to the dining room that evening after practicing by myself in the Forgotten Gardens for several hours. Footwork, sword routines, swings and arcs, all ran through my head. My shoulders ached from the work, but I enjoyed it. Merrick and I hadn't gone for a run in Letum Wood ever since our talk and I was happy to leave it like that.

Two maids walked past me in the hall, whispering in low tones.

Well, the night maid said that the High Priestess declared war during the Council meeting.

They say that the West is trying to infiltrate from the Borderlands.

I heard the Southern Network heard our bugle as well.

Gossip about the possibility of war rang through the castle all day, leaving me with a dour feeling. None of it meant anything, but that didn't seem to matter. Witches would believe any information to gain some sense of control over a moment in their lives. I knew the feeling, even if I didn't understand it.

I steered myself into the dining room with a sigh and headed toward the food table, my stomach growling. Night had fallen, and the candles and torches flickered from a breeze whistling through the open windows, winding around the wooden tables and chairs.

After piling a plate high with roasted potatoes, a chicken leg, a mound of buttery corn, and a dinner roll, I snatched the last brownie before they disappeared. Michelle sat at our usual table with Nicolas at her side. He had a swatch of brown hair on the back of his head that ran against the rest of his mop and, as a result, stuck almost straight up. It looked endearing in a boyish kind of way.

"Merry meet," I said, sitting across from them.

"Merry meet, Bianca," Michelle said in her quiet voice. Nicolas smiled at me, his baby blue eyes lighting up.

"Merry meet, Miss Bianca. It's good ta see ya this evening."

I smiled at him. Unlike the other witches from Chatham City, Nicolas had an undeniable warmth in his accent. Michelle's cheeks flushed to a bright red, and she ducked her attention back to her plate.

"Where's Camille?" I asked.

"By the Guardians," Nicolas said.

I looked up to find Camille sitting in the midst of a table of off-duty Guardians. Brecken sat several chairs away, ignoring her completely. Camille made an obvious point of never looking his way.

"Where's Leda?" Michelle asked. "I tried to find her earlier but couldn't. She wasn't in the Witchery or the library."

"I'm not sure," I said vaguely. "Maybe she's doing something with Miss Scarlett."

"Have you heard about the forest dragons?" Nicolas asked. A fluffy little cloud of mashed potatoes sat on the end of his fork. "Word is just getting out about them tonight."

Michelle smiled a little. "Nicolas loves dragons," she explained. "Actually, he's quite obsessed with them."

"No," I said with a little curl of worry. "What about them?"

He shifted in his seat, moving a little closer. His voice lowered to an excited, conspiratorial tone. There was a bright spark in his eyes.

"Two dragons were spotted flying over Letum Wood yesterday, after Almack died. That's as good as a signed declaration of war, if ya ask me."

"How so?" I asked.

"The dragons only come out if there's danger headed for Chatham Castle. With the Southern Network doubling their guards at the wall, not ta mention the issues with the West, there can't be any other assumption, can there?"

A bleak spirit slid into the conversation, and I nudged at my pile of corn dismally. Nicolas dropped his fork back to the plate with a little clatter and gave himself wholeheartedly to the tale.

"Witches started spotting the dragons at odd times the past week or so. I saw one myself in the distance, flying over the boundaries. They're beautiful animals. I've read about them my whole life. And just think: I might get close enough ta see one flying by!"

Michelle shot me a secret smile.

"Yes," I drawled. "That would be unforgettable, wouldn't it?"

"But mark my words," he finished in a sour tone, "bad things are coming ta the Central Network if the dragons are out. I don't want anything bad ta happen, but I do want ta see a dragon."

Dragons in flight, Miss Mabel's use of Almorran magic, and Papa's head on the chopping block with the Council tomorrow. Could anything else go wrong?

A loud chorus of laughter interrupted my grim thoughts. Camille shot to her feet, desperately reaching across the table at which she sat. A Guardian named Luther held something out of her grasp, taunting her. The witches at their table laughed uproariously while she swiped for it.

"Come get it, Camille!" Luther taunted.

"Please," Camille pleaded, looking worried. "Give it back. It was my mother's. Please! Oh, don't break it! It's all I have!"

"You can have it as soon as you can get it!" another Guardian said, holding up his hands for it. Luther tossed it to him over Camille's head. The necklace glinted as it flew through the air between the two of them. I pushed to my feet, my chest flaring with anger, when Michelle stopped me with a hand on my arm.

"Wait!" she said. "Look at Brecken."

Brecken stood up from the other end of the table, grabbed Luther by the back of the neck, and whispered something in his ear. The laughter at the table dwindled. Luther scowled, but his face turned pale beneath his display of bravado. He surrendered the locket to Camille, shoved away from Brecken, and stormed out of the dining room.

Camille grasped the locket in her hand and took a step back, her eyes wide. Brecken sat down and resumed his previous conversation as if nothing had happened.

"Wow," I whispered, lowering myself back to the bench. "He's good."

"Really good," Michelle agreed.

Camille left the Guardians and walked over to our table.

"Merry meet Bianca, Michelle, Nicolas. How are you?" Camille asked, her eyes distant.

"Everything all right, Camille?" Michelle asked.

"Just grand!" she cried with her usual gusto, but her eyes snaked over to Brecken, who still ignored her.

"Are you angry with Brecken?" I asked.

Her lips pressed together. "We aren't on speaking terms right now. We had a little argument over algebra the other day."

"Oh," Michelle said quietly. I silently offered Camille my roll. She reached right past it to grab my brownie and then bit into it with an angry vengeance.

A shout from the kitchen forced Nicolas to his feet.

"I got ta get back," he said with a sigh. "Thanks for eating with me, Miss Michelle, Miss Bianca, Miss Camille." He nodded to each of us, gathered up his plate, and disappeared. Michelle stared at his broad back with a pathetic little sigh. Like Camille, she drifted off into a different place with a glazed look on her face. I turned back to my food, burying myself in thoughts of forest dragons, war, and the Council meeting to come the next day.

Reliable Stella

"May I speak with you a moment, Bianca?"

Merrick and I looked up from our silent walk the next morning in surprise. Stella stood on the garden path in front of us, a long burgundy dress with a dark lace overlay sweeping the top of the stones at her feet. The bright sun shone on her graying auburn hair, making her look very lovely.

"Yes, Miss Stella," I said, slowing to a stop in front of her. Merrick cast me a questioning look, nodded once to Stella, and continued on his way. She waited until he was out of earshot to continue.

"I don't have much time," she said, folding her petite hands in front of her. "The Council meeting to vote over the decision regarding your father is about to start."

"Yes," I said, my eyes flickering up to the windows in the West Wing. "I know. I've been track—"

"I came to see if you'd ever been to the basement of the West Wing," she said quickly, cutting me off.

"Yes, I've been in there a few times," I drawled, startled by her question.

"There's a little office in the lower floors that Mildred and I used to work in long ago. I think there is something that you may be interested in there, if you can keep a secret."

A small square of paper appeared in her right hand.

"Yes," I said, clearing my throat. "I can keep a secret."

She smiled. "Wonderful. Then this is all you need. If I were you, I'd head there now."

I took the proffered slip of paper. Her eyes sparkled with a mischievous little edge.

"Be careful," she said. "And keep your ears open."

With that, Stella disappeared, leaving me staring at the little piece of paper in disbelief.

The paper—which had turned out to be a set of directions—led me to the lowest floors of the West Wing, an area dedicated to storage and offices for the lowliest assistants. No other witch haunted the quiet halls with me, leaving me to run through the silence with the wraiths of witches who once lived there. An unknown drive pushed me, hurrying me along. Whatever this would lead me to, I had a feeling it involved the Council meeting for Papa.

Hurry, hurry, the quiet hallway seemed to say. *The Council is starting.*

"Right here," I whispered, stopping at an old door on my left. The ornate carvings around the edges held pockets of dust. The tarnished silver handle and deep groove lines in the wood indicated it hadn't been visited in some time.

The door swung into the room with a groan. Dust coated the floor and walls, tickling the inside of my nose. Cobwebs swathed the corners, swooping about the bookshelves and tapestries. A dusty light settled through a couple of high windows, muted from grime on the inside of the panes. A feeling of forgottenness pervaded the room, as if the owner had just stood up and walked away without looking back. Feathers, half-opened scrolls, and old books littered the desk.

Elaborate tapestries hung from the stone walls between each bookcase. I couldn't make out the pictures through the coating of powder, but had a feeling they were rare. The aged, bitter smell of rotting parchment overwhelmed me. If Camille had an office, I imagined it would look just like this.

I looked down at the note.

Beneath the big tapestry. Declan should open it.

I ran my fingertips along the stone wall to find a seam and a subtle rift in the rocks caught my eye. No doubt it hid a secret passage. A castle this old likely held her own secrets. I muttered an opening incantation in the Declan language under my breath, letting my fingers trail along the cool stone facade. A squat doorway soon gave way with a great groan, spilling light into a corridor that surely hadn't seen it in years.

"Oh," I whispered, raising an eyebrow. "Interesting."

The palpable darkness felt like a room filled with only black curtains. I held my hands out to feel my way. A dirty wall met my fingertips, damp and cold. The air smelled like rot and mildew. My toe hit the bottom of a stair, and within moments, I was slowly climbing upwards in a tight spiral, the walls brushing my shoulder on each side. I counted each step as I went.

The disjointed, steep stairs led up and up. The decaying wood felt weak in some places. With a whispered light spell, a bright ball of light formed on my fingertips and drifted above me, illuminating the path. I immediately regretted it. The close stairway felt more claustrophobic and frightening once I saw its narrow confinement. A long white object against the wall caught my eye, and I forced back a scream when I realized it was a bone.

"Cease," I whispered, and the light evaporated into a puff of smoke. I pressed onward, hoping I didn't encounter the rest of the skeleton along the way.

"Where do I stop?" I whispered, reassured by the sound of my own voice. "Surely there must be—"

A single ray of light distracted me. I continued up the stairs until I came eye-to-eye with the small beam. It was exactly my height and about the width of a marble. I peered through to find it looked into a room I didn't immediately recognize. I saw a wall, and heard a couple of voices. Then another beam of light caught my eye to my right, and I realized that there were several smaller holes in various spots in the stone.

Keep your ears open, Stella had said.

I pressed my eye back to the cool wall, looking at a blood red tapestry adorned with twisting black designs. A familiar face moved by. Stella. My gasp echoed off the narrow walls.

The Council Room.

A bell broke through the low chatter. "Witches welcome," Jansson said. "Let us join in an invocation for wisdom before we begin the Council meeting."

A quiet chant reached through the cold stones. Positioned just right, I could hear every word the Council Members would say. A little thrill ran through me. Reliable Stella!

Once they finished the invocation, the meeting began.

"The first issue for discussion," Jansson's voice rang through the air, "will be presented by the Chatham City Coven Leader. Clive, the floor is yours."

A slight shuffle of movement came next. I could see half of Stella's face and half of a Council Member I didn't know through the peephole. Clive made short work of getting right to the point.

"I won't take up much of your time, esteemed Council Members," he said. "I would like to submit a petition on behalf of the witches of Chatham City. They, along with myself, ask that you consider removing Derek Black from his position as Head of Protectors. It's quite simple," he concluded, "with war on the horizon, can you trust him?"

The question sat in the air for some time before a low murmur ran through the room. The other Council Member in my line of vision stood, a silver mug with steaming contents in hand, and disappeared out of sight.

"He's lied to us and the High Priestess these seventeen years," one Council Member called. "Clive is right. Can't be ignored. He's the only witch to have ever, in centuries of ruling, broken one of our traditions."

My stomach turned. In an effort to spare the High Priestess backlash, Papa had told the Council that she had not known of Mama or me. Although she had severely chastised him for not allowing her to take responsibility, she saw the necessity of his plan. If the Network knew she had any part of it, they'd demand she step down as well. Now Papa bore the whole burden himself.

"Can't be trusted."

"And who else would you put in his position? He may have lied, but Derek's the best Head of Protectors we've ever had!"

The arguments continued for several minutes.

"Let us not forget," Stella's voice called above the rest in a cool tone, "that Derek served us more than faithfully those seventeen years. I call upon any of you to recount a single incident for which he should be rebuffed."

Silence descended. My heart swelled in gratitude and hope.

"That is a subjective observation," Clive pointed out. "There could be many such incidents that he's lied about, just like any Head of Protector may have also done in the past."

Another chorus of agreements, but this time with less gusto.

"By that argument we could also say that he is not the first witch to have broken tradition," Stella said. "He may have just been the first witch that was caught."

The room was silent now.

"We are talking about honorably maintaining a family instead of casting them to the dogs," Stella said. "It's hardly subterfuge. Besides that, we have the obvious question of whom you would place in his position. There is no one ready to command the secretive side of war."

"You insult our Protectors," Patrice, the Council Member for the wealthy Ashleigh Coven, said in her nasally voice. "Any of them are skilled and capable witches. It's a question of trust, Stella."

"The Protectors will not replace Derek unless he stands down," Stella said.

"How could you know that?" another voice called. It was a female, with a thin, thready tone.

"Because I asked them."

Another murmur passed through the group. How I wished I could see their faces! Stella's chair scraped against the ground as she stood. I could barely make out her face. I imagined Clive at the receiving end of her intimidating glare.

"I oppose all of it," Stella said in a voice of solid granite. "You have no grounds."

The back-and-forth banter continued for the next fifteen minutes. Some paced, splitting off into side discussions. Others sat, saying nothing. I could only catch a snippet here and there before straining to distinguish words gave me a headache.

"I think he should be exiled. Both Derek and that wild daughter of his."

"Indeed. Out of control."

"Exile seems like a harsh punishment after all his service. He has kept us safe these seventeen years."

"Exile. Send him to the North."

Jansson broke through the melee in a commanding voice that quieted all the rest.

"Be calm, Council," he said. "We cannot stand divided. We must make a decision now."

Slinking like injured cats when they crossed in front of the peephole, the Council Members returned to their seats. My heart hammered in my chest.

"We will vote once. The final tally goes to the High Priestess for her ultimate decision. Those in favor of keeping Derek Black as the current Head of Protectors, raise your hand."

I strained to see, though I knew it was pointless. Stella's hand rose tall and proud, but I entertained little hope that enough of the other Council Members would vote with her. I didn't know my hands shook until I put them to my flushed face.

"Those against."

A long silence fell.

"There you have it," Jansson said in a quiet voice. "The Council votes to remove Derek Black from his position as Head of Protectors six to four. Let us move onto the next point of business; our suggestions for nomination of the new High Priest."

His low drone continued in the background. I pulled away from the peephole, disgusted. It was just a tradition. But they couldn't let go of it, and they never would. I recalled Merrick's words from a previous lesson.

Tradition isn't always a good thing. Keep that in mind.

I was beginning to understand exactly what that meant. With a frustrated sigh, I turned away to tell Papa their decision, my heart heavy.

An Ideal Solution

"You can't be surprised by the Council's ruling," Merrick said as we walked back to Chatham Castle. He'd allowed me to sleep in that morning before our lesson, so the day was already bright with an angelic blue sky. I carried both buckets of rocks at my sides while he strolled next to me, unburdened and enjoying it. "You already knew they were out to get him."

"That doesn't make me like it," I muttered, grunting when my forearm wrenched and threatened to cramp in pain. Merrick agreed with a lift of his eyebrows. A quiet shuffle off to the left, tucked in the back of the gardens, caught my attention. I stopped and set the rocks down.

"Did you hear that?" I asked.

"A bird," he said dismissively. "I've got to get going. I'll see you tomorrow."

Merrick disappeared with the soft sound of transportation. I abandoned the buckets and crept silently toward the sound. Last time I'd seen something out of place here, a dragon popped up. A low murmur of voices met my ears the closer I approached the hedged garden. I knew it well. Inside was a fountain with angels spouting water from their mouths. Several trellises lined with blooming white flowers formed a ceiling above it, filtering little snippets of light through their thick petals. It was rumored to be the High Priestess's favorite garden.

"I don't like it," Ambassador Marten said in a firm tone. "I don't like it at all, Mildred."

I slipped down onto my stomach and peered just around the corner. Marten and the High Priestess stood in the back of the small garden, their hands clasped and bodies pressed close together. The High Priestess's face angled away from me with a sad, rueful expression.

"It's not an ideal solution, Marten, but at least it's something," she said, but her voice didn't have its usual sting.

"I don't agree," Marten replied. "You can figure out another way to solve it. This isn't the only way. You've encountered more difficult situations before and come up with better answers."

A bit of her spine returned. She stiffened and shot him a haughty look. "I think I know what I'm doing. After all these years together, don't you trust me?"

"I've always trusted you."

"I'm the one to make the final decision in the end," she said with impressive resolution. "This is how I plan to move forward. It's the best thing for the whole Network."

"And Stella?" Marten asked in a vehement voice. "What did she think?"

"She thinks I'm right. She doesn't like it, but she sees the wisdom in it. It won't happen any other way. I think you know that too; you need to come to terms with it."

His shoulders slumped as he capitulated to her words. "Yes. You're right. I can't stop you. But I just . . . I want more time to try to make this work. I don't want to lose you, Mildred."

"Have you ever really had me, Marten?"

He reached up and touched her face with the tips of his fingers. She closed her eyes and leaned into his palm. Their voices fell too low to distinguish, but I wouldn't have wanted to hear what they said even if I could. My heart stalled in my throat as I crept away, eyes wide.

The High Priestess had a lover.

That was the only way to describe the scene: the look in their eyes, the quiet way they touched each other. The intimate scene I'd just witnessed rocked everything I thought I'd known about the High Priestess.

Should I tell anyone? No, that would violate her privacy. I respected her too much to do that. How long had they been together? What did it mean? Like the Head of Protectors and Head of Guardians, the High Priestess could not have a spouse or a family. But clearly she'd maintained a lover all these years.

I toiled with my questions on my way back to Chatham Castle, still reeling. Would *Mildred's Resistance* have details about the High Priestess's secret lover? No, that would be madness. She'd never allow something like that printed. If I told anyone else what I'd seen, it could turn the Council against the High Priestess in such a way that could threaten her life. Not even Leda could know.

I shook my head, hoping to clear my thoughts. No wonder the High Priestess took pity on my father all those years ago, letting him take position in defiance of tradition. She must have known what it felt like, loving without being able to live it.

No, I decided. This secret would remain my own, like the others I held in my heart.

Betrayer

"Please, Camille?"

"Bianca, you're mad!" Camille said, peering into a little mirror hanging on the wall as she put the finishing touches on an elegant braid in her hair. "I'm not taking you into Chatham City today. Except to run with Merrick, you're not supposed to leave the castle grounds and you know it."

"I just need to get away for awhile," I said, sitting on the edge of the divan. I'd fallen into a desperate melancholy the past two days, ever since the Council's vote. Waiting on the High Priestess's final decision, and keeping her secret tryst to myself, made me irritable and snappish. Even Merrick had noticed my distraction during our practice that morning and stopped our session early. I rubbed the bruise on my forearm from when I hadn't anticipated an obvious lunge. "Please?"

"What if we get caught?"

"Then I'd get in trouble, not you."

She rolled her eyes. "That's what I'm worried about! You don't need any more trouble. Oh, hullo!" she sang under her breath, peeking out the window to the lower bailey. "Brecken just took his shirt off. I can see his muscles from here. Goodness! He's so handsome."

She gave a happy little shudder, as if she'd just taken a bite from a delicious pastry, and sank back onto the window seat to pull her slippers on. She wore a new dress from Henrietta. Pale pink flowers decorated a white fabric with a scooped neckline and rounded sleeves. It was feminine and classy and looked perfect on Camille's tan skin.

"Please?"

"No," she said with a firm shake of her head. "You can't come."

"Fine," I concluded with determination. "I'll just transport ahead of you. I'll stop by Miss Holly's Candy Shop first and buy all of the vanilla-flavored caramels before you even get there. Then I'll give them to the gypsies."

Camille shot me a glare. "You wouldn't," she whispered, her eyes narrowing. I gave her a cheeky smile.

"Oh yes I would and you know it! Merry part!" I called.

"Bianca!"

"I'm already on my way. In fact, it will probably be easier to sneak out without you." I started walking down the turret stairs.

"Wait!" she said after I'd made it down ten steps, scrambling to catch up. "Fine, I'll let you come with Michelle and me. But you aren't allowed to talk to anyone!"

Chatham City surged around us an hour later, teeming with witches, dogs, and a bitter smell that made my stomach turn. Tall brick chimneys huffed black soot into the air. A couple of scrollboys stood on the corners of the street, arms flailing.

"High Priest announced tomorrow," their squeaky voices called in melodic tones, waving newsscrolls at anyone passing. "The Council votes 6-4 against Derek as Head of Protectors. High Priestess to announce Head of Protectors! Cast your bet on the new High Priest and Head of Protectors at Owen's Pub!"

"This is pandemonium," Camille hissed, dodging a witch walking unusually fast and nearly falling into the gutter for her trouble. "I don't know why I agreed to let you come! What if someone from the castle sees you out here? Everyone knows that you're restricted to the castle grounds. There was an article about it in the *Chatterer*."

"No one is going to recognize me. They can't even see my face when I'm wearing my hood."

"Fine, be reckless. In the meantime, I need to find a ribbon for the ball," Camille said, gazing around. "Do you see any shops? Let's go to

Miss Holly's last. Then I can look forward to it. Anticipation always makes the caramels taste better."

Finding a ribbon was the last thing on my mind, but I didn't say so. I followed along behind without any trouble. When ten minutes had passed and no one jumped out of the crowds to point me out, Camille seemed to relax.

"Oh!" she cried several minutes later in front of a shop. "That's just the one. Look, Michelle. That one would match your dress! Henrietta will be so happy."

Camille hurried Michelle inside, leaving me out on the street. The castle was prison enough for me; I couldn't fathom finding anything in the stuffy, over-perfumed shops that I'd want more than a brownie from the gypsies.

But the anxiety in my chest tripled now that I stood alone in the heart of Chatham City. Perhaps coming here hadn't been the best idea. *Chocolate,* I decided, ignoring the tense magic. *Chocolate will make this terrible mood all better.*

The gypsy markets began one street over, and I peered at them through the whip of carriages and horses legs speeding past. No one would know me there, and if anyone recognized my face, they wouldn't care. A small group of gypsies gathered in a circle, laughing and dancing with a careless disregard I envied. When I turned and gazed in the shop window, Camille had her back to me, ten different ribbons already in her hands.

Knowing I'd have time to run over, buy a treat, and come back before Camille finished, I dodged across the street. A gang of young witches nearly ran me over as they kicked a ball down the road, oblivious to the heavy traffic.

Like my friend Jackie from Miss Mabel's, the gypsies had skin the color of caramel and hot chocolate. Their bright yellow, red, and orange silk robes were a far cry from the earthy greens and blacks I normally wore. Most of them made their living as Diviners or merchants, selling lustrous beads, gowns, and headdresses on the streets of Chatham. Their wares were expensive and garish, but strangely fascinating.

I wandered amongst the hastily constructed stalls, running my fingers over the jewelry and scarves. Some of the beads were as big as broaches. A Diviner girl with a green dot just above her right eyebrow smiled at me, making her tattoo crinkle.

"Ya like?" she asked, pointing to a broad, metallic necklace piece of gold laced with multi-colored gems. Her husky Chatham accent sounded off-kilter in comparison with the usual heavy tones of the gypsies.

"It's very pretty," I said. Her gaze grew troubled when we made eye contact. She took a step back, suddenly wary.

"Go," she cried, jerking her head. "Leave!"

I obeyed but cast an uneasy glance over my shoulder as I went. Her accusing eyes followed me until I was out of sight down the way. A tent made from layers of bright green fabric caught my attention. It smelled like fresh cotton. When I peered inside, a hand shot out from between the folds of silk and grabbed my wrist. I gasped but didn't pull away.

The wrinkled face of an old woman came into view. Her deep brown eyes appeared nearly as black as her thick hair. Wires of white ran through the tight, small curls. A flowing robe of lavender and mustard silk, stained with old sweat marks, clung to her ancient body. Candles with emerald flames burned inside the tent. My breath caught.

A Diviner.

"I pull your cards," she said, with the clacking accent and incomplete sentences of the gypsy dialect. "Stay."

"No." I pulled my arm from her soft hand. My last experience with Divination at the hands of my friend Jackie, a would-be Diviner at Miss Mabel's, had left a bad taste in my mouth. If Jackie, with her amateur skill, could detect the darkness in my heart, what would stop an experienced Diviner? Perhaps this old lady already had, just like the gypsy that demanded I leave.

"Oooh," she crooned, her lips forming a small o. "Fear. Anxiety."

She reached up and tapped a finger over my heart. It seemed to ping inside me like a door knocker, stirring the magic. I swallowed.

"Yes," I said. "I don't want to know my paths."

The Diviner frowned.

"No?"

"No."

Her eyebrows crashed together.

"Blind!" she whispered, but it was a sharp accusation. "You choose blindness. Fool. Fools choose blindness."

I shifted back a step.

"I'm no fool," I insisted, but it came out with less conviction than I'd hoped.

"Ya look at sky," she said, motioning up with her finger and taking a deep breath through her nose, "when snakes at ya feet. Ya see? The cards say."

My stomach lurched when I saw three cards displayed in her hand, taken from the top of the deck. The raven, the High Priestess, and the fool. Three of the cards Jackie had drawn over five months ago.

Death, mourning, and denial.

The air in the tent suddenly seemed hot and overbearing. The powers woke inside me with a roar of fear, making my fingertips tingle. The green flames of the candles flared with a gust of violent wind. The Diviner stood up, terror in her eyes that battled my own.

"Betrayer! The power in ya heart!" she screeched. "Go from us, betrayer! Go!"

Her squawks rang out through the air and I stumbled back, nearly upsetting the entire tent.

"Nan!" a voice called out. A girl rushed into the tent. "Nan, calm down."

The horrified cries ceased and the candles died down. The girl spoke in the gypsy language, soothing her grandmother with the warm cadence of their words. Forgotten, I turned to go when I caught a glimpse of the girl's face.

"Jackie?" I whispered.

She whirled around. Her eyes widened in disbelief when she took me in.

"Bianca?"

Nan muttered something under her breath, reaching for one of the many jeweled necklaces she wore and waving it in the air toward me. Her accusations burned in my heart.

Betrayer! Power in ya heart!

"Meet me outside," Jackie said, reaching for a squat little pot of tea that sat on a small table in the middle of the tent. "I need to calm her down."

All too glad to escape the suffocating smell and odd darkness of the tent, I slipped between the flaps. Chatham City continued on outside, no one any wiser for Nan's hysterical outburst.

My hands trembled as I waited. Nan had pulled the same cards as Jackie. Surely that meant something. I wasn't sure how long I studied the soot-stained Chatham City skyline before Jackie ducked out of the tent. She looked at me with concerned, reserved eyes.

"Are you all right?"

"Yes," I said, somewhat shakily. "I don't know what—"

"Nan's a bit sensitive lately," Jackie said, fidgeting. "It's the issues in the West. She can feel the building evil."

"I didn't know you were a gypsy," I said in a desperate attempt to change the conversation. *Building evil. Issues in the West.* Did I have some part of that evil? Is that why Nan called me a betrayer? I hadn't realized how strong the magic burned inside me until then. It ran through me in long currents, wanting free.

Jackie cast a rueful eye along the tents on the street and the half-dressed children running around in bright turquoise and pink pants.

"I'm not ashamed of being a gypsy," she said. "But it has never helped me when people knew my heritage, so I don't talk about it. Many witches judge us to be heretics stuck in the ways of our predecessors. Or they say we don't want education and progress just because we stay close to the land and sleep under the stars. That's not the truth. I want to help destroy that belief."

"That's why you enrolled at Miss Mabel's," I said. Nan started singing something in the background in throaty, melodic tones. Jackie nodded.

"I want to get us representation in the Network."

All of our time together at school, what little we'd had, had been lighthearted and fun. But here in Chatham City, standing with her people, I saw a different side of Jackie. She was strong, authoritative. I felt a little awed by her.

"I've been keeping track of what's happened with your father," she said. "We hear the rallies all the time. Clive has a good deal of Chatham City angry over it."

Yes, the rabid dogs.

"I'm sorry that everyone is reacting that way," she continued when I said nothing. "It's amazing the power tradition holds, isn't it?"

"Or frightening," I quipped with no small amount of bitterness. Jackie took that in with a long, solemn gaze.

"Listen, Bianca, I can't speak for all my people, not yet anyway. But I can say that we don't agree with Clive in removing your father. Not a single gypsy signed that petition, and not just because the gypsies don't hold by the same traditions the rest of the Central Network clings to. While Clive went around garnering signatures, the Factios robbed most of the gypsy camps and killed two of our Elders."

My eyebrows lifted.

"What?"

Jackie's formidable expression spoke to a maturity far beyond our age.

"It's true. We sent our last Elder to Clive with a plea for help against the criminals, but he ignored him and sent him away." She gazed over the bright tents and down the alley. "If violence like this continues, if Clive doesn't stop the Factios before they get out of control, Chatham City will soon be divided. The gypsies will side with whatever leader offers the most protection. That's why Nan is so sensitive right now."

"I'm sorry, Jackie," I said, not knowing what else to say.

"It's not your fault. It's just part of life, isn't it?" Her full lips split into her familiar pearly white smile, one that extinguished the sudden gloom upon the conversation. "You look terrible, Bianca."

I couldn't help but grin. It was a relief to move back toward the familiar side of our friendship, away from the darkness.

"I know."

"Come visit again," she said. "Just avoid Nan, okay?"

I managed a half-hearted smile. "Agreed," I said and left, grateful to put the gypsies and their bright swatches of color at my back.

I'm Sorry.

I waited outside the High Priestess's office the next morning with my heart in my throat.

My wrists hurt from an intentionally early lesson with Merrick. He started it before light, telling me that working off the anxiety over the High Priestess's decision would help control the magic when I heard the outcome. A greenish bruise popped on my right forearm from a wayward whack with the stick. I'd been distracted through the whole lesson. Merrick finally made me run up and down the lower bailey stairs until I could barely move. The muscles in my legs still throbbed.

Tiberius stood next to me, staring at the floor. Neither of us spoke but I took comfort from his burly body anyway. Donald sat outside at his little desk, murmuring to himself. Feathers flew around him like independent little birds, scrawling notes on scrolls, books, and pieces of parchment alike.

After an eternal wait, the door opened. I straightened, my stomach churning in fear. Papa came out first, his face pale but stoic. The way his lips pressed together and his eyes seemed to look past me told me all I needed to know.

I stepped forward. The coiled magic released and flooded my chest with a dragon-like roar. He shook his head to indicate I shouldn't speak, put a hand on my shoulder, and nodded to Tiberius.

"When are they removing you?" Tiberius asked, his tone as hard as flint.

"Today," Papa responded. The sadness in his eyes hit my heart. I had to look away, to take a deep breath and gain control of the inner dragon. The High Priestess appeared behind Papa, standing in the doorway.

"I'm sorry, Derek," she said in her business-like tone. There was no inflection and no apology behind it. "You may not agree with me, but trust me when I say that this is for the best."

He gave a curt nod.

"Come on, B," he said, turning me around to leave. "Let's go."

I looked over my shoulder and locked eyes with the High Priestess. She watched me go, an inscrutable expression on her face.

That afternoon, the most solemn assembly of witches I'd ever seen gathered for the announcement of the new High Priest.

Bodies filled the high and low baileys, stretching past the wall, all the way down Chatham Road. Witches lounged in the trees surrounding Chatham Castle, their bodies infusing the branches with specks of white and brown. Maids opened the windows so that those working inside could hear. Not a single witch within a day's travel would miss this announcement, and some came from even further. Those who could transport came at irregular intervals, landing outside the Wall to control who stood in the baileys. Protectors scattered throughout the crowd in disguise. I thought I recognized Merrick amongst them, although I couldn't be sure. Guardians stood sentry at every entrance.

At one minute to three, the High Priestess stood at the edge of her office balcony, facing the whole bailey. Papa, Tiberius, Marten, Zane, Stella, and I stood just behind the High Priestess. Stella's unwavering demeanor gave me strength. Papa stood back with Zane, talking quietly in the shadows they so loved.

The High Priestess spoke the moment the clock finished striking the hour.

"Today," she called, "I will announce several pieces of business. First, I release Derek Black as Head of Protectors."

My heart stalled in my chest. Although I knew it was coming, it still hurt. Clive wasn't within sight, arranged that way on purpose, no doubt. Papa lifted his chin, drawing in a deep breath. I tried to rally my strength, but found I could not. The building powers prevented it.

"I institute Zane Thomas in his place."

Zane stepped forward to stand next to the High Priestess. The crowd didn't move. I wasn't even sure they were breathing. The magic whipped through me with all the power of a gale. Stella put a stabilizing hand on my shoulder, linking me back to reality. A wave of calm rested on me, but even that couldn't subdue the magic for long.

"It's okay, Bianca," she said in a quiet murmur.

"The next High Priest," the High Priestess said without preamble, "will be Derek Black."

I wasn't sure when it happened, when the moment of hearing turned to understanding, when my heart comprehended what my head couldn't. I knew it when my blood turned to ice and my knees buckled beneath me and I reached out, holding to the wall for purchase. I knew it because cries of excitement and alarm rang out around me, but none so great as my own.

No matter what ruckus they made, no matter how loudly the Guardians and congregated witches cheered or booed, nothing could compete with the seductive voice in my head.

Your task is to kill the next High Priest.

The next thing I knew I was sprinting down the corridor, past the arched windows that allowed fresh spring air to pour inside. Alone in the long halls, I ran through Chatham, my feet echoing on the floors. The magic threatened, so I ran faster.

No, no, no, no.

The blackness that meant I was transporting came, and I fell forward with a clear image of Miss Mabel's bungalow in my mind. The wind pressed against me, moving stronger than I'd ever felt. The force was so heady that for a moment I imagined it would press my eyes into the back of my head.

Miss Mabel's voice was the next thing I heard.

"I've been expecting you, Bianca darling."

Reckless

I tumbled head over heels onto the red cave floor, slamming into it with a heavy thud. The moment I landed I sprang to my feet.

"What have you done?" I demanded. Miss Mabel lounged back on a chaise, a bored look on her face. A wooden chest stood on the floor next to her with a small, silky reticule waiting on top.

"Merry meet. How are you?"

"I won't do it!" I cried, storming toward her. "I won't kill my father for you!"

She tilted her head back and laughed. "Oh, Bianca. You're too much fun, really."

"You knew, didn't you? You knew all along who the High Priestess was going to pick."

Miss Mabel sighed and sat up.

"It's Mildred's own fault. She so bloody predictable, Bianca. Who else would she choose? Don't tell me you thought it was Marten. Or Jansson? What a bore."

The cloying, teasing tone of her voice almost broke me.

"I won't do it!" I yelled in desperation. "I won't kill my father!"

Miss Mabel stood up.

"You signed the contract."

"Then I'll die!"

Miss Mabel smiled and made a tutting sound with her teeth.

"A lovely story it will make, don't you think? You kill your father and spare me the annoyance of having to do it. Or, since you insist on being so noble, you die on your seventeenth birthday and your father, so upset, wallows in misery and can't save the Network. In the meantime, I kill Mildred and take control. A happy ending for everyone! Do you understand your purpose now in all of this?"

"You'll never beat the High Priestess," I snarled. "She's stronger than you and you know it."

Miss Mabel's eyes blazed with a sudden fire.

"There may be someone in the Central Network stronger than me, but it certainly isn't Mildred, you daft idiot," she cried. I flew back with a violent slam, hitting the wall with a grunt of pain.

Her words poured through me like poison, shriveling what little life I still had inside. Gone, all of it was gone. Grandmother dead, Mama killed. Now I would die, which would destroy Papa. Would he be able to cope with my death and function as High Priest at the same time? If he couldn't then the Central Network, already bruised, would fall to pieces.

"Why are you doing this?" I demanded, shoving away from the wall, loathing my guttural desperation. "Why?"

Her eyes flashed again.

"Because I can."

"That's a lie!" I cried. "You're doing this for a reason. You have to be!"

"Oh Bianca," she drawled, rising to her feet with the smooth grace of a specter. "Aren't you tired of unqualified witches holding power? Mildred had her day. Now it's my turn."

"It's about May, isn't it?" I asked, pressing into the anger with wild abandon. "You never lived up to her expectations, did you? You weren't good enough! So you left her at the castle to die alone while you celebrated. You didn't even see her before they killed her for treason."

Miss Mabel moved so fast all I saw was a flash of white before my back slammed into the wall behind me again. Her hand wrapped around my neck and anchored me there, my feet dangling an inch from the floor. Despite her fury, her eyes remained calm and cold.

"Don't meddle in things you don't know anything about," she whispered. "May had the power to crush your soul. She deserved to die alone. She earned her traitor's death."

She released me with a flick of her wrist. I crumbled to the floor, gasping for air. All the emotions in my heart boiled, building up inside me, threatening to explode. Maybe I'd shatter from the inside out. All this power would vent through self-destruction, and the only thing that would break at the end of the day was me. *Yes,* I wanted to beg. *Let me break. Let this agony end.*

"Was it because Angelina didn't want you?" I asked, coughing. "Was it jealousy that May had power, but you didn't?"

Miss Mabel's nostrils flared into a sneer.

"You know nothing, Bianca."

"I know you hated May," I said, struggling to my feet. My inner dragon roared, pushing me to goad her more. "Probably because you were so much like her but still not good enough."

An explosion threw me backwards. I collided with the wall again, only this time several books fell on top of me—one dropped onto my nose and another hit the side of my head, slicing open my ear. Once the barrage of books stopped, I extricated myself and stood up, dizzy. A warm trickle of blood ran down my upper lip.

"Had enough?" she snarled. "You've turned reckless, Bianca, and it's made you stupid. All that power doesn't mean a damn thing if you don't use it properly."

Reckless.

"I'll never kill my father for you," I said, wiping the blood off my face. "I'll never kill anyone for you."

Miss Mabel rolled her eyes.

"Then die on your birthday. I certainly don't care. I have my own plans in motion, and they don't hinge on you."

My fingertips curled into my palm, stinging and painful. What would happen if I let myself go? Would I try to destroy her?

Would it destroy me instead?

"Keep fighting that power, Bianca. It certainly is growing, isn't it? I can't wait to see you when I get back. No doubt you'll really be out of control by then."

She picked up the little reticule on her box with a sly smile. I looked around the room, realizing that several of her belongings were missing from their places. Empty spots littered each bookshelf in an unusual disarray.

"Back?" I asked, nearly choking over the word.

"I have business to take care of elsewhere for the next couple of months. I will come visit you in the Central Network on your birthday, of course, to see the fulfillment of our contract. Whether that means your father's death or your own, I really don't care. I'm sure it'll be fun either way."

The cold tile ripped away from my feet, and my surroundings turned to inky blackness as she transported me away. I fell into it, grateful to leave, and let the magic go.

The emerald canopy, so tall above me, seemed to wave and wink. *Wake up, Bianca,* it sang. *We've missed you.*

I blinked three times, trying to recollect myself. Like at the rally in Chatham City, my memory of what had happened after the power took over had dissipated into snippets.

Miss Mabel's face. *Darkness.* Falling on the ground in Letum Wood. *Darkness.* Trees flashing past as I ran. *Darkness.* My chest aching. *Darkness.* A pair of yellow eyes, a loud snort. *Darkness.* Tripping, skidding across the dirt. *Darkness.*

My heart clenched.

Yellow eyes.

My head pulsed when I sat up, and I had to squint through the dull thuds. Pain shot through my right leg. I looked down, my vision blurry, to see the big toenail on my right foot dangling off to the side, with only a red mush in its rightful place. Scratches raked my legs, and I reached up to feel blood on my face. Clearly I had started running, consumed by the power, and now had no idea where I had landed. I shot to my feet, my body still trembling.

"Where are you, dragon?" I called out, circling.

A few birds took flight from the nearest tree, scattering into the high branches. The eerie silence that followed broke with the snap of a twig. I whirled around but saw nothing more than mossy tree trunks. The darkness of the forest meant that hours had passed. Papa must be half-mad with worry. Giving in with a sigh and a whisper, I closed my eyes and initiated the transportation spell.

The blackness pressed on me for only a second, maybe two, before releasing, dumping me onto the floor of the apartment with a thump.

"Jikes!" I cried, grabbing my leg when the naked toe slammed into the floor. A nauseous roll grew in my stomach, threatening to spill as the white-hot pain danced up and down my bones. I rolled onto my side, my eyes screwed shut. "I'm going to be sick," I muttered.

"What happened?" Papa's concerned voice broke through the haze of pain. I opened my right eye and then my left to find him standing above me. "Are you all right?"

I dropped my head back to the floor.

"I'm fine," I lied. "Just ripped my toenail off on a run."

He stood and moved to a small cupboard near the window. The sound of glass vials clinking together followed.

"This is going to sting," he said quietly, and seconds later fire ravaged my foot. I ground my teeth together to keep from crying out and waited for the pain to subside. After several minutes it calmed enough that I could take a deep breath.

"What happened?" he asked.

"I went for a run in Letum Wood and tripped over something," I whispered, closing my eyes. I couldn't bear to lie to his face again. A stab of guilt pierced me. He deserved so much better than this.

I've lied to you. I ran away because I'm supposed to kill you and I don't deserve your trust.

"Can you stand?"

"Yes."

He helped me to my feet. The potion had already taken effect and numbed the top of my toe.

"Let's talk out here," he said, motioning to the balcony. I started forward, hobbling on a sore leg, my hip aching. The breeze brought me back into reality. We stayed in the quiet silence for minutes, studying the skyline. Witches milled around the high bailey and Chatham Road.

"There's no celebration," I observed.

Papa chuckled, but it was filled with something heavy.

"No. No one wanted to celebrate the High Priestess's choice. She's meeting with the Council right now. Several Members are threatening to walk away."

"Good," I muttered. "Let them go."

Papa didn't say anything in response.

"I'm sorry," I finally said, swallowing. "I shouldn't have run out like that. I should have been there to support you. It just . . . it took me by surprise."

"You weren't the only one," he muttered, his face tight with anxiety. An impossible thought occurred to me. Was Papa frightened?

"When did she ask you to do it?"

"This morning when she told me that she was going to remove me from the Protectors," he answered. Not knowing what to say, I fell silent. I had so many questions I didn't know where to start.

"I'm sorry I didn't tell you," he continued. "I should have at least warned you so it wouldn't be such a shock, but she forbade it. Understandably so. There are a few witches who don't want me in power."

There were many. Would Clive still fight Papa now? What would all those angry people in Chatham City have to say about it?

"When will she empower you?"

The Empowerment ceremony would confer the power of the High Priest on Papa, along with the charm, a bracelet, that signified the title.

"Just before the Network ball, on your birthday. There's a lot to do before then, things to get straightened out. The High Priestess wanted to give the Central Network time to adjust before I took the official oath."

"Wise," I murmured. "Especially with so many displeased Council Members."

"Yes. Understandably so."

"Are you scared?"

"It's a big responsibility," he said, shooting me a sideways glance. "The High Priestess isn't an easy person to turn down."

I'll do it for you, I wanted to say. *I'll tell her no. Then we can leave, just disappear. Maybe we'll go north, into the mountains, where no one can find us. Exile wouldn't be so bad, right?*

The dream faded. I wouldn't live long enough to enjoy that life anyway. Papa would take the role of High Priest and it would be his life. I would die protecting him from myself.

"But now that there's a war . . ." I trailed off.

"I would have been even more involved in the war if I was still Head of Protectors."

"Will you be happy doing this?" I asked, looking up at him. If it brought him some degree of joy, of progression, I could bear dying in three months. He let out a half-smile and tucked a stray piece of hair behind my ears.

"If you're with me, B, I'd be happy living in a shack, on the beach, exiled from the Central Network."

I snorted.

"Living on the beach hardly sounds like a punishment."

"Exactly," he said, winking.

"You're going to be working all the time as a High Priest, even more than you do as a Protector. Will I ever see you?"

I felt like a little girl again, looking up at him, seeking the reassurance that even though he had to leave, he'd always come back. I wanted to pretend that his strength could keep the frightening world at bay. Only this time, I wasn't a little girl, and I knew that he couldn't hold back reality forever.

"Yes." He hooked an arm around my neck and pulled me into his chest, then pressed a kiss on top of my head. "We'll always be together."

Not always, my heart whispered, and the magic gave another little stir.

Desperate Enough

Magic threatened to burst through the walls of my heart that night.

If I had let it, the power would have spilled out in a wave of blood and bitter regret, consuming me and everything I touched. I locked myself in my room, away from my friends and anyone else, pleading exhaustion. They let me retreat without a word. I sat on the edge of my canopied bed and stared out the arched window with a lifeless gaze.

The next High Priest will be Derek Black.

So many thoughts ran through my mind that I didn't know how to organize them. I just let them go. The jumbled mess eventually narrowed, tapering into the memory of Isadora's creaky old voice.

You've underestimated her before.

My hands trembled where they rested on my lap.

I stayed there for hours, not moving, just thinking. My life would either begin again or tragically end in a battle with Miss Mabel. Of that I had no doubt. This time it would be different. She gave me power when she killed Mama, and now I was going to use it.

Perhaps she'd underestimated me as well.

When the first fingers of dawn lightened the edge of the sky, I straightened up. My muscles and knees, stiff from holding the same position for so long, protested. I slipped into a pair of breeches and an old shirt, tied my hair with a small strip of leather, and drifted out of the apartment without a sound.

By the time I padded my way through Chatham's quiet corridors and back staircases, the looming top of Letum Wood looked black against the milky blue sky. The darkness of the trees met me like an old friend. With a confident stride forward, I headed deep into the heavy shadows and hit the trail at a hard run.

My frantic breathing soon saturated the early morning, accompanied by the gallop of my heart. Merrick's advice sounded in my mind as I flashed through the trees, my legs flying.

Just let it happen.

Stop trying to control it.

Although I wasn't entirely certain what he meant, I thought I had an idea. I braced myself, expecting the worst.

Once I'd warmed into the run, the magic started its usual war on my heart. Memories flickered from the buried depths of my mind. Running through Letum Wood with Mama and Papa. Picnics in the warm sunshine. Giggling underneath white sheets with Mama in the morning. Instead of pushing them away, I let the memories come. A flood of pain followed, but I didn't try to stop that either.

Just let it happen.

I crested a hill to see Mama's memory waiting near the top, a smile on her face. She caused a painful spasm in my heart.

Bianca! the memory called.

I sped past a boulder heaped with moss, hoping to ease the pain in my chest. Mama's voice brought a flood of emotions I hadn't prepared for. Grief, despair, pain, sorrow.

Bianca!

Yes, Mama, I thought, embracing the recollection. *I hear you.*

In my mind I became a little girl hiding behind a tree, stifling my laughter with a hand over my mouth. The leaves swayed overhead, dappling my skin with sunshine and shadow. Birds warbled from a nest nearby, and the musty smell of earth emanated from the sun-warmed dirt. Any second now and Mama would find me. The delicious anticipation made me shudder and giggle at the same time.

The stab of a rock in the middle of my foot wrenched my next step, jolting me back into reality. My strides stumbled but didn't stop. I leapt a boulder and dodged a low-hanging vine. The memory faded, replaced by another one.

Mama appeared ahead of me on the trail again, her arms spread wide, her hair streaming around her shoulders like banners.

You're back! she called, laughing. *I missed you. Did you have fun with Papa?*

I miss you, Mama, my heart replied.

The little girl laughed and ran past me on the trail, throwing her wispy body into Mama's arms. A sob lingered in my throat as the two ghosts of my past twirled around, so happy together. I'd never see that smile on Mama's face in real life again, outside this vague world of ghosts and shadows.

Oh, how I miss you, Mama!

Despite the lurking dangers of the early morning forest, I lost myself in the motions of running with disregard. The only way to endure the sorrow of missing Mama would be to find a greater pain, so I ran until my lungs burned. My knees ached. My heart beat so hard it threatened to crack my ribs.

I remember, my heart wept. *I remember!*

The grief opened up, flooding me with spikes and barbs and wretched sorrow. I let out a cry and slowed my pace. It was the first time since Mama's death that I'd given the grief any kind of respect, and it threatened to rupture me. My legs gave out. I lowered to my knees.

"Mama," I sobbed, pressing my face into my hands. "Mama!"

Like the mourners in the West, I wailed my torment. The cries came from deep in my belly. I held nothing back. All my ugly heart scars opened and I bled. I cried for minutes; it could have been hours. My eyes had almost swollen shut when I heard her voice again.

It's going to be okay, Bianca, Everything will work out.

I looked up to find Mama standing a few paces away, her eyes focused on a spot in the distance. She looked calm and lovely in the white mourning dress she'd worn to Grandmother's funeral. It had been the last time I'd really seen or spoken to her. The words came again, but from farther away this time.

Everything will work out.

Mama began to fade, first from her feet and then her hands. The ethereal substance trickled away, born on a gentle wind. She gazed down on me and smiled. The last thing I saw was her gray, gentle eyes.

I love you, Bianca.

Mama was gone.

"I love you, Mama," I whispered, but she had already disappeared. The words choked in my throat. "Always."

Something new clicked inside me, filling me with warmth. I felt spirited and strong. I lifted a hand and pressed it to my heart.

The magic.

It moved inside me with calm, languorous waves now, settling next to the swollen part of my heart that still mourned Mama. The magic and I were enemies no more. Startled by the swift change, I stood. It moved through my body, strengthening the muscles and sinews. I started to run and the magic ran with me.

It felt wonderful moving along the trail without struggle. I reached out to a dead, overhanging tree branch and let a little of the magic go. A shot of light spiraled through the dead mass. The wood trembled, shifting from the deep, dead gray to the same vibrant brown as the surrounding forest. I pressed my palm to the branches blackened from a dragon's breath. They sprang back to life, jolly and green again.

"Yes," I whispered with a smile. "Yes!"

I took off again, springing up hills, dodging low branches. I would have run forever, reveling in the magic, if a narrow pair of yellow eyes hadn't startled me. My foot caught on a root and I pitched forward, rolling down a hill until I crashed into a pair of gleaming claws the length of my arm.

When I looked up, I gazed into the eyes of five towering forest dragons.

Really Quite Simple

"**B**lessed be," I whispered, my chest heaving.

The dragons loomed so far above me that I had to crane my head back to see them. Their scales glittered with marbled veins of sapphire, crimson, emerald, and a deep mauve, seeming both colorful and dark. Heat radiating from their bodies flooded over me.

I crept to my feet, keeping my eyes trained on them until I had finally straightened, unable to determine if they meant me harm.

The smallest dragon, one with longer wings and mauve scales, leaned toward me, his nostrils flaring. He stomped and shuffled a second step closer. His great head came within an arm's reach of me, nearly obstructing my view of his body. Beneath his mighty claws, the ground gave a little shudder. He suddenly backed away as if I'd touched him with something hot, then roared, sending a spray of fire into the trees directly in front of him.

A dark feeling spread from my heels up through my spine.

Let's not frolic with the dragons tonight, Bianca, I thought. *They don't play nice.*

I dodged a stomping claw and ran a few steps, but the long tail of a dragon hidden in the trees whipped around to block my escape. When I changed direction, another claw landed a few paces away. It didn't take long to realize they had me hedged in, each dragon taking their turn sniffing at me and roaring to the treetops. The ground shuddered as two dragons barked, attacking each other with teeth bared. Their spastic movements catapulted me onto the end of a stray tail.

The heat of the warm scales nearly sizzled my sweaty palm. I jerked away with a cry.

A new pair of sunburnt orange eyes and pulsing nostrils lowered right next to me. This dragon had a red tinge running through his scales like little flecks of blood, turning the ebony into a dark, seething black, like a breathing chunk of coal. I froze, unable to look away. Three of the other dragons screamed, fire bursting from their nostrils, while the red dragon and I continued to stare at each other.

Just when I thought this surly forest dragon would be the last creature I'd ever see, a shout broke into my thoughts.

"Lay off, you rotten lizard! She's no harm to you. Bianca, stay behind me." It was Sanna hobbling over, yelling in a surprisingly calm voice. "They are quite agitated tonight, the dirty rotten—"

"Sanna?" I gasped.

"Yes. Who else did you expect? Isadora? I told you, she's a wimp. Do as I say. Unless you want your bowels hanging out."

I preferred my bowels where they were.

The red dragon threw his head back and let out a scream, setting the leaves above us on fire. I ducked behind Sanna's hunched form, feeling like a coward for putting a blind old woman between myself and danger.

"Are they planning on eating us?"

"Nah. They wouldn't eat me. They'd eat you, yes. But not me. Not a bad way to go, though. You wouldn't feel a thing."

"Oh," I muttered, staring at the long fangs dripping from the red dragon's mouth. "I think I'd feel something."

Sanna bellowed in a language I didn't recognize. It sent the dragons into a stomping rage, and she chuckled. "They hate it when I say that."

The emerald dragon snapped at the mauve one, her teeth dripping with pearly saliva. The mauve dragon was not amused, and screamed in response. I stumbled, but Sanna didn't waver. She shouted something else, and the other dragons screeched.

"Can I transport out of here?"

"Sure," she called. "Go to my house. I want to stay and see what happens. It's been awhile since I've seen this many in one spot."

"Are you mad?" I cried. "They'll trample you."

She waved a hand through the air. "I'll be fine."

"But Sanna, you're blind."

She smirked, tapping her finger against the side of her head. "Not to everything. Go on. They'll get pretty rough here soon."

Grateful to escape, I transported away. The spell dropped me onto a familiar patch of forest near her gurgling stream. I rolled off a rock with a grimace, thinking that I really needed to work on my transportation skills, and slowly made my way up the path. Sanna appeared on her porch just as I arrived.

"That red one is fierce," she said with a little tutting sound. "Fierce, fierce. Those teeth? Jikes! One hell of a set, if you ask me. Well, come on already. No sense waiting out here."

Sanna turned into the house, waving me in after her.

Despite the massive dragon talon on the wall, the rest of Sanna's house was nondescript and tidy. She had a small table, a narrow bed, a fireplace, and a few pots hanging on the wall. She motioned for me to sit in a chair at her rickety table and I obeyed.

"Thank you for saving me from the dragons," I said. She gave me a toothy smile, seeming quite pleased with herself. Tucked away in her little cottage, and more comfortable with monsters than with witches, I doubted she got into society much. "Can you explain what's going on? Why are the dragons following me?"

"Your power," she said, reaching for a teapot. I marveled that she didn't just use magic to call all the things that she needed to her. "The dragons are drawn to it."

"To my power? Why?"

Sanna poured a cup of tea into a nearby glass and took a sip.

"It's really quite simple, Bianca," she said in a long suffering tone. "Forest dragons love power. It calls to them."

My hand covered my heart, which had begun galloping. "How do you know about my power?"

She scoffed with a gruff, scraping sound. "It doesn't take a witch like Isadora to recognize strong magic. I've been around for a long time too. I sense it, and so do they."

My eyebrows lifted halfway to my hairline.

"All these dragons coming out of Letum Wood are my fault?"

"Blessed be, no. Kind of an arrogant child, aren't you?" she muttered. "One little girl like you couldn't make the dragons this nervous. But the old powers are awakening. That's what draws them out near the city. But once they're closer to you, the power, which is quite strong, calls to them. It's lucky for them that you're also a lovely little snack. At least I think you are. I can't see whether your face is lovely or not. You could be quite ugly."

I brushed aside her snarky tone to pry at something that concerned me far more.

"What do you mean by *the old powers are awakening?*"

"The old powers, you know!" Sanna cried with a surly wave of her hand. "The dark magic is in Antebellum again. It's all just beginning."

She reached up and rubbed one of the scales on her necklace and a tattoo on her wrist was visible for just a moment. It wasn't a circlus like mine; Sanna's wrist boasted the furled wing of a dragon, the sign of the Dragonmaster. It stretched across her wrist in a black, swooping design.

"Why is dark magic bringing them from the deep forest?" I asked, peeling my eyes away from her tattoo. "What part do they play besides protecting the castle?"

Sanna smiled. "Let me tell you a story," she said, as she settled into a chair with her teacup floating beside her.

"It starts back in the days of the Mortal Wars, when the Almorran priests banished the humans from Antebellum and sent them across the ocean. Most of the forest dragons were allied with the Almorran priests in what is now the Western Network. Once we destroyed the Almorran race, and separated from each other into the Network system, each Network murdered the forest dragons living in their lands, just to be sure the evil was really gone. Each Network, that is, except for ours."

A little twinkle appeared in her eye: she must appreciate the underhanded, rebellious spirit. She took another sip.

"A man named Damen, my distant ancestor, stepped forward and spoke for the dragons who hadn't aligned with the Almorrans. He convinced Esmelda to spare them on the condition that they protect the castle, and her inhabitants, whenever they sensed the old powers. In years of peace, the dragons could live amongst the deep shadows of Letum Wood without disturbance. But when the old powers stirred, the forest dragons would be obligated to come out of their repose and protect the castle."

My thoughts flew back to Miss Mabel and her partner. There was little doubt in my mind that they were somehow linked to the rising evil in Antebellum. I hoped the dragons didn't sense part of Miss Mabel in me, like the gypsies had.

"The dragons are stirring because Chatham Castle is in danger."

"Yes." Sanna seemed a little too at ease with the conversation for my taste. She leaned forward with a conspiratorial whisper. "I'd not go into Letum Wood if I were you."

"If they are bound to protect Chatham Castle, why did they mean me harm? Don't they like witches?"

"No!" she spat, recoiling. "Most of them hate us. The dragons don't appreciate their bondage. They may protect our castle, but they don't have to like it. Some are lukewarm about humans, but not many."

"I recognized one of them," I said, scooting to the edge of my chair. "I saved him from some poachers awhile ago. The blue one."

Sanna leaned back in her seat. The teacup set itself onto the table nearby.

"Yes, yes. He's nice enough at times. A bit emotional, really. His attitude has always turned on a hat pin."

"Is there a way to resurrect Almorran magic? The priests have been gone for centuries."

"Yes, there is," Sanna said, smacking her lips carelessly. "There always is. Witches may die, but magic does not. Especially not the old magic. For the sake of every witch in Antebellum, let's hope that's not what happens. I'm not sure we'd survive that kind of resurrection."

Her sudden shiver brought a little lump of fear into my heart.

"Yes," I whispered, slumping back against the seat. "That's what I was afraid of."

Viveet

Merrick sat next to me the next morning and blew out a long breath of air. Neither of us spoke for a long time as we stared out at Letum Wood, lost in thought. I wondered if he'd still want to do a lesson today.

"So that's what happened," I said, swallowing. A few birds twittered by, disappearing into the ragged wall of green leaves that surrounded us. I was grateful to be sitting. It made it feel less like the world was moving too fast around me. "I finally let the memories come and everything changed."

He'd remained quiet during my entire recounting of the previous day, including my time with Sanna. I'd even told him of my mother's ghost, and how my reluctance to run stemmed from seeing her in the forest. Now he just stared out, his eyes stewing.

"I can tell that your magic has settled," he finally said.

Settled, yes. That was it. The usual restless knot of anxiety, the cagey dragon in my chest, all of it had calmed. It seemed to purr like a content kitten.

"I'm still trying to figure out what happened," I said, breaking the silence. "I think I understand it, but I'm not sure."

His intense green eyes met mine.

"Tell me what you think happened."

"I think that my refusal to remember or think or talk about Mama just built the powers. Then, when I got angry or scared, the emotions amplified an already volatile magic, and it took over."

He nodded and asked, "So what did you do that changed the pattern?"

I paused for a moment, reflecting back.

"I didn't stop myself from remembering."

"Or feeling," he pointed out.

"Yes," I said slowly, thinking it over. I had felt a lot of emotions, brutal emotions that I'd never given time to before. "I suppose you're right."

"Denying your emotions only increases your powers until you can't handle it anymore. Accepting the grief, even the pain, allows us to control it and stops it from expressing itself in more destructive ways."

"Couldn't you have just told me that?" I asked sheepishly.

"Would you have listened?" he shot right back.

"No," I admitted after thinking it over. "I wouldn't have."

His voice dropped, and he regained some of that distant intensity in his green eyes. "Be prepared to really start experiencing the grief now that you've faced it. Everything you've been putting off will come at you full force. As long as you recognize that emotions are power, and you don't prevent yourself from feeling it, you'll get through."

"Thanks," I said, managing a small smile. He nodded.

"It'll be okay," he said. "Just remember that."

"I will."

Merrick stood up and began to lope at an effortless jog toward a leather parcel near the back wall of the garden.

"I brought this today but wasn't sure if you were ready," he said over his shoulder. "Now that I know you've figured out enough about controlling your powers that we can start working on it, I feel good about starting with swords."

That piqued my curiosity. I stood and joined him on the other side of the garden.

"With swords?"

The leather flaps fell away to reveal a gleaming sword. Swirls of ivy patterns that reminded me of Letum Wood ran the length of the silver blade, which was about as long as my arm. A deep blue snaked through the ivy leaves and down the hilt.

"What is it?" I asked.

"A sword," he replied in a wry tone. "Your sword. Pick it up. It won't bite."

Hesitant, I reached out and wrapped my hand around the hilt. The moment it touched my palm I felt a thrill rush from the tips of my fingers through my shoulder. A sapphire blue light zipped through the leaves on the blade, disappearing so fast I thought I'd imagined it.

"Where did you get it?" I asked.

"I didn't," he said, running his narrowed gaze over it. "Your father had it made for you. He told me to give it to you when you were ready."

"When did he have it made?"

Merrick shrugged. "Must have been a while ago. Swords like that can take years to finish. See the letter *A* carved into the metal near the hilt? It's a distinct signature from the swordmaker Andrei. I've seen his work before. He lives in the Southern Network and uses a special kind of metal that's only mined in a few places in the South and West. It's known for making exceptional swords that are never brittle."

"What?" My head jerked up. "The South? We aren't allowed to trade with the South."

"That's a Southern blade, all right. Your father must be a friend of Andrei's. If Andrei gave it as a gift then it wouldn't violate the prohibition on trade. Turn it over. See the writing on the back?"

Instead of asking how Papa had even met Andrei—a pointless question, given the travels he'd been on in his job as a Protector—I did as Merrick said, flipping the sword around and resting it on my palm. The twisting vines near the top of the hilt spelled out a tiny word.

Viveet.

"That's the name of the sword," Merrick said. "Every good sword-maker names each sword based on their experience in creating the weapon. Since every sword is forged differently, they all have their own personality."

"Viveet," I whispered, my eyes narrowing on the word. I looked up to Merrick. "That's the language of the Ancients."

Merrick nodded, an expectant look on his face.

"It means *protector,*" I said.

"It'll be interesting to see what kind of personality Viveet has, then."

I ran my hand along the smooth edge. It lit up in the same shade of sapphire blue it had before and faded again when I pulled my hand away. The metal felt chilly, like it had been submerged in a bucket of ice. Merrick sheathed his sword, which was longer than mine and etched with a purple filigree. He reached for Viveet, and when I reluctantly gave her up, inspected her with a deft ease that could only come with years of experience.

"A good sword is like a shield," he explained, testing the weight with his firm grip. "The more you train with it, the more it responds to you. The magic that comes with using a sword will become stronger as well, so keep that in mind."

He stepped back and ran through a few routines, swinging it in wide arcs. The blade sliced through the air like a song.

"Am I going to use Viveet now?" I asked, hoping to get rid of the cumbersome wooden sword he'd been making me practice with every day. I had so many splinters in my hands that my palm was starting to scar.

"Yes. Now that you know how to keep yourself under control, I'll trust you with a real blade."

Merrick, all business now, pulled his own sword from the sheath and handed Viveet back.

"We're going to go through the sword positions again, but this time with Viveet. The weight and balance is different, so we'll keep it slow for now. The last thing I need is the wrath of your father if you get hurt. Here's Viveet's sheath; put it on. You'll need to practice drawing your sword and sheathing her in one smooth motion. Until you build that muscle memory, it's not as easy as it looks."

He tossed me the hard leather sheath, complete with a belt to buckle around my hips. I obeyed his directions, then inspected Viveet's light metal frame and easy grip. I swung her through a few positions, enjoying her light, nimble movements. Compared to the clunky wooden sword I'd learned with, she felt like fighting with a puff of air. Perhaps Merrick did know what he was doing. But of course that was an admission I wasn't likely to concede to yet.

"Are you ready to learn how to put magic and sword fighting together?" Merrick asked, one eyebrow lifted. His face had returned to its usual focused, brow-pulled expression.

"Yes," I said, feeling like I'd been handed a key to my own life. It was empowering and terrifying at the same time. Miss Mabel would be back on my birthday. I might not be perfect, but I could be strong. "I think I'm ready."

"You are."

I met his eyes.

"Then let's get started."

A Bracelet and a Shop

The days faded into weeks and then months. Every hour blurred into the next. Training, running, aching muscles, calloused hands. Viveet sang under my hand, guided by Merrick's persistence and talent. I learned from him every morning, and practiced alone every evening, sometimes far into the night.

Enduring the pain of Mama's death instead of trying to ignore it made me the master, and the magic my minion. Once I stopped fighting the grief, the power flowed into me, swift and strong.

As Merrick promised, my emotions took on a higher range. Acknowledging the feelings had a way of amplifying them. Sometimes it frightened me, the enormity of what I felt. One minute I could be laughing, and the next fighting back tears. My lows became very low indeed. I cried myself to sleep at night, and occasionally locked myself into a melancholic seclusion. Other days it let me go, gave me a break, allowing me to laugh and live and heal another small corner of my heart before the next onslaught.

A flurry of activity surrounded Papa day and night. Except for our ritual breakfasts, I rarely saw him. Witches came to protest his upcoming reign every day at the front gates of Chatham Castle. The Factios provoked rallies against him throughout Chatham City. I no longer doubted whether they worked for Miss Mabel or her partner: I could see it in the darkness of their eyes. The protestors shouted Papa's name so loud I could hear it from the Witchery. Papa and the High Priestess didn't seem to notice, but I did. The rage and discontent settling over Chatham City terrified me.

The High Priestess scheduled the Empowerment on the morning of my seventeenth birthday, the same day as the Anniversary Ball. The castle started preparing months in advance. I took it all in with a detached air, living for one thing: learning to meld magic and sword fighting so I could defeat Miss Mabel.

Leda graduated from her first-year and immediately dove into her second-year courses just as spring finished. Brecken left for a three-month assignment guarding the Borderlands, leaving Camille behind. She avoided her classes even more dutifully than before and went on long walks in the rambling gardens alone. Michelle spent more time blushing, and more time in the kitchens with Nicolas, than ever before.

The ebb and flow of life seemed to elongate into one long river that moved me closer and closer to my birthday. I moved with it, gaining strength and power with every day that passed until it dumped me firmly on the doorstep of my demise. Before I knew it, spring had become summer and three months had passed.

One hot summer afternoon two days before my birthday, the heat drove Camille and I deeper into the cold, unexplored passages of Chatham Castle. She let out a dramatic sigh. We were staring at a painting of two water nymphs trying to woo a young witch into the water. Once he gave into their song, they would devour him and use his bones to make the walls of their house. Camille stared at it as if it were a road map for her life instead of a vulgar painting with half-naked women and an enamored young man.

"I'm sad today, Bianca," Camille admitted, finally abandoning the painting. We walked down the dank corridor side by side. Her normal enthusiasm had waned, and today she seemed quite depressed and dull.

"Why are you sad?" I asked, running my fingers along a faded gold frame that left a light coating of dust on my finger. The painting was of a woman with long auburn curls billowing around her. She had a thin face with high cheekbones and a confident expression. Esmelda, our first High Priestess.

"I don't know," Camille said in a low voice, brushing past a velvet seat along the side of the hallway. "I'm just sad."

"Even with the Anniversary Ball coming up in two days?"

"Yes."

"Does this have something to do with Brecken?"

"Brecken?" Camille murmured with a little too much innocence in her tone. "W-why would this be about him?"

"Well, you haven't seen him for several months now."

I expected her to shoot me a sharp look and a curt expression, but she just sighed instead.

"You're right."

Startled, I turned to look at her, confirming now what I had suspected for weeks.

"I miss him. He's been gone for three months, and I haven't gotten a letter from him in two weeks."

"You like him a lot, don't you?"

"Oh, very much! To make matters worse, several more Guardians have asked me to the Anniversary Ball, and I just don't know what to do. There's a chance he could be back in time to attend with the rest of the Captains, but he doesn't know for sure. He may not. I certainly can't wait around for him to figure it out."

"Then don't go with anyone," I said, peering down another hallway on the right. An occasional window shed light on the wooden floors, highlighting a few old paintings and dusty divans. "Just go without a date."

"Without a date?" she asked slowly, as if she'd never pronounced the words before. "Are you mad?"

I shrugged. "Just an idea."

"Oh, I don't know what to do!" she wailed in a forlorn voice, running her fingers along the wall. "I'll decide later. I'm too tired today and—"

She trailed off and didn't pick the thought back up again. I hid a smile. The pathetic worry on her face was so innocent, so sincere, that I couldn't help but think of a lost little girl.

"I'm sure you'll figure it out."

"Let's head back. I'm tired of thinking about boys. Michelle is supposed to bring lunch to the Witchery. I hope she brings chocolate," she muttered. "Gobs of it."

We walked back to the occupied region of the castle in silence, both lost in our own reveries. I thought of Miss Mabel, of my birthday just two days away, and allowed the usual feeling of dread it brought. The emotions made me feel jittery, but I embraced them instead of turning them away.

I'm nervous and scared, but I'm also strong and determined. I can beat Miss Mabel.

The fear soon faded as I thought about running through Letum Wood to work the energy out. *Tonight,* I thought, instinctively reaching to my side where Viveet usually rested. She wasn't there now, I'd left her in my room to avoid suspicious looks and Mrs. L's probable wrath. I wished I could take her everywhere with me. I felt safer with Viveet in my hand.

Camille started prattling about something she'd overheard while on a walk in the gardens, but I didn't pay attention until she said, "Jikes, Bianca! I almost forgot."

I looked up to see Miss Scarlett walking toward us.

"Do you have a test?" I asked.

"Yes," Camille said with a heavy breath. "I didn't realize how much time had passed."

"Aren't you worried?"

"No," she said with uncharacteristic confidence. "It'll be fine."

Miss Scarlett's broad frame cut into the sun from the windows. She wore a long sleeved navy blue dress and her black hair in a bun at the nape of her neck. The low, singing tones of her bracelets preceded her.

"It's good to see you again, Bianca, Camille," Miss Scarlett said as she approached us.

"Merry meet, Miss Scarlett," I said, curtsying.

"Not much has changed, I see," she said, eyeing my poor display. "I hope that's not the way you curtsy for the High Priestess."

"Yes, it is. She finds it deplorable."

Her pursed lips and narrowed eyes told me she had her opinions about my etiquette at the castle. Now that summer had come Miss Scarlett spent most of her time at Chatham Castle. Rumor had it that the High Priestess planned on making her the next Head of Education. Miss Scarlett turned to Camille.

"Are you ready for your test?"

"Yes, Miss Scarlett," she said. Miss Scarlett stared at her in unmasked surprise.

"No hysterics?" she asked. "No begging or pleading to delay it?"

"No," Camille said, as if they discussed the weather. "I'm ready."

"Well, very good. Let's go to the library then. I'll meet you there after you gather your things."

Miss Scarlett turned to me as Camille walked away. "How have things been for you lately?" she asked. "I haven't seen much of you. It seems that you're always outside training."

"It's kept me very busy."

"Have you come to terms with your father's new position?"

I thought my response over before answering. "No, Miss Scarlett. I'm not sure I ever will."

"I think that's a very normal response," she said, bestowing a silent approval I couldn't help but be grateful for. Despite her rigid rules and high expectations, I respected Miss Scarlett and wanted her to like me. "Do you know where Leda went? I'm having a hard time finding her."

Join the club. Leda had been more elusive and slippery than ever. Although I knew she had to be doing more than just working for Jansson, I couldn't peg down what she did or where she went. When I asked, she brushed me off and changed the subject.

"Have you checked the library?" I asked.

"I was just on my way. Let's walk there together."

"Yes, Miss Scarlett," I said, following behind her.

"Scarlett," said a male witch who tipped his head when he passed us. She replied with a nod, her steps never faltering. As always, I was in awe over her ability to glide with her spine so straight and her gait so perfect. Surely a more composed witch never walked these halls.

"Miss Celia told me that you stopped by and talked to her about Mabel back in the spring," Miss Scarlett said, interrupting my silence. My throat squeezed in a nervous spasm. That had been so long ago, almost like another time, that I'd almost forgotten.

"Yes. I just had a few questions."

"About Mabel?"

"Yes."

"Why did you ask about her?"

I shrugged, telling only a half-truth. "I guess I just wanted to understand why she killed my mother."

To my surprise, I found the magic stirring inside me as I spoke. Miss Scarlett's shrewd eyes said she didn't believe me, but she didn't press the matter further. Taking it as a draw, I turned to the right, grateful to see the library close. Leda glanced up as we moved in, turning her two mismatched eyes on us.

"Merry meet, Miss Scarlett," she said, bobbing a curtsy I was sure looked more awkward than my own had. I smiled.

"I came to give you and Camille your tests," Miss Scarlett said. The eye she cast on both of us really meant, *I wanted to make sure you are representing yourself with the utmost decorum and ensure you aren't wasting your time here.* As usual, Miss Scarlett had her mind set on upholding the rules.

"Yes, I'm ready," Leda said, quill in hand, taking herself altogether too seriously.

"How are things going with Rupert and Jansson?" Miss Scarlett asked.

"Things are going well for me, Miss Scarlett." There was an extra chirp of happiness in Leda's voice, one that could only mean she'd been studying for hours and thought she was in heaven. "I've just finished the analysis on the Mansfeld Pact and its implications on our upcoming war."

"Very good. What are your views?"

Leda just stared at her.

"My . . . views?" Leda asked, taken aback. Even I stared at Miss Scarlett in surprise. She had never solicited our opinions before.

"Yes," Miss Scarlett said, as if she didn't notice our gaping mouths.

"I-I think the Eastern Network will stick to the Mansfeld Pact," she said, slowly warming to it. "They won't get involved in any business or war that doesn't directly involve them."

Miss Scarlett turned to me next.

"And what do you think?" she asked.

"I think Leda's right," I said, pulling myself together enough to form a coherent response. "The East will wait for the Western Network to get through us before they get involved. Why put their witches in danger when they can hide behind us?"

Miss Scarlett thought our assessments over with pursed lips.

"What of the Southern Network?" she pointed out. "They've been training their army for months now. Will they break the pact?"

"I don't know," I said.

"I think the South will break the Mansfeld Pact and form an alliance with the West. Both will advance on us, and then the East will follow. That's my assessment," Leda piped up, her voice thick with gloating. She shot me an expectant look and I scowled.

"Very interesting," Miss Scarlett said. "Leda, here are your tests. Please sit at an empty desk to take them. You have no time limit."

Leda took the proffered scrolls just as Camille came bouncing into the room, her face flushed.

"Find a table," Miss Scarlett commanded. "You have one hour, Camille."

Miss Scarlett handed Camille a daunting scroll, one that may have been as big as all three of Leda's combined. I felt a twinge of pity for her. To my surprise, Camille took it with a self-assured nod. "Thank you, Miss Scarlett."

I wasn't the only one startled by her reaction. Miss Scarlett studied Camille again and responded with a slow drawl.

"You're welcome. Best of luck to both of you," she said. "Bianca, come with me."

Camille shot me a wink as Miss Scarlett started to walk away.

"I just found this in the Witchery when I got my things," Camille whispered to me, motioning to the corner of a small envelope in her skirt pocket. "I got a letter from Brecken!" She squeezed my hand and headed to a free table with a little spring in her steps, humming under her breath. I smiled and caught up with Miss Scarlett.

We moved to the other side of the library where a large map of Chatham City covered the wall. Though the map had been there for ages, many of the shops were still in business. Market Street, normally crammed with the vendors from farms and the outlying cities, was one of the five main roads. Miss Emma's Bakery, Miss Holly's Candy Shop, Owens Pub, and a few others, were still open on Market Street today.

"If you seek answers regarding Mabel, perhaps I can help. I can't verify this for you with any certainty," Miss Scarlett began in a low tone that only I could hear. "But I will tell you that there's a little pub here, toward the outskirts of Chatham City, which Miss Mabel went to infrequently."

I wanted to ask Miss Scarlett how she knew but bit my lip. Miss Scarlett, while a talented and devoted teacher, had been a spy for the High Priestess all the years that she worked at the school. She must have followed Miss Mabel more than a few times, trying to figure out her wicked plots.

"Who did she meet there?" I asked.

"It's hard to say," Miss Scarlett said with a frown. "I never followed her inside, but I'm certain she went there to meet someone."

Miss Scarlett ran her finger along a road just across from Letum Wood in the seediest part of Chatham City. "Here," she said, tapping the little square that represented the pub. "This is it."

I looked from the map to her. "How will this help me find answers?"

"I can't be sure it will," she said and I thought I heard regret in her voice. "But I felt like I should tell you all the same. There may be a few breadcrumbs there. Of course, as your teacher, I cannot support the breaking of any rules." She gave me a severe glance. "But I cannot be held responsible for what I don't know."

"Then why are you telling me?" I asked, searching her eyes. I'd never known Miss Scarlett to bend the rules. To my surprise, she softened just a little.

"Let's just say that I know how haunting unanswered questions can be," she said in a steady tone. She reached to her wrist and slipped one of her bracelets off. The crimson beads gave off a dull sheen in the light. "Wear this when you go. It will protect you."

I hesitated. "Protect me?"

"It's a charm. The High Priestess gave it to me when I started working at Miss Mabel's for extra protection. I give it to you now."

Miss Scarlett walked away before I could thank her. I watched her go, uncertain how I felt about this new information, and what the roiling in my chest meant, if it meant anything at all.

Finding the pub Miss Scarlett directed me to proved easier than I expected. I wasted no time getting there. The moment Miss Scarlett turned away, I left the library, ran to the Forgotten Gardens, and transported to the outer wall of Chatham City.

Though it blended in with the rest of the aging, decrepit hovels that surrounded it, something drew me to the correct building. It had no porch, no stairs, and only one window at the front. I stood across the street in the alley, watching to see what kind of people walked in and out. When no one had entered or exited after I'd held vigil a full ten minutes, I wasn't sure if I felt relief or greater fear.

"Now or never," I whispered to myself. Miss Scarlett's bracelet clung to my right wrist, pressing up against my circlus. Without the rest of her bracelets to clank against it didn't sing, but every now and then I felt a little shiver of warmth from it.

Despite the section of Chatham City I was in—no one would recognize me here—I kept my head down and walked quickly across the street, hoping to keep my courage. Once I stepped inside the small pub, the world outside seemed to fade away.

The interior didn't fare any better than the outside in my estimation. Four moldering tables and about twice as many chairs were scattered across the small hovel, which was completed by three booths across the back wall. A middle-aged woman stood behind a counter that stretched along the left wall. Glass jars filled the counter space, holding various shades of gold and amber liquid. It smelled sour, like stale yeast.

"Whatchya want?" the witch called as she flipped her hair over her bony shoulders. Light blonde roots at her scalp told me that black wasn't her real hair color. She was thin. Too thin. Her pale skin stretched over her jutting bones, and her eyes hung down in bags.

"I have a few questions I'd like to ask," I said, my voice sounding small despite my attempt to project it. She sized me up, her eyes narrowing.

"What kind of questions?" she asked, drumming the tops of her fingers on the counter.

"About your customers."

She sucked on her front teeth, then gave a bored shrug.

"Sure. For a pentacle or two."

Although I had a few coins and no plans to use them for anything else, it annoyed me to give them to her. But I needed her to talk. I pulled three pentacles out of the pocket of my olive green dress and held them up for her to see. She straightened, suddenly invested in the conversation, and extended her palm.

"One for security," she drawled, her voice taking on a nasally intonation. "My name is Dahlia, by the way. What's yours?"

I tossed her the coin.

"Doesn't matter. Has a woman named Mabel come in recently? She has blonde hair and blue eyes. She's very beautiful."

Dahlia rolled her eyes around in thought.

"I have a lot of witches with blonde hair come in," she finally said.

"Sure," I said. "But are they all so beautiful it almost makes your eyes hurt?"

And do they all have enough evil power to incinerate you into ashes?

Dahlia stewed on it again. "Ya. I've seen her several times. Not for a few months now, mind ya."

"Does she come in with anyone?"

"No."

"Does she sit alone?"

Dahlia puffed out her cheeks while she thought the question over.

"No. Another witch always comes and meets up with her. Sometimes the other lady comes first, but not often."

I tried to keep my heart from racing with excitement but failed. My thoughts flickered back to the woman I'd heard Miss Mabel talking to in the West. Could it be the same witch?

"Oh?" I asked evenly. I must not have done a very good job hiding my enthusiasm because Dahlia lifted one eyebrow and held out her hand, twiddling her fingers in expectation. I flipped her another pentacle.

"They sit in that booth." She motioned to the back with a jerk of her head. "Neither of them take any food or drink, but they always leave a few sacrans behind so I don't mind letting them in."

"How often do they come?"

She shrugged her thin shoulders. "Couple times a year, sometimes less. For a while they came once a month, and then it slowed down again."

"Have they been coming here a long time?"

"Years now. Ever since I started working here."

"What does the other witch look like?"

"Dunno. She keeps her hood on. I've never actually looked her in the eye. All I can tell ya is that the woman has black hair and a figure I'd kill someone for. Nice hourglass shape and everything."

My heart hammered a little bit faster. What was it Miss Celia had said? *Angelina looked just like May. Black hair, curvy figure, and eyes that could cut.* Was Miss Mabel working with her mother? It shouldn't have been a surprise.

"What did they talk about?" I asked.

"I may have heard a thing or two," she said, jingling the coins in her hand and raising her eyebrows. I set the last pentacle down on the counter. She snatched it and all three disappeared, vanishing into thin air.

"Like what?"

"From what I remember, they talked about a book."

My expression must have betrayed my confusion because she shrugged. Her eyes narrowed.

"Doesn't make sense ta me either, sweetie, but that's what they talked about. I heard a few snippets now and then, but not much. Best I can tell ya is that they're looking for a book." Dahlia gave a little shudder. "And let me tell ya, both of them give me the creeps. I don't care how pretty they are. Something isn't right about them."

"Do they ever talk about dark magic?" I asked, breathless now. Dahlia's eyes showed true trouble for the first time.

"Ya. Once or twice. Mostly just historical stuff, ya know.

Speculation over the Almorrans, that one nasty High Priestess . . . what's her name, Evelyn? Oh, and dragons. Stuff like that. Between ya and me," she said, leaning in closer, her eyes darting around and her breath engulfing my face in a blast of what smelled like pickles. "I swear I saw a dragon over the castle the other day. No one believes me, but I know what I saw. Bad times are coming."

"Is that all?" I asked impatiently. "Nothing else?"

"Ya!" she cried, recoiling as if I'd burned her. "Look, it's not my business what they want ta talk about. They pay, I'm happy. Although I'm happier when they leave. Got it?"

Sensing that she didn't have any more information to give—and I was out of pentacles anyway—I ended the conversation. Dahlia had told me more than she could have possibly known.

Almorrans, Evelyn, dragons.

"Thank you, Dahlia," I said. She waved me off with another twiddle of her fingers and I left the close little pub, grateful to get out of the dark corners and the overpowering smell of vinegar.

My thoughts whirled as I walked back to Chatham Castle under a cloaking incantation. Once I made it to Letum Wood, I found a familiar trail and jogged back to the Forgotten Gardens. The distance helped me work out some of my frustration and think clearly. The conclusion I came to was so dark, so frightening, I didn't entertain it for long. I allowed it only in manageable blips and snatches, worried it would ignite my soul and consume me in Miss Mabel's—and Angelina's—evil.

I'd hear them talk about a book from time to time.

Instead of going to the Witchery, I headed to the library.

Book of Spells

"**C**an you keep a secret?"

Leda's lips twitched: I'd interrupted her studies. She didn't move from her hunched-over position at the long table.

"What is it about?" she asked with a long-suffering sigh.

"I need help," I said. "You're the first witch I came to."

"Yes, you do need help," she agreed, looked down at her book and mumbling, "more than I can give."

"I need help finding a book," I said. "Or, at least, a book about a book."

"You want me to help you find a book about a book?" she repeated in disbelief, her eyes cutting into me with a look that said, *You're joking, right?*

"Yes, and I won't go away until you help me."

She considered that with a glower. I was nothing if not determined. Perhaps she was using the chance to look into the future and see that I was being honest: I wouldn't leave until she helped me.

"Fine," she muttered, closing *Witches of the East* and folding her arms across her chest. "You have fifteen minutes."

"It's a history book," I explained. Time was ticking, and Leda would hold me to the minute. "An ancient history book."

"As ancient as the Mortal wars?"

"Yes! But maybe a little before that."

Her pale brow wrinkled over her eyes.

"Before the Mortal Wars?" she asked in disbelief. "Bianca, there's almost no information that predates the Mortal Wars. It was all destroyed. Remember?"

I rolled my eyes. "Right, but there has to be something."

Leda shook her head.

"Not here in the Central Network. We have some old scrolls, but not many. Almost all the Almorran books were burned."

Her words made my heart catch. *Almost all.*

"Can you show me what we do have?"

Leda glanced around. "Fine," she whispered, leaning in close. "But you have to follow me without question and don't make a sound. I'm not supposed to know where they are. If the librarians catch us they'll ban me from coming back to the library at all, and I'll make your life a nightmare. Understand? A nightmare."

"Agreed."

Leda stood up, pushed away from the table, and started toward the far corner of the library without another word. She wound through several rows of bookshelves, leading me into a back area I'd never seen before. Once there, she glanced over her shoulder, reassured herself that no librarian had followed us, and whispered an incantation in front of a bookshelf of old scrolls labeled *Findings from the Southern Covens.* The shelf swung toward us with a low groan and Leda waved me inside ahead of her.

We stepped into a room beneath the grand stairs. The sloped stone ceiling gradually slanted upwards. A few beams of sun spilled into the room from a high window, illuminating the walls with dusty light. Bookshelves were cut and chiseled into the walls themselves. Leda strode into the gray room without hesitation, ducking when she turned a corner. I wondered how many times she'd been there before.

"How did you find out about this place?" I asked, running my fingers along the chilly walls as I followed behind.

"I made friends with one of the librarians, Rachael. She showed it to me. Don't tell anyone!" she hissed, shooting me another glare. "They'll banish me from the library."

"Relax," I muttered. "I'm not going to tell anybody your secret. The last thing I want is you sulking around without any place to go but the Witchery."

"Over here," she said, gesturing with a jerk of her head to a lonely bookshelf against the far wall, swathed in shadows. She pulled a wooden chest off the bottom shelf. "The oldest records that the Central Network has are here. They are mostly first-hand accounts of the Mortal Wars. Rachael told me that the High Priestess has Esmelda's journal."

My eyes popped open. "Esmelda's journal? Really?"

Leda nodded.

"That's what Rachael said. I don't know if it's true or not." She grabbed the lid and pulled it open. It protested with an ominous groan. Dozens of scrolls tied with twine or leather strips awaited inside.

"No books," I observed, my hope sinking.

Leda shook her head. "I told you we didn't have any. Besides, they used mostly scrolls back then. The magic and culture were different back around the Mortal wars. It was a rougher, less precise magic. They used it for big things, not little ones."

Probably more powerful that way, I thought of saying, my mind slipping to Michelle's reluctance to use magic for anything but what was necessary.

I knelt in front of the chest and pulled a scroll out. Miss Mabel had me learn several of the ancient languages while earning one of the marks in my circlus, the Esbat. I'd studied Almorran and Declan, two secret languages that few people inside or outside our Network ever cared to learn. It wasn't until now that I realized how strange it was that the Almorran language was even a part of the Esbat curriculum. Why would they want us to learn the language of a race destroyed because of inherent evil?

"Are any of these scrolls written in Almorran?" I asked.

Leda's face clouded over.

"Perhaps. Mostly Declan, I think. In addition to the common tongue that we speak now, Esmelda and her people spoke Declan. The Almorrans used their own language, of course. What book are you looking for again?"

Her eyes had taken on a suspicious glint.

"I'm looking for a book about a book," I corrected, shuffling through the scrolls, avoiding her studious eyes. Surely there had to be some information in the aged papers. "It's an Almorran book."

Leda bit her bottom lip. "Are you sure it's not a scroll?"

I recalled the conversation between Miss Mabel and the mystery woman in the Western Network. It was hard to know what I was working with. Really, I sought a legend, a tale conjured in the darkest night meant to scare children. But I couldn't be sure anymore that reality wasn't just an extension of what I once thought was fantasy.

Honestly, how difficult can it be to find a book?

"I'm sure."

One particularly ragged scroll stuck out. I grabbed the thin paper and unrolled it while Leda shifted on her feet and dazed out into one of her visions. The paper of the scroll was brittle. It had been curled so long I had a difficult time holding it open without shattering it. The ink had faded, but I could just make out a few words in Almorran.

"It's a letter," I said. Leda shook her head, snapping out of her vision. She stood up.

"I have to go," she said. "Come on. We need to leave."

"No!" I cried too loudly and lowered my voice. "I can't go yet. I just found a scroll that may help."

"I have an appointment I can't be late for," Leda said.

"I'll stay without you. I promise I'll be quiet and leave soon. Please, Leda?"

She hesitated, one foot already headed toward the doorway.

"What are you going to say if a librarian finds you in here?"

"I'll tell them that I overheard the incantation from a different librarian. I'll be fast, I promise. I just want to look through these scrolls."

"Fine," she muttered, one finger raised in warning. "Make it fast."

She cast one last look at me over her shoulder, then left by the entrance we'd come in through. It whispered shut behind her and I dove into the tattered scrolls with earnest. Most of them were letters. Fathers to sons. A witch to a mortal, warning of a raid on his village. A few lovers. Two of the scrolls were notes from a meeting with Coven Leaders. I couldn't read at least five of them. Time and humidity had taken their final toll, blurring out the words entirely. The pile of unreadable scrolls grew, as did the pile of scrolls that didn't help me at all. It wasn't until I unfurled the second to last scroll that I found a clue, a little note hidden in a line of a letter from an Almorran witch to his wife.

There was a great fire in the library, Anjel, started by our enemies. Almost all the books are gone. Oh, how I wept! The Great Histories of the World, as transcribed by Coven Leaders of the past, all burned into ashes. A few of our Almorran treasures have been lost as well, the Book of Spells amongst them. I tried to salvage as much as I could from the wreckage, but most had turned to soot and cinder. The loss of our connections to those that have gone before us are deep and devastating indeed. We can never regain our lost knowledge. No, never.

I sucked in a deep breath. The *Book of Spells*. Like the wicked Almorran priests of legend and lore, it was almost a myth. The dark magic that defined the Almorran race was reputed to have existed in one grimoire. All the spells and incantations, all the secret potions and charms, gathered as a single volume. But, as the letter said, it had been lost.

Or so the stories went.

Many witches throughout history claimed that they had found the book and resurrected the magic. Most of them had been stuffed into dungeons, regarded as heretics or insane. But what if they had been right? What if the *Book of Spells* wasn't lost after all?

The power contained within would certainly draw a witch like Miss Mabel. If she resurrected the old Almorran powers by using the *Book of Spells*, all of Antebellum would fall. We only escaped the wicked black magic of the Almorran priests by sheer luck and tenacity during the Mortal Wars. What would save us this time?

I released the scroll. It bounced back together with a little hiss and I set it aside, a cold feeling of dread holding onto my heart. All the ugly arithmetic of Miss Mabel's vile plans began to line up.

The real question now was whether Miss Mabel had found the *Book of Spells* yet, and if she had, what was her plan?

Do You Feel Stronger?

"Your birthday is tomorrow, isn't it?" Merrick asked the next morning. A blanket of hot air sat on the new world. Since spring moved out and summer stormed in, Letum Wood had boiled to life. Green walls of ivy surrounded the Forgotten Gardens on all sides, eradicating any sign of stone. Tufts of grass grew in between the rocks below in a thick carpet. The air, too heavy and hot to allow a breeze, just hung. Sweat caked my back and neck, dripping down my face in long rivulets.

"Yes," I said, attacking the wooden dummy Mikhail again. Viveet's glowing blade bit into the wood, chipping off a piece that flew through the air and landed a few paces away. I took another swing, arcing Viveet up through the air to slice up through the arm. It fell off with a loud thud. Merrick waved his hand and the limb leapt up, adhering itself back to the dummy. He cast me a concerned look I ignored.

"Worried about something?" he asked.

Yes. I will die tomorrow if I don't kill Miss Mabel first. Oh, and I think she's resurrecting an ancient evil magic to wipe out the world but I can't tell anyone about it because my secret binding won't let me.

The thought gave me a second surge of power. I used it to lop Mikhail's head off. Viveet's blue flame danced in slow licks until I set her aside. The light and power faded as soon as I released her. She rested on the stone wall, nothing more than a sharp piece of metal without me.

"No," I lied. "Just practicing."

"Let me guess: You don't like birthdays?" he asked, lifting one eyebrow. His green eyes matched the emerald flora. Sweat poured off him too, darkening his sandy hair at the roots. The lightest shade of a blonde beard ghosted against his strong jaw.

"Not really," I said. "When I was growing up, birthdays only meant I'd get older."

"I guess when you have an Inheritance Curse threatening to kill you, the day loses some of its excitement. This year you should celebrate. It's your first birthday without fear, right?"

Oh, how I wish.

"Sure. When are the Protectors going to vote on you?" I asked, hoping to change the subject. The thought of tomorrow weighed enough on my mind that I didn't want to discuss it with other witches. "Isn't that supposed to be soon?"

An unmistakable tension crept into his shoulders.

"Yes," he said. "Any day the Protectors want to vote."

"You mean they don't tell you when?"

He shook his head. "They could be voting right now, in fact. They won't say anything. They'll just inform me as soon as they've decided."

"So you have to just keep working in the meantime?"

"Yes. Speaking of work, it's been a few days since you and I have had a proper spar. Let's see what you can do."

Yes, I wanted to agree. *Let's see if I have any hope of defeating Miss Mabel before she kills me tomorrow.*

"Sure," I said, forcing a sarcastic smile. "Let's see how sad you are when I prove that I'm better than you."

Merrick never announced the beginning of a fight; he just started it and expected me to pick up the defense. Today was no different. He came at me with a high swing. I called to Viveet and she flew to my palm just in time to block his sword from slicing me in half. Although Merrick's strength was twice my own, my powers quickly bounced to life and held him at bay.

We fell into a familiar, but always changing, attack-and-defend dance. He moved forward, I worked back. My feet never crossed, my sword never dropped. Viveet and I sang, whirling, twirling, and dancing in a sweet kind of symphony that could only come from the interplay of swords and magic.

Despite all my work over the past several months, I couldn't beat him in skill or speed, and probably never would. Near the end of the sparring session, when the sweat on my roughened, calloused hands made it difficult to grip Viveet's hilt, Merrick kicked her from my hand and snatched both of my wrists, holding them behind my back.

"This is one of the most common holds you'll see," he said right next to my ear. "They'll get both hands behind you and twist them up your back until your shoulders pop out of socket. You'll be almost useless."

He took both my wrists and pushed them up between my shoulder blades. I bit back a yelp of pain by grinding my teeth together.

"How are you going to get out?" he asked. "You can't transport because someone else is touching you."

I tried to wrench free my left hand, the weaker of the two, but he just held onto it and laughed. When I struggled further, he shoved them higher up my back.

"Not going to work."

Each time I tried to stomp on his toes, he simply moved his feet back and pushed harder on my arms. My muscles started to protest in earnest now.

"Don't focus on the toes. Go for something that will make them release you and not be able to grab you again. If your opponent is in pain it will be harder for them to use magic to fight back."

"A curse?"

"They can counter it without letting you go. Think bigger."

"A head butt?"

"They might be taller than you."

I gazed down.

"Your knee?"

"Exactly. If someone has you from behind and you can't break free, do a back kick. Reinforcing it with magic will make you strong enough to break their leg or at least shatter their knee. Even if they anticipate it, they'll have to step back, which moves their focus."

He released my arms. I shook them out with relief, tired from the early morning workout and long sparring session. Merrick, however, looked fresh and ready to fight again. Unwilling to back down and admit my weakness, I brushed the fatigue aside and waited for his next lesson. He grinned.

"Now," he drawled. "Let's talk about poking someone in the eye."

Our conversation came to a sudden halt when a folded piece of messenger paper zipped in front of my face. The purple ink on the front nearly stopped my heart.

Miss Mabel.

"Who's that from?" Merrick asked. I snatched it from the air and stuffed it into the pocket of the breeches I wore.

"No one," I said, breathless. "Eyes, right? Poking them out and such."

Merrick held my gaze.

"Is it from Derek?"

"Doesn't matter," I snapped. "Let's get back to work."

The question in his eyes seemed to move like the cogs in his eyes as he decided whether he should press the question. I waited, hoping that my face remained impassive.

"Fine," he said. "If someone attacks you from the front and . . ."

His words faded into the background. I listened to the rest of the lesson, but could hardly pay attention, doing little more than mimicking his motions until he finally dismissed me with a frustrated growl. Once free, I forced myself to walk back to Chatham Castle at a normal pace until I made it into the back stairwell and bolted to the top of the Witchery at a sprint.

Both Leda and Camille were in the library working on their classes, so I tore into the envelope immediately, my heart pounding.

Dearest Bianca,

How time flies! I so look forward to seeing you tomorrow. It will be a joy watching you fulfill your part of our little contract. Keep your eyes open. A ball is certainly an easy place to hide, isn't it?

I'll see you soon, darling girl.

Miss Mabel.

In the aftermath of her message, my heart stuttered over and over again. I crunched the message in my fist. Our confrontation finally felt real now in a way it hadn't felt before. I glanced up to the wooden blocks on the mantle with a grim clench of my teeth. Their numbers taunted me.

Tomorrow.

Letum Wood enveloped me that evening in a humid, damp hug. I transported from my bedroom once Papa fell asleep, gently snoring on the old divan. The dark night filled the world like the liquid in an inkwell as I walked down a forest path. Viveet rested at my side, her constant presence reassuring my anxious heart. I wore a pair of loose pants just in case, more comfortable with my fluidity of movement when I didn't have a bunch of skirts dancing around my ankles. Once I saw the lights of Isadora's cottage through the wood I let out a long breath.

"Come in, Bianca," Isadora said when I stepped onto her porch. She sat in a rocking chair, her hands folded in her lap. She wore a light pink dress with white lace around the collar and her hair tucked back away from her face. I moved inside, leaving the door open to the night, and gasped. Candles scattered across her shelves lit up her once-lost china collection. Every square, cup, tray, and pot sat where it had a year before, when I first met Isadora.

"Your china is back."

"Yes. Sit," she said, motioning to a chair across from her with a nod of her head. "Now that your power is under better control I can trust you with it."

"You took it down because of me?" I asked, gaping. She nodded once.

"You were very angry that day and didn't have your powers under control yet. There were too many possibilities, so I did the safest thing. In the end, you got away without breaking anything."

I didn't know what to say.

"I'm sorry if it's too late to come speak with you."

"It's not too late," she said. "I knew you were coming. I'm not allowing Miss Mabel's to open for school in the fall, so I haven't been very busy."

"I'm not surprised," I admitted. "Not with things in Antebellum getting worse. What will the students do?"

"Learn at home. They'll have the option to learn the marks still, just not here. What can I help you with tonight, Bianca?" Isadora asked.

"I came to talk to you about Miss Mabel."

A flicker of something dark passed through her eyes, disappearing a moment later. She peered at me through the dim light.

"I can't give you want you want, Bianca. Unlike my sister, Sanna, I cannot save you by yelling at your monsters and scaring them away."

"Sanna told you we met?" I asked, smiling with one corner of my lips in a sheepish way. Isadora nodded.

"There isn't much that Sanna doesn't tell me. She gives me a headache, most days. But that's not what we're here to talk about."

My eyes fell to the floor as I thought over why I had come to talk to her. Tomorrow brought my birthday and possibly my death.

"What do I want?" I asked, hardly aware of it myself. A heavy jumble of guts, nerves, and fear sat inside me. If I hadn't learned to control the magic the past three months, I would have been a walking explosion.

"Reassurance," Isadora said. "You came for reassurance."

She was right. I wanted her to tell me that I wouldn't die tomorrow, that I'd be strong enough to kill Miss Mabel before she killed me. I wanted to know that my friends would survive the many hells that Miss Mabel and Angelina, if my suspicions were correct, would release on the Central Network. But even those weren't my biggest fear.

I want you to tell me that Papa won't die, I wanted to say. "Yes," I whispered instead. "I suppose you're right. I do want reassurance."

"I can't give you that."

"You can't help me at all?" I asked, clutching to hope. "You can't tell—"

"No." She shook her head. "I can't."

We sat in the silence while I tried to collect my thoughts.

"Did you see it?" I asked, finally giving voice to the question that had plagued me for over six months. "Did you see Miss Mabel killing my mother when you first interviewed me?"

Isadora's aged face turned down, the wrinkles elongating into a sad expression.

"I saw much grief and struggle. I saw many graves. I saw sadness and fire."

Many graves. The words echoed through my head.

"Will you tell me what you see now?" I asked, though I already knew the answer.

"No," she said in the same firm tone Leda used. "I will not."

I couldn't blame her, not really. Deep down, I didn't want to know the future. What if I saw something I'd never planned on? What if it frightened me into inaction? But although I'd had this conversation with Leda plenty of times before, for some reason it hurt more tonight. Perhaps I simply had more to lose.

"You said that I had strengths that Miss Mabel didn't," I said, recalling our last conversation. "Am I any stronger?"

Isadora paused, glancing down at my right hand, which rested on my lap near Viveet. The circlus sat there, unchanged.

"Do you feel stronger?" she asked.

"Physically, yes."

"How about here?" Isadora tapped her heart with the top of her fingers. I pressed my hand over mine, not sure of how to answer. Was my heart any stronger? I had better control over my powers, but the wrathful dragon still paced inside me, the living embodiment of my rage for Miss Mabel. I still woke up every day wanting my mother back. I still dreaded the night and longed for the morning.

"I don't know," I answered honestly.

Isadora stared at me. Seeming to relent under some invisible pressure, she let out a sigh.

"I see more than you think and more than you can comprehend right now," she said. "I can only tell you to watch and be valiant. There is much death coming, much death."

Her voice faded, sounding morose.

"I figured that."

"There's more to fear than just the West, Bianca. You already know that."

I stared back at Isadora for a moment, debating over whether I should trust her with my latest conjecture regarding Miss Mabel and Angelina. Then again, if I couldn't trust Isadora, who could I trust?

"Isadora, I have suspicions that I can't share." The protective magic of the binding sent a cool grip around my voice, a warning. Isadora's brow fell low as she regarded me. I gave her the space to sift through the memories in my head.

"Yes," she finally said. Her face darkened, like a storm had just moved over it. "I can see what you want to talk about. You think that Mabel has found the Almorran *Book of Spells* and plans to use it to take over Antebellum?"

I nodded.

"There's no proof that the book really exists. It's all hearsay and speculation."

"The scroll in the library—"

"Yes," she murmured. "I know. It says it was lost, not destroyed. There's also the matter of Angelina."

Her eyes glazed over again, going distant. When she came back to the present, she drew in a deep breath.

"I need to do some seeing. It may take time but I should be able to gain more information about the *Book of Spells* and Angelina."

Knowing that someone heard my fears took a great burden off my chest. If I died tomorrow, at least Isadora could press forward with the information I'd given her. I sank back against the chair in relief.

"Thank you, Isadora," I whispered.

"Blessings on you, Bianca. You're going to need all the strength you have to make it through what's coming."

A stark sense of impending doom crept up on me as I hiked back into Letum Wood, Isadora's at my back. Unable to talk myself out of the melancholy, I transported to the trails outside Chatham Castle, as familiar as the warm veins of blood on the back of my hand. My anxiety drifted into my run. Rushing past the dark trees, leaping over the boulders, and navigating the maze of tree roots cleared my head. Letum Wood made me feel strong again. Or was it the magic? Sometimes I couldn't discern the difference.

By the time I made it back to the apartment, the night had advanced. The late shift of Guardians patrolled the Wall. Double that number flanked every floor on the grand staircase and the entrances. The Royal Hall teamed with Guardians and Protectors, those visible and those not. Perhaps the High Priestess knew what I could not say.

Miss Mabel is coming. Soon. She'll be here soon.

After washing my sticky skin and changing into a cool blue linen dress with cap sleeves and a swooping neckline trimmed with white ribbon, I started up the Witchery stairs, barefoot. The anxiety from talking to Isadora had turned into a nagging headache, but I ignored it and climbed to the top anyway, hopeful that my friends were still awake.

If this is it, I thought, gazing around the familiar turret walls, *if I die tomorrow, I'll live my last night in style.*

Camille stood in front of a mirror, practicing curling her hair, wearing only her binder and a set of light knickers. She let out a yelp when the door slammed into the wall and I burst into the room. Michelle jerked, overturning an inkwell. Leda slowly glanced up from a book, annoyed.

"I'm going to stay up all night," I declared, breathless. "Who's with me?"

Camille dropped a curl and spun around.

"What?"

"Let's stay up all night!" I said, exhilarated with the idea. "We can go raid the kitchen and bring all the food back here and play games."

Camille gasped for joy.

"I've always wanted to stay up all night talking!" she cried, throwing herself onto a pillow. "Oh, it sounds wonderful. We can talk about the ball and braid each other's hair. Ooh! Let's sneak into the library and un-alphabetize the books." She let out an evil giggle. Leda rolled her eyes and tucked herself back into the tome she was studying.

"I'm working early tomorrow so I can get off in time to get ready for the ball," Michelle said, watching the thick pool of spilled ink gather back into the bottle with a collection incantation.

"I don't do well without sleep," Leda replied carelessly.

"Oh, come on!" I pleaded first to Michelle and then to Leda. "It'll be fun! Plus, Fina will never miss it if we steal some goodies because they're making so many for tomorrow. What's more fun than stuffing our face with chocolate and brownies?"

"Nothing!" Camille squeaked. "Nothing at all! I'm in!"

"Please?" I begged. "Do it for me."

Because I may never have another chance.

Michelle seemed to have read my thoughts. "Bianca," she whispered. "I forgot. Tomorrow is your seventeenth birthday."

The room fell silent, destroying the amicable mood I'd tried to force. Leda set aside her book and straightened.

"Tomorrow?" she demanded, her lips pinching in a tight line. "No, it can't be tomorrow."

Camille's joy died into an instant set of tears.

"What? It's tomorrow?"

"No!" I cried, frantically trying to get the jovial air back. "No! We aren't doing this. We aren't! I just . . . I just want to have one fun night. Just in case. Okay? We won't act like I'm going to die tomorrow." Camille's lower lip began to tremble, and I tacked on, "Because I'm not." The silence grew cumbersome, then awkward.

"Right," Leda declared, standing up. She met my eyes with a small, resolute smile. "The High Priestess promised you that she'd sort it out, and she will. Let's have a fun night. Brownies it is!"

Michelle stood. "I'm in," she said. "I-I'm not sure I can stay awake all night, but I'll try."

Camille clapped, sniffled, and stood up, her eyes still sparkling with unshed tears.

"Indeed! The High Priestess will have it put to rights. We'll think of nothing but having fun for the rest of the night!" she declared. "Let's go swim without clothes in the pond! I've always wanted to try."

We started our celebration by sneaking into the kitchen by the back staircase. Michelle created a distraction while the rest of us filched brownies, tarts, lemon bars, a bottle of fizzy water, and a handful of cranberry poppy seed muffins, piling our ill-gotten gains onto a tray. I stuffed a loaf of bread, a hunk of cheese, and a few other goodies in a pillowcase. Then we left, running back up the stairs with hushed giggles and Leda's panicked threats that we'd be found if we didn't hush up. When Mrs. L saw us from the other end of a hall and called out, we ran for the turret and threw ourselves into the safety of the stairwell before she caught us. I put a protective incantation on the stairs to keep her out, just in case.

"Oh, don't forget to try the lemon bar," Camille sighed an hour later, her eyes closed as she savored the sweet-and-tart pastry. We sat around the table, our fare spread out in a lavish feast before us, the turret windows thrown open. "It's simply divine."

Michelle tried a bit of croissant glazed with strawberry and chocolate. Leda, who for once didn't have a book within arm's length, dove into a berry tart and didn't speak for minutes. The remnants of our food hurricane were scattered on the floor around us. Camille had stripped all the way down to her knickers and binder again, and her hair was pulled away from her face in a high ponytail.

"They are going to serve fifty different kinds of pie tomorrow," Michelle said, picking out a chunk of sponge cake.

"The Central Network has always celebrated with food," Camille said, sucking the frosting off her fingers. "Which is precisely why I shall always consider it home. At least I know I'll be in good company. I do hope there's a Milton berry pie tomorrow."

"There will be," Michelle said with a happy sigh.

I eyed a square brownie loaded with frosting. I'd just finished a slice of chocolate cake. Should I?

Might as well, I thought, and snatched it before Leda could. She changed course and went for an eclair instead.

"Oh, I'm so excited to go to the Anniversary Ball!" Camille said, recovering her usual breathy tone. "I'm just going to die when I have to leave to go back to school in the fall."

"What if they don't start school back up?" I asked after swallowing a thick bite of brownie. All three of them stopped chewing to stare at me.

"What do you mean?" Michelle asked. "Why would they stop school?"

Realizing that I had spoken up too soon—I couldn't explain what Isadora told me without having to explain why I went to Isadora in the first place—I tried to dance around it.

"With war becoming more and more likely," I said in a musing tone, "Isadora may not deem it safe to run the Network schools until the danger subsides."

Camille waved it off.

"I'll just stay here with you and Miss Scarlett. It would be amazing!"

"I don't think it will happen," Leda said in a cool tone as she took another bite of eclair dripping with cream filling. A drop fell and plopped onto her hand. She sucked it off. "It will all work out."

"You aren't worried?" I asked. I wondered what she saw that she wasn't telling me. Leda avoided my eyes.

"No."

"Let's play a card game, shall we?" Camille asked, grabbing a deck of cards. "Zeke taught me a really fun one. Then, once it's really late, we'll sneak to the pond and go swimming."

The cards spilled all over the floor when she opened the flap, scattering into a hundred different places. The mishap broke the strand of tension in the air and all of us dissolved into laughter, reclaiming the joy we'd felt and forgetting that it could be our last night together.

The Empowerment

All of us fell asleep shortly after Michelle went to work in the kitchens, just before the sunrise. I woke to Camille slapping me while she mumbled in her sleep, and I plucked a reed out of my hair from our wicked trip to the pond. Leda was nowhere to be found. I got up with the sun and quickly dressed, tucking my hair into an orderly braid and tossing it over one shoulder. I had an Empowerment to attend.

Two Guardians stood near the grand staircase as I walked past. The added security set my teeth on edge. With the ball tonight, and all the Coven Leaders and their families here, Papa and Tiberius had taken every safety precaution. Miss Mabel's letter ran through my mind, and I shuddered. I wished again, for the hundredth time, that I could send out a warning of what may come. I'd tried, only to find cold silence tightening my throat.

I sucked in a deep breath and steered myself for the Royal Hall. The Guardians stood in the path, barring any entrance. Before I could explain my presence they parted, letting me through.

The Throne Room stood at the end of the hall, just before the High Priestess's office. The double doors contained our history in a quick glimpse. I stopped long enough to study the elaborate carvings that started at the top and worked their way down. Esmelda filled up the left corner at the top, and the rule of High Priests and Priestesses moved across the door. A black x marked Evelyn's spot.

I turned away with a shudder.

The doors to the Throne Room groaned when I pushed against its bulky weight, exacerbating an already pounding headache that hadn't gone away since I left Isadora's. A line of crimson and gold carpet ran from the doors up to the stone stairs that led to the thrones. The two massive chairs sat next to each other, elevated on a platform above the rest of the room. The High Priestess's throne sat ahead of the High Priest's, indicating that she held more power. Papa would never exceed her in power as long as she was alive. Once she died and a new High Priestess took her place, his throne would move forward.

Papa lounged in the Dragon Throne, his eyes trained on a distant spot on the wall above me. A run of paintings depicting previous High Priests and Priestesses circled the entire room, their faces peering out like old specters. A blank, empty spot stood where Evelyn's painting should have been. No painting would rest there as an ugly reminder of the dangers of dark magic and evil purposes.

"Papa?" I asked. The door whispered to a close behind me as I ventured a few steps into the mostly empty room. My bare feet made no sound as I walked. Papa drew in a deep breath and tore his eyes away from the spot at which he'd been staring on the wall.

"Come in," he said, scooting over to make room for me. "Let's talk."

The Dragon Throne was wide enough to fit both of us side by side. Carved scales ran along the legs and claws supported the bottom. The back of it resembled the long neck of a forest dragon, with shiny black scales that looked like a bruised blue and black at the same time. An angular head roared at the top, teeth bared. The gruesome thing made me shudder. I slid onto the seat next to Papa and we sat in the silence for a few minutes. He smelled like peppermint and it comforted me.

"I'm not sure how I feel about doing this," he said, gesturing to the throne and looking at me with one eyebrow lifted.

"It's too late to back out now. They've already made your favorite desserts in the kitchen."

He chuckled at my poor attempt at humor.

"Yes. Fina wouldn't be happy."

For the first time since I made the vow with the High Priestess, I wondered if lying to Papa had been for the best. If I failed to defeat

Miss Mabel, would he be able to move on knowing that I'd given myself up for him?

"How did this happen, B?" he asked, finally looking at me. I wanted to reach out and smooth the wrinkles around his eyes away, but I didn't have that power. This kind of constant pressure and stress would be his life from now on. Papa would serve the Network until death took him.

"You'll be great, Papa," I said in a breezy tone, as if this kind of thing happened all the time. "You're the best man to lead this Network through the war and on to victory."

He didn't seem convinced. The uncertainty in his eyes made him seem too human, too breakable, and I wanted to look away and tell him to stop. I'd never seen Papa like this, and I didn't want to ever again.

"The Council doesn't want me in this position," he said, although his tone was more musing than fearful. I thought back to Clive's rally, to the witches in Chatham City protesting his Empowerment. Would the Central Network ever know peace again?

"Do you want this position?"

"Would anyone?" he shot back.

"No," I murmured. "I guess not. Are you scared?"

He thought about it for a minute, his eyes tired.

"Yes," he said. "I'd be a fool not to be."

"Do you think everything is going to be okay with the Council?"

"Eventually, yes. They'll accept it because they have to. Don't worry about them, B. You let me take care of that."

But I would worry about it. I'd worry about it every time the Council voted. If I lived long enough, I'd worry about it every time Papa made a decision.

"I think they just want someone to blame because they're scared," I said in an attempt to make myself feel better. "And they've chosen you because you're so strong."

His eyes lit up for just a second.

"That's an incredibly adult thing to say," he said in a quiet tone. "Are you sure you're not turning thirty today?"

"Don't put me there yet," I said, forcing a wry smile to put him at ease. "I'm not officially seventeen until 11:54 tonight."

The clock seemed to tick all the louder in the background, calling back to mind how little time I had left. I would miss Papa more than anything. Or would I? What happened after death? Mama and Grandmother believed we continued on. I hoped they were right.

"I'm sorry your birthday has to culminate on a ball," he said, pulling me from my thoughts. "You should celebrate by playing in the mud. That sounds more like you."

I tilted my head back and laughed.

"Only if I can rub your face in it."

"I don't want to drown out the excitement of turning seventeen with something as boring as politics. This is the first birthday you're free," he said, his expression sober. "You should enjoy it."

I'm never free, Papa. Never.

"Boring?" I giggled. "Papa, you're making history. Mama would have been so proud of you today."

He smiled with a warm undertone that brought me comfort.

"You're just like your mother, B. Marie wanted nothing but adventure wherever she could get it."

While it wounded my heart to hear her name, it healed another ache I didn't know I had.

So many little bruises. How will they all ever heal?

"She also loved going barefoot and the smell of rain," I said, recalling the memories with perfect clarity. "She told me every night that her biggest adventure started the day she met you."

Papa chuckled under his breath.

"Do you remember the time we found a cave and your mother wanted to go inside? It was early summer, I think, and we were walking through Letum Wood in the north of the Network, near Newberry."

The memory flittered back through my mind.

"Yes!" I cried. "She went in and then came running back out, chased by a couple of small bear cubs."

Papa let out a hoot of laughter.

"You weren't laughing then!" I poked him in the arm. "You were terrified that the mother bear was going to attack. I had to transport back home."

"Well, you were just a cub yourself. I had no choice. Your mother would have taken the bear home as a pet."

"She always did take in stray animals."

The mirth settled into a comfortable silence, leaving both of us to our memories. Life had always been an adventure with Papa.

"I'm starting to forget what she looked like, Papa," I whispered, wishing with all my heart that I could recall the lines of her face. I should have appreciated the living memories when I'd had them. "It frightens me."

I hadn't admitted it out loud before, and saying it made me feel fragile, exposed. Perhaps all this darkness would spill out of my heart and I could put it back together without the dragon inside. He took my hand in his and threaded our fingers together.

"I guess I'm lucky," he said. "I get to see your mother every day." I raised an eyebrow in silent question. He brushed a stray lock of hair from my face and tucked it behind my ears. "Every time I look at you I see Marie."

"I love you, Papa," I said, squeezing his hand. "No matter what happens, just remember how much I love you. I'm so proud of you."

Tears welled up in my eyes. He chucked me softly under the chin, giving me the smile that Mama had fallen in love with so many years before, then pulled me in close and tucked me into his side.

For just that moment I let my heart melt, absorbing everything I could. I forgot about Miss Mabel, about the possibility that I could die or send the Central Network into a spiral that it couldn't recover from. Because I didn't know if it would be the last time he'd ever hold me, I thought only of his strong arms and the smell of peppermint.

Tiberius's massive size gave me strength.

We stood together in the Throne Room, waiting for the Empowerment to begin. Papa had switched back into Protector mode and stood near the Dragon's Throne with his hands folded in front of him, his face stoic.

Though Antebellum was deteriorating into war and panic, all of us could see that Papa didn't fear. Any remnants of the worry he'd expressed to me had vanished. He looked calm and confident, just the way we needed him to be. The rest of the Protectors stood behind Zane in a line, their hands folded behind their backs. Merrick stood at the far end.

"Tiberius," I leaned over to him. "Did the Protectors accept Merrick?"

He nodded once with an annoyed scowl.

"They voted this morning. He's taking the open slot."

I grinned down the row at Merrick, but he stared straight ahead and didn't see. His jaw had a tighter clench, his eyes more focused than I'd seen before. I wondered if he was afraid.

The small group of thirteen projected an air of authority, but the wide range of their appearances was almost comical. Grizzled beards stood next to faces as smooth as a baby. Some of the Protectors were lean and strong, while others had paunchy bellies and bulky shoulders.

Ambassador Marten walked up to join Tiberius and me. He shot me a reassuring smile that helped quell the nervous fear in my belly, and nodded to Papa, who returned it with a wry grin.

"Derek Black," the High Priestess said in her usual crisp manner the moment she walked into the room. "Because this is a private ceremony, and I've run out of patience for old traditions, I'm going to cut through most of the fluff."

My lips twitched with a concealed chuckle as she passed.

In honor of the ceremony, she wore no crown, no jewelry, no embellishments at all. Instead of her ball gown she wore one of the yellow dresses that made her look ages older. Papa wore a pair of brown leather pants, sewn by Henrietta herself, and a black shirt with a black vest over it. Neither of the outfits were anything special. The lack of glamor was intentional: it represented that the heart of being High Priest or Priestess was character, not adornments.

The High Priestess turned to those attending, running her eyes over us. Her gaze lingered on me, seeming to burn a hole in my head. I looked away, unable to bear it. Even if she fulfilled her part of the vow tonight, it wouldn't matter. The binding still kept a noose around my neck, one that only I could loosen.

Papa will be safe to save the Central Network from war if I die, I reassured myself. *He'll be able to move on, to stay busy, to remain afloat.*

The thought of giving him another reason to mourn pained me. The nagging headache I'd had all day intensified when the High Priestess began.

"Derek, today you will receive a blessing of Empowerment reserved only for those who take the responsibility to care for the Central Network as High Priest upon their shoulders. It is not a position you may ever leave. In pledging to serve your Network, you give the rest of your life to it."

"I understand," he said. His voice rang through the room without hesitation. A few of the Protectors smiled; the rest frowned. The High Priestess held out her hand and a swirl of glowing sapphire dots rose from her palm, whirling around an ebony bracelet on her palm. It was the High Priest's bracelet, inscribed with the language of the Ancients.

SAC ERO DOS SUM MUS

A nearly identical bracelet rested on the High Priestess's arm, although hers was silver.

"You will wear this representation of your power every day of your life," she said. "It can only be removed upon your death. As one of the strongest charms in all of Antebellum, it will provide an extra protection should you need it. The power that comes with it is great. Should anyone try to take it from your wrist while you live, it will kill them."

Papa nodded.

"I understand."

"Then let us empower you."

The High Priestess closed her eyes and began a low chant, whispering the blessing under her breath. No one else could hear the exact words she spoke except Papa, and he'd have to memorize them on the spot, committing them to memory to repeat later if he brought in a new High Priestess.

A bright white glow illuminated the words on the bracelet. The sapphire dots gathered into three long, slender ropes that pulled the shimmering charm into the air. It swung toward Papa and fell onto his awaiting hand. He placed it on his left wrist, over the sign of the Protector's Brotherhood. The High Priestess's incantation broke.

Papa drew in a long, shaky breath. His face paled and the muscles of his jaw tightened. He stood with white-knuckle fists, then stumbled and fell to one knee, gasping. His nostrils flared and neck spasmed.

Tiberius grabbed my shoulder when I started forward to help him.

"He needs to do this alone," Tiberius whispered. "Leave off."

"Overwhelming, isn't it?" the High Priestess asked Papa in a quiet tone. "This endowment is a heavier burden than anyone will ever know you bear. The power you feel will soon calm."

My heart rested somewhere near my throat, fluttering like the wings of a hummingbird in nervous anticipation.

Papa remained with his head bowed, his shoulders trembling, for several minutes. Then with one mighty move, he shoved away from the floor and stood to face us again, accepting the full weight of his duty. The magic from the blessing caused him to glow with a golden shimmer from the inside out. The stretch of his shoulders seemed broader, his legs more powerful. He took my breath away. This was a new Papa, a new witch.

I knew then, in my heart, that *he* was the one Miss Mabel feared.

There may be someone in the Central Network stronger than me, but it certainly isn't Mildred.

"Are you ready, Derek?" the High Priestess asked, breaking into my thoughts.

"Yes," he said. The moment passed, and the glory dimmed back: he was his usual self again now, but with a new air of power. A surge of pride overwhelmed me. I leaned into Tiberius's side and he put a big hand on my shoulder. The High Priestess turned to the other Protectors.

"You have not lost your leader," she said. "You've simply seen him gain further progression, as all of you strive to do. By taking this position Derek continues to fulfill the creed of your brotherhood."

Zane rested a hand over his heart.

"As I have before," he said to Papa, "and will forever more, I pledge to you my protection, loyalty, and assistance, brother."

Each Protector would say the phrase with his hand over his heart: as the youngest, Merrick would pledge last. Instead of putting his hand on his heart to accept their pledge, Papa stepped forward, grabbed Zane by the left arm and gripped his shoulder.

"Live and die together," he promised. "You have my word. I am your brother."

He went down the line with the same routine, then lightly chuffed Merrick on the side of the head with an affectionate smack. When he finished, the High Priestess stepped forward.

"We have a ball to prepare for and attend," the High Priestess said. "Please be on your guard. Reports from the South indicate that they have been calm all day, and so has the West. I don't trust calm things. This would be a prime opportunity to attack and weaken the Central Network."

Yes! I wanted to shout. *Yes, Miss Mabel is coming!*

The High Priestess's eyes fell on me when she finished. A flash of anxiety prodded the powers, resurrecting the surly dragon that still lived in my chest.

Wake up, I thought. *Wake up, wake up. I'll need you later.*

When Miss Mabel shows up.

Closer

"You don't seem like a young witch that's about to go to her first ball," Henrietta remarked, bustling behind me with a needle and thread in hand. I stood on a step stool, staring out at Papa's empty apartment. Now that the Empowerment was over, maids had already started packing our belongings to move us into the High Priest's suite in the middle of the castle, not far from the High Priestess's personal quarters. The apartment seemed small and empty without swords and daggers decorating the walls.

"I guess I don't feel like a young witch attending her first ball," I said.

Henrietta shot me a surprised glance. The usual flood of pins and needles bobbed in the air around her, tailing her wherever she went.

"Why not?" she asked.

Imminent battle with my worst enemy, possibly death. The usual.

"Something of a headache," I said, and it wasn't a lie. The herbal tea Grandmother used to give me for headaches hadn't worked, though I'd drunk nearly a pot of it since the Empowerment. I wondered what my friends were doing in the Witchery. Was Camille lamenting about her hair? Fussing over Michelle? I couldn't wait to see Leda in a ball gown. Henrietta, giving up on conversation, patted a few places, added a stitch here and there, and stepped away.

"There it is," she said. "You look a wonder. Far cry from the wild child that runs in the woods. It's not ladylike to go barefoot, you know."

A mirror lifted into the air from where it rested by the door and drifted toward me. A gasp caught in my throat. For a flash, a brief second, I thought I saw my mother in the long black hair and slender body that looked back at me. All the work with Merrick had given my shoulders a toned, sculpted appearance. The deep sapphire material of the gown covered my shoulders and arms just to my elbow. Lace as black as night decorated the ends of the sleeves and the scooped neckline. Except for the grief in my gray eyes, I wouldn't have known it was me. I looked away when Henrietta clasped something around my neck, saving the mirror from another unfortunate accident.

"I know you miss her tonight," she whispered. "And although it's against tradition, I thought you should wear this again. It will make her feel a bit closer."

The weight on my breastbone told me all I needed to know. Mama's memento. A little silver ball with a locket of her hair inside, usually worn on the anniversary of her death. Tonight it would be pressed against my heart, exactly where I needed Mama to give me strength.

"Thank you, Henrietta," I whispered, clasping the memento in my fist. A longing for Mama ran through me in a long current, painful and stinging. *This is why I used to push it away,* I thought. *It hurts.* But beneath the grief came a subtle rise of power. I held the magic in my heart, drawing strength from it.

Soon. Miss Mabel will be here soon.

Henrietta, so unaware of my thoughts, smiled and patted my shoulder.

"Now," she said in a bright tone, casting a wary eye on my hair. "What are we going to do about your hair? It doesn't look quite as wild as usual, which gives me hope that it can be contained."

"Nothing," I said, tucking a strand behind my ear. "I plan on wearing my hair just like this."

Henrietta's expression dropped.

"You what, dear?"

I smiled. "I'm going to wear my hair like this."

"Like *that?*" she cried, pointing.

"Indeed. I washed it, brushed it, and Camille helped me curl it a little with some kind of potion she made. It's very shiny, don't you think?"

I toyed with a lazy curl that rested just past my shoulder, but Henrietta didn't seem to notice. She opened her mouth to protest, and seeing the stubborn look on my face, closed it again. There would be no winning this fight. If I would die tonight, I'd do it my way.

"Don't tell me," she drawled, casting a fearful glance at my feet with her doughy face. "You aren't going to—"

"I am," I declared proudly, sticking one bare foot out of the dress. "I'm going barefoot. I refuse to wear shoes to the ball tonight."

Henrietta's face flushed, then went pale.

"You wouldn't. Not for the Anniversary Ball. Not for the biggest night of your father's life."

"I would," I said breezily, moving off the stand. "He won't mind. He'll just laugh. Besides, Henrietta, who will notice? No one will be looking at my feet, and if they do, whatever they find is their own fault."

"Not right in the head," she muttered, turning away from me. "Addled. Too much heat. Needs to spend more time at something productive. Sewing! Sewing is good for the mind."

Her prattling faded away as she moved out of the room without a farewell, obviously too bothered by my lack of restraint to say goodbye. I watched her go, then bustled over to the window. The sun started sinking beneath the trees of Letum Wood. In the distance, I thought I saw the flicker of a pair of wide, dark wings rising from the night.

The clock above the grand stairs rang ten times as I walked past it toward the High Priestess's office. The ball started promptly at eleven in the evening and would run until dawn. Most of the Council Members, Coven Leaders, their families and the lesser leaders had congregated in the dining room for a lavish dinner that I'd passed on. I could just picture Fina's red face flying around the kitchen, barking orders, making sure every dish looked perfect.

Less than two hours until my Inheritance Curse completes.

The thought set my nerves on fire. I shook my head and tapped on the door with my knuckle just once, but the High Priestess was already calling to me.

"Yes, come in, Bianca."

She sat behind her desk, intent on writing a letter with a small gray feather. The open windowpanes allowed air to drift in, filling the room with the silky scents of grass and summer. The linea fabric of my dress kept me cool. I felt like the heat was just a silly mirage. When I moved into the room she gazed up, looked me over, and went back to her letter. It all felt the same, and yet, something was different.

"You look very nice," she said.

"Henrietta would like to club me over the head and do my hair while I'm passed out," I replied, settling on the chair. The soft rustle of the fabric against my legs felt like moving through a cloud. A more perfect last dress didn't exist.

"Don't give her the satisfaction," the High Priestess muttered. "She has no talent for hair."

I waited for her to finish her letter. When she finally did, her gaze slammed right into mine.

"I want to know how you feel about your father taking over as High Priest," she said with her usual abrupt gravity. "This change will possibly affect you more than him. We never talked about it, and I apologize. Things have been busy."

Taken aback, I sat there for several moments, trying to decide what to say.

"I was frightened for him," I admitted. "But not anymore."

"Why not?"

I thought back to the Empowerment, to the look in his eyes, the electric power in the air. Then I thought of Miss Mabel, of our conversation, and the sense I had that she feared Papa.

"Because he's strong," I finally concluded. "The strongest of all, I think. He may be one of the only witches Miss Mabel actually fears."

"Your father is quite possibly the most talented witch and the most powerful Protector we've ever known. That's what I want to talk about with you tonight. There's a reason I allowed your father to break tradition and have a wife and daughter."

My eyebrows rose.

"Why?"

The High Priestess let out a heavy sigh.

"I love the Central Network. I always have. I've given my life to her. I see all her beauties, and all her flaws. We've created a powerful Network, but we've also created a monster. All of our traditions keep us rooted in the past. The witches of our Network hold to them for comfort, not realizing that those traditions are the very thing that will bring about our downfall."

Her words set my heart into a gallop.

"Downfall?"

"Derek is the only witch I know that's brave enough, and powerful enough, to go against tradition and allow change. Mabel's campaign against us will be successful if we don't let go of how things used to be done. She knows our traditions. She's already using them against us. She will continue to do so until our deeply entrenched habits become the very things that destroy us. Your father is intelligent enough to alter the way we do things in a way that Mabel can't anticipate. After all these years, Mabel knows me too well. She's studied me enough to understand how I think and what I will do. That's why I went against the Council to put him in power. We need your father. He's strong in ways I never can be."

I thought over what she said with a somber heart. Her admission felt like a heavy secret. I knew she was right and it frightened me. Hadn't Miss Mabel correctly guessed the High Priestess's choice for who would be the next High Priest?

"I see," I said when the silence stretched too long. She narrowed her eyes.

"No, you don't. Not yet. But you will, eventually. And when you really understand, I want you to think back on this conversation and draw comfort."

I fidgeted with the lines of my dress, trying to draw some courage. "May I ask you a question?"

She nodded.

"What happened after my mother died?"

The tense lines of her face relaxed just a little.

"You don't know?"

I shook my head.

She thought for a second. "Four of us came to assist Derek. Stella, Donald, Marten, and myself. When we arrived, you were screaming and holding Marie. We couldn't get you to stop, and you wouldn't let go. It was Stella that first noticed your broken hand. I put a calming incantation on you so we could fix it. Then Stella and I rode with you in the carriage back to Chatham while Marten tried to find Mabel. Scarlett helped Derek take care of Marie while Donald informed Miss Bernadette and Miss Amelia of what had occurred and what to tell the students."

Tears filled my eyes. When I looked down, away from the intensity of her stare, two hot tears dropped down my cheek, skipping like a rock across the surface of a lake.

"Henrietta and I took care of you in my personal apartments until Derek came back late that night," the High Priestess continued. "Then he took you back to his apartment and that's where you woke up the next day."

She allowed silence to fill the room in the aftermath of her explanation. Instead of the usual burn of agony and regret, I felt the cool balm of knowing I was loved even if Mama was gone. Through my darkest hours I was still surrounded by witches who cared. Now, standing apart from the shock and horror of those moments, I could appreciate how much that meant.

"Thank you," I said, gazing up to her. That simple phrase encompassed so much more than I could ever verbalize. The High Priestess's face softened, looking so much like Grandmother's that another pang of longing swelled inside me. I knew I'd never question her again; the High Priestess understood far more than I ever gave her credit for.

"You're welcome."

I wiped the tears off my cheek, and the High Priestess directed the conversation elsewhere.

"I'm sure you are wondering about our vow," she said, her tone becoming clipped and businesslike again.

My breath caught in my throat.

"Yes, of course."

"Do you still trust me?"

"Yes, Your Highness."

The High Priestess leaned back in her chair.

"Good. Then I would ask you to extend that trust another hour."

A flicker of hesitation, perhaps uncertainty, moved across her face. I wondered what kind of magic she would have to use to make this come about, but I forced the thoughts from my mind. I had to focus on my part and trust that she knew what she was doing.

"I'm proud of you," she said, taking me by surprise. "You've come a long way in the past couple of months. The good gods know that nothing has ever been easy for you, but somehow you've made it out alive."

Don't get ahead of yourself, I thought.

"Thank you."

"Whatever happens tonight, Bianca, I want you to accept it. Do you understand? The things that will happen to the Central Network over the next months or years are bigger than either one of us."

Miss Mabel is coming. Do you know? I wanted to ask, but the words stuck in my throat.

"Yes, Your Highness," I whispered instead, not entirely certain I understood what she meant. Did it matter? No. Not tonight. All that mattered tonight was staying alive and killing Miss Mabel before she killed me.

"That's all," she finally said, her gaze lingering on me. "You may go."

"Thank you for the dress," I said, standing up. "Henrietta said you chose the material. It's lovely."

"You look like your mother in it."

"Yes," I agreed with a slight smile. "You're right."

"Go," she commanded, turning back to her scroll. "I have a few things to attend to here."

When I looked back over my shoulder, she remained in the same position, focused on the scroll. Regal, a touch haughty, and probably the most influential witch I'd ever met. I wondered why she looked so sad.

I hope I make you proud tonight, Your Highness, my heart whispered.

With a preparatory breath, I turned and steeled myself for whatever might come next. I didn't know how Miss Mabel would come, or when, or if she'd even look like herself, but I knew she'd be there.

And I had to be ready.

She's Here

"Isn't it too wonderful?" Camille asked in a breathy voice. "I think I might just die from happiness. It's all so pretty!"

The four of us stepped into the ballroom together. Although I couldn't tell them, having my friends at my side made me feel strong. Being in control of the power brought a great deal of hope and light to my heart, but not as much as their persistent friendship. A wave of anxiety welled up from deep within. I embraced it, letting it roll through me, feeling it expand my magic.

Yes. Make me strong. Let me feel it all tonight. This time the emotions will make me mighty.

The massive ballroom had been decorated with such a natural elegance that it took us several minutes of staring to take it all in. Tables laden with food lined one wall, boasting at least fifty different pie offerings, as Michelle had promised. Sprawling paintings of Letum Wood filled every other wall in long murals of green and brown. Golden trim swept along the ceiling, while mirrors reflected the burning torches, and elaborate sconces dripped with golden Letum Ivy. Above it all loomed an emerald-laced forest dragon painted on the ceiling, breathing fire and banishing our enemies.

The High Priestess and Papa stood at opposite ends of the room, Papa on the right, the High Priestess on the left. Standing together made them too vulnerable. Even if they didn't know or act like Miss Mabel was coming, they were certainly taking every precaution. Two thrones, smaller replicas of the real thrones in the Throne Room, had been placed at the end near the High Priestess. Later, when toasts were made from the Council Members to Papa, they'd sit there together. A few strategically placed Protectors hovered near both of them, occasionally blending in with the crowd, appearing and disappearing whenever they wanted. I searched for Merrick, hoping to congratulate him.

"It is beautiful," Michelle said, looking awkward and thick in her high-waisted pink gown. Camille had pinned Michelle's coarse brown hair up on her head with sprays of small white flowers and curls, making her face look wider than ever.

"Really, Bianca," Camille huffed, casting another wary look at my hair. "You should have let me do something more than just that potion. It's a ball, you know."

Despite her demands, Camille hadn't been allowed within arm's length of me after Henrietta helped me with the dress. She'd spent most of the afternoon getting herself ready, and the time paid off. Her dishwater curls looked bright and blonde, formed into perfect ringlets that bounced whenever she turned her head. Her dress, an elaborate ivory piece with layers of lace and chiffon, made her look royal and elegant.

"My hair is just fine the way it is," I said, watching a few couples spin past us. Council Member Patrice wore an extravagant green gown with so many ruffles I almost couldn't see her beneath it all. She pranced away with another Council Member, giggling.

Leda let out a hefty sigh next to me.

"How are you, Leda?" I asked. "Is your curse beating you up?"

"It's tolerable," she said with a grimace and put a hand to her head. She spaced out again, her eyes distant. The light blue dress that Henrietta had sewn for her actually complemented her fair hair and skin. Tonight, Leda looked petite, pale, and lovely.

"Are you going to make it for very long?" I asked once she snapped out of it. A crowd of this size must be giving her a headache as walloping as mine. My own head pulsed and raged. Leda looked at me from the corner of her eyes, her face unusually pinched and her jaw clenched.

"I'll be fine."

I searched through the crowd with the fear that I'd see Miss Mabel's suave grin and sparkling eyes peering out from amongst the innocent spectators. Perhaps she'd transform herself so no one recognized her, or pull me off to the side to deal with me in private. I hoped for the latter.

"Oh no," Camille said under her breath, chewing on her bottom lip. "Here comes Luther."

"You don't want to dance with Luther?" Michelle asked.

"No!" she breathed, turning away and pressing her hand to her flushed cheek. "I don't mind, I-I just hoped to dance with Brecken first."

"Is Brecken back?" I asked.

"I don't know!" she wailed under her breath, turning away as if she hadn't seen Luther. "I haven't seen him or heard from him. Oh, dear."

My eyes widened as a familiar pair of broad shoulders and unruly brown curls stepped into Luther's path, cutting him off.

"Camille," Brecken said in his rolling, low voice. "You aren't crying over me, are you?"

Like the other Captains, Brecken looked handsome in a deep red shirt underlying a black overcoat. Colorful emblems stitched onto his jacket indicated his achievements as a Captain of the Guards, silent testimonies to his years of work. Camille whirled around, wide-eyed and shocked.

"Brecken?" she whispered.

He grinned with a wicked smile.

"As if you ever doubted that I'd come," he said and whisked her onto the dance floor without another word. The two of them disappeared, absorbed into the teeming mass of bodies.

"Michelle?" came a voice from behind.

Michelle and I looked back to see Nicolas standing there, slightly hunched and burly. He stood several inches taller than Michelle's towering frame, with beefy shoulders and hands to match.

"I almost didn't recognize you," he said, smiling in his soft, quiet way. "You look wonderful tonight. More beautiful than I could have ever imagined."

A dazzling blush crept over her face when she ducked her head down.

"Merry meet, Nicolas," she whispered so quietly the violins in the background absorbed her voice. He smiled and then bowed once to me.

"Merry meet, Miss Bianca. You look lovely in dark blue."

I smiled. "Merry meet, Nicolas. Thank you."

A cumbersome silence followed. Michelle opened her mouth to say something, decided against it, and looked to me with a wide-eyed plea for help.

"Would you do me a favor, Nicolas?" I asked.

His eyebrows rose in surprise. "I would love to."

"We were just on our way to get something to drink," I said. "But I have a terrible headache and don't plan on moving very far. Would you mind going with Michelle? It's not good manners to walk around alone at a ball."

A smile so wide I thought it would split his head met my request.

"I would love to help! If Michelle doesn't mind, of course."

Michelle looked up, startled.

"No!" she said too loudly. She calmed her response. "I mean . . . I'd love it if you walked over there with me."

He offered her his arm and she took it, sending me a secret, grateful smile over her shoulder.

Two friends taken care of, I thought, circling back around to face the dance. *One to go.*

"Well," I said to Leda, gazing around, "I guess we'll just be stuck here waiting to dance together."

"Speak for yourself," she scoffed. "I have a dance or two lined up."

To my disbelief, Rupert moved toward us with a hand out to Leda. His red mustache gleamed in the candlelight and looked so proper that I wondered if he'd actually brushed it before the ball. Leda took his hand and disappeared without a glance back.

"Good for you, Leda," I murmured with a smile that quickly faded. I hoped this wasn't goodbye.

All for the best, I reminded myself. Dancing wasn't my idea of a good time. At any rate, I had plans.

I was scouting out the ballroom when a hand captured my wrist and tugged, twirling me around until I stood face-to-face with

Merrick. I didn't comprehend for several seconds that we were danc-ing, but soon realized that he glided me along without me even know-ing it. A little flutter of butterflies moved deep in my stomach. Did they teach all the Protectors how to dance so smoothly?

"Merry meet," I said, clearing my throat, mortified to feel a blush rising to my cheeks. Like the rest of the Protectors, Merrick wore a simple outfit that blended in; in his case, black pants and a white shirt with a black jacket over it. It was formal enough to get by, but not nearly as stuffy and pompous as some of the other witches. His hair, freshly washed, was pulled back into a ponytail. The sandy streaks of brown and blonde looked especially bright in the ballroom lighting. His shaven face looked temptingly soft. I curled my fingers into my palm instead of reaching up to feel his cheek. He hadn't even changed his appearance for the Ball this evening. "I hear that congratulations are in order."

He smiled with that wry quality I'd come to appreciate so much, like he constantly knew something no one else did.

"Thanks."

"Are you relieved?"

He lifted his eyebrows. "A little. Now the hard stuff really begins. You look different tonight. Is it your hair?"

"Different?" I repeated.

"Okay, beautiful."

"Uh . . . thanks. Who taught you how to dance?"

His eyes clouded up like a thunderstorm. "My mother."

"You don't talk about her much," I said, surprised to hear her mentioned.

"That's no accident," he said, his forehead wrinkled, getting right to business. "Listen, I wanted to tell you that I have a bad feeling about tonight. Something's wrong. Something's off."

A shudder skimmed my spine.

Yes. I'm probably part of that reason.

I opened my mouth to tell him to try to get the High Priestess out of the ballroom, or at least to take my father far away, but the bind-ing's magic activated and stopped the words in my throat. I drew in a deep breath and looked away, frustrated. My eyes latched onto the

High Priestess at the far end of the room. She wore a white dress with feathery extensions that looked quite atrocious on her. My eyes trailed to the nearer side of the room, where Papa stood with several witches around him, in deep discussion. The open windows streamed summer air into the stuffy room. Beyond the night I thought I saw a shadow shift in the air, momentarily blocking a star. Dragons?

"I was just outside and saw your little friend," Merrick said, following my gaze.

"My little friend?"

"Your dragon. The sapphire one."

My eyes narrowed. "He's not mine."

"He certainly seems to like you."

"They're out tonight?"

"Three of them are circling the castle in the air right now."

My stomach twisted. "Have you told Papa?"

"He knows."

My heart gave a little tremor.

"It's not a good sign," I whispered in a distant voice. Suddenly, all of this seemed very overwhelming. It left me short of breath. But after months of preparing, I couldn't deny feeling a certain relief that the time had finally come. At least I wouldn't stress over it anymore.

"From the time it was built, the ballroom has been protected by an old magic that the original builders of the castle used. A foolish one in my opinion," Merrick said in a grim voice, his brow low over his beautiful green eyes. "It doesn't allow anyone to transport in. Or out."

"So if something did happen—"

"We'd be trapped inside, unable to transport out. You have Viveet, right?"

"Of course," I said lightly, smiling at an elderly woman that waddled by. Viveet was strapped to my right thigh, feeling ice cold. "I never leave her out of sight."

"Take this. Wrap it around your ankle. Just in case you need it later."

He stopped us where we were on the edge of the crowd and handed me a small dagger, similar to the one I lost in the Western Network when I tried to stab the *Book of Contracts*.

"Now?" I asked, gazing around.

"Yes. Now."

Flustered, I knelt down and tied it to my left ankle. When I straightened back up, no one seemed any wiser.

"Good," he said. "Just keep an eye out. I'm going to look around. Let me know if you see anything suspicious."

"You look nice tonight, by the way," I blurted out before he pulled away.

"Thanks." His eyes met mine, and, if I didn't know any better, looked amused.

"I-I've felt the same way you have all night," I said then, wanting to break the awkward tension. "It's not just you."

"The other Protectors feel it too," he said, his tone dropping low in a warning. "It always means something."

The pain in my head took a turn for the worse, making me suddenly dizzy. I turned away from the twirling mass of bodies with a grimace, feeling lightheaded just being near the motion.

"What's wrong?" Merrick asked, stepping back toward me.

"A headache, that's all. I'll be fine. Go. Go look around. Be alert to any changes and protect my father, please."

I stumbled over the words, barely able to release them before the magic took my throat hostage again. He hesitated, but soon disappeared, expertly blending into the crowd.

Grateful that he'd left, and moving as if blind, I pushed through the substantial crowd of witches along the edges of the ballroom, my eyes half-open. How would I ever look for Miss Mabel while combating such an explosive headache? It felt like someone had a spike to my temples and was driving it in with a large hammer.

The first scream rang out seconds later.

At first I thought I'd imagined it. Maybe one of the violinists had missed a note while playing. But then it happened again. I came to a dead halt. No one else seemed to have heard. The dresses continued to whirl by in dizzying streaks of chiffon and lace. Witches, already getting rummy on ipsum, tilted their heads back and laughed. Perhaps I had picked up on something outside.

Unwilling to bet on so simple an explanation, I spun around and sought my father, confident that he would have heard it as well. Barely able to see him above the crush of people, I caught only a brief glimpse of his tense face. He ignored those nearby, his eyes darting throughout the room. My heart pounded. Papa had heard it too. A damning confirmation that all was not well.

Just across from him, Zane moved into fast action, slipping along the walls behind the ring of people around the dance floor, headed for the High Priestess. Another bad sign. The high-pitched scream came closer, exacerbating my headache. I forced myself to shove through the crowd. This was it. I could feel it.

She's here.

I had the inexplicable urge to start screaming, to tell people to leave the ballroom, but who would listen? A few witches behind me stopped to gaze around when a third shriek sounded, asking each other, "Did you hear that?"

The next high-pitched sound split through my head, making me see white. I stumbled, barely catching myself before I fell to my knees. The violins squawked, the flutes stumbled, and soon the whole ballroom had tuned into the sound. Witches looked wildly about the room, trying to discover its source.

Then the windows shattered in a fine spray of glass.

I wasn't sure what was louder: the screams of the witches in the ballroom or the shrieks of the bats that swarmed in. Glass rained down in a glittering shower. The doors to the ballroom slammed shut, sealing us inside an opulent tomb. I ducked underneath a table to hide from the glass and froze, my eyes staring at the shards on the ground in horror.

No shoes!

The bats continued to stream into the room, their long wings fluttering just above our heads. One of them whipped down and scratched me on the cheek with the tip of his wing, drawing a thin line of blood. Another bat grabbed a witch by the hair and pulled on it until she screamed. Nearly paralyzed with fear, the witches in the room ducked, throwing their arms over their heads to protect them from the awful lashings of the heavy wings.

Focus. Focus, I told myself, taking in a deep breath. *Find Miss Mabel. The sooner you kill her, the sooner this madness will end.*

My eyes frantically studied the floor, locating a few spots bare of glass shards. I pushed through the crowd again, elbowing people to the side when needed to, and hopped from spot to spot, back toward the middle of the room, the bats flapping above me.

I spilled into the center, where every couple had curled down on the dance floor for protection. Merrick's eyes met mine from across the room, his sword glowing a dark purple hue in his hands.

Viveet!

My heart took courage at the thought of her. I hauled my skirt up, grabbed the sword from her strap against my thigh, and yanked her free just as the bats settled in the rafters. She glowed in my hand, making me feel stronger. A witch curled into a ball at my feet tried to coax me down with them, but I waved her off. Several witches near the doors banged on the wood, attempting incantations to no avail, desperate to get out. Council Member Patrice let out a half-hiccup, half-cry from near the dessert table. Otherwise, the room was silent.

Come on, Miss Mabel. I'm not afraid of you.

The High Priestess, now protected by my father and a small army of Protectors, stood at the top of the room, looking both furious and terrifying.

"Leave!" she commanded the guests. "All of you!"

At the High Priestess's words, the sound of turning locks reverberated through the near-silent room.

"Not until I say so."

The alluring, silky voice that haunted my nightmares rang over the crowd, sending chills down my spine. My headache that once hurt now exploded. I fell to my knees with a groan. My gut ached; my heart recoiled.

Miss Mabel is here.

You Underestimate Me

The crunch of Miss Mabel's shoes clicked toward me, breaking glass with every step. A black silk dress, dark as the night, billowed out behind her. Her blonde hair hung free. Diamonds in their glittering brilliance hung around her neck and dripped off her ears. The tattered *Book of Contracts* lay in her left arm, held tight to her side.

No, I thought, digging into the power in my chest. *You will never bow to Miss Mabel.*

I forced myself to my feet, ignoring the pain that rocketed from my head to my neck and back in sharp streaks. Her chilling sapphire eyes provoked the furious dragon in my heart to a roar. I let him rage, feeling it out, using my wrath for Miss Mabel to build my own strength.

"Merry meet, Mildred," Miss Mabel called, her sensuous lips pulled into a grin. She stopped just in front of me, giving me full view of her perfect profile.

"What exactly are you trying to do here, Mabel?" the High Priestess called. "Dictate the terms of your death?"

"I'm doing well," Miss Mabel sang. "Thank you for asking."

"You have business with me and no one else. Let's settle this in private."

"Oh, let's not."

"You took long enough to arrive, now I get to dictate the terms. We go to my office."

"Or what?" Miss Mabel asked, her eyebrow lifted in challenge. "You're going to release your Protectors on me? Do it. I dare you.

My little sweethearts will rain from the sky and teach your innocent followers just how serious I am." Miss Mabel's sweet, malevolent grin spread.

"If you won't settle our matter in private, you have three seconds left until I kill you on the spot," Mildred said in a calm voice.

"I'm in charge here," Miss Mabel cried with a bright blaze of her eyes. "I came to accept your resignation."

"You came to accept your own death."

"Is that a no?"

"This is a no," the High Priestess said. The massive chandelier where the bats waited, hanging upside down like ghosts from the underworld, burst into white-hot flames. The ghastly animals took off, screeching. Some of them fell to the floor in fiery plumes, dead. Miss Mabel didn't turn around to look at them, but her eyes had visibly hardened.

"I wish you hadn't done that, Mildred. Now we can't bargain at all, can we?"

The bats swooping around the room morphed into flowing ebony wraiths with charcoal black plumes following them until they settled into an almost-human form.

"Clavas," I whispered in shock, recalling the vile painting in the hallway where Mrs. L had caught me.

Clavas transform into humans from their bat-like form. Very powerful fighters. It's Almorran magic.

Almorran, of course. Miss Mabel's signature style. My mind sped back to the Almorran *Book of Spells* with a flash of fear. Had she found it already? Was Antebellum doomed to her wrath? I didn't have time to dwell on it. Once the Clavas touched the floor, they began an immediate assault.

"Away from the windows!" Merrick jumped on top of the dessert table and bellowed. "Move away!"

Streams of Guardians burst into the ballroom from the already broken windows, swords at the ready. The crowd of witches surged forward, desperate for freedom. A forest dragon bellowed from the outside, followed by a plume of fire and smoke from the southern windows.

Viveet leapt in flame as a half-transformed Clava landed near me. I slashed his outstretched hand. Black blood poured out of his severed limb in globs. He shrieked and morphed back into a bat, flying away on an injured wing. I rushed forward, intent on Miss Mabel, but she disappeared, fading into the hiss and clash of metal on metal.

"No!" I yelled. "Where are you? Your fight is with me!"

Another Clava landed in front of me, a leering grin on his half-transformed face. He held a black sword in his hand, sharp, but covered in rust and what looked like black tar.

"I'm not afraid of you," I muttered with a surge of power, falling instantly into the fight when he advanced on me. After dodging his half sword, realizing it seemed almost like a club, I stabbed him in the thigh, yanked the blade free, and then pushed Viveet into his stomach. He staggered back with a groan, falling away from my sword. His black blood sizzled on Viveet's burning metal.

A flash of hazel eyes caught my attention.

"Bianca!" Camille screamed, reaching for me with one arm. A streak of bright red blood dripped from her elbow, staining her beautiful ivory gown. A Clava nearby had her dress in his long claw and was pulling her toward him. "Bianca, help!"

I dodged through a tangle of witches and slammed my shoulder into the Clava, knocking him over. Viveet cut through his leathery black flesh, removing one of his arms and biting into his neck. He screamed as I pushed off the ground and cut his head off with a quick swing. Shards of glass stuck to the bottom of my feet, but I only briefly registered the pain. Brecken stood just in front of Camille, locked in combat with two of the black wraiths.

"Are you okay, Camille?"

"I-I'm fine, I think. Are we going to die?" she asked, her eyes wide with terror. "We're locked in!"

"No!" I yelled. Viveet flared, her flames licking high into the air. "You won't die! Come on," I said taking her trembling hand. "Let's get you somewhere safe."

"Where?" she wailed. "Nowhere is safe!"

Frantic, I looked around. The Clavas concentrated most of their efforts on the Guardians and Council Members. A few of the hideous beasts plucked escaping witches off the walls, tossing them back into the crowd like rag dolls. My eyes fell on the edges of the ballroom, where several heavy couches sat against the wall.

"There," I said, nodding with my head. "We'll get you to hide behind those until you can get outside."

"What about Brecken?"

A Guardian from the windows fought his way next to Brecken, who cut the leg from one Clava as his friend decapitated the other.

"He'll be fine," I said.

"Where's Leda?" she cried, stopping me. "We can't go without her."

"I'll find her!"

Hands locked, we plunged into the fray. I staved off a few stray swords and spears with Viveet. My bare feet seemed to find every stray piece of glass still littering the floor, but even that pain wasn't as great as the dull thud of my headache. I gritted my teeth and pushed through both.

"Bianca!" Camille gasped. "Your feet!"

"It's fine," I said, refusing to look at the bloody footprints. A witch nearby let out a hollow cry. I whirled around to see him fall on his face, blood pooling out in a balloon behind him. Camille froze, her eyes riveted on his dead body.

"GO!" I yelled, shoving her behind the couch. I pushed it as far against the wall as it would go, then stuffed her inside and put the pillows on top of her head. "I'll go find Leda."

Leda found me. I whirled around and she was there.

"Bianca!" she cried in relief, grabbing my arms. "There's—"

"No time!" I said, pushing her down. A bat came winging right at us, teeth bared in razor sharp fangs, aimed right at my face. I sliced it in half with Viveet and the two pieces crashed to the ground with a squish. Blood stained Leda's pale dress. She stared at it in shock.

"You've got to hide!" I said. Camille let out a cry of relief and reached for Leda.

"Stay here," I told them both.

"Wait!" Leda said. "I need your dagger!"

I stopped, grabbed the small dagger from my ankle that Merrick had given me, and handed it to her hilt first. Already hunched over,

I pulled three shards of glass out of the bottom of my feet, feeling instant relief once they came out. Blood flowed over my fingers, making them sticky.

"Use the dagger if you need to," I told Leda, who stared at my hands, looking paler than ever. "Don't move until I come back!"

"Bianca!"

Leda's cry died behind me as I left, only one thought on my mind: I had to find Miss Mabel. This would continue until she died.

This was between her and me.

My eyes glanced up at the clock. 11:38. *Sixteen minutes left.*

I tuned back into the fray as I pushed my way through. Guardians still streamed into the room from two windows. The dragons roared with fire outside. Witches in their lavish gowns and elegant suits tried crawling out the glass-strewn windows, assisted by a small contingent of Guardians. A few witches lay gasping in their death throes on the floor. One man had a fit of spasms and jerked, a foaming bite mark on his face.

"Bloody madness," I whispered to no one.

Guardians and Protectors battled with the wraiths, which all wore the same impassioned, cold expression and attacked without rule or regard. Unable to break through the pockets of fighting to get near the top of the room, I shoved a cake off one of the dessert tables and jumped up onto its spot.

In the midst of the fighting, the High Priestess and Miss Mabel now faced off, oblivious to the pandemonium. They twirled, walking in a slow circle around each other. My throat nearly choked. A Mactos. The High Priestess was in a Mactos with Miss Mabel.

Blighters zipped back and forth between them, mere blurs of color. I'd never seen so many moving so fast in my life. It made my pathetic attempt at fighting Miss Mabel last winter look like a child's game. The streaks of light from the blighters came to a sudden stop, evaporating into little clouds of color. Miss Mabel and the High Priestess stood across from each other. The High Priestess spoke, her shoulders tilted back and head high. Whatever she said I couldn't make out. Miss Mabel lifted one eyebrow with a coy smile.

Panic, pure and hot, ripped through me.

What are they talking about?

Viveet glowed a vibrant blue-white. I could feel her heat resonate in my hand, nearly searing my palm. Then the High Priestess and Miss Mabel both looked right at me. The High Priestess met my gaze with a calm, expectant air. She nodded.

A shot of chilly realization made my knees weak and my dragon rage. Suddenly I understood.

Mabel knows me too well. She's studied me enough to understand how I think and what I will do.

"No!" I screamed. "No!"

The High Priestess turned to Miss Mabel and nodded again. Miss Mabel grinned and closed her eyes. Her lips moved. Something inside me broke, like a great rending inside my soul. I gasped, fumbling to stay on my feet. A heaviness rushed through my chest, my arms, my legs, and disappeared out my toes, removing a burden from my soul. Without it, I felt light and free. It could only be one thing.

Miss Mabel had just removed the Inheritance Curse.

"No! NO!" I screamed.

I leapt off the table, throwing myself on the back of a Clava and knocking him over. The Guardian below him shoved a sword through his spine and the wraith went limp. I jumped off without another thought.

It took me too long to bounce my way through the mess, to hack at the bats that swooped down to attack me. The closer I moved to Miss Mabel, the worse it became. Two Guardians moved aside as I barreled through.

"Move it!" I yelled. "Move!"

I spilled into the Mactos circle.

"Ah, yes, Bianca. Just in time. Mildred is just about to fulfill her end of our bargain." Miss Mabel purred, smiling at me. The High Priestess stood tall, her chin tilted back, shoulders squared.

"Don't do it!" I yelled in desperation. "Please!"

A flash of light slammed into the High Priestess's chest with a bright spray. She stumbled and fell to her knees. I heard my scream before I knew it was there. It reverberated through my pounding head. Was this a dream? A terrible dream.

"Your Highness!"

The High Priestess crumpled to the ground. I skidded to a stop at her side, sliding on my bloody feet. But I was too late. The High Priestess's blank eyes stared out, lifeless.

Not again. Not again. I won't do this again!

I pressed my hand to her heart. She didn't stir, didn't move. She'd fulfilled her part of the vow with her own life. The High Priestess had died for me. A rush of power and rage boiled through my blood. I embraced the bitter pain, the horrible agony of watching another loved one die.

"Why?" I cried. "Why?"

"Oh, Bianca," Miss Mabel drawled. "Do get up already. You're pathetic, you know that?"

With all my might I released the magic expanding in my chest and threw Viveet at Miss Mabel, aiming for her face. Viveet whipped through the air like a flaming dart, the blue-white flames dancing high. Miss Mabel ducked at the last second and Viveet soared past, biting into the High Priestess's throne. Her luster faded; the flame died.

Miss Mabel's wild eyes danced with delight.

"Oh darling girl," she crooned. "I had no idea you'd be so happy to see me tonight. Are you ready to fulfill your part of the bargain? Or will I have to do that for you?"

The pain in my head magnified again. I fell to my knees with a cry, my eyes shut.

"Never," I snarled. I tried to stand but fell back to my knees, unable to bear it. The fury and agony came, as I knew it would. I was glad for it, embraced it, because I'd never be strong enough to fight her without the pain. Magic, pure and uncontrolled, soared through me.

"Never? Oh, very well," Miss Mabel said, clicking her tongue. "That's too bad. You could have been great. You're so bloody determined, even to the point of your own death. I'll have to kill your father myself."

Her eyes flickered past me. I didn't have to look. I knew she saw Papa.

"No," I called with a strength I didn't know I had. "Your fight is with me."

The world went silent.

Viveet flew back to my hand as I sent a wall of glass zipping around us in a flurry of light, traveling all the way to the ceiling, surrounding us in an impenetrable circle, sealing off everything outside. The hysteria and chaos continued, but we heard none of it.

Miss Mabel studied me with a curious gaze.

"Very interesting, Bianca. But I must ask, why? I've already fought you and won. Everything you love is in the palm of my hand."

"Not everything," I said, looking at the clock, barely able to make out the hands. The pulsing in my head was so great I could barely concentrate. 8 minutes. "Not yet."

Her lips curled into that infuriating, slow smile.

Yes, I thought. *Fight me. You underestimate me.*

"It will be a pleasure to kill you, Bianca. Although I doubt anything will feel as good as killing Mildred."

My shield appeared at my side, obeying the surges of magic that my instincts commanded. Miss Mabel sent a volley of white blighters in a fast arc through the air. The last time Miss Mabel shot a white blighter at me, it broke my hand. Now she sent a small army of them, none of which would stop until they slammed into me like a cloud of death.

I braced myself with my shield, shuffling through several incantations in my mind. Moments before they would have hit, the white blighters cracked in midair, separating into harmless pieces that bounced against my shield like little shards of ice. The percussion of it shook me, sending my headache into another painful spiral. I looked down to see Miss Scarlett's bracelet glowing on top of my circlus.

Miss Mabel lifted an eyebrow with a flash of her eyes.

"Very interesting," she murmured. "Scarlett's been helping you out, hasn't she? I recognize that charm. It has an exceptional power to repel blighters and curses."

"Looks like the disadvantage is yours," I said, and shifted into a defensive position. The movement sent me into a dizzy stumble and I had to right myself. "Are you up for a real fight?"

"I would be, but you aren't."

My vision blurred and my stomach revolted as the headache took an unbearable turn. I leaned to the side and dry heaved, falling to my knees. My loyal, faithful shield tumbled for a second and popped back up.

"Do you understand what's happening?" she asked. I opened my mouth to curse her, but couldn't keep a thought that long. My brain felt swollen inside. I could barely comprehend what she said and had to focus on one word at a time. "This is the power of the binding, Bianca darling. You see, you had a long time to complete the task, but you didn't. And now, well, you'll die."

I looked up to find Papa outside the wall, throwing his fists into the glass, his face contorted in a livid yell. Merrick wasn't far away, banging the bottom of his shield into it. No matter what they did, the wall never weakened. I willed it to be stronger.

No Papa, I wanted to say. *It has to happen like this.*

The magic flickered inside, drawing strength from my pain. This is how I'd die.

For Papa.

"You'll have a few more minutes of miserable coherency left before you black out. You'll die in a coma the very minute you turn seventeen. If I don't cut off your head first, of course. Which I will," she promised in a melodic taunt. "With your own pretty sword."

She stood over me. At least, I thought she did. My vision failed, throwing me into darkness. Blood, warm and thick, dripped from my nose. I heard it drop onto the cold tile floor.

"Actually, no," she continued in a thoughtful tone. "I don't think I will kill you. I'll let you suffer, destroy yourself in your last moments while dear Papa watches. Oh, Bianca. It's more delicious than I planned!"

My thoughts began to scatter, becoming ragged and disjointed. Leda teaching Camille. Michelle with flour on her face. Papa laughing. The High Priestess. Were these memories? Was I imagining them? The gray eyes. Who had the gray eyes?

Minutes must have passed, filled with only fragments and images. Green leaves and a high canopy. The blue flash of a sword. A pair of knobby old hands. Miss Mabel's voice existed somewhere in the background, the music to my last moments.

This is it, I realized. *Miss Mabel wins again.*

The blackness overwhelmed my chest, encompassing it in a blanket of night. The pounding of my heart made a staccato against my ribs. When I was ready to give myself over to the edge, to escape the misery of mortality, I felt another rending inside. It rippled through my body with physical pain, like my muscles had been torn apart. The headache ceased immediately, my vision cleared. A pressure I didn't know was on my chest released, setting me free.

"What's this?" Miss Mabel hissed.

With a gasp I lifted my head to see Leda standing just outside the wall, the *Book of Contracts* in her arms. A torn page of paper burned in her right hand. The flames danced toward the ceiling, highlighting the triumphant smirk on her face.

"Leda," I breathed in a rush of exhilaration and fear. She'd saved me. Leda had found and destroyed the binding. Miss Mabel's eyes constricted, turning a dark, furious color.

"Kill her!" she screamed, although the Clavas couldn't hear us. "Kill the vile bitch!"

At first attracted by the tall flame, and then noticing Miss Mabel's livid eyes, three Clavas rushed Leda.

"Leda!" I yelled. "Run!"

Leda looked to the side and her eyes widened. She stumbled back a few steps, threw the *Book of Contracts* at one Clava that dropped in front of her, and tried to run. Miss Scarlett, her thick hair falling around her face and singed on the ends, stepped in front of Leda just as a cloud of Clavas swooped down. Both of them disappeared into the midst of the black wraiths.

"No!" I screamed.

"Stupid little monster," Miss Mabel spat. "She'll get what she deserves. I'll see to it. You and your friends make me sick."

The magic roared to life in my chest again, as powerful as I'd ever felt it before. Now the real fight would begin.

I shot to my feet, summoned Viveet, and ran toward Miss Mabel with a guttural cry. Her shield appeared in front of her at the last second, protecting her from the force of my sword. I dropped to my knees, then my back, and swung my legs around to trip her, but she transported away. The power of the Mactos circle overcame the magic of the ballroom, which allowed her to transport within our glass confines and put me at a disadvantage.

"Back here, Bianca," she called from just behind me. "I do so love to see you this angry."

I raised myself into the defensive crouch Merrick had drilled me on since day one. Miss Mabel and I were too far apart for me to engage her with Viveet. I'd have to close the distance. Before I could act, Miss Mabel disappeared, a bored look on her face. I ducked away from where I'd been standing, but moved too late. When she reappeared she had her hand around my throat. With superhuman strength she picked me up off my feet and slammed me into the glass wall. It cracked behind me but didn't break.

"Maybe this is the best way for you to die," she hissed, her eyes wild. "Then I can see the life ebb out of your eyes."

The magic gathered near my heart, and I released it in a powerful jolt. Miss Mabel soared across the Mactos circle and collided with the glass across from me. Viveet flew back into my hand, leaping into instant flames.

"We'll see about who's going to die tonight," I growled.

Miss Mabel grinned, but it was cold and calculating. She disappeared, and I whirled around, arcing Viveet out as far as she'd reach in a circle around me. Miss Mabel transported into middle of the Mactos circle, leaning just out of Viveet's reach, with a sword of her own in hand. The steel was black, but fresh and sharp.

"Then let's spar, Bianca darling."

I advanced first. Sparks flew when our swords collided, sending out a spray of white and blue. She dodged my advance. The top of Viveet snagged her skirt, setting the material on fire.

"Not bad," she drawled, extinguishing the flame. "You're doing an admirable job. It's not anything like what the Guardians learn, is it? You're a far cry from the desperate little girl that came to my school a year ago. Too bad, really. I could have taught you greater things than your special kind of fighting found only in the Northern Network."

"Great things like what? Almorran magic?" I spat, stepping to the side with a smooth shuffle. Merrick's instructions spun through my mind. *Never cross your legs. Sword up. Your shield will follow, so don't give it more attention than you give to Viveet.*

Miss Mabel and I circled each other. Blood stained the ground from my still bleeding feet, making it slippery.

"Oh, yes. You would have been wonderful with such a strong magic like the Almorrans'," she said, forcing an innocent tone. "I should have started you on it when you were earning your marks, as my grandmother did for me."

"I'll never do anything like you," I muttered, dodging an advance and forcing her back. "Is that how long you've been planning to take over the Central Network? Since you were a teenager?"

She laughed in a throaty, deep chuckle.

"Bianca, I was made to control Antebellum. Don't you see that yet?"

"You'll never succeed in taking over the Central Network. The Almorran magic will be too much for one witch to wield alone."

I was guessing now, desperate to find a weakness.

"You think I only want to rule the Central Network? Dear girl, you do underestimate me."

Not anymore.

She transported away. I quickly circled, the shield protecting my back, but not before I felt a slice of heat searing through the back of my left arm. Miss Mabel laughed, and the sound echoed off the walls. Blood oozed down my arm in a warm trickle to my elbow and stained the tip of her sword. Unlike her, I couldn't transport as fast or as precisely as she did. I'd have to stay, anticipating her moves.

"You want to take over all of Antebellum," I said, gritting my teeth. "But you can't."

Her amused expression quickly morphed into annoyance. Her emotions were as volatile as ever.

"Oh, can't I?"

"Not alone, you can't. So you teamed up with the one person you hate more than anyone: your mother, Angelina."

Her grip on the black sword tightened and her knuckles blanched white.

"But neither of you can do it yet, can you?" I continued, stepping to the side, waiting for the right moment when I properly distracted her attention. She moved with me. "Because you don't have the *Book of Spells*. I heard the two of you talking in the West. Until you find the incantations of the Almorran priests, you'll never have the power to defeat the Networks."

Miss Mabel's eyebrows lifted in mock surprise.

"You think you know so much, do you?"

I lunged toward her with a fast hacking motion, hoping to cut her arm off at the elbow. She hit me away like an impatient nanny swatting at a child and lunged for me. My shield shot up, blocking my face and absorbing the heavy blow.

"You think you've got it all figured out, Bianca? It just shows how little you know. You haven't the faintest idea what Angelina and I are doing."

I swung Viveet in a low arc, power flowing through my sword. Miss Mabel blocked it, but the magic surged into her body, throwing her back. She hit the glass wall with her shoulder, then swung back around to face me with a hiss.

"I know that you're desperate!" I said, hooking my shield back onto my arm once she retreated. She had a caged, agitated look in her eyes I hadn't seen before. *Every witch has a weakness*, Isadora's voice whispered from the depths of my memory. "You haven't found the book. Is that the task Angelina set for you? That's why you were gone for so long, searching for it. You still haven't found it because you're completely incompetent at anything that doesn't involve controlling other witches."

The last comment was another guess, a wild card thrown out in hopes of being on target. She smiled, but it had a flicker of gravity and rage that I didn't miss. Rage meant I struck a sore spot. Miss Mabel wanted the Almorran *Book of Spells* for certain.

"Oh, how little you know about the evil in our world," she crooned.

I swung my arm, sending my shield at her like a javelin. She covered her body with her own shield, but the power behind my throw sent her back against the wall again. I rushed forward with Viveet, blue flames dancing high, but Miss Mabel rolled out of the way and the tip of my sword hit only glass. My shield returned to its position in front of me.

"I know you," I said, panting. "Which means I know more about evil than I ever cared to."

I ran at her again, sword flying. She fended me off, locking us into a battle of back and forth around the whole length of the circle. My instincts took over the motions while the power made me strong. I nicked her cheek, burning some of her hair and setting the fabric at her neck on fire. Seconds later I felt a deep bite of pain in my wrist. Viveet clattered to the floor, smoking and lifeless.

I grabbed my hand and gritted my teeth. Blood seeped fast from the wound. My head began to feel light, so I dropped to my knees. How much blood had I lost? I redirected the magic to my arm, whispering a healing incantation under my breath. I had no hope without a sword to fight her off. My shield protected me, but it would do little alone.

"Oh, I do love to see you bowing before me," she murmured with wicked delight, then leaned her head back and laughed. Heat filled my wrist, my hand. I felt the ebb of blood slow. The sticky liquid stopped spilling around my fingers. It worked.

Miss Mabel sauntered around to face me. "There isn't a single witch in Antebellum that I care for except myself, and I never have. I shall find great joy in watching the life leave your body, you arrogant little rat."

She disappeared. I whirled around, grabbed my shield, and pulled it over me just as Miss Mabel brought her sword down on top with a heavy blow. I sent power into the shield at the same moment. Her sword shattered into a hundred pieces on the floor while my shield cracked in half, a great fissure forming down the middle. I opened my injured hand and called Viveet. Miss Mabel grabbed my shoulder from behind and jerked me up just as I caught the sword. She burst into a white-hot flame, dancing high and fast.

"I'm much stronger than you think," Miss Mabel hissed, grabbing my sword arm with supernatural strength. Viveet fell to the ground again, inert. I tried to force Miss Mabel away by magic alone, but her power overwhelmed me. She yanked my arms up my back, squeezing until I thought the bone would shatter. The only thing that prevented her from grinding me into dust was the resistance of my angry, roiling power.

"This could go on forever, you know," Miss Mabel goaded, right next to my ear, pushing my arm up so far it would soon dislocate from my shoulder. "We could be locked in the Mactos circle for an eternity, fighting. Both of us are so driven by hate that the magic may never stop."

Just beyond the glass stood Merrick, his chest heaving, purple flames dancing on his sword. He tilted his head down imperceptibly.

Do it, his eyes seemed to say.

"No," I said to Miss Mabel. "I'm stopping this now."

I lifted my foot, and with all the focus I had left, I kicked back into her right knee. The bone broke with an audible *crack* and Miss Mabel dropped to the ground. I whirled around, grabbed her hair, yanked it back, and forced her to her knees. Viveet leapt to my free hand as Miss Mabel released a scream of pain. The white, pearly skin of her neck glowed against Viveet's searing blue blade.

"Don't move," I whispered.

She stared at me with glimmering sapphire eyes, then lifted one side of her lips in a challenging smile.

"Well played again, Bianca," she whispered, her nostrils flaring in pain. "Go ahead. Take your revenge. I would have taken everything from you."

I pulled on her hair, tightening my sword against her neck. The skin pulsed at the base of her throat where Viveet sat. A thin line of blood appeared. She smiled with a cold evil that touched right to my soul.

"I shall find great joy in watching the life leave your body," I said.

"Angelina is already watching you, Bianca Monroe. You and your father. Killing me will only bring her on you faster. Consider yourself warned. She doesn't take lightly to people interfering with her plans."

"Good," I hissed. "Let her come. We aren't afraid of Angelina."

Miss Mabel smiled. "You will be. She'll destroy you."

"You've earned your grave, do you understand that?" I asked, yanking her hair again. The muscles in her neck tightened, pulling her face into a grimace. "No one will cry over you, a heartless fool."

Our eyes locked. She dared me in a silent challenge.

Do it.

I hesitated, Viveet pressed to her neck. The chance I'd dreamed of for so long had come. I was free. The shackles that anchored me to death had fallen. I held Miss Mabel's life in my hands, as she had always held mine. The memento burned against my chest. Mama would never live again, but she'd want me to live happy. To choose to live free, not burdened with guilt and questions.

"You would have taken everything away from me," I said, staring Miss Mabel in the eye. "But I will never be like you."

I cast a paralyzing incantation, pulled Viveet away, and took a step back. Miss Mabel's body jerked and fell to the side, limp.

Her eyes, staring out at the ballroom, didn't move.

Where's Leda?

My mind, almost lost to shock, could think of only one thing the moment after Miss Mabel fell.

"Leda?" I cried, whirling around. "Where is she? Leda!"

The glass wall dissolved in a shimmer of white, unwinding and falling to the floor in a fog. Papa ran to me just before I collapsed onto my hands and knees, catching me in his arms. Suddenly my whole body hurt. My feet, my head, my heart.

"I'm f-fine," I said, but couldn't find my voice. "F-f-fine."

"Just sit down, B. Sit down."

"Where's L-l-leda?"

"She's with Camille. Nicolas carried her up to the apothecary. Merrick and Brecken fought the Clavas off."

Camille, yes. Good, I wanted to say. *Camille will know what to do. She'll stay with Leda.*

Three Guardians rushed past us and surrounded Miss Mabel. Zane whispered a few more incantations to strengthen the paralysis. Her body lifted into the air, bound by cords of iron, her right leg twisted at a grotesque angle to the side.

I turned away.

"Tell me Leda's going to be okay," I demanded. "Tell me she's okay!"

Papa responded immediately. "Yes," he said, in control and confident. He pressed a hand to my forehead, whispered a blessing under his breath, and a wave of calm passed through me. My mind reorganized itself and I drew in a deep breath.

"The High Priestess," I said. "Sh-she died because of—"

"We'll talk about it later. We need to get you upstairs."

His words faded into the background with all other sound. Beyond his right shoulder lay the High Priestess, motionless on the ground. Eight Protectors, tattered, bloody, and bruised, formed a wall around her body. Her hand rested at to her side, limp. A tear fell out of my eye as I stared at it, transfixed.

Gone.

"Bianca? B? Listen to me."

Papa's voice came from far away. He slapped me on the cheek, but I hardly felt it.

"Bianca, I need you to look at me."

"Yes, Papa," I said, closing my eyes, then opening them on him. The calming feeling swept through me again, reinforcing my strength. "I'm okay."

My voice evened out, my frantic breathing calmed. I looked at the carnage around me, the dead bodies, the bleeding Clavas with their pale skin and black blood, with a sense of surreal detachment. Everything had crumbled into chaos and pain. I wasn't alone in my mourning anymore.

"I want you to go to the apartment," he said.

"No," I said, a lump growing in my throat. "I want to help."

"You're a mess, B. I'm worried that—"

"No!" I cried. "I can't be alone right now. I can't do it. Let me help, please!"

Papa hesitated. He must have seen the desperation in my eyes, heard the pleading in my voice. The cries and moans of everyone in attendance suddenly seemed louder than ever. If I could just think about something else I wouldn't see the High Priestess falling. I wouldn't remember the moment when I was ready to give into that eternal sleep—

We need your father, the High Priestess had said. *He's strong in ways I never can be.*

"You need to stay here," I said, using his arm to pull myself to my tender feet. I ignored the pain, drowned it in the aftermath. Right now, the pain felt good. It felt like life. "The Central Network needs a High Priest."

He turned to face the ballroom. A small river of blood ran down his leg, soaking his pants, his stocking. A gash across his right temple seeped blood, and his lip split down the middle in a dark line. He gazed around, his eyes rapidly assessing, seeking the remnants of danger.

The only Clavas that remained were dead or badly injured. The rest had fled when Miss Mabel had been overcome. A small troop of weary Guardians moved through the carnage, killing any Clavas that still clung to life. The witches that hadn't escaped through the window and somehow survived the massacre stared up at Papa from the bloody ballroom floor with pale faces and wide eyes. Merrick stepped out of the crowd, limping slightly on his right leg. Papa wouldn't let go of me.

"I'll stay with her until you can," Merrick said, matching Papa's intense gaze. "I swear it on my life, Derek."

Papa hesitated, but released me with a single nod. Merrick reached out a hand and helped me down from the elevated platform where Miss Mabel and I had fought. Like the rest of us still alive, blood and sweat marred his clothes.

"Thank you," I said, clenching my jaw to hide the pain. My feet continued to leave bright red footprints as I hobbled.

"You did good, Bianca," he said, studying me with his serious emerald eyes. "I'm proud of you."

I looked away, my eyes filling with tears, and gazed up at my father. He stood in between the two thrones, his sword clenched in his fist, glowing with a bright crimson flame.

"Witches of the Central Network!" he called. His voice rang over the ballroom, spilling out into the gardens where contingents of Guardians waited, listening. "I stand before you today not as a fellow witch, not as a leader, but as a brother-in-arms. We've been attacked, but we have prevailed!"

He held his sword above his head, his jaw tight.

"We have prevailed!"

The Guardians raised their swords and joined in his cry. The maids and kitchen servants sniffling in the corner came out of hiding. The Protectors lifted their broken fists and joined in the call. Their shout spread from the ballroom to the gardens. The contingents of Guardians outside bellowed, augmented by the livid roar of the dragons circling the castle in the air.

"We will continue to prevail," Papa said, "until we are safe. This I promise you, as your High Priest. We will honor Mildred's name and her legacy." His voice faltered, but he regained it with a determined ferocity, his nostrils flaring. "We will not fear. We will fight. We will win. We will live!"

The cries and shouts of the Guardians continued, ringing around us. Several witches collapsed into sobs. Papa stood above it all, strong and powerful, mighty in ways we could not be. I stared at him in a mixture of awe and fear.

"It's begun, hasn't it?" I asked.

"Yes," Merrick said. "It's begun."

Leda didn't wake up until late the next morning.

I lay curled up next to her on the bed, staring at her face, willing her eyes to open. Michelle had bandaged my feet and my arm, and helped me wash the bloody stains off my body. Stella, tousled but alive, worked a special magic with her healing oils so I didn't feel any pain when I walked. The three of us worked into the early hours of the morning in the ballroom and kitchen. Merrick, true to his word, didn't leave my side, but helped with the rest of us. Then Papa pulled me away before dawn. I recounted everything to him, Tiberius, Zane, Marten, and Jansson. The vow with the High Priestess, the visits to Miss Mabel in the West, the binding to complete an unknown task, and our newest threat, Angelina.

Four Council Members were dead, the eccentric Council Member Patrice amongst them. The rest of them had been injured to varying degrees. The tally of bodies hadn't yet been finished, and I didn't want to know the final number. The bloody battle would haunt my dreams for years.

A large bump had bubbled up from the left side of Leda's head, spreading a light black and blue bruise down her eye and cheek. The apothecary had sewn shut a deep cut on her neck and cheek with twenty perfect little stitches. The dried blood seemed especially dark against her creamy white skin. Camille's handwork with a brush had left Leda's hair washed and braided in two short braids.

Camille had finally dropped into sleep around daybreak, curled up on Leda's other side, holding her hand. Michelle sat in a chair behind me, her eyes trained forward. She rocked back and forth, back and forth. For a long time, the only sound was the creak of the wood as it moved. It was anchoring, reassuring, or else the silence would have been too overwhelming and I would have screamed.

"I'm going to go check on Nicolas," Michelle said in a wooden voice. She had a dazed expression on her face, her eyes fixed and unseeing. Her lips barely moved when she spoke. I didn't say anything, just watched her disappear down the stairs wearing only one shoe. Someone would tell her. And if they didn't, what did it matter?

Leda's pale eyelashes slowly fluttered open.

"Bianca?"

I let out a long breath of relief, as if I'd been holding it all that time.

"What are you doing?" she asked. "Why are you staring at me?"

"We're waiting for you to wake up," I whispered.

She glanced around but didn't move her head. Shadows and fatigue stained her eyes.

"Where are we?" she asked.

"The Witchery."

Her foggy eyes didn't clear. She blinked several times.

"Oh," she whispered, dazed. "I remember." Her eyes widened in a panic. "Camille! Where's Camille? Is she okay? I had to leave her—"

I held a finger up to my lips to signal her to be quiet.

"She's right behind you, holding your hand. She just fell asleep so don't wake her up."

Leda looked at her right hand, intertwined with Camille's, and relaxed back against the pillow. My throat tightened with unshed tears.

"You saved my life," I said.

"I know," she remarked with a dry grin, gazing at me from the corner of her eyes.

"Thank you."

Leda let out a breathy laugh, then winced and grabbed her side, her face twisted in pain.

"You broke a couple ribs," I told her. "You also have stitches on your face and neck, not to mention a mild head injury, so you're supposed to rest for several days. Miss Scarlett brought your mother here. They are both downstairs right now, helping the apothecary. She's very nice, by the way."

"Mama came?" Leda asked, blinking rapidly, unable to hide the relief that crossed her face. Her eyes misted.

"Yes."

"Is Miss Scarlett okay?" Leda asked, swallowing her emotion. "All I remember is her standing in front of me, and then everything went black."

"She's fine. A little roughed up, but Merrick and Brecken helped her fight all the Clavas off both of you."

"Did you beat Miss Mabel?"

I quietly filled Leda in on the details she'd missed. When I finished she let out a long, pained sigh.

"I'm sorry about the High Priestess, Bianca," she said. "You were close to her."

Instead of fighting off the wave of grief, I welcomed it. It crashed through me, drowning me in a sorrow that had become all too familiar. I didn't respond. Leda seemed to understand and didn't protest when I changed the subject.

"How did you know about the binding?" I asked. "How did you know what to do?"

A sheepish smile came to her face.

"Miss Scarlett taught me to transport when I first got here. I've been going to Isadora's a couple times a week to learn how to control my curse ever since I figured out transportation well enough to be safe. You showed up in the middle of one of Isadora's lessons one day. I didn't want you to know because I was embarrassed, so I hid in her pantry and overheard your conversation. Isadora explained it all to me after you left."

"Isadora told you?" I asked in disbelief. "But she said she wouldn't tell."

"No," Leda corrected me with her usual prim tone, all too happy to be condescending again. "She said she wouldn't tell the High Priestess."

I thought back to that day with a grim feeling. Perhaps Isadora's wisdom was far greater than I'd imagined.

"Where was the *Book of Contracts?*" I asked. "Miss Mabel wasn't holding it."

"Brecken came to check on Camille and I told him that I had to find it. Ever since I've been working with Isadora, I've been better able to see future possibilities, even with Miss Mabel in them, although they're still vague and grainy. I'd seen a possibility that I could burn the binding for you, so Brecken went with me to find the *Book of Contracts*, and both of us ended up wrestling with a Clava for it. Eventually Brecken cast a curse and I grabbed the book. I feared I was too late."

"You almost were," I replied quietly, recalling that moment of capitulation once again. The intense pain, the crushing feeling in my mind. Camille stirred next to us, her eyes fluttering open, pulling me from the deep waters of fear and grief again.

"Leda?" she whispered, blinking.

"Yes, Camille. I'm okay."

Camille stretched her arms in a lazy arc above her head and wrinkled her face in pain. Her eyes shot open. She bolted upright, a look of panic on her face.

"Leda!"

"Calm down," Leda said in a soothing tone. "I'm fine."

Camille took one look at her, turned her gaze to me, and burst into tears.

"Leda, we've been so worried!" she said, burying her face in her hands. Leda grimaced, something I assumed was meant to be a reassuring smile. "I thought you had died. I was so scared!"

"It's okay, Camille," she said, awkwardly patting her back. "I'll be fine. Where's Michelle?"

"She went to check on Nicolas in the apothecary," I said. "He got a couple of deep cuts on his forehead from the Clavas."

Footsteps came up the stairwell just then, and Leda's mother, a quiet, warm woman walked in, followed by Papa, who looked weary. Stitches closed the large gash on his temple, although dried blood still stained his face.

"Oh, Leedee," her mother breathed, rushing over. "You're awake!"

I stood and embraced Papa, grateful to see him in the light of day. He brushed the hair off my face and pressed me close to his side.

"Camille," Papa said. "There's a Captain waiting for you at the bottom of the turret. He's concerned and wants to make sure you made it through the night. He said he won't move until he's heard from you."

Camille's eyes widened. "Really?"

"If I know Brecken," Papa said with a smile, "he'll wait all day."

She disappeared down the stairs in a flash of bouncy blonde hair and watery eyes. Papa held me close.

"You okay, B?" he asked.

"Yes, Papa," I said with a deep sigh, holding him close. The ties that had once bound me to death no longer existed. For the first time in my life, I could embrace him without question, without fear. "I'm okay."

A Network At War

The crowd that gathered to pay their final respects to the High Priestess had one thing in common: determination.

The clenched angles of their jaws, their set stares, their tight lips all stood out to me. We'd been attacked on the pulse of who we were as a people. Even the gypsies shuffled by, a strange light in their eyes. They didn't agree much with any authority, but it was obvious that they felt the fire as well. Mildred had always been a friend to their people.

I stayed tucked back in the shadows, my back pressed against the castle wall, watching it all unfold. Leda, Camille, and Michelle had all gone home to see their families, leaving me at Chatham Castle alone. I welcomed the chance to get all the events straight in my head and spent most of the past couple of days wandering through Letum Wood.

Most of the witches walked past the High Priestess's stately, regal form with emotionless faces. Many of them, especially the foresters and gypsies, dropped springs of Letum Ivy. The growing pile threatened to overtake her.

Across the high bailey near the Ranks flickered a little shadow that sent my heart racing. Instantly on alert, I straightened to see better. A familiar pair of foggy eyes met mine, and then another. Isadora's hunched frame stepped out of the shadows, followed by Sanna. Both of them looked right at me, and I wondered if Sanna could see after all. We stared at each other, and I could see the mourning in their eyes. Isadora set a white lily on the ground, met my eyes again, and nodded once before disappearing.

I kept my eyes on the lily for a long time before turning back to the High Priestess. I wanted to see her sit up, snap at someone to stop staring at her, and take her place on the castle balcony with her usual sallow haughtiness. I'd give anything to hear her reprimand my curtsy. I'd even learn the correct way to curtsy if she'd just come alive again.

I sat there, my knees pulled into my chest, my scabbed, bandaged feet tucked underneath me, waiting for her to move.

But she never did.

Once everyone left, after thousands of witches traipsed through the high bailey, Papa, Tiberius, and I stood on the Wall near the Gatehouse. A contingent of Guardians, led by Marten, marched the High Priestess out to a protected graveyard that was nestled deep in Letum Wood. The Captains had already amassed their Guardians in the lower bailey to give them verbal preparations for the flood of new Guardian hopefuls coming the next morning, motivated by the attack on our homeland.

"What are you going to do now, Papa?" I asked, a hollow feeling in my heart.

"We are going to train and fight," he said. "The West will need time to gather themselves back together. Dane will have to figure out what to do now that Mabel, and the West Guards, have failed."

The Western Network had attempted an advance on the Borderlands, hoping to seize it for their control, at the same time Miss Mabel swooped in with her bat-like hordes. The Guardians held them back with a supreme combination of magic, skill, and brute strength.

"Will the war end with Miss Mabel's capture?"

He scoffed, a short, quick breath packed with meaning.

"No," he said. "This war never did begin nor end with Mabel."

"So now we fight Angelina," I said with a frustrated sigh. "A woman more powerful than Miss Mabel but twice as invisible."

"Yes," Papa agreed, his jaw tight. "If she is as powerful as you think, that is."

He doubted Angelina's role in all this, I could tell. Part of me couldn't blame him. Angelina was virtually unknown, more ghost than witch. How could they fear a witch they'd hardly heard of before?

Perhaps that was the most frightening part of all.

"We've got something she wants," Tiberius pointed out. He meant Miss Mabel, and the very idea sent a chill through me, reminding me of something the High Priestess said last year after Mama died.

This is a lot bigger than just you or me, Bianca. It has been for awhile. I only kept the obvious wolves at bay when I overthrew Evelyn. Now is the time to flush them all out. It will be a painful, dangerous process.

"Marten will remain our Ambassador," Papa said. "He's hoping to go to Diego in the Eastern Network to discuss what all this means. They must take some kind of action before it's too late."

"The Mansfeld Pact is still in place," Tiberius said with a dark mutter. "Diego isn't going to break the contract to help you. Not to mention that Mikhail is running low on metals for his army and the West has them in abundance."

"They'll violate the Mansfeld Pact and form an alliance, won't they?" I asked, and Tiberius nodded with a quick jerk of his head.

"What about the Eastern Network? Will they fight?"

Tiberius snorted.

"They aren't going to do anything. Diego is in denial. He holds to the Mansfeld Pact more tightly than any Network ever has because it originated there. There are no rules in war," Tiberius muttered. "Diego loves rules. Bloody fool."

Tiberius had been like a bank of coals since the night of the ball, burning and hot. Any attack on the Network enraged him, but such a successful campaign was a personal insult. Papa's eyes narrowed, but I knew he wasn't seeing the lower bailey, the formations, or the shouts.

"And the North?" I asked. "Who is going to warn them?"

"No one," Papa said. "The North doesn't care about what's going on down here. They'll take care of themselves."

"But—"

"We're going to fight this war the best way we can, B," he said, intercepting my thought. "We'll exhaust every avenue."

"Including Angelina and the missing *Book of Contracts*?"

Papa pulled in a deep breath. Zane had personally scoured every inch of the ballroom and was unable to find the *Book of Contracts*. We had no idea where it went after the chaos on that devastating night.

"Yes, B. Every option. Don't worry, okay?"

But I did worry. I worried about him, about me. About the Central Network and my friends. Would Michelle's brothers go to war? Would Leda's father still be able to support his family? What about Tiberius and Merrick?

"Yes, Papa," I said. "I'll try."

Papa and Tiberius walked me back to the Royal Hall, where we parted ways. They went to join the broken Council, already tasked with replacing their dead, and I veered off to our new apartment.

Busy maids and attendants bustled inside, trying to find something to do to keep busy. I slipped past, ignored, as I wanted to be. Except for several swords, a few pairs of armor, and four heavy chests that no one but Papa could open, we had very little to bring with us to the new lavish rooms. I stepped out onto the large balcony jutting off from the High Priest's chambers and drew in a deep breath.

The dying summer heat settled in a sticky layer on the rolling emerald hills of the Central Network. They unfurled in front of me like the white banners rippling from every turret, signaling Chatham Castle's mourning for our lost High Priestess. From the Witchery flapped our own white flag. The words *The Wits* were invisible from so high in the air.

A lonely, empty ache gnawed at my bruised and brittle heart, keeping me company. From such a beautiful summer evening, I drew very little joy. The solitude left my thoughts free to roam to the High Priestess, replaying the moment of her death again and again and again.

There's always more room for pain, isn't there? I thought. *Joy is so fleeting.*

"Mildred hated the summer."

I looked up to find Marten come up to my side, his hands resting on the stone railing separating us from a fall several stories high. Guardians bustled in the lower bailey below. Witches moved back and forth on the wall, some of them laughing, some of them talking. It all seemed so normal. Didn't they know what all of this change meant? The flapping white banners, the Council assembled in the West Wing, discussing what should be done with the Southern Network and the

Borderlands. Would the East help? Would I be able to convince Papa that we should fear Angelina the most, that we should find the *Book of Spells* first?

Why didn't they see the battles we faced?

"I don't blame her," I said, feeling a trickle of sweat fall down my spine. "The heat is relentless."

His lips twitched in a little smile. "She didn't like the winter either. Too cold, she'd say. She didn't like waking up with a chilly nose."

The High Priestess's voice, full of snap and vinegar, played through my mind, bringing a small smile to my face. I couldn't imagine feeling any humor over her passing, and then realized that I was smiling to keep from crying.

"She wasn't an easy woman to please."

"No," he agreed with a deep breath. "But she was the best leader we've had since Esmelda."

The little stirring of pain in my heart agreed. *I'll miss you, High Priestess,* I thought. The magic whispered. I left it alone, neither using it nor pushing it away. My powers and I now lived with a mutual agreement of tolerance.

Marten stood next to me for several minutes in a companionable silence, surveying the landscape. I wondered if he sought the inevitable dark wings rising from Letum Wood that I did. The forest dragons had been circling Chatham Castle every night and morning since the High Priestess's death. We might have had Miss Mabel locked away, but the danger had only increased.

"I loved Mildred almost the moment that I saw her, you know," Marten said in a musing tone. "Our life together was far from conventional, but it was worth it."

I caught a gasp.

"You—"

His eyes twinkled just a little as he looked down at me.

"You've proven to be an exceptional secret keeper. I heard you in the gardens that morning. Mildred didn't. At least I don't think she did."

A blush crept up my cheeks, along with a feeling of relief that I'd kept their secret.

"Why didn't you say something?" I asked.

"I knew I wouldn't need to."

The lingering smile on his face disappeared as his chin quivered and his forehead wrinkled. "I don't know what I shall do without her. Mildred and I could never officially vow our hearts to each other the way your parents did, but she had mine all the same."

I observed him in silence, recognizing the same sorrow in his eyes that Papa tried to hide in his own. Marten shook himself out of his bleak, morose thoughts.

"I came to fulfill a promise," he said. I looked up at him in question. He held a small piece of rolled parchment in his hand, sealed with a dollop of wax and a piece of tied twine. "The High Priestess has asked me to explain to you why she chose to have Miss Mabel kill her, and so I shall. The very night she made the vow with you she tasked me with the job of finding a way out of your Inheritance Curse. I searched for months, but found nothing in the way of magic to remove it. Eventually we grew desperate. I went to the West as an Ambassador and spoke with Miss Mabel."

My breath caught. "You went to her? Why didn't you just kill her right then?"

"As an Ambassador under the Mansfeld Pact, I am bound by a very strict magic. I could not bring harm to Miss Mabel while bringing the message from Mildred, as much as I wanted to. It's an unalterable law."

His eyes narrowed on the horizon with a deep breath.

"Mildred knew that Mabel would bargain for the chance to kill her, but likely not much else. I gave Mabel a couple of options, one of which was Mildred's life in exchange for yours. Mabel said she'd let us know."

My mind returned to the ballroom. I heard the High Priestess speaking again. *If you won't settle our matter in private, then you will have three seconds left until I kill you on the spot.*

"Miss Mabel didn't respond to your offer, did she?"

Marten shook his head. "No. She disappeared. We were at her mercy, for Mildred refused to let you die or to kill Mabel."

My eyes widened in shock.

"Why? Why would she refuse to kill her?"

Marten drew in a deep breath. "Mildred believed that we need Mabel in order to end this. Mabel wasn't the beginning or the end of the evil grasping for control of Antebellum, but she may be our only chance to end it."

"Angelina," I whispered. "The High Priestess knew about Angelina."

"She suspected," he said. "But never could confirm it. Mildred asked me to continue our search for the *Book of Spells* and for Angelina once she passed on, something I mean to take very seriously."

I looked up at him.

"I'm glad," I said with relief. "I've been afraid no one would believe me."

He gave me a warm smile.

"Now, this is for you." He handed me the small scroll. "Mildred wanted you to have this. In fact, she was so worried about it that I took a vow that I came to fulfill. Consider my duty done. I shall be in contact with you, Bianca. Very soon, I think. I'm in the market for an Assistant, if you're interested. I'll need someone to help me search for the *Book of Spells.*"

"Sure," I said. I'd have to get a job eventually anyway. Papa wasn't going to let me mope around the castle anymore. Not that I wanted to, anyway. "Thank you, Marten."

Once I took the scroll he walked away, his hands clasped behind his back. I stared at it for several minutes before breaking the seal. The tiny message crackled as I unrolled it. Four words in the High Priestess's thin writing met my eyes, sealing off the portion of my heart that would always belong to her.

The choice was mine.

My jaw tightened. I read it twice, then crumbled it in my hand. The High Priestess chose to die so that I could live. I'd always mourn the High Priestess, like I'd always mourn Mama. She'd been one of my best friends in her odd, severe way. Missing them would always be a part of me. Perhaps this was how it was always meant to be, perhaps not. It didn't matter anymore, because I couldn't change what happened.

The paper caught fire in my fist, smoldering from the heat of my magic. My eyes lifted back to the verdant hills of the forest of my home.

We are a Network at war. A world about to be divided.

I no longer stood on the edge of something grand and horrible. The Central Network had taken a step into the chasm as one, and we plummeted toward the bottom together.

About the Author

Magic captivated me the moment I held my first book. I lived many lives as I scoured story after story. Now, I write fantasy books so you can seize the light, hold magic in your fingertips, and forget the shadows of real life to live your wildest adventure.

Printed in Great Britain
by Amazon